THE MIDWIZARD OF COSCONIA

ZACK SCHOPPEN

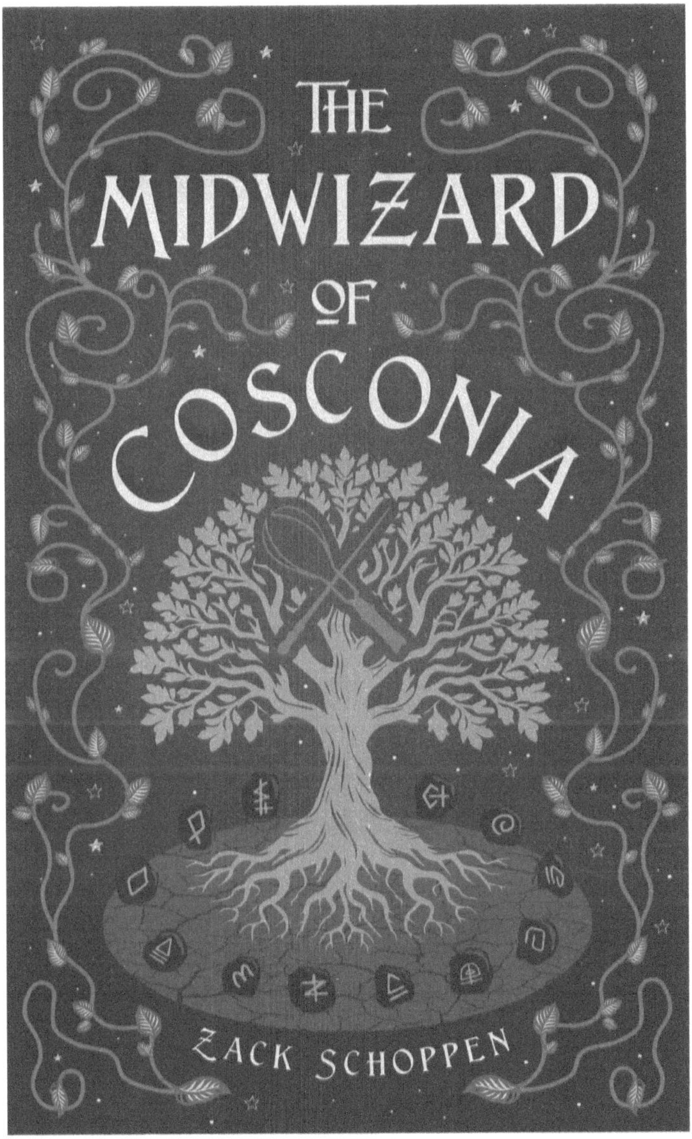

THE MIDWIZARD
OF COSCONIA

ZACK SCHOPPEN, MD

Table Of Contents

Chapter One: A Giant Problem 1

Chapter Two: Dejombro 16

Chapter Three: Unicorn Eater 21

Chapter Four: Changeling in the Air 35

Chapter Five: The Majalir 49

Chapter Six: A Fae Mood 62

Chapter Seven: The Water Palace 71

Chapter Eight: Royal Pains 79

Chapter Nine: The Ritual 93

Chapter Ten: Infertile Crescent 108

Chapter Eleven: The Coronation 121

Chapter Twelve: The Little Mermaids 135

Chapter Thirteen: Sea Monsters Inc. 151

Chapter Fourteen: Halls of Stone 165

Chapter Fifteen: Hi Ho, Hi Ho, It's to the NICU We Go 183

Chapter Sixteen: Letters From an Orcish Prison 199

Chapter Seventeen: Baby Factory 212

Chapter Eighteen: On The Road Again 224

Chapter Nineteen: The Elf, The Mithor, The Legend 242

Chapter Twenty: Postterm Gestation 261

Chapter Twenty-One: Wedding Before War 272

Chapter Twenty-Two: A Bid for Peace 285

Chapter Twenty-Three: Becoming the Monster........................295

Chapter Twenty-Four: The War Begins 309

Chapter Twenty-Five: A Misguided Attempt 322

Chapter Twenty-Six: The Beast Returns........................335

Chapter Twenty-Seven: Maternal Magic 349

Chapter Twenty-Eight: An Unexpected Visitor........................360

Chapter Twenty-Nine: Blood Sprites 370

Chapter Thirty: War Rages 384

Chapter Thirty-One: An Indecent Proposal........................396

Chapter Thirty-Two: She's Gonna Be All Right........................408

Chapter Thirty-Three: Reconciliation........................417

Chapter Thirty-Four: The Mind Mage 429

Chapter Thirty-Five: All Wars End 439

Chapter Thirty-Six: Era of Peace 456

Chapter Thirty-Seven: A Day in the Life 468

Epilogue 480

Acknowledgements........................484

Development Edit by Emily Dahl

Copy Edit by Zoe Cochlin

Cover Art by Book Cover Design by ebooklaunch.com

Map of Cosconia by Alec M

Map of Gravipar by Melissa Nash

Front and Back Artwork by Book Cover Hub

Interior Formatting by Sumaiya Mukta

For Rachel, my favorite frele in the world. You are the kindest and best human I know.

None of this—the book, the condo, the dogs, the travel, our entire incredible life—would be possible without you. I love you and Penny and Desmond more than I love Shrek and Nickelback.

A Note from the Author / Trigger Warning
PLEASE READ!!

First off, I want to sincerely thank you for picking up this book. This idea has been percolating in my head for years, and I can't believe it's a reality. As an OB/GYN and fantasy lover, this concept combines two of the things I love the most in life. Second, this book has some heavy stuff in it. Like, seriously heavy. Infertility, miscarriage, preeclampsia, poor pregnancy outcomes, and maternal and fetal mortality. Even though these things happen to elves, orcs, and changelings, it still might be triggering, especially for anybody who has experienced trauma related to pregnancy. To you, from the bottom of my heart: I see you. While of course I've never personally been infertile or had a miscarriage or lost a child, I've supported countless people dealing with extremely difficult pregnancy and delivery related problems. I've cried with patients. I've sobbed in my car after work. Some of those bad outcomes sit with me for months or years. I've seen the most beautiful, joyous moments in a family's life, and I've seen the worst. Nobody knows your trauma like you do, but as much as any man can, I understand it.

If you have pregnancy trauma and reading about depictions of pregnancy complications seems like it would be too hard, I understand if this book isn't for you. Pregnancy trauma is all too common, and we don't talk about it nearly enough. Did you know nearly 20% of pregnancies end in miscarriage? Or that 5% of pregnancies are complicated by preeclampsia? Or that postpartum hemorrhage is the leading cause of maternal mortality worldwide? I hope this book brings awareness to some of the issues those who identify as women in our world face but don't feel like they can talk about. Pregnancy gets so little representation in society, and this book aims to change that. Plus, I promise if you keep reading, it will pay off :)

While pregnancy, labor, and delivery are nowhere near as dangerous in our world as in Cosconia, and this book is not meant to be an allegory of the real world in any way, there are many similarities that bleed through. Pregnancy is wonderful and beautiful, but it can also be dangerous and scary, especially for people of color. Maternal morbidity and mortality (aka women who have bad outcomes or die during the pregnancy, delivery, or postpartum process) in the United States is unacceptably high. I see the consequences of this every day. It places an undue burden on patients, their families, and the healthcare workers who care about them. Please consider donating to an organization that is committed to improving women's health in your area. For all of 2025, I will be donating 100% of e-book proceeds (not profits because I don't think indie authors make those!) to Cherry Health and Sojourner House, two excellent organizations committed to helping women.

Finally, you may be asking yourself "why the hell a dude is writing a book about pregnant women and having babies?" It's a fair question with a simple answer: I love it. Even after a 24-hour shift, I'm excited to go into work the next day. I love obstetrics and gynecology. I love delivering babies. Sometimes I still tear up, even thousands of deliveries later. I love talking about birth control. I love making sure women are up to date on all their screening. I love helping women take control of their lives by teaming up and treating their heavy or painful periods. I love helping somebody transition who doesn't feel comfortable in the body they were born in. I love changing somebody's life by removing a bothersome ovarian cyst or a fibroid uterus. I love everything about labor and delivery, and this was the best way I knew to share it with the world. I want to be the biggest male advocate for women's health. Women have had their voices silenced for too long, and I hope I can use my voice to amplify theirs. I hope this opens a door for writers of all gender identities to explore some of the more... *uncharted* concepts in a fantasy world like I have. If you think I've misrepresented the experience or need to understand women better, please go to my website, www.themidwizard.com, and let me know! You can also sign up for the newsletter, receive bonus content, info on upcoming releases, and special offers there too.

TL;DR: lots of crazy pregnancy shit happens in this book—make sure you're ready!

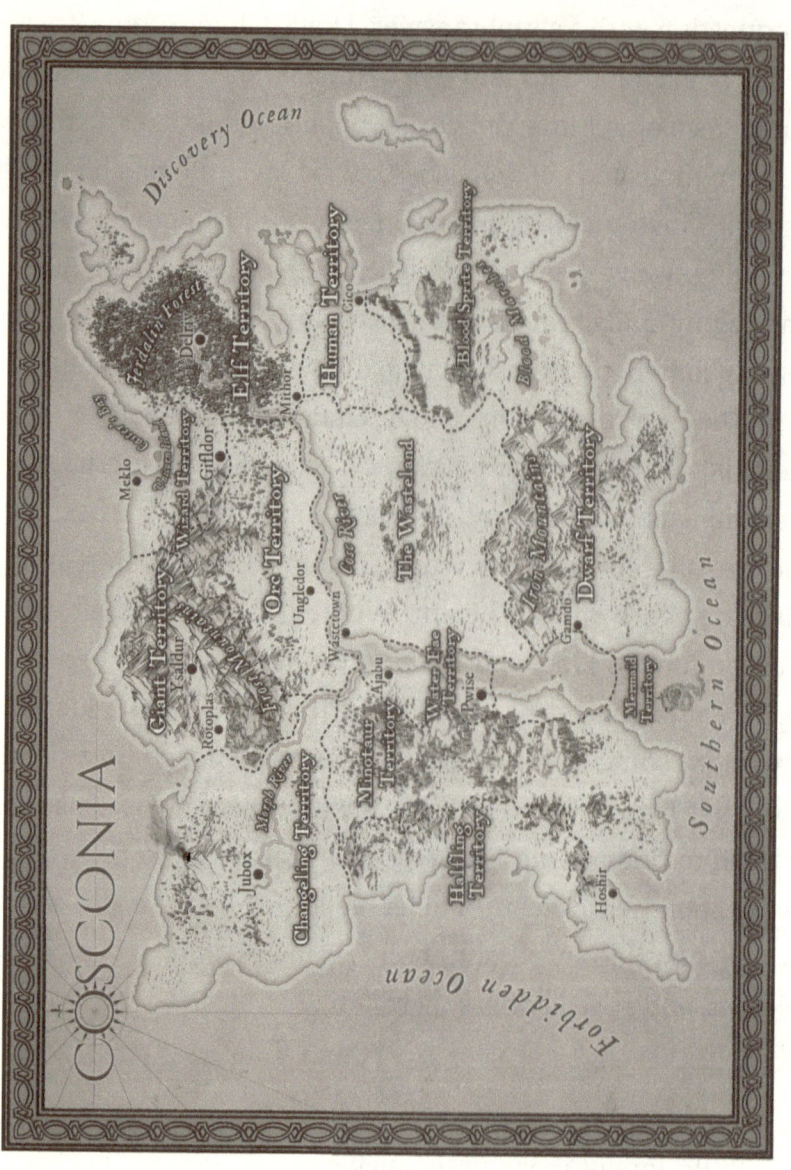

CHAPTER ONE

A Giant Problem

---

*They say that the Giants aspired to the
sovereignty of Heaven, and piled the mountains,
heaped together, even to the lofty stars.*

—Ovid

---

50 years before the Twelve Race War
Rotoplas, Giant Territory

"PUSH!" Izzie screamed for what felt like the one hundredth time that day. The baby giant's head had been crowning for at least six hours, and the midwizard was starting to get worried this baby wasn't coming. She knew this was a potential complication, but it was the first time she'd actually seen it in real life. The textbooks and simulations couldn't prepare you for the real thing.

This baby wasn't coming out. She could feel it in her gut. It wasn't unusual for a giantess to labor for weeks and push for upwards of an entire day, but the twenty-four-hour mark had just passed with no end in sight. Izzie tried to envision what her professor had taught her about giantess pregnancy complications in midwizardry school.

Size is the giant's greatest asset and their biggest downfall, Professor Vylt had lectured. *The average giantess, who is typically taller than her partner, is twenty-five feet tall. Of the many types of giants—rock giants, frost giants, and even the fabled fire giants—the rock giants are the smallest in stature.*

This lecture is a giant *pain in my ass,* Dalfa whispered to Izzie.

Shhh, Izzie stifled a giggle and shushed her best friend, playfully smacking her under the desk. *This is going to be on the test!* Izzie knew the mind mage would ace the exam no matter what, but Izzie wasn't as naturally book smart.

After a gestation of nearly two years, Professor Vylt continued, *a giant baby—pardon my oxymoron—will usually weigh around sixty pounds.* The entire class gasped at this. Giants were only the second race they had covered so far in midwizardry school, and after starting with dwarves and their three-to-four-pound babies, a sixty pound baby was incomprehensible. They went on to learn that giants would give birth to babies up to five feet tall.

Damn, Dalfa whispered again. *That's lanky as hell.*

Now, Izzie looked up at the sweating giantess. Even though she had cast a spell on herself to increase her own size to help with the delivery, Sydyr still towered over the wizard. Sydyr, the youngest sister of the Giant King of Rotoplas, was considered to be one of the smaller giantesses, clocking in at about twenty-one feet by Izzie's estimation. Part of being a midwizard was meeting her patients where they were at, which sometimes included physically changing form. Since Izzie was the height of a normal wizard, about six feet tall, there was no way she could deliver a baby nearly the same size as her. For this reason, all midwizards were required to learn the spell *corporus gigantorum*, which effectively doubled their size.

Sydyr, like most rock giants, had rough, gray skin. She wasn't sure if it was her imagination, but Izzie thought her skin looked even grayer right now, like the ash left over after a fire. That wasn't a good sign. Her strong jaw was set with determination, but it was clear she was in pain.

The giantess's coarse, black hair was plastered against her anguished face. Her breaths were short and gasping, and her typically imposing presence seemed diminished. Weak. Scared. Her older sister sat by her bedside with a massive hand resting gently on her shoulder.

"Take a break for a few minutes," Izzie told the giantess. She looked deeply into Sydyr's dark, shadowed eyes. She could tell how exhausted she was, but in spite of that she remained resolute. "How are your energy levels doing, Syd?"

"I'm fine," Sydyr grunted. "I can do this." Izzie knew she was putting on a brave face. Her normally thunderous voice was barely above a whisper. "I know I can do this," she reaffirmed with a bit of her normal thunder returning. "What do you need me to do?"

Izzie pondered on this for a moment. She was trying her best to appear as a calm, reassuring presence, but she was terrified. She knew if this baby didn't come out soon, there was a high probability both mom and baby wouldn't make it, and she couldn't let that happen.

The midwizard pulled her wand out of her pocket and tapped it against Sydyr's chest. Izzie had something special that set her apart from other wizards—a blood magic Affinity. All wizards were born with an Affinity for a specific type of magic, like how Dalfa had a mental Affinity. As far as Izzie knew, she was the only wizard in Cosconia with a blood magic Affinity. She came from a long line of blood wizards, but her father had abandoned the family when she was young, and her mother had died giving birth to her little brother. He hadn't survived either. Izzie was nowhere near the level of power of some of her ancestors who had fought in the War for Cosconia, such as her great-grandmother, but after the ritual failed, she preferred to use her blood magic for healing instead of violence.

There were three essential aspects to performing magic. The first was Affinity, which made doing blood magic come naturally to Izzie. The second was Skill. A mage of any sort had to train for years to become sufficiently Skilled in a spell. The more Skilled you were in a particular spell, the easier it was to perform and the stronger the spell would be. Finally, an effective spell needed the proper Intent. This was the hardest to define when teaching new wizards, since it was a nebulous mix of emotion and circumstance.

With a simple tap of her wand, she used the *vitalangra* spell to ascertain important information about Sydyr's current status. She was in bad shape. Izzie closed her eyes and envisioned she was the black blood flowing through the giant's body. She arrived at her heart, which was the size of Izzie's head. She could sense that it was unlike her own four-chambered heart; the giantess had a six-chambered heart instead. She had learned in her anatomy classes that giants had an extra two chambers purely for the storage of blood. Rock giants were slow, sedentary creatures. Though they lived for many centuries, they rarely left their own small communities. A giant's heart usually beat around twenty-five times per minute, which was plenty sufficient for their slow, day-to-day tasks. However, the nearly five liters of blood stored in their extra chambers was ready at a moment's notice to supply the rest of their massive bodies with the vital oxygen and nutrients required to move quickly if they needed to defend themselves or escape a dangerous situation.

Sydyr's heart was beating at a blistering seventy-five beats per minute. It was an ominous sign of impending disaster, but Izzie persisted as she navigated through the rest of the giantess's body. She found nothing else amiss, but she knew an extremely fast heart rate was sometimes the only warning sign prior to the heart stopping completely.

She could not let that happen. For two reasons. The first was that Sydyr was her patient. Pregnancy was hard, and it was scary. Izzie's dark past had awakened in her a deep desire to walk this path with scared freles. Though there had been some recent advances in midwizardry, maternal mortality remained high in many communities, especially giant communities. Izzie had learned at the beginning of midwizardry school that about a fifth of giantesses died in labor, almost always taking their babies along with them. By the time she graduated twelve years later, the rate had increased to nearly a quarter. Nobody could explain why.

The second reason she couldn't let Sydyr die that day was a little more selfish—she *also* didn't want to die that day. Sydyr's older brother, Grodge, had hunted Izzie down in the nearby capital of Ysaldur, where Izzie had been living in the community to learn more about giant pregnancies. Izzie discovered giants could nearly always predict the arrival of a baby to within a month. Sydyr being three months past the "due date" was unprecedented. Even though she had informed him she was barely out of midwizardry school, he didn't care. He just wanted somebody there for his sister. She couldn't blame him. At first, Grodge, the giant king of Rotoplas, seemed like a scared, overprotective brother. The situation took a turn when they got close to Sydyr's home.

"I have not been truthful with you, wizard," he had boomed in his gravelly voice. There were many myths about giants being stupid or unintelligent, but this wasn't true. They spoke slowly and used few words, but they were far from unintelligent. "Sydyr is special. There was a prophecy. Foretold by the elders hundreds of years ago, after the Great Divide. They told of a leader who would refuse to enter the world, but if he did, he would lead the giants through times of war."

That's weird, thought Izzie. *Cosconia has been at peace for centuries.*

"Sydyr's son will go on to lead not just our kingdom, but the entire giant race. Skygyr is to be our savior—and you must save him. If he doesn't make it, neither will you." Izzie shuddered as his ominous words seemed to shake the earth.

"How do you even know the baby is a mele?" she asked the giant king, trying to keep her composure. He towered over her in her normal form, being over twenty feet taller than her. She felt like a child in his presence, and his ember-like eyes glowed with silent anger. She was rapidly trying to make sense of the situation, because though her profession required facing life and death, it usually wasn't her own.

"I just know," he responded after a long pause. "Skygyr is the chosen."

Those were the last words Grodge had spoken to her, and now the king stood menacingly near Sydyr's bed. "You must save the chosen one," he reminded Izzie.

"How many times do I have to tell you, Grodge," Sydyr grunted between painful contractions. "My baby is not chosen. The prophecy is not real. It's just from some dumb book written before any of us were born. I knew the risks when I got pregnant."

"NO!" the giant king shouted, making Izzie nearly jump out of her skin. "No," he said more softly after he saw his sister look at him with fear in her eyes. "She will help you. You will not die today. I will not allow it."

"Get out, brother," Sydyr snapped. "The delivery room is no place for a mele. Especially not my screaming brother."

Grodge looked as if he was about to say something, but he held back. He looked at Izzie again. "Save her. Save him." The implied threat was clear. There was no other option.

She was out of time. She knew if the giantess's heart rate reached 100 beats per minute, she would die and not be able to get the baby out. Izzie pulled a hair tie out of her robes to push back her silvery hair. As always, the stubborn scarlet streak tried to point the opposite direction of the rest of her hair.

"Sydyr, I have to be honest with you. The situation is dire. At this poin—"

The giantess cut her off. "I have made my peace. Our mother will protect you from Grodge. He cares too much. Thank you for all you have done."

"What are you saying?"

"Do you have any children, midwizard?"

A sharp pang of sadness tore through Izzie's soul, but she suppressed it. *Not the time.* "No. But I think being a mother is one of the most important things you can do."

"Sometimes a mother must make the ultimate sacrifice."

"I'm not going to let that happen," Izzie said.

"Can you at least save my son?"

"Do you trust me?"

"Do I have a choice, wizard?" Sydyr grunted.

"You always have a choice. But I think I can do this." She turned around to look through her enchanted medical bag. She hadn't cast an enlargement spell on it, so everything seemed tiny while she was double her normal size. As a gift for graduating midwizardry school, every graduate received a bag like this. The enchantment allowed unlimited storage. She couldn't even begin to understand the magic behind it, but she had filled it with as many medical devices and gadgets as she could find before setting off for Ysaldur.

"Damn, you're enormous, Isadore," the bag whispered to her.

"Don't you know that isn't the kind of thing you're allowed to say to a lady? Also I've told you a thousand times to call me Izzie now," she muttered in reply. Most students enchanted their bags with a basic speaking charm. In their profession, the days were long and the nights were longer, and with the travel between communities and the time spent waiting in labor, sometimes it got a little lonely. These charms didn't give the bags sentience exactly, but usually they could hold a casual conversation and help you find what you were looking for inside the bag.

Unfortunately, she was terrible at charms. She had no Skill or Affinity for them, so she had to brute force it with Intent alone. Something had gone wrong with her spell, and even though the enchanted bag did gain the ability to speak... well, it was a bit of a dick.

"You are sooooo effed here, bruh." *Bruh? What did that even mean?* For some reason, not only was the bag rude, the way it talked didn't even seem to be of this world. It used strange words she didn't understand and had a casual way of speaking that didn't make sense half the time. Still, she got the gist of what the bag was saying.

"Very helpful. Can you just help me find what I need for once?"

"I could, but will it matter? That giant emperor or whatever is gonna make a soup from your freshly peeled skin! Shave your liver! Squeeze the jelly from your eyes! I've heard it's quite good on toast..."

"What's going on down there..." Sydyr asked sleepily. "Who are you talking to?"

"Uhhh nobody!" she laughed nervously. "Just a minute!"

Izzie tried to whisper quieter, but she was terrible at being quiet. *If I had a* penor *for every time I was told to keep my voice down, I'd be the richest midwizard in Cosconia.* Izzie was known among her colleagues as being the life of the party, mostly due to the fact that she was usually the loudest in the room. "First of all, you're thinking of ogres, and they were wiped out in the War. Giants are peaceful creatures."

"I bet he makes an excep—"

"Second of all," she interrupted the bag. "How about a little faith? You've seen me pull through dozens of times!"

"It's actually only been seven times, by my count."

"What do you mean your count? You've been counting the times..." *Damn it.* How did she always let that damn bag goad her into an argument? She loved the thing, but she was in the middle of a very tense situation. Even though the bag was bottomless, it seemed like the tool she was looking for was somehow always at the bottom.

"I'll give you a mouse if you shut up right this second and help me find the spoons." For some reason, the bag had developed a taste for mice and she could use them to bribe it. She didn't think it was eating them, but she wasn't sure exactly why it wanted them. And just like that...

"Here it is!" she exclaimed, making the tired giantess perk up for the first time. She pulled out two items, mirror images of each other. "This is a lost art among many midwizards, but I was lucky to have a professor who was an expert in one of the most effective methods of delivery, especially for giant babies."

She thought back on Professor Vylt. She had been one of Izzie's mentors at school, and Izzie had done a lot of shadowing of the professor's work in giant communities. Just before graduation, Vylt had revealed the exciting but shocking news— she had become pregnant herself. It wasn't particularly hard for giants to get pregnant, but many avoided it due to the mortality rate. Despite the large size of Ysaldur, communities throughout Giant Territory were shrinking rapidly due to this fact. In spite of all her knowledge and practical experience, Professor Vylt didn't survive her own pregnancy. Like so many before her, the baby got stuck coming out.

Izzie shook off the gloomy thoughts of her late professor. "These are forceps. They're basically like giant spoons that go on the baby's head so we can pull him out." Izzie realized she'd started referring to the baby as a mele too, even though as far as she knew, there was still a fifty percent chance it would be a frele. That was one thing that was common to all races with two sexes she knew of—there was never a race who produced more of one than the other. A strange quirk of biology that tied everybody together. Freles, like Izzie and Sydyr, were the childbearing sex of any race, be they elf, halfling, wizard, or orc, and the other sex was called mele. The only race that broke convention were merfolk, since mermen laid eggs and mermaids didn't. In her opinion, society placed far too much importance on what was between somebody's legs.

The forceps were made of steel, like most good swords. There were two separate pieces to the forceps, which looked like giant spoons. They interlocked with each other when applied correctly. The forceps had long metal handles for the midwizard to hold onto, and curved blades to exactly match the curvature of a baby's head.

"These are what we use to deliver babies who won't come out."

Sydyr looked at the forceps skeptically. "Those would barely fit around my baby's foot, much less his head."

Izzie chuckled, slightly embarrassed. "Ah, yes, well. Of course." She muttered a spell, *cosarus gigantorum*. It was a slight modification of the spell she used to make herself big, and it turned the item to exactly the size needed to deliver Skygyr. It was an easy spell to cast with Skill alone. "There we go!"

Sydyr was slightly pacified, but still unsure. "You are too small to pull my baby out. I am three months late. He is likely almost as big as you."

Izzie wasn't quite sure that estimate lined up, but she didn't say anything. "You're right. I'm just guiding and pulling. You're doing all the work."

"I'm too tired," the giantess said simply. "I can't do it."

This was where Izzie's idea got a little dicey. "I know. But I have my blood magic, which may be able to help." Being the only blood wizard in Cosconia, much of what Izzie did was self-taught. She had spent many years studying blood magic before she enrolled in midwizardry school, but she hadn't had many opportunities for practical application. Now that she was out refining her craft, she could experiment with her abilities a bit.

The giantess looked at her skeptically. "What are you going to do to me?"

Izzie explained her idea, and the giantess grunted with displeasure.

"You're in control here, Sydyr. You can say no. But I think I can save him."

"Do whatever you need to do to help my baby."

Izzie closed her eyes and envisioned herself within the giantess's heart again. Her heart rate was up to ninety beats per minute. *Cect*, she thought to herself. It wasn't a guarantee Syd's heart would stop if it got over one hundred beats per minute, but the chances were high. Too high. Her intuition told her Sydyr was not going to be one of the lucky ones.

"Take a few deep breaths for me," she said out loud. Taking deep breaths didn't actually do anything, as all midwizards knew, but it was something you said when you wanted a patient to relax.

She could feel the giantess's breathing slow. It was a good sign that she still had enough control to do so. Once she established the connection with Sydyr's blood, she opened her eyes. "You ready to be a mom?" Izzie asked the giantess.

She nodded. Izzie set her jaw, which everybody always described as sharp. She wasn't sure if it was a compliment or not. Sweat poured down her pale skin, which rarely saw the sun because of how much she worked.

"Alright, Syd. I'm moving the blood from your reserves. You might feel a little lightheaded, but push through it. I'm sending half of it to your uterus, and half of it to the vessels that supply your heart." The *sangrimovi* spell worked perfectly for this. Sydyr's heart rate was now at ninety-five, but Izzie didn't tell the giantess. She couldn't let her lose focus. "That way, more oxygen goes to your heart, and we can protect you during this process."

Izzie's goal was to give a boost to Sydyr's uterus, which contained the presumably massive baby, so they could get this baby out with the assistance of the forceps. She took the first forcep, the left one, and cast a spell on it. *Lubricado*. All midwizards learned this spell on day one of their twelve-year midwizardry education. This spell lubricated the blade to minimize any discomfort for the already miserable giantess. Since she could see the crown of the baby's head, hence the term crowning, she pressed the blade against the baby's head and slid

12

it into place. The late Professor Vylt had always told her a forceps-assisted delivery was as much an art as it was a science. You couldn't see where the blade ended up, since it was inside the body along the side of the baby's head. Everything was done by feel. Izzie could feel the blade go exactly where she wanted it to. *Twelve hells yeah*, she thought to herself.

After casting *lubricado* on the second blade, she slid it into place on the opposite side of the first one. Again, it found exactly the right place. Izzie knew it was the right place, even if she couldn't exactly explain why. Maybe it was Maternal Magic. Maybe it was good training. The locking mechanism clicked into place with an extremely satisfying sound.

Though she hadn't mentioned this to the giantess, she had a final spell to cast, though this one would be on herself since she knew Sydyr's weakened body wouldn't be able to handle it. *Enforza corporus*. It would strengthen her entire body, but she knew that after it wore off, she would be extremely weak. Spells to strengthen the body weren't in line with her Affinity, but she had a fair amount of Skill and more Intent than ever since three lives were on the line. It was worth it. She had learned the spell specifically for instances such as this.

"Alright Syd. This is it. Time to meet this kid. You ready?" Izzie asked, power coursing through her body. "On the count of three, you're going to give me the biggest push you got. Every bit of energy you have left. You've got this."

"Three…" Izzie felt the giantess's heart rate increase to 102 beats per minute. She was committed, so there was no going back. There wasn't any spell she knew to prevent the giantess's heart from giving out. "Two…" The midwizard tightened her grip on the forceps, feeling the strength in every single muscle in her body. "One…" She took a deep breath in and prepared to pull with all her might.

With an earth-shattering roar, Sydyr pushed with a power the wizard had never seen in her life. Even with her magically enhanced body, the power emanating from the giantess was far greater. This is something the midwizard had observed many times over the years. Maternal Magic. There weren't any textbooks on it. It wasn't officially recognized as a school of magic. Many people (mostly meles) didn't even believe it existed. But Izzie had seen it dozens of times. A strength that transcended known science. A baby pulling through against all odds. She could see it on full display in front of her. As Sydyr pushed, Izzie used her enhanced strength to pull harder than she'd ever pulled before. She knew there were risks to a forceps delivery, like injuries to the baby's head, eyes, mouth, or even brain, but she wasn't worried. The forceps were exactly where they needed to be.

For the first time in what felt like days, she felt the baby move. She could see the baby descending right in front of her. It was working. It was working!

"Yes! Syd! Don't stop; keep this push up and you're going to meet this baby!" The baby continued to descend as Izzie pulled. She knew her enhanced strength wouldn't last much longer, but she would pull until she dropped.

Finally! The baby's head was completely out. The giant baby had a thick coat of brown hair on his head. The forceps had been a smashing success! She had saved him. *Maybe this really is a special baby*, she mused.

Now that the head was out, the hard part was over. She removed the forceps since they'd done their job, and she just had to put gentle downward traction on the head and the baby's giant shoulder would pop right...

No. No no no no. This can't be happening right now. We were so close. This was what Izzie had been worried about from the beginning; she'd just pushed it to the back of her mind because labor wasn't progressing. *Size is their biggest asset and their greatest downfall.* Like many medical terms, the word for this one was in the old language. *Dejombro.* The baby's head was out, but the shoulder was stuck.

* * *

Dearest Izzie,

I hope your time in Giant Territory is going well! I can't imagine how hard it is for you to be there after what happened to Prof Vylt. How are you? Meet any cute meles yet? I'm here in Halfling Territory, and it's even more bleak than we learned about. I swear I lose more babies than I save. But I did successfully deliver quintuplets the other day; you'd be so proud of me!

Western Cosconia is beautiful right now; I bet you're jealous since you're probably freezing your ass off in Ysaldur. I miss you, and I hope we can see each other really soon.

Love, Dalfa

P.S. You are so lucky you have a blood magic Affinity. My mind magic is practically useless for delivering babies. Why the hells did I become a midwizard again?!

CHAPTER TWO

Dejombro

"Life is loss," the giant said. "Aye, that it is."

—*John Gwynne*

---

50 years before the Twelve Race War
Rotoplas, Giant Territory

"Grodge! Come help!" Izzie screamed. She'd recognized the *dejombro* in a heartbeat, and even though she knew what to do, she was still terrified. This was pretty much the worst complication that could happen to a giant. All midwizards had a healthy fear of *dejombro*, which was when a baby's shoulder got stuck after the head was delivered. The rest of the baby was smushed into the birth canal, cutting off the blood supply to the umbilical cord. No blood meant no oxygen, which made this a true emergency—no creature could live for more than a few minutes without oxygen.

"What?" Sydyr asked, fear evident in her voice. "What's happening? I thought my baby was out. Do you need me to push harder?"

"No!" Izzie practically screamed at the giantess. "Stop pushing right now." If the giantess kept pushing, the baby would be even more stuck.

Grodge lumbered into the room at a shocking speed, clearly using his own reserves for the extra energy boost. "Is he—"

Izzie cut him off. "Grodge—take her right leg and pull it as far back as you can toward her head. Glyndyr," she addressed Sydyr's sister, who had been quietly supporting the laboring giant. "Do the same thing on her other side!"

Once the giantess's siblings pulled her legs back to open up her pelvis and create more room for the baby, Izzie once again put downward traction on the baby's head. The baby didn't budge. *Still not working.* She could see his face starting to turn blue. Her magically reinforced strength was fading, and there was no chance she would be able to deliver this baby without it. Izzie was worried she may collapse into unconsciousness with how much energy and power was circulating through her body right now.

With her last burst of strength, Izzie pressed down as hard as she could just above the giantess's pubic bone. She knew if she pressed hard enough here, she could actually push down on the baby's shoulder from the outside and get it to slip out. As she pushed down with all of her strength, she felt a *POP!* and all of a sudden she could feel the head start to descend again.

Just like that, the shoulders delivered and the rest of the baby started to slide out. And it kept coming. And coming. Until finally, she saw the giant baby's feet, practically as big as her own. She did it. The baby was here. He was...

"Syd," Izzie said softly, her strength completely sapped. "We were all wrong. It's a girl!"

Grodge and Glyndyr helped her hand the baby to the new mother. Sydyr wept as she pulled her daughter in close. The massive baby was practically as tall as Izzie. Both mom and baby looked happy and healthy. Izzie, on the other hand, collapsed to the floor. Nobody even made a move toward her. *This is the life of a midwizard, I suppose. They need me here before the baby comes out, but as soon as we saw those feet, everybody forgot I was even here.* As she collapsed, thankfully retaining consciousness, her strength and enlargement spells both wore off, returning her to her normal height in a state of weakness.

"You look like hot garbage," she heard her bag say from the table above her. She rolled her eyes. *Couldn't even give me credit for the most insane delivery I have ever done.*

"Would you knock it off!" She reached up, pulling the bag off the table.

"AHHHH!" it screamed, like it could feel pain. It couldn't feel pain, right? But nobody heard it over the sound of the screaming giant baby.

"Hey! I was enjoying the show! Now I can't see the new baby!" the bag whined.

"You hate babies! You've told me that a million times."

"Yeah, but I still like to be part of the action."

Me too, Izzie sighed internally as she gazed longingly at the mother and newborn. Tears gently cascaded from Sydyr's dark eyes as she looked at her baby for the first time. Even though Skygyr was enormous, seeing the fresh baby filled Izzie with longing for her own.

She laid on the floor for a few minutes, gathering what little strength she had left. Finally, Grodge looked over, away from his new niece, and realized Izzie was on the floor. He gently helped her up, and she barely came up to his knees now that her enlargement spell had worn off. Neither of them spoke. Izzie looked up at the giantess and her daughter and rested her hand on Sydyr's leg.

18

"Syd…" She trailed off. Something wasn't right. Unwittingly, when she set her hand on the giant's leg, her blood magic activated and she knew something was wrong. She closed her eyes and felt the giant's heartbeat. It was barely moving. It was beating at four, maybe five beats per minute. How was the giantess still conscious and talking?

Maternal Magic. It had to be. There was no other explanation. They only barely covered the concept of Maternal Magic in midwizardry school since so little was known about it. There wasn't even any proof it was real. It was what midwizards used to describe any unexpected outcome. A ten-pound dwarf baby? *Maternal Magic.* An orc delivery without a drop of blood? *Must be Maternal Magic.* A giantess talking to you after her heart had practically stopped?

"Syd," she started again, but the giantess cut her off.

"I know. I can feel it."

"Let me—"

"No," the giantess said softly. "This was my destiny. Brother, you were right. *She* is the chosen one. Get the measuring rope." Since the giants valued size so greatly, checking the height of a new baby was one of the first things they did after delivery.

Grodge, confused, did what she asked. He carried the baby over to the wooden crib in the corner of the room and measured her. Izzie heard him gasp. "Impossible." He picked the baby back up and carried her over to her mom, setting her back in her arms.

"I love you so much, little one," Sydyr whispered to her daughter. Izzie let out a soft half laugh, half sob under her breath, since the giant baby was already much taller than the midwizard. In fact, this was by far the largest giant baby she had ever seen.

"You will do so much good in this world. You will *be* so much good in this world. Fulfill the prophecy. Make me proud. I love you."

With that, the giantess took her last breath.

Tears flowed down Izzie's face. She had known this was a possibility. She knew this came with the job. She knew not to get too attached. She knew even saving one of them defied the odds in a situation like this. It didn't matter. There was now a little girl who was going to grow up without a mother. Without her rock. Izzie knew what it was like growing up without a mom. *At least if I never have a baby, I can't leave it motherless,* she thought darkly, even though she didn't truly believe it.

She looked over at the giant king, fearing the worst. *I hope the bag was wrong*, she mused. Grodge rested a massive hand on her shoulder. She could feel the weight of it, pressing down on her already weak body.

"There is a second half of the prophecy, wizard," he said, not unkindly. "The chosen leader would enter this world standing taller than any who came before. But the child would steal its strength from she who bore it. I was afraid this would happen, and that's why I called you here. Thank you, Izzie. Your name will not be forgotten."

Before her consciousness lapsed, Izzie was assaulted with memories of her past.

CHAPTER THREE

Unicorn Eater

---

*I recognized you instantly. All of our lives
flashed through my mind in a split second. I felt
a pull so strongly towards you that I almost
couldn't stop it.*

—*J. Sterling*

---

84 years before the Twelve Race War
Gifldor, Wizard Territory

"Ma'am?" Isadore must have dozed off while reading, as she often did. It was after hours, so she wasn't even supposed to be here anymore. She figured she'd ignore the voice and continue her snooze until it went away.

"Excuse me? Ma'am?" The voice became more insistent.

"Go away," she mumbled. "We're closed." Yet again, she had fallen asleep reading *The Definitive History of the Wizards of Cosconia* for what had to be the fiftieth time. Isadore was reading the book for one singular purpose: to find any clues she could regarding wizard reproduction.

After graduating from the Wizarding Institute of Gifldor, the WIG, where they received a mandatory seven-year education on the basics of magic, most wizards ventured out into Cosconia to hone their Skill, practice their Affinity, or set out in search of adventure. She never wanted any of that. Isadore just wanted to live a normal life. She didn't care about growing in power or discovering the intricacies of her Affinity. She wanted to settle down. Get a job. Maybe meet somebody. And what she wanted most of all was to raise a family.

Isadore had always known the odds were stacked against her. Wizards rarely reproduced, and when they did, it was usually by dumb luck. Her mother having two children was exceptionally rare—and it had cost her her life. Statistically, Isadore knew she was quite unlikely to ever get pregnant, but it was still her goal. She figured that if she was fertile, she certainly would have gotten pregnant during her years-long on-and-off relationship in wizarding school since she purposely never took any precautions to prevent pregnancy. *Even though those barely exist.*

So instead of settling down like she wanted to, she set out to learn everything she could about wizarding history, specifically wizard families, children, pregnancy, or anything that could even remotely help on her journey to becoming a mother. She started by staying on at the WIG for an extra three years to work in the library. She scoured every single book in the library that even mentioned wizards. She barely spoke to another person for the entire time. Every night, she would fall asleep reading. Every morning, she would pick up where she'd left off and read as she walked to the library. She almost got fired several times for being too busy doing her own research to help a student find a book in the library, and the only reason she kept the job was because nobody else wanted it.

The Definitive History of the Wizards of Cosconia, as the title indicated, was the most comprehensive history of wizardkind. The massive tome contained over five thousand pages, much of which was genealogies and useless information. Though she learned a great deal over her time at the library, she didn't feel much closer to her goal. She knew that obviously she would need another person to be part of this process of creating a baby, but in a perfect world, she would figure out a way to use her blood magic to do it herself. She'd certainly never meet anybody by staying up late in the library every night, refusing to speak to anybody.

She only had one hundred pages left of the book, which briefly covered the last few decades of wizard history. This would be her last time reading it. She practically knew it by heart at this point, and she didn't think she would be able to get any more information from it. Isadore knew it was time to move on. She'd gotten all she could from this place, and she knew she would have to leave the safety of Gifldor, her hometown and the location of the academy, to venture into the world and uncover all the secrets there were to find. If she could just get through these last...

"I'm sorry, but I need that book." Isadore still didn't peel her face off the page it was stuck to, but the kind voice had become more insistent.

"We're closed," she grumbled again, becoming impatient with the student. "Come back and ask the librarian for it in the morning."

"I would, but I think you may be using it as a pillow..."

Isadore shot up, her face tearing the page it was stuck to. Thankfully, it was just a page about some stuffy old wizard mele. *He was probably an asshole anyways.* "You must be confused. This is *The Definitive History of the Wizards of Cosconia*. I've worked here for three years and I'm the only one who has ever touched this book. What book are you actually looking for?"

"No, ma'am, that's definitely the one. I've attempted to check it out dozens of times, but it's always gone. I guess now I know where it was."

Isadore blushed slightly. She *had* been hoarding the book, thinking the answers she was looking for were buried deep inside. For the first time, she actually looked at the student standing in front of her. He was taller than most wizards. Much taller than her, to be certain, which was rare, since she was "tall for a frele," as everybody liked to tell her. *I'm practically a dwarf compared to the rock giants*, she would often protest.

Most wizards had long, gnarled beards and flowing hair, but not the one standing in front of her. He had deep black hair, another rarity among wizardkind, light hair like her own being much more common. It was closely cropped at the sides and much longer on top. He smiled quizzically as he looked at her. Even though she almost never noticed physical appearances, she could see how striking his jawline was when he smiled.

"Um, hello?" *Cect.* How long had she been staring at him? Was this all just a hallucination, brought on by too many late nights at the library? "Are you really here?"

The mele in front of her laughed. Not a nervous, are-you-crazy kind of laugh. No. A genuine laugh from deep in his belly. His eyes squinted closed almost completely as he laughed. Had she ever heard such a beautiful sound? What was happening to her? She needed sleep, desperately.

"I'm pretty sure I'm really here, though I suppose one can never be one hundred percent certain of anything. Are *you* really here?" he asked, wiping a tear away from his eye after his outburst of laughter. She looked into his huge eyes, which were forest green, like somebody had painted them with the same brush they used for a pine tree. His eyes were gorgeous, but there was something in them that she couldn't quite identify. A sadness, maybe? *No, determination. But for what?* The look passed as quickly as it came.

"What a preposterous question. Of course I'm here!" she responded indignantly, aware it was a reasonable question since she'd just asked him the same thing.

"Well, I'm glad we've got that settled! We are both, in fact, here. Now... are you finished reading that?"

Isadore looked down at the book in front of her, which contained a very conspicuous spot of drool in the middle of the torn page. She slammed it shut. "I... just have a few pages left. I'll return it tomorrow and then you can ask the librarian to check it out for you. Now, you really shouldn't be here after hours."

"Say, haven't I seen you around here before? You look really familiar."

Isadore sighed. She'd worked in the library for enough time that pretty much all of the students at the university should at least recognize her, but she had made a point to stay isolated. "Yes, I work in the library. That's why I'm here late. Which, again, *you* aren't supposed to be. What did you say your name was anyway?"

The boy smiled, revealing dimples set into his tan cheeks, yet again making her heart skip a beat. "I'm Syrel. It's a pleasure to meet you, Isadore."

She didn't remember telling the boy her name, but she was still half asleep and wanting to get out of his strangely intoxicating presence, so she didn't give it a second thought. Was that vanilla she smelled? "Nice to meet you, Syrel. Now you have to get out of here before somebody blames me for letting you in after hours. Like I said, you can talk to the libr–"

"How about you just give me the book over dinner tomorrow?"

Aside from the fact that giving somebody else a book *she'd* checked out would be a blatant disregard for proper library protocols, she had decided to leave Gifldor. There was nothing left for her here, and there was no point going out to dinner with a boy. Even if he was more attractive than a fae prince. She couldn't form any attachments that would make it harder to leave. She had a mission, and she was determined to find as much information as she could, no matter where it took her. Although, there really was only one way to find out if she could get pregnant...

"I'll take your shocked silence as a yes. I was just using the book thing as a segue—I wouldn't ask somebody to give me a book they'd checked out, completely violating proper library protocols. I'll meet you at Hidgem's tomorrow for dinner. Bye, Isadore!"

And just like that, he was gone in a swish of his robes. Isadore was left dumbfounded by the entire interaction, specifically the part where he accepted his own invitation on her behalf, which she found extremely presumptuous and rude. But also slightly... alluring? Which was odd, because she hated being told what to do. Especially by meles. On the other hand, she hadn't been bedded in quite some time. Plus, he *did* respect proper library protocols, which was *particularly* arousing.

The next day, Isadore returned *The Definitive History of the Wizards of Cosconia* and told the librarian she was moving on, which was met with about as much emotion as the old frele was capable of. After that, she packed up everything she owned, which wasn't much. A few books she thought might still be relevant to her search. Some casual and dress robes, both of which were falling out of fashion in favor of simpler garb.

All in all, it took about three hours to clean up everything her life had become over the last ten years, which was a little depressing. She'd saved up quite a bit of money, so she wasn't worried about finding inns or taverns to sleep at, and with her wizard's constitution, she didn't need to buy food frequently.

Throughout the entire day, she couldn't stop thinking of Syrel. Somehow, he'd managed to impress her with his literary taste at the same time as he'd offended her by assuming she'd want to go out with him. What a strange interaction it had been. Originally, she had made up her mind there was no point in going out with him before she left. Then again, maybe she shouldn't pass up the opportunity to get a fresh unicorn steak from Hidgem's...

As a strong, independent frele, Isadore had no problem being treated to a free meal and perhaps a bit of adult fun before she left Cosconia. The only other stop she would make would be at the graves of her mother and the brother she never got to meet. She wasn't even sure where she would go, but wizards were at least *tolerated* by most races in Cosconia, so she wasn't particularly worried about safety—a privilege she knew not all twelve races had. There was a reason the twelve territories were spaced far apart with distinct borders. She figured the best place to start might be with the water fae, who were known, like wizards, to have great difficulty with conception. Maybe they would have more resources for her fertility research.

As she walked toward the restaurant, she could see Syrel waiting outside for her. He had traded his student's robes for a thin, long-sleeved shirt, which looked to be made of a white silk-like material, and the new "pants" humans had introduced to Cosconia just a few decades prior. The shirt was unbuttoned to just above his sternum, revealing a dark patch of chest hair peaking out. Even though dress robes were usually the only way to dress formally, he somehow looked dignified without being overly ceremonious. Casual, but in a comfortable way rather than a way that implied he didn't care. In fact, it looked like he cared quite a bit about how he looked based on the fact he was checking his reflection in a washing basin outside the restaurant.

When he looked up, he spotted her approaching, and a smile cracked across his face, accentuating the same jawline that was half the reason she had decided to show up. From behind his back, he pulled out a flower. It was the most brilliant pink color she'd ever seen. It didn't even seem like a color that could possibly exist in nature. Now within arm's length of him, she was more focused on the flower than she was on him. She reached out to touch it, but the flower disappeared in a puff of smoke.

"Umm... I think I broke your flower."

He laughed. Again with that genuine laugh that made her feel like the funniest person alive. *Which I am, but he doesn't know that yet.*

"Don't worry; it was just a trick."

Isadore scoffed. "So you brought me a fake flower? Classy."

He grimaced. "Well, technically, it was a fake orchid. But they are real! You can't find them anywhere near here, so it was hard to procure one on such short notice."

"Well, good to know you're always willing to go the extra mile." She rolled her eyes.

"No fair!" Syrel protested. "You can't find an orchid within three hundred miles of here!"

"Okay fine, so you aren't willing to go the extra *three hundred* miles to impress me," Izzie retorted, trying her best to throw him off balance.

He remained unfazed. "I guess I just don't know if you're the kind of frele who is worth an extra three hundred miles."

Okay, it looks like he can give as good as he can take, so maybe this dinner won't be terrible.

"I'm just going to tell you the truth right now before we even go inside. This is my last night in Gifldor. I quit my job, I packed up my apartment, and I'm setting off tomorrow. I decided to show up tonight partially to humor you, but mostly because I want a free unicorn steak. So if that's not going to work for you, tell me now and I'll take mine to go."

The beautiful mele just grinned. "Let's eat."

* * *

"Y'know," Isadore spoke through a mouthful of steak, not even pretending to have any decorum, "unicorns are so prevalent in the forests of Cosconia that if you don't hunt them for food, their populations grow out of control and they start hunting sentient beings."

Syrel, with one eyebrow raised in concern, appeared slightly nauseated. "You know that's a myth Big Unicorn wants you to believe, right? Unicorns are vegetarians, like me. And they've been significantly overhunted in Cosconia."

Isadore interjected. "Who is hunting vegetarians?"

He laughed heartily. "You know what I meant. Some experts say if we continue the consumption of unicorn meat at the rate we have been, they could become extinct some day."

She scoffed. She couldn't imagine a world where unicorns didn't exist. Unicorn Island was full of them, but they were very shy creatures who darted at the first sight of any other creature.

"Is that really true? How have I not heard about this?"

"Did you not see the protesters outside the restaurant when you walked in...?"

"Okay now that is just ridic—" he cut her off by drawing her attention outside the windows, to where a group of people with signs were walking around the restaurant. She could make out one that said *I'm 'horn'y for saving the unicorns!* Was she really so hypnotized by him she didn't notice a genuine protest going on...?

She looked at the plate in front of her, no longer finding it particularly appetizing. She slid the half-eaten steak as far away as she could. "Fine. I am rarely willing to admit this, but I suppose I may have been wrong. You mind splitting your potato stew with me? Or is there something ethically wrong with potatoes now too?"

"Well now that you mention it..."

"Stop. I don't want to know. Slide it over here."

As she slurped up the remains of his meal, she finally asked the burning question. "Okay. What gives? Why did you ask me out? And when I said I'm skipping town tomorrow, why did you stay?"

"I've been wondering when you were finally going to ask me. I didn't realize all it would take is me going hungry and giving you my meal!"

She just looked at him. She wasn't going to entertain any games here because she legitimately wanted an answer to the question.

"Okay okay. Well the answer to the first question is easy. I asked you out because I thought you were stunning. You were drooling into a five-thousand-page book in the middle of the night at the library, and you were somehow the most breathtakingly gorgeous wizard I'd ever seen in my entire life."

Isadore's face turned bright red at this. "Wait just—"

"I'm sorry," he interjected. "I won't be taking any comments or questions at this time. Please save them for the end." He grinned at her. She was pretty sure he was kidding, but she figured she wouldn't push it.

"The answer to the second question is a little more complicated. In short, well... I'm leaving too."

Neither of them spoke for a minute. Isadore assumed he was thinking the same thing she was—what the hells were they doing here? They were both setting off on their own adventures and clearly didn't have time for any funny business. She was going to thank him for his time, leave a few *penores* for her half-finished unicorn steak, which she'd probably never eat again just in case these claims were true, and get on her way.

They both started to speak at the same time. "Can I be fully honest with you?" he asked while she was trying to gently end the date.

Luckily, it appeared he hadn't heard her. *Typical mele, too caught up in what he's saying to listen to me.* She internally rolled her eyes. "Uhh, I suppose. Sure. What do you want to be fully honest about?"

"You're looking for something. I don't know what it is, but I know you're looking, and you haven't found it."

Isadore went cold inside. It wasn't some grand secret she was searching for answers around wizard families and fertility—she'd sought insight from plenty of people around the university. It still felt weird to have this mele make strange accusations, and she certainly wasn't planning on talking about her deep desire for a baby while she was on a first date. *Not again.*

He continued before she could protest. "I know, because I'm looking for something too. My Affinity."

"What do you mean you're looking for your Affinity?"

"I don't have one. Well, I'm sure I have one. But I don't know what it is."

A wizard without an Affinity? Was that even possible? Isadore supposed it must be, but she'd never heard of it. Even though Affinities couldn't be predicted based on lineage, most wizards discovered theirs at a young age. When she was a girl, probably no older than eight, her friend had fallen down and cut his knee. He was too young to know what was happening. She saw the blood start to drip down his shin, and she instinctively grabbed the wound. The second she came in contact with the blood, she felt something strange pulse through her. When she pulled her hand away, the bleeding had completely stopped. She ran in to tell her aunt, who recognized a blood Affinity. Since Isadore's father was absent—most likely dead—and her mother had passed, she was raised by her "aunt." It wasn't really her aunt, but rather a neighbor who took her in after the death of her mother. She was a cruel frele.

"How can you be a wizard without an Affinity?"

He chuckled, though she could hear pain in the laugh. "Well, I'm certainly not a very good one."

"What have you tried?"

"All the big ones. I have no elemental control. I can't talk to animals. Definitely can't do any mind magic. My apparition skills are shit. Hells, I've even tried blood magic and I definitely can't do any of that."

"So how can you do any magic at all?"

"Well, I've practiced most basic spells a great deal, so the Skill is there. And I think my lack of Affinity puts even more strength behind my Intent." Isadore supposed that may be true, as Intent was the most crucial component of performing powerful magic.

"But you have to have *something*, right?"

"That's what I'm trying to figure out. I've never been out of Gifldor, and I know the answer has to be out there. If only there was a book that had every single piece of information about Cosconian wizards..."

Isadore gulped. "Yeah... sorry for being selfish." She wasn't really sorry, but it seemed like the right thing to say.

He gently set his hand on her arm, sending chills down her spine. "I forgive you," he winked.

She hated winking, but she wasn't going to tell him that. "So what are you going to do?"

"I'm going to get out of here. There has to be an answer somewhere. And I'm gonna find it."

"So what are you going to do first?"

"Between you and me," he whispered conspiratorially, "I'm planning on taking *The Definitive History of the Wizards of Cosconia* with me."

Isadore gasped. Of all the strange things she'd heard from him so far, this was by far the wildest. "You're going to steal... from a library? From *my* library?"

Syrel grinned nervously, running his hand through his already tousled hair. *He is* damn *cute for a book thief,* she thought.

"Maybe I wouldn't have to if *somebody* wasn't hogging it for the past three years!"

"Hey! Who are you calling a hog?"

"Wait—no! That's not what I meant!" Isadore laughed, having finally gotten a rise out of the seemingly imperturbable wizard.

"Damn it," he muttered, looking ashamed for rising to the bait. "Should have known to expect that kind of behavior from a unicorn eater."

"Okay *now* you're pushing it. Can we get back to the matter at hand? Why are you telling me about your lack of Affinity?"

"Ahh yes, sorry for getting off topic. I figured you'd have put it together by now." His tone was slightly condescending, but she figured she'd let it slide. This time. "I was just guessing you were looking for something, but the look on your face confirmed my suspicion. I don't even care what it is you're looking for. We're both looking for something, and the answers clearly aren't in Gifldor. Come with me, Isadore. Let's find the answers together."

Izzie's jaw fell open. "What—Why—Who—" she sputtered, having too many half-formed questions. She took a deep breath and tried to gather her thoughts. Isadore felt like one of her greatest skills was her ability to analyze a situation empirically and without emotion, so she tried to think rationally about the situation. She had learned a bit about Syrel throughout their conversation over dinner, but she still knew remarkably little. He had just graduated this year, making him probably only a few years younger than her. He had grown up in a small town near Gifldor, and apparently he was the only wizard she'd ever met who didn't have an Affinity.

"Okay," she said calmly. "Let me get this straight. Even though we met less than twenty-four hours ago, you think I'm allegedly 'looking for something,' and you want me to accompany *you*, a strange mele, across Cosconia so you can find your Affinity, which you somehow don't know?"

His face broke out into his widest smile yet. "Yep, that about sums it up!"

What the hells, she thought. "Alright. I'm in."

CHAPTER FOUR

Changeling in the Air

As a changeling I can switch to any race that I have physically touched.

—Matt Dinniman

---

38 years before the Twelve Race War
Jubox, Changeling Territory

Izzie took a long sip of coffee, her third cup since she'd sat down in the coffee shop. It was a rare day off for the midwizard, since she had completely thrown herself into her work from the moment she arrived. After six years in Jubox, her time in Changeling Territory was coming to an end. It was bittersweet, which surprised her—she'd thought for sure she'd be ready to move on to Water Fae Territory by now. It was hard to believe she'd already almost finished her time with two out of the twelve races in Cosconia, first the giants and now the changelings, even though it had been over ten years since she had graduated midwizardry school. Decades didn't feel particularly long to a wizard like Izzie, who would probably live for nearly a millennium, but it still felt like time was flying by. She worked for upwards of eighteen hours a day and felt like she was constantly learning. Though she faced many stressful situations, none were as terrifying or heartbreaking as Sydyr's delivery and subsequent demise nearly twelve years prior.

Midwizardry school had taught her a lot, especially the simulation illusions the headmistress mind mage created to test them, but there was nothing like being in the trenches working with pregnant freles day in and day out. After finishing midwizardry school, graduates were expected to spend at least six years in each of the communities they planned to specialize in. Some midwizards would only spend time with a few races, but Izzie's plan was to become an expert in the pregnancies and deliveries of every race in Cosconia. Maybe then she could finally find an answer to the questions that had plagued her for so many years.

A book sat on the table in front of Izzie. The title read *Sangrila*, which was the word for blood magic in the old wizard tongue. She'd inherited the book from her great-grandmother, a powerful and ancient wizard whom she'd only met once—the day she received the *Sangrila*. A note on the inside cover read, *Isadore, use your power to do good for those who deserve it, and don't hesitate to use it to do ill to those who don't.* Most of the book was far beyond her understanding, and even with her Affinity, she didn't have the Skill with blood magic to perform many of the spells.

"Woah," she said out loud as she stumbled across a strange spell, *sangresorba*, that detailed how to absorb somebody's blood to gain their Affinity. There was no way she would ever be powerful enough to perform something like that, if it was even actually possible, but there were lots of helpful tips in the book. She studied from it constantly to learn more about her craft and figure out ways to use blood magic for good.

She was working on a spell that would stop early labor, but she hadn't quite figured out how to do it yet. Nearly half the day she'd spent here, long enough to feel guilted into buying three cups of coffee, and she still wasn't making any progress. She kept getting distracted by her surroundings. Changeling culture was *fascinating*. Just looking around the coffee shop, she saw a human, a minotaur, a halfling, an orc, and several changelings in their natural state.

The natural state of the changeling is a 'blank slate' for a humanoid creature, Professor Seres had taught.

Humanoid. Izzie rolled her eyes, directing a comment to Dalfa. *Humans were the last to arrive in Cosconia and somehow they're the standard?*

Have you ever met a human? Dalfa asked. *They're just so... bland.*

The last human Izzie had interacted with was Vera, who had inspired her to attend midwizardry school.

I know, she whispered, hoping the professor wouldn't overhear them. *Can you imagine not having any magic? No Affinity?*

Dalfa made a gagging noise. *I wouldn't wish it on my worst enemy.*

The changeling professor continued her lecture, delving into a bit of Cosconian history.

The humans were the last race to arrive in Cosconia millennia ago, but their language, Fingol, became the language of the land. In those days, all the races of Cosconia lived together in harmony, which made speaking the same language necessary. Ancient tongues died out as society became integrated, but even after the Great Divide, each race continued to speak Fingol, in spite of being in their own separate territory. So now, thanks to the humans, any bipedal creature with two legs and two arms is referred to as 'humanoid.'

Wouldn't 'wizardoid' be a better term? Izzie asked Dalfa, and her friend stifled a laugh.

These days, Izzie couldn't imagine two, much less twelve, races living together. The racial segregation was profound in Cosconia, and Izzie was concerned there would some day be a breaking point.

The changelings in their natural state were various shades of solid gray. Their skin was smooth in appearance, but Izzie knew from experience it felt almost exactly the same as her own. Changeling faces all shared similar characteristics: a small gray nose, pale lips, and two tiny ears. They never had hair in their natural form, but many changelings throughout Cosconia had taken to wearing wigs even in that state to blend in with other races, though this was much less common in their own territory.

Their eyes, on the other hand, were as striking as they were diverse. A changeling frele, which Izzie could only barely differentiate from a changeling mele even after spending six years among them, was sitting next to her, and Izzie surreptitiously examined her eyes. Like all changelings, her eyes were massive, taking up nearly a third of her face, which was what differentiated them the most from other humanoid creatures. The frele next to her had eyes of a brilliant shade of purple she usually associated with royalty in old paintings. The deep purple was interrupted by streaks of gold in swirling patterns around her irises. It made Izzie self-conscious about her own eyes, which were but a dull charcoal, though in the right light they contained flecks of crimson.

The changeling looked up, making direct eye contact with Izzie, who quickly turned to inspect her coffee like it was the most fascinating beverage she'd ever seen.

"Can I help you?" the changeling asked nervously.

Changelings not only adopted the appearance of the creature they changed into, but they also gained some of their natural abilities and powers. A changeling blood sprite could perform a little blood magic. A changeling who spent most of their time as an elf would have a much longer lifespan. A changeling water fae could control water to a limited degree. A changeling wizard could even perform magic, though they would of course lack an Affinity. On the flip side, they also adopted their weaknesses. A changeling orc would bleed out quickly on the battlefield. A changeling minotaur would have the low intelligence associated with their race. A changeling human... Well, humans didn't have any particular racial weaknesses, but they didn't really have any strengths either.

"I'm sorry for staring; I was just lost in thought. But I did notice your eyes are absolutely stunning."

Izzie imagined that if the changeling could have blushed, she would have.

"You are too kind. I'm new here. I was worried there were more changeling wizards?"

"More? Besides who?"

"Oh, um, I meant the king and queen. Just them," she answered hurriedly. "Sorry, I'll leave you alone now."

Izzie knew the changeling king and queen, who were beloved by their constituents, were considered Apex Changelings, meaning they could morph into any of the other eleven Cosconian races.

"No need to apologize. My name is Isadore, but everybody calls me Izzie. Welcome to Jubox—as you can see, I'm not a native, but I have been here for the last six years helping deliver babies. I'm a midwizard. Tomorrow is actually my last day in town."

"A midwizard? Here in Jubox?" The changeling's words made her seem surprised, but her face indicated this wasn't news to her.

Izzie chuckled, knowing her kind were few and far between in Cosconia, so most people would likely never meet a midwizard in their lifetime. There were only two midwizards in her graduating class. "Yep, in the flesh. I'm here to learn about changeling pregnancies and deliveries. It's been... a tough few years."

The frele nodded. Even if she was new to Jubox, she wasn't new to being a changeling. She would know the dangers associated with pregnancy for changelings. "I don't know how you do it. I'm Pyke, by the way."

"Hi Pyke, nice to meet you. What brings you to Jubox?"

The changeling lowered her voice. "Actually... I was looking for you."

Izzie looked at her quizzically, wondering why on earth some random changeling in a coffee shop would be looking for her. Her time in Changeling Territory taught her that complications in changeling pregnancies were even more common than for giants, which was flipped from what she had learned in midwizardry school.

"That sounds a little ominous, if I'm being honest. Why were you looking for me?"

Pyke glanced around the coffee shop, clearly taking note of each patron. "Can we talk about it somewhere else?"

Izzie closed the *Sangrila* and sighed. She wasn't learning anything new that day either way, so she might as well see this through. She looked back at the changeling and nodded. Unlike in Giant Territory, where she had performed all of her deliveries in the giants' homes, here there was a small building in the middle of town that acted as a gathering place for laboring patients. She had a small "office" in the building, which was what she called the tiny room she could sleep in when she didn't want to walk home after a late night.

As the pair walked out, Izzie bid farewell to the barista, a changeling in human form. Coffee was popular in all of Cosconia, but especially in Changeling Territory. Like their language, humans had introduced the wonderful beverage upon their arrival to Cosconia, and it had immediately permeated the entire continent. The barista at her favorite coffee shop had adopted human form and spent years working in different places in Human Territory to learn the art of coffee-making, and it had certainly paid off.

Walking through Jubox was always a surreal experience for Izzie. It was like living in an alternate history where all races lived together in harmony, just like they did before the Great Divide. Elves walking side by side with orcs—a sight that would be utterly shocking if they weren't changelings—mermaids and water fae children playing around in the fountain, and even a few halflings running around. It made Izzie long for the time in the distant past when the races had lived together in harmony. Instead, she lived in a time of increasing tension between the races and constant border disputes and skirmishes.

At any given time, a minority of changelings in Jubox stayed in their natural forms, but many of them spent much of their time "morphed," as they called it.

"Where were you before Jubox?" There was a long silence before the changeling answered.

"I was in Gifldor."

"Wait... you were in Wizard Territory? My homeland?" Izzie was shocked. Though there was some intermingling of races— she was a prime example, though customs were naturally different for midwizards—one rarely saw any other races in

Gifldor. *But maybe...* Before Izzie was able to ask her a follow up question, Pyke quietly asked again if they could talk about this in private. This was getting weirder and weirder.

Upon entering the small office, Izzie sat the changeling down. "Alright, this is getting downright strange. What's going on?"

Pyke sighed and launched into her story, staring down at her hands instead of looking Izzie in the eyes. "I grew up right here in Jubox. My parents were both purists." Izzie knew from experience what that meant—they didn't morph. There was a small cult of changelings who thought morphing into other races was a betrayal to their own race. Why spend half your time as another race instead of embracing your own? The purists were squarely in the minority, but they were a very vocal minority. Their presence was quite small in Jubox, since the large capital city was rife with changelings who were constantly morphing, so most of them lived in the more rural areas of Changeling Territory.

"It was awful. They wouldn't let me *spruminga*."

Izzie winced. She knew forbidding *spruminga* was popular among purists, but she also knew it was considered barbaric by most other changelings. Since changelings could only morph into creatures they'd touched, there weren't a lot of options if they never left Changeling Territory. So, on their fifteenth birthday, changelings were given permission to leave the territory and wander Cosconia. Most tried to find as many other creatures as they could to touch and add to their repertoire, but most other races were wary of changelings.

"I'm assuming you didn't listen?"

Pyke smirked. "No chance. The day I turned fifteen, I ran away. I started in Halfling Territory, which gave me false confidence since it was so easy to befriend halflings and add them to my repertoire. From there, I traveled right to the plateaus of Minotaur Territory. I acted like an injured halfling and lured a minotaur to try to grab me and eat me, but I was able to get away right after he touched me. After that, I quickly made my way through the Dwarf and Human Territories by playing the changeling in distress, and just like that I was nearly halfway done."

"What about blood sprites?" she interjected. She couldn't imagine how dangerous it would have been for Pyke to enter their territory, much less try to touch one.

A distant look crossed the changeling's face. "It was... not what I expected. But I can't talk about that."

"Can't? Or won't?"

"Both, I guess. " She shrugged again, showing a nonchalance that didn't match her face. "Anyway, by that point, I was seventeen and full of well-earned confidence. I spent a while in Elf Territory, wandering from village to village in the Jerdalin Forest. It was easy to touch an elf, but I also wanted to learn from them. After that, since elves maintain such good relations with the mermaids and water fae, those two were easy. I don't want to talk about my time in Orc Territory, but I did what I needed to do. I went back to my halfling form to touch a giant, which was almost too easy—they barely notice you're there when you don't even come up to their shins. Then..."

"You only had one place left to go," Izzie finished her sentence. Could this changeling in front of her really have done it? Made herself into an Apex? "What happened in Gifldor?"

"I... don't think you're going to like this part of the story. Do you promise not to kill me if I tell you?"

"*Kill* you? " Izzie was taken aback. "I'm a *midwizard*. I bring life *into* the world. Why on earth would I *kill you*?" Izzie was starting to feel more and more uneasy about the situation she'd found herself in. For a moment, she wondered if Pyke somehow knew about her past, but that wasn't possible. *Was it?*

"You promise you won't hurt me? No matter what I tell you?"

"I would never hurt anybody!" Izzie answered, exasperated. That wasn't *strictly* true, but Pyke didn't need to know that. Izzie would never hurt anybody *again*. "Yes, I promise. Spit it out."

"Okay, but remember you promised. By the time I arrived in Gifldor, I could feel the power coursing through my veins. Most changelings gain two, maybe three morphs in their lives. I was probably already more powerful than everybody except the king and queen."

Izzie started to feel sick to her stomach.

"I waited for nightfall outside the university and changed into my blood sprite form. I knew normal blood sprites weren't powerful enough to kill wizards, but by this point, I was far more powerful than a normal sprite. There was a wizarding student wandering home drunk in the middle of the night. He never saw it coming. I didn't plan to kill him—all I wanted to do was touch him and move on, but he was so frightened after he felt my touch that he panicked and tried to attack me. I cast one little blood magic spell and…"

Izzie didn't know what to say. She now understood why Pyke had made her promise. Wizarding custom dictated the penalty for slaying a wizard was death, and it could be exacted by any wizard at any time without consequence. *So she really is an Apex. I have to tread carefully here.* "So you're an Apex. Are you here to overthrow the king and queen?"

Pyke exploded with laughter. "Ha! I have no interest in leadership. They can keep running this Territory, I don't give two shits." The meek, shy changeling Izzie had met in the coffee shop was gone, replaced by a creature who clearly knew her own power. She wasn't sure which one was the real Pyke.

"Why are you telling me all this? You don't even know me."

"I've never told anybody, and I needed to get it off my chest."

"Even though technically I should kill you for murdering a wizard?"

" Should? Sure. Can? You'd have to be pretty powerful to kill me."

Izzie's blood magic had grown stronger since graduating, but she still didn't feel particularly Skilled, especially in offensive magic. "What does any of this have to do with me?"

"Unfortunately, the story didn't end there. Once I turned into an Apex, I was drunk on power. I spent years in wizard form, learning magic. My goal was to grow powerful enough to come back here and put an end to the purist cult once and for all. Nobody should be forced to remain in their natural changeling state for life. We can become so powerful—who would give that up?"

"You still haven't answered my question. I don't want to get involved. I won't even be in Jubox this time next week. Why did you seek me out?"

"Well, my plan was to come back here and do away with the purists. I was almost done with my studies in Gifldor. And then I met a mele."

Realization dawned over Izzie. She looked closer at the changeling in front of her, who was wearing a long, baggy top over an oversized pair of pants. Pyke wasn't staring down at her hands while she talked. She was looking at her belly.

"You're pregnant," Izzie said. It was a statement, not a question. It was painfully obvious now that Izzie was paying attention. *What kind of midwizard doesn't even notice when somebody is pregnant?*

Pyke nodded, her eyes filling with tears. "When I found out I was pregnant, I started asking around about midwizard care. I would have stayed in Gifldor, but I knew Nesbreth wouldn't be happy when he found out the truth about me being a changeling."

"I assume he's the baby's father?"

Pyke nodded again. "He was a professor there. I was his student."

"Did you tell him?"

"I was terrified. I knew once the baby came, he would know I was a changeling, not a wizard. So I left without telling him. I went to the midwizardry school to seek help. I heard they were willing to help freles in trouble. I talked to somebody named Seres—a professor there."

Izzie's face lit up. "Professor Seres! She was our changeling professor who taught us about your pregnancies."

"She was the one who told me to find you. She knew your schedule would have you in Changeling Territory for a few more months, so she said I could come here and find you. And that's exactly what I did. This baby is special."

Izzie mentally rolled her eyes. Everybody thought their baby was "special." How many times had she heard that now? "So what now? If he doesn't know about the baby, shouldn't you be safe?"

Pyke bit her lip. "That's what I thought, but right before I left town, I heard he was looking for me. That he was going to find me."

Izzie stood up and started to back away. "Oh no. I'm not getting involved in all this. I've already had more drama than any midwizard ever should."

"I know what's in your bag."

"What are you talking about? There's all kinds of stuff in my bag."

"I know you can show me my baby."

Izzie went pale. How could she possibly know about that? She hadn't taken it out of her bag in years. "Who told you?"

Pyke grimaced. "I may have been somewhat... forceful with your professor. But I need you to do this." Minotaur horns sprouted from her barren head, and Pyke pointed them at Izzie. She wasn't asking. Izzie could tell the changeling wasn't used to being threatening, but pregnancy had a tendency to change you.

Izzie almost gave in, but she couldn't do it. She wouldn't be bullied by anybody, even a powerful Apex Changeling. Before Pyke had a chance to react, Izzie cast *bajasangra*. The changeling fell unconscious, and Izzie ran away as fast as she could.

* * *

Dear Izzie,

Orc Territory has been pretty tough for me. These postpartum hemorrhages are brutal. You wouldn't think an orc would even have that much blood, but I've seen so many freles not survive the labor process. I bet your blood magic would be a huge help here, but I feel more useless every day. It's like I can't save anybody anymore. Thankfully, I met an amazing soldier here named Kurai. He's such a nice mele! I brag about you to him all the time. Remember that time you used your frijangre spell to freeze my blood when that mele slipped something into my drink at a party? He really got a kick out of that story!

Kurai says he's a pacifist, but apparently the orcs are gearing up in case Cosconia ever goes to war again—crazy thought right? I tried to read the mind of one of the orc lieutenants, but he caught me before I could find anything out. My skills are getting better every day though! I also found out how to create a copy of myself the other day, which was super fun.

Anyway, I hope you're doing better than I am. Being a midwizard is really hard, and I miss you dearly.

Yours truly,

Dalfa

CHAPTER FIVE

The Majalir

Perilous to us all are the devices of an art
deeper than we possess ourselves.

—*J.R.R. Tolkien*

---

38 years before the Twelve Race War
Ajabu, Water Fae Territory

Izzie reread Dalfa's letter when she finally settled into the first water fae town she could find after getting the hells out of Changeling Territory. They had cast a spell in midwizardry school that would ensure their letters always found each other, so they could easily write to each other. She was worried about Dalfa. The bleak outcomes for both mothers and babies in Cosconia was enough to humble even the most levelheaded person, and Dalfa was known for having big feelings and even bigger reactions to said feelings. Though it had been years since she'd seen her best friend, they kept up their correspondence via letter whenever possible. She was glad Dalfa had a new friend she could trust, but Izzie had to admit the warmongering orcish culture made her nervous. It had been a bit since she had time to write a letter in return, but it was at the top of her to-do list.

She felt bad for making the pregnant Pyke pass out by diverting all the blood away from her brain with her *bajasangra* spell, but the last thing she needed was to be wrapped up in drama like she had been in Giant Territory. Her hair was a mess from her frantic departure, and the pesky red strand fell in front of her face like always. She could feel her forehead breaking out, likely from the stress. She'd wandered into town in the middle of the night, and the only lantern lit in the whole place had been in front of this building. Based on the number of houses she saw on her way in, this town couldn't have more than a few hundred people. Since she had been planning on leaving Changeling Territory the next day anyway, she already had a destination in mind. She'd been communicating by letter with a water fae physician in a city named Pwise, which she thought was about a three-day trip from Ajabu.

Izzie rested her head on the straw pillow of the inn she'd checked into just a few hours prior. It looked like the sun was going to be up in a few minutes, so she'd sleep for a bit and then set off for Pwise. Just as she drifted off to sleep and the first dream—or, more likely, nightmare—began to play in her mind, she awoke to a frantic pounding on her door. *You've gotta be kidding me.* She wondered who could possibly be at her door since she didn't know anybody in this town, and she'd specifically instructed the innkeeper not to wake her until midday.

She briefly considered asking who it was before opening the door. *But*, she thought to herself smugly, *I am a blood mage. So I'll probably be fine.* While she was in the coffee shop in Jubox, she'd actually uncovered the key to a new offensive blood magic spell. She hoped she would never have to use it, but was willing to if necessary. She opened the door to see... herself? It was like looking in a reflecting pool. Before she had a chance to panic, the wizard in front of her shifted to the natural changeling form of Pyke.

"Sorry," she huffed, out of breath. "I convinced the innkeeper I was your twin sister. He'd never seen a twin before since I don't think fae have them, which was why he let me come back to find you."

Izzie raised her wand. Even though it was a replacement wand for the one she'd lost on the worst day of her life, it got the job done. She hadn't used any offensive magic in decades, but she would protect herself if push came to shove. Before she had the chance to shoot off a spell, her wand was flying out of her hand across the room. Pyke had a genuine wizard wand pointed at her. Izzie slowly raised her hands in a sign of surrender.

Pyke grimaced like she was ashamed of herself. "I'm so sorry I had to do that to you. Please, you have to show me my baby."

"Why?!" Izzie shouted with no regard for the late hour. "Why should you get special treatment?"

"Do you believe in Sparilism?"

Izzie felt like she got whiplash from the sudden change in topic. She sat with the question for a moment. She was never particularly religious, but she understood the basic tenets of Cosconia's prevailing religion. Its evangelists said every soul would be reincarnated in the next life as a different race based on their actions in this life. There were twelve gods for twelve races, each of whom presided over their own heaven and sentenced those not worthy to one of the twelve hells. Sparilists believed every soul would be reincarnated twelve times, once for each race. At the completion of the twelfth life cycle, one's actions over those cycles were all added together, and the good was weighed against the evil. If the sum of one's actions was net positive, they could choose the heaven in which they would spend eternity. If not, the gods conspired to choose which hell to send them to.

"More or less," she lied. "Why?"

"Do you know what Sparilism says about changelings?"

Izzie shook her head. She barely knew what it said about wizards.

"The more creatures a changeling has in their repertoire, the stronger they become, but at a high cost. Each new morph splits the changeling's soul anew, which is both physically and mentally painful. Sparilism tells us each time we gain a new morph, the part of our soul that would have been reincarnated into that race is consumed."

"What does that mean?"

"This life is it for me. I've morphed into every race. I'm not coming back."

Izzie wasn't sure she believed anybody would be reincarnated, as there was no scientific proof of such a phenomenon, but she could understand how scary the trade-off must be.

"Well that was your choice. You could have skipped *spruminga* like your parents wanted."

"I know. I was young and dumb. But now I'm going to be a mother." A single tear fell down Pyke's face. "At least, I hope I am."

For the first time, Izzie felt true sympathy for the frele.

"I have to know. I promise, if you show me, I'll leave you alone. You'll never hear from me again. I just need to know." Pyke's wand was still pointed at Izzie, but the tremor in the changeling's hand was evident.

Unlike giantess pregnancies, changeling pregnancies weren't dangerous for changeling freles—it would be unusual for a changeling to die during pregnancy or delivery. Unfortunately, the same couldn't be said for their babies. Izzie had learned in midwizardry school that nearly ten percent of all changeling babies were stillborn, meaning they passed before they even took their first breath in this world. However, she had kept detailed notes during her time in Jubox, and she'd observed the rate to be closer to twenty-five percent. Just like how giantess pregnancies were more deadly than she'd learned. Izzie supposed the information she'd learned in school was out of date, but she was starting to become worried there was something more ominous at play. Maybe Cosconia's Maternal Magic was fading or dying for some reason.

I don't really have a choice here, do I? "Swear you won't hurt me. Swear that once I do this, you'll let me go in peace. Swear it on the baby."

The changeling hesitated for a moment, but she relented. "I swear it," she said, placing her hand on her belly. Izzie pulled the *majalir* out of her bag.

"Then I'll do it. But I have to warn you—there can be some... unintended consequences."

In an ideal situation, a changeling baby was born looking like a miniature version of a changeling in their natural form—a precious gray blob with gigantic eyes. All changeling babies were born with gray eyes, making them very hard to differentiate from one another, but they would eventually develop into the striking and unique patterns their race was known for. Most of the time, the changeling baby would enter the world as a little gray blob, much to their parents' delight.

The rest of the time, the parents weren't so lucky. The one feature in common to practically every stillborn changeling baby was the presence of a body part from another race. A mermaid tail. Elven ears. A dwarven beard—adorable but deadly. As far as she knew, the mortality was one hundred percent when a changeling baby wasn't born as a pure changeling.

Ironically, this was where the changeling purists were lucky. If a changeling had never morphed in their lives, their baby would be born perfectly healthy. This was part of their entire philosophy—if they were meant to morph, why would it be so bad for their offspring? It was a reasonable argument, but since most changelings felt like asking them not to morph was like asking them to cut off their own hands, it was just an accepted part of life. If you wanted to morph, it was a risk you'd have to take.

Izzie hesitantly opened her bag, knowing exactly what was about to happen.

"This idea is dumber than the time you tried to rip off a prostitute in a nightclub," her bag kindly informed her. Pyke looked at her quizzically, a question forming on her lips.

"Don't ask." She turned her attention back to her bag. "Okay first of all, that was a complete misunderstanding. Second of all... I asked you not to bring that up anymore!"

"Fine, but your mother and father will be hearing about this young lady!"

"My parents are dead!"

"That's another thing! You've been inside me how many times and you never talk about your past?"

"Okay gross, you make that joke every day. It really never gets old for you does it?"

"You're going to give me a hard time about being old? Old Gandalf-ass bitch..."

"HEY! Language! What does that even mean? Just hand it over, alright?"

Finally relenting from its verbal beatdown, the bag produced a smooth crystal ball about the size of Izzie's head. The ball itself was light as a feather, but it carried an almost palpable supernatural weight. The room darkened as it seemed to suck in the light from the torches on the wall.

Pyke reached out to touch it, but Izzie yanked it away from the pregnant changeling. "Don't even think about it. I promise you don't want to."

"That's it? That's the maj-thingy?"

"The *majalir*, yes," Izzie corrected her. "One of only a few dozen remaining in Cosconia."

"Where—"

"Nope. Not getting into that. None of your business where I got it. You shouldn't even know I have it."

The magical device in front of her had many purposes, tailored to the specific user. Though it wasn't its original use, Izzie had a special use for hers. She rarely ever used it, since she knew *majalirs* were rare and powerful enough it would put a target on her back. Some used it to see the future. Others to spy on their enemies. Izzie used hers for a *very* different purpose.

"Are you sure you want to do this? Even if we find out your baby is affected, there's nothing we will be able to do." That was why Izzie hadn't used it at all in Changeling Territory. Even if she identified a fetus that would be stillborn, there was nothing she could do about it. She was there to help deliver babies and support the freles with babies who didn't make it.

"I know," Pyke answered quietly, the atmosphere in the room tense. "I just have to see."

Izzie had developed a magical technique she referred to as "ultrasound." She was able to use a spell to vibrate her wand at a frequency so fast its vibrations were audible to her finely tuned ear, though most creatures with normal hearing couldn't hear it. She'd never tried it on an elf, but she suspected they would be able to perceive the sound with their heightened senses. Izzie would be lying if she said she knew exactly how it worked other than simply "magic," but when she placed her wand on the belly of a pregnant patient, she could feel the vibrations bounce off the baby inside. It wasn't in line with her Affinity, but her training as a midwizard gave her the Skill necessary, and there was certainly no lack of Intent in a situation like this.

This was where the *majalir* came in. Many years before, with the help of Professor Seres (who was now on her shit list for getting herself overpowered by Pyke), she was able to rig the device to receive the vibrations and display a picture of what was inside of the uterus. The picture was shockingly crystal clear to her trained eye, but it would look like a blurry gray mess to anybody else.

Izzie gently placed her wand on Pyke's abdomen, her other hand resting on the *majalir*. Goosebumps appeared on the frele's skin.

"*Vibro ultrasonorium.*" The midwizard cast the spell under her breath. Immediately, the wand started vibrating so fast it wasn't visible even to her sharp eyes. Pyke gasped but quickly controlled her breathing, focusing her vision on the *majalir*.

A fuzzy grayscale image started to form—Izzie still wasn't able to figure out how to get the image in color. The first thing that became clear was a large pair of definitively changeling eyes. A good start, since Izzie had seen plenty of stillborn changeling babies with the small eyes of a human or the slanted eyes of an elf. Besides the ability to morph into any other living creature, another characteristic unique to changelings was the length of their pregnancies—they were completely variable. She'd seen pregnancies that lasted only three months, about the length of a halfling pregnancy, all the way up to nearly three years, the average length of an elven pregnancy. She couldn't tell how far along the changeling was. Knowing Pyke wouldn't be able to make any sense of the images on her own, she narrated her findings.

"Okay, I see a set of changeling eyes. No beard. No pointy ears. So far, so good," she said, and she could see the changeling's demeanor slowly start shifting from apprehension to relief. "I've never seen any torso anomalies except in rare minotaur cases, but this is obviously not a minotaur torso. A minotorso, if you will," Izzie joked, trying to lighten the mood with her clever portmanteau.

The changeling glared at her. "Seriously? I'm on the run from a powerful wizard and trying to figure out if my baby is going to die, and you're making puns?"

"Even I have to say that was a *bag* one," her bag chimed in unhelpfully.

"I've gotta remember to close that fucking thing..." Izzie mumbled, though she secretly loved the snide comments. It was a bag after her own heart. She still didn't understand exactly *why* Pyke's former paramour was chasing her—if any of her story was even true—but she didn't want to know the details. "Anyway, everything looks great thus far. Baby is definitely moving around a lot!"

At this, the changeling lit up. Though Izzie was still extremely unhappy she'd been forced to do this, she had to remember that at the end of the day, Pyke was just a scared mother hoping her baby was okay. Even if she didn't approve of the methods, she couldn't blame anybody for wanting to ensure their baby was safe and healthy. Izzie thought about what she would do if she could get pregnant. Would she threaten a powerful wizard to make sure she was healthy? *Of course I would. I'd threaten Cect himself if I thought it would save my baby.* Izzie was glad she hadn't made the comment aloud, since she tried to avoid uttering the name of the wizard god, even if she wasn't sure she believed in him.

She got the sense Pyke wasn't actually the power hungry monster she came off as.

"Those are two stubby changeling arms I see wiggling about!" Izzie moved her wand around a little, trying to find the legs and officially confirm this would be a healthy baby. "There they are! While the ultrasound magic isn't perfect…" Izzie smiled. "Congratulations, Pyke. You're going to have a healthy baby." Izzie pulled her wand away, ready to put this whole situation to rest.

The changeling broke out into a tearful smile, which immediately faltered. "Wait a second. Can you see the… y'know?"

"Cash and prizes? Scrumdiddlyumptious? Hooha? Eggplant emoji?" Izzie's bag chimed in before getting a swift kick.

"Really? You're going to force me to use an ancient magical tool to figure out what kind of genitals your kid is gonna have?" Izzie replied, exasperated. The changeling nodded her head sheepishly, so Izzie placed her wand back on Pyke's abdomen and recast her spell. Thankfully, there was no uncertainty. "Looks like you're going to be a boy m—"

The black and white image of the changeling baby disappeared from the *majalir*. All of the light seemed to be sucked from the room. Izzie tried to move the device, but it was firmly stuck in place. Vivid color images began flashing across the crystal ball. A bloodied orc. A massive battalion of elves, bows in hand. A herd of minotaurs charging into battle. A pile of slaughtered fae. A massive building somehow made of… metal? With Izzie herself standing in front of it. Twelve individuals, one of each race, gathered in a circle. And a hooded… something. A human? A changeling? Maybe an elf? This image lingered in the crystal ball. It seemed somehow known and unknown at the same time.

As quickly as they started, the images stopped. Neither of the pair said a word, processing the shocking and confusing images that had just flashed across the *majalir*.

Finally, the silence was broken by her bag. "What the bloody hell was that?"

Pyke responded, voice breaking with emotion. "That's my baby's father."

* * *

83 years before the Twelve Race War
Lactut, Minotaur Territory

"Fire?"

"Nope. Still have a burn on my ass as proof."

"Mental?"

"I can barely control my own thoughts, much less somebody else's."

"Hmmm. Beast?"

"Our family dog didn't even like me."

"Awww you had a puppy? What was its name?"

"Sawyer. Chompy little bastard. Did you have any pets?"

Isadore shook her head. "Wasn't allowed. My aunt was a... harsh woman."

"You were raised by your aunt?"

"Not really. My mom died giving birth to my little brother, so our neighbor reluctantly took me in."

"What about your dad?"

Isadore shrugged. "Never met the mele. Never wanted to. He abandoned my mom while she was pregnant with my brother."

"No other family?"

"Are you a Sparilist Inquisitor? Why does it feel like you're interrogating me?"

Syrel laughed, which forced a smile out of Isadore. Talking about her family was always difficult, but even in the few months since she'd met him, Syrel's laugh always brought joy to her soul. "You just asked me like a hundred questions!"

"I'm trying to help you figure out your Affinity! Isn't that the whole point of this excursion?"

"I can assure you, I've tried them all. Besides, the point of this excursion is to get you pregnant." He cast her a sly smile.

She glared at him. After they'd set out from Gifldor, she'd reluctantly shared with him that she was infertile and trying to figure out how to become pregnant. "No," she retorted, her tone falsely firm. "We're trying to figure out *how* to get me pregnant."

"I can think of at least one way." He winked at her.

She smacked the back of his head, tousling his already tousled black hair. "If it was that simple, my ex would have gotten me pregnant long ago."

"But—"

"And you *know* I hate winking."

"Why do you think I do it so much?"

Isadore groaned. "So why are we starting in Minotaur Territory? How is that going to help you find your Affinity?"

"It's not. We're here for you."

She cocked her head, awaiting further explanation.

"The current herd leader, Labtira, has fathered over a thousand offspring. I figured maybe he would know a thing or two about fertility."

In a moment of inspiration, Isadore grabbed Syrel by his chin and pulled him into a kiss. Normally first kisses were awkward, fumbling affairs. Not this one. Her lips met his in an explosion of sparks like sword hitting shield. She gently cradled his cheek in her hand as he pulled her closer by her waist. Before she could get too carried away, she reluctantly broke contact.

"W-what was that all about?" Syrel stuttered breathlessly.

"I dunno. I was just overcome at how sweet and thoughtful it was for you to immediately take us somewhere that might help on my quest."

"But you told me on day one of this journey this would be *strictly* platonic. I think your exact words were 'I'd rather lick the inside of an orc's armpit than be romantically involved with you.'"

"And then you told me you wished you could be an orc's armpit." She rolled her eyes.

Syrel laughed at his past joke, which was annoying and endearing. He continued, "And then you said 'If you try anything, you'll wish you were on the receiving end of a blood sprite curse."

Isadore shrugged. "I changed my mind. I think I like you."

CHAPTER SIX

A Fae Mood

Faeries are fallen angels, cast down out of heaven for their pride.

—Cassandra Clare

---

38 years before the Twelve Race War
Ajabu, Water Fae Territory

"I knew getting involved with that changeling was a bad idea, Izzie!" her bag protested as she quickly threw the few items she'd unpacked into it. "She's been nothing but trouble since the moment you awkwardly stared at her in that coffee shop!"

"You think this was *my* idea?! Do you realize how powerful she is? I had no choice in the matter! Besides, she hunted me down." As soon as Izzie had heard that the terrifying figure she'd seen in the *majalir* was involved with Pyke, she had kicked the changeling out of her room and started getting ready to get the hells out of town. From what she understood of the story, Pyke had needed to flee to escape this wizard, who was clearly powerful enough to strike fear into somebody who was secretly one of the strongest creatures in all Cosconia. The details were a bit fuzzy, but Izzie wasn't sticking around to get to the bottom of it.

She couldn't stop playing those images from the *majalir* over and over in her head. She tried to forget them, but they were permanently seared into her brain. The first several images were clearly related to warfare. That made Izzie nervous given the rising racial tension in Cosconia. A bloody orc made sense—the different factions were always warring with each other, but that violence rarely spilled out of Orc Territory. Even minotaurs charging into a battle wasn't completely shocking. But the sight of an army of elves gave her chills. Her experience with elves was that they were gentle, peaceful creatures, but ruthless and strong when necessary. *What would have to happen to get the elves to gather into an army?* Izzie wondered.

The most surprising thing she'd seen was naturally the assembly of a creature from each race communing together. It had probably been millenia since all twelve races were together in one territory, much less one room. Maybe it was just a group of changelings—could that be why she saw it when she was with Pyke? She certainly had the power to upset the entire changeling governmental structure. And a metal building? Of course swords and shields and plenty of other smaller things were made of metal, almost all of which was mined by the dwarves and sold to other races, but an entire building made of metal didn't make sense.

None of those compared to the last image that had stayed in the *majalir* for what felt like ages. It looked foreign yet familiar. Like her favorite painting, drastically warped by the elements over time. And Pyke had *slept* with him?

"I'm still out here, you know," a muffled voice carried through the door. "I'm not going anywhere until you tell me how you know Nesbreth and help me figure out how I can escape him."

At this, Izzie stopped packing and swung the door open in rage. "You have got some nerve chasing me here. How would I possibly know your baby daddy? I *told* you using that godsforsaken device could have unforeseen effects. I *told* you it was a bad idea, and *you* forced me to use it anyway. Now you're the one who has to deal with the consequences. Not me. It's not my fault you have bad taste in partners." She wasn't in the mood to be extending any mercy to somebody who had manipulated and used her. "Isn't it enough I helped you find out your baby was going to be fine?"

Just before she could slam the door in the changeling's face yet again, the door of the only other room in the inn opened up a crack. A sleepy voice drifted out. "What's all the racket out here? It's the middle of the night."

Pyke looked unashamed, but Izzie felt bad. She was already upset about being woken up in the middle of the night, and now she'd done the same to the only other occupant of the small inn. The door opened up further, revealing the most stunning creature Izzie had ever laid her eyes on.

Matching Izzie's tall stature and towering above the small changeling, who had morphed back into her natural form, the water fae practically glowed with ethereal beauty. Her skin was whiter than the snow Izzie had trudged through in Giant Territory. Alabaster hair cascaded down her shoulders all the way to her narrow waist. Her eyes glowed the vibrant blue of sunlight shining down on the ocean.

"Um... sorry. Hi, I'm Lulu."

Izzie responded before Pyke could. "I was just leaving. Alone. I'm sorry to have woken you, but I assure you there will be no more disturbances." She turned to the changeling. "I'm going to Pwise."

The fae lit up. "I'm actually on my way to Pwise too! I'd be happy to take you there!" Her warm smile illuminated the dark night in the small town.

"We'd love some company!" Pyke responded cheerily.

Izzie exploded. "*WE*? There is no WE! I don't know you. I don't *want* to know you. *I* will be going off on my own before *you* ruin my life." The changeling shrank in response to her words.

A pained expression crossed Pyke's face, making Izzie calm down a bit. "I'm sorry," she added reluctantly. "I just... I need to go." To Izzie's great shock, Pyke broke down before her eyes. Tears cascaded from her vivid purple eyes down her featureless face. At first, Izzie resisted feeling sorry for her. This was the same creature who had forced her to perform dangerous magic she didn't even want to use, and now she was paying the consequences.

"I'm scared," she whispered, barely audible. Tears still flowed down her gray cheeks. "I'm so scared and alone and I don't know what to do. I'm afraid he's going to take my baby for himself."

Izzie's stomach sank. She wasn't acting like a midwizard—she was acting like a monster. She shouldn't be mad at Pyke. She *couldn't* be mad at Pyke. Pyke was the *victim* here, not the aggressor. She was just a scared frele, doing whatever she could to protect her baby. On the run from a wizard who seemed hellsbent on finding her. In an instant, Izzie's perspective on the changeling shifted—and her perspective on herself changed too. She was a *midwizard*. Somebody who had dedicated her life to protecting and serving freles. Yet she was being cruel to a frele who had sought her out to be an ally, not an enemy.

Lulu, who had watched the exchange wordlessly, set her hand on Pyke's shoulder, slender fingers squeezing the changeling's featureless shoulder in a comforting gesture. She didn't ask the girl any questions, but gently guided her into her own room, shutting the door behind them.

Izzie stood dumbly in the hallway. She didn't blame the fae for getting Pyke away from her. She tried to put herself in Pyke's shoes. Pregnant. On the run. Terrified. Alone. Being screamed at in the middle of the night by the one person she'd come to for help—even if her methods were questionable.

"That was pretty brutal, Iz," her bag said softly. *Damn*, if that punk thought she was being mean, her explosion must have been worse than she realized.

"Was I really that angry?" she asked, dreading the answer.

"I would say on a scale from Darrow after Eo's death to Violet when Shadow Daddy Xaden does literally anything, I would say you clocked in at 'man walking in to find out he's been cucked.'"

"... Okay I didn't get any of that, but I'm assuming the moral of the story is that I came off as a huge asshole, yeah?"

"Oh yeah. Big time."

Izzie was disgusted with herself. Determined to make the situation right, she gently knocked on Lulu's door. She'd been standing in the hallway reflecting for at least half an hour, and the sound of tears drifting through the door had stopped.

"Go away," came the sound of Pyke's voice, raspy from crying.

Izzie knocked more insistently. "Please, let me come in. I need to apologize."

The water fae opened the door a crack. "... I don't think she wants to see you right now. She's in rough shape."

"I know. I need to apologize for my outburst. It was completely out of character."

Lulu was visibly skeptical.

"I don't blame you for not believing me, but can I just come in and say I'm sorry? If she never wants to see me again, that's okay." Izzie was inwardly amused at how quickly she'd gone from telling the girl to leave her alone to begging to see her one last time.

The door opened all the way to reveal Pyke in water fae form—changelings commonly morphed to match the appearance of those around them when possible. She was no longer crying, but her eyes were puffy and her face red. "Didn't you just tell me you were leaving? *Alone?*" Izzie winced at the jab, even though it was completely valid. Pyke was spitting her own words back at her.

Instead of speaking, Izzie pulled the changeling into a tight embrace. Pyke resisted, immediately attempting to withdraw, but Izzie didn't let her go. She pressed the girl's face into her shoulder, which quickly became wet with tears as Pyke began crying again.

"I didn't think I had any more tears left in me," she choked out. Izzie's own tears fell into the changeling's now white hair, which Izzie stroked in long, smooth motions. She didn't know why she was crying. Part of her felt deep sympathy for the pregnant changeling. Part of her was jealous Pyke was pregnant and she wasn't.

"Shhhh. Shh. I know. It's okay," Izzie comforted the changeling.

Several minutes into perhaps the longest hug Izzie had ever participated in, she felt another set of arms wrap around the pair of them. Lulu had joined their embrace, placing her strong arms around the both of them. The trio stood there quietly, Izzie and Pyke both weeping openly.

Finally, Lulu stepped back and spoke up. "Don't get me wrong—I'm all for helping out a frele in need. But what the *actual fuck* is going on here?"

Pyke stepped away from Izzie's hug, and for a moment all three were silent. Then Pyke burst out laughing. This ignited an immediate chain reaction, as the wizard and the fae also broke down in raucous laughter. None of them could regain control as the explosive laughter continued, a different kind of tears now streaming down each of their faces. Lulu collapsed to the floor in gasping peals of laughter. Here they were, three strangers, with a case of the giggles at a random inn in the middle of the night.

Just as the laughter started to die down, a loud rapping on the door shut the freles up in a heartbeat. Lulu cautiously opened it to reveal the fae innkeeper's red, angry face in the doorway.

"What in the name of the gods is going on up here? It's the crack of dawn and my husband and I can't sleep with the sobbing and laughing and laughing and sobbing. This ain't tea time; people are trying to sleep for crying out loud!" At that moment, the innkeeper seemed to realize he hadn't initially noticed the other two in the room—his only other guest, and the "twin sister" he'd let visit. It looked like he was about to protest her presence, but he just shook his head. "Keep yer mouths shut or you'll all be asked to leave." The door slammed shut.

Lulu slowly turned around to look at the other two. They remained silent for another moment before simultaneously bursting forth in another fit of laughter, poorly attempting to do so quietly. Finally, Pyke regained control and wiped the tears away from her eyes. "I think you're going to want to sit down for this."

As the sun rose in the sky, Pyke shared the same story with Lulu she'd shared with Izzie just days before, except this time, she shared significantly more detail. Like the stories often seemed to go, Pyke's relationship with Nesbreth was a storybook romance at first. He worshipped the ground she walked on. He was exactly the kind of guy she'd always been searching for. They fell in love quickly and deeply. She didn't think it was possible for her to get pregnant with his baby, her being a changeling and him a wizard, but it happened so quickly. After she found out she was pregnant, she just needed space to think about what to do, so she took off. While she was taking shelter at the midwizardry school, she started hearing rumors about Nesbreth being hellbent on finding her. She was afraid he'd found out she was a changeling and would take her son as his own.

Once she had told her tale, Izzie shared her own. She started with midwizardry school, not wanting to get into the complicated time before that, and talked about her time in Giant Territory and Changeling Territory. "As a midwizard, my plan is to spend about six years with each race learning everything I can about labor, childbirth, and basically all things freles' health. My next one is supposed to be in Pwise, where I've been communicating with a local doctor." She paused, internally confirming she truly meant what she was about to say. "Would you two like to join me?"

Lulu and Pyke both grinned.

"It's a little ironic," Lulu answered. "Pyke is running from her baby daddy, and I'm hoping to reunite with mine. Well, one day. I hope."

Izzie raised her eyebrow. "Oh? What's his name?"

Lulu had stars in her eyes when she answered, "Thelonius."

"Why did you leave him?" Pyke asked, looking jealous of the healthy relationship.

"It's... a long story. It's probably better if I just show you."

* * *

Izzie,

Twelve hells, I hope you're having a better experience than I am. No wonder nobody wants to be a midwizard; we're useless. Besides you of course—I'm sure you're out there saving lives every day. I was just telling Kurai the other day how powerful your blood magic is. I talk about you so much he really wants to meet you!

I have to be honest, Iz. I'm struggling. It's so hard watching freles die every day. I'm a bit ashamed to admit this, but I've taken to using my mind magic to convince some of the orcs not to get pregnant. It's the only way I can save them. How come nobody told us it was going to be this hard? Or did they and I just wasn't listening? I'm starting to think maybe goofing off together in class all the time was a bad idea. But we just had so much fun! Remember during that lecture in our halfling unit when we secretly took shots every time the professor said the word "tiny"? We were so drunk we were seeing triple. Speaking of triple, can you believe I can use my mind magic to make two copies of myself now? Crazy!

I miss you. Reminiscing on our good times together helps me through the tough times on the road. Hope to see you again soon.

Dalfa

CHAPTER SEVEN

The Water Palace

Sublime wonders lie in store,

I am shown a regal residence;

a mighty kingdom, an empire

with more grandeur than before...

—*E.A. Bucchianeri*

---

38 years before the Twelve Race War
Pwise, Water Fae Territory

"Then what happened?" Pyke chuckled as Lulu told her story. The three freles had become fast friends on their journey from Ajabu to Pwise. Izzie sensed the same thing in Pyke and Lulu that she felt herself—a sense of loneliness. Each of them had been on their own journey, alone, before they came together. They spent the entire trip telling stories, laughing, crying, and bonding. It was evident they all needed companionship.

"What do you think? I put my clothes back on, stepped over the ruins of my bed, and got the hells out of there as fast as I could."

Izzie laughed uproariously.

"I thought I was going to have to use my water magic to blast my way out of there." Each one of the fae's stories was wilder than the last.

Lulu led Pyke and Izzie through the winding streets of Pwise, the largest water fae city in Cosconia. The city sprawled outward from the banks of the Cosc River, with natural and fae-made channels and streams crisscrossing the entire city. Water magic, the only type water fae could practice, practically oozed from the city, with fountains and water sculptures that defied the laws of nature. Each fae they passed, mele and frele alike, was more beautiful than the last. Many were swimming and dancing in the waterways they crossed over. Every house had an offshoot of a waterway running directly through it, water being essential for fae survival. They weren't like mermaids, who couldn't live outside the water, but they were just as comfortable inside the water as outside of it. Water fae could hold their breath underwater for hours, but they didn't have gills, which was why they needed to live outside the water.

After several hours of walking, barely speaking as the two newcomers took in the splendor of the city and its inhabitants, they arrived on the bank of the Cosc. The river, which Lulu had explained was named after the water fae word for magic, was the namesake for the entire continent. Pwise was located at the widest portion of the river—it was nearly ten miles from shore to shore. Izzie could barely make out a few dozen buildings on the other side of the river, which was where the Wasteland started, but most of Pwise was located on this side of the Cosc.

The trio wandered down the banks of the river for nearly an hour until they found a small shack with a boat tied up outside. It was a small rowboat, but it would certainly fit the three of them. Since fae were so comfortable in the water, there was really no need for boats, and sure enough, a human mele—or male, as they called themselves, since they *had* to be different—sat outside.

"Hello!" Lulu greeted him cheerfully. During their journey from Ajabu to Pwise, Lulu's relentless joyfulness had never once waned. She was the most optimistic, genuinely kind person Izzie had ever met. Lulu still hadn't shared much about herself, insisting it was better she show them. "Would you mind if we borrowed your boat?"

"Of-of c-course," the man stammered, clearly caught off guard. "Take anything you want, please. I'd be happy to drive the boat for you, ma'am." Izzie felt like this was an overly formal, if not downright deferential response, but she supposed maybe this man lived in water fae territory because he had some kind of weird obsession with fae.

"Thank you, sir!" Lulu said, setting her hand on his head.

"You honor this poor man by your presence. Thank you for blessing me by taking my boat."

Okay, Izzie mused. *This is just getting weird.* Lulu gave them a wry smile, but didn't say anything as she hopped in the boat.

"Not to quote a crazy hot water fae... but what the *actual fuck* is going on here?" Pyke asked, genuinely confused.

"Do you live on the other side of the river?" Izzie could see with her sharp vision it was not the nice part of town, most of the structures looking rundown and ramshackle.

Remaining silent as the other two climbed into the boat, Lulu reached her hand down into the water. Immediately, the boat started cruising as the fae used her water magic to propel it forward. The strong current of the river flowed in the opposite direction as the boat, but this didn't seem to be a problem for Lulu. Though the water was flat as far as she could see, Izzie began hearing the distinctive rumbling sound of a waterfall. By the time they were a mile from shore, the sound was practically deafening, but no matter where she looked, there was no evidence of any falling water.

Then, as if a veil was lifted, Izzie saw the water a few hundred feet in front of the boat disappear as it cascaded down into a massive... hole? In the middle of the water? The circular hole in the center of the river had to be at least eight miles across, meaning it was equidistant from both riverbanks. She couldn't see what was at the bottom quite yet, but whatever it was was at least a hundred feet below the surface of the river. Water rushed down from the river around the entire circumference of the hole. Pyke and Izzie screamed simultaneously as soon as the hole appeared, making Lulu smile even wider than she had before.

"Holy shit! Why is there a hole in the water!" Pyke shouted, looking back and forth between the shore and the approaching edge of the river before it fell into the chasm. "We have to turn back!"

"You're an Apex Changeling!" Izzie shouted over the thunder of the water. "You can just turn into a mermaid! What the hells am I supposed to do?" This slightly calmed the changeling down, but she still looked wistfully back at the shore.

Lulu laughed maniacally as her two passengers panicked, the edge nearly upon them. "Hang on tight!"

Izzie's bag started singing in a strange voice. "Is it raining? Is it snowing? Is a hurricane a-blowing? Not a speck of light is showing! So the danger must be growing! Are the fires of Hell a-glowing? Is the grisly reaper mowing?" The nonsense somehow made the terrifying situation even more tense.

The bow of the boat tipped over the edge of the waterfall as Izzie and Pyke grabbed each other and the side of the boat; then the rest of the vessel followed as they plunged down the enormous cascade. Thankfully, Lulu had the situation under control. Reaching her arm further into the water, she lifted the bow so they wouldn't fall out and slowed the progress of the boat to a gentle drift. Izzie opened her eyes, which she had squeezed shut as soon as they careened over the edge. If there had been any breath left in her lungs when they landed on the bottom, it would have been taken away.

A massive palace rose from the water at the bottom of the hole, which was far calmer than it should have been for being at the bottom of a giant circular waterfall. Looking like a tiered wedding cake, the circular tower was broadest at its base, with eight sequentially smaller rings ascending toward the top of the chasm, though it only reached about halfway up. It was a brilliant green, like the sprawling grasslands settled by the humans. It appeared to be made of a shiny substance that looked somewhat like a green pearl.

Lulu guided the boat to a gentle stop at the bottom of the waterfall, and then started propelling the boat toward the tower. "That was fun! That's the first time I've ever taken a boat down Fae Falls; it's way more exciting than just swimming!"

Pyke glared at her, slack-jawed. "You've never done that before? Are you crazy?!"

She giggled. "It certainly wouldn't be the first time I was accused of that!"

The boat cruised into a large hole cut into the side of the bottom tier of the tower. The narrow waterway they now glided along inside the tower was lined with water fae, all of whom looked at Lulu with confused expressions. They continued sailing until they reached what Izzie approximated should have been the center of the tower.

"Get ready for my favorite part of the castle—the elevwater!"

"The what?" Pyke and Izzie asked in unison just before the boat shot toward a hole in the ceiling. They didn't even have time to scream as they shot upward . As the boat slowed down, Lulu explained the ambient water magic was so dense in this tower that the most powerful water fae, herself included, were basically able to do whatever they wanted with the water. The fae hadn't even built the tower, which Izzie had never read about or heard of in all her studies of Cosconia, as it was here when they arrived on the continent millennia before.

Finally, they reached the top of the water, the boat resting on a water spout Izzie couldn't see the bottom of, and Lulu guided them to step off the boat onto the floor of the top ring of the tower. Pyke dramatically fell to her knees and kissed the ground, eliciting eye rolls from the other two.

A group of uniformed guards approached them, all bowing deeply. Their leader, a beautiful dark-skinned man with rippling muscles, greeted them. "Princess Luxor. Welcome back. The king will be very eager to see you."

Izzie and Pyke both gasped loudly. "Princess?!"

* * *

82 years before the Twelve Race War
Hoshir, Halfling Territory

"I still can't believe Hoshir Halfling Library had a book on Affinities we didn't have in Gifldor," Isadore commented.

"Wizards and halflings have long been unlikely allies. I just wish it had given me more info," Syrel responded.

Isadore sighed. "I know. But at least we know now there *is* more information out there. We just have to find it." She grabbed his hand and squeezed it. "And we will, even if it takes forever."

Syrel leaned over and kissed her forehead. Her cheeks turned red as she smiled at his touch.

"So where should we head next?"

She shrugged. "Dwarf Territory? But I don't know what we would find there that would help either of us."

"We have to go everywhere. We've already found knowledge in the most unlikely places. We're going to figure out a way to find my Affinity and get you fertile."

"Can I be serious with you for a minute?"

Syrel chuckled nervously. "Sure... Did I do something wrong?"

Isadore smiled "Quite the opposite. I know we've skirted the issue as our relationship has been developing, but I think it's time we finally address it. Syrel: If we're ever able to figure out how I can get pregnant, will you be the father?"

He put his hand to his chest in mock surprise. "Me? Your baby daddy? I thought you'd choose some hunky human or a sexy fae!"

"We're being serious right now!" Isadore replied with mock outrage.

"Okay, I'm sorry. Isadore, I want nothing more than to raise a child with you. You're my dream frele. I love you."

Isadore was shocked into silence. Even though they'd been officially dating for about a year, they still hadn't said the L-word. Somehow, it seemed to Isadore that telling somebody you loved them was more serious than asking them to have a child with you. *That doesn't make any sense at all though, does it?*

"I love you too," she whispered, choking up with emotion.

"What was that? I didn't quite hear you." He grinned.

Isadore swiveled her head to ensure nobody else was around on the isolated beach outside of Hoshir. Once she confirmed they were alone, she shouted, "I LOVE YOU!"

Syrel laughed and shouted it back, kissing her on the lips between each word. She pounced on him, pinning him to the sand and tearing his shirt off. "I love you," she said again, this time in the most seductive voice she could produce. Isadore slid out of her robes. "I love you," she said once more, and then let her body do the rest of the talking.

CHAPTER EIGHT

Royal Pains

---

*Faerie might be beautiful, but its beauty is like a
golden stag's carcass, crawling with maggots
beneath his hide, ready to burst.*

—Holly Black

---

38 years before the Twelve Race War
Cosc River Water Palace, Water Fae Territory

Izzie had to admit that Lulu—or Princess Luxor,
apparently—was right about one thing. This whole thing had to
be seen to be believed. She sat next to Pyke at a large banquet
table surrounded by a dozen gorgeous water fae. Lulu's father,
King Tidor, sat at one end of the banquet table, and her mother,
Queen Nuptia, sat at the other. Prior to the lavish dinner, Lulu
had explained the family structure to her companions so they
wouldn't be completely lost.

Tidor and Nuptia, who had ruled Pwise and therefore all of
Water Fae Territory for over five decades, had four children—all
daughters. According to water fae royal tradition, each princess
was betrothed to a suitable mate, chosen by the king and queen,

at the age of twenty-one. Lulu's oldest sister sat at the right hand of the king across from her betrothed, and the rest of the table was seated in a similar manner, from oldest to youngest. Lulu, being the youngest, sat at her mother's left-hand side, the seat across from her being conspicuously empty. Izzie and Pyke, who had stayed in her water fae form, were plopped right in the middle of the table between the two middle sisters and their betrothed.

"Lulu, my precious daughter," the king boomed. He looked like the mele version of Lulu, the fae princess clearly taking after her father. Fae looked like a beautiful crossover of humans and elves, somehow taking the best features of both races. "You have finally come home. We have all missed you dearly for the past years. The Palace isn't the same without your radiant presence." Lulu beamed, but her face fell when her mother spoke up.

"Yes, my darling husband is right that the Palace hasn't been the same since you abandoned your family and your betrothed without telling anybody. We were worried sick, and by this point, we'd given up hope you'd ever return," she admonished.

"I never gave up hope," her father added, winking at her. "I knew you'd return to us some day."

"Wow, Dad. Be more blatant with your favoritism," Lulu's oldest sister, Jandor, said, rolling her eyes. "She's been gone for years and you still treat her better than the rest of us. I bet you'll still give her more gifts for her birthday than the rest of us, too." This got a few nods of agreement from her other sisters.

"Hey, that's not fair! Dad's not allowed to be happy I'm back? At least somebody is," Lulu fought back, giving a sidelong glance at her mother. It was the first time Izzie had observed Lulu being anything but kind. She couldn't blame her, as she was sure this was not the kind of reception she'd been hoping for.

The queen waved her hand, dismissing her youngest daughter's comments. "I see you're as dramatic as ever, Luxor. I suppose some things never change."

"My dearest bride." Tidor gritted his teeth. "Can't we just be happy our prodigal daughter has returned home at long last? I'm sure she had her reasons for leaving, didn't she?" He gave her a conspiratorial grin.

"As a matter of fact, Father, yes I did. I needed to see more of our territory. I wanted to meet the common folk. We were barely allowed to leave the Palace, much less Pwise, and I felt like a fish in a cage."

"See, Nuptia?" the king laughed merrily. "A good monarch needs to know her subjects. How can you expect one to rule if she doesn't know the common folk over whom she rules?"

"How can *you* expect somebody to rule when they can't even *follow* the rules?" her mother shot back.

Lulu winced at her dad's obvious favoritism, which must have isolated her from her sisters.

"Seriously?" Imelda, her second oldest sister, asked. "How will she ever rule when she runs off, leaving her betrothed to bang every other fae in the city?"

Izzie was starting to see why the princess had left. This was one of the most toxic families she'd ever had the displeasure of interacting with.

"Sounds like Timu is just as charming as ever," muttered Lulu, just loud enough for everybody at the long table to hear.

"Speak of the devil," said a fae who rivaled Lulu for her beauty, which far surpassed that of her sisters, as he set his hands on her shoulders and kissed the top of her head, "and he shall appear. Hello, fiancée."

"Total season one Chuck Bass vibes," Izzie's bag said loudly enough for her ears only.

The royal children also weren't allowed to marry until a child had been produced—their marriage and coronation would take place simultaneously. This meant that starting on their twenty-first birthday, they were engaged to a mate chosen by their parents, and they would remain betrothed until they were parents, or die before their wedding day ever came.

In fae culture, fertility was valued above all. Only about twenty percent of fae were able to get pregnant; infertility was rampant. The only reason their societies remained large and their race lived on was that they lived for hundreds of years— still shorter than wizards, but longer even than the lifespan of an elf. When they were able to get pregnant, their pregnancies and deliveries were actually quite uncomplicated, especially by the dismal standards of Cosconia. As evidenced by Queen Nuptia, fertility was usually all or nothing for the fae. You either couldn't reproduce no matter how hard you tried, or you popped out babies left and right.

There was an extreme amount of pressure on the royal couple's children to reproduce, because a new king and queen couldn't be named until an heir had been born. That was why Tidor and Nuptia had been ruling for fifty years—neither Lulu nor her three sisters had reproduced, in spite of years of trying.

Lulu visibly recoiled at his touch. She jumped out of her chair and gave a withering glare to the newcomer, who Izzie correctly assumed was Timu.

"Mom..." the princess said, backing even further away from the table, where her betrothed had just sat in the chair left vacant for him. "Did you seriously invite this cheating bastard to dinner?"

"Oh come now, Luxor. We all know the real reason you left. But it doesn't matter. You will resume your engagement with Timu and immediately begin trying to reproduce. Obviously there isn't much hope for your sisters." Izzie pushed her half-finished plate away from herself. She felt viscerally ill due to the judgmental and rude comments the queen kept making. Lulu's sisters didn't respond, accustomed to her behavior.

"Yes, sweetheart. Why don't you sit back down and finish your dinner?" said the obnoxious fae, who was apparently betrothed to Lulu.

Izzie had been around for centuries and met a lot of people, but she was pretty sure Timu was the cringiest mele she had ever encountered. *Yuck.*

"Who are your lovely companions?" he added. Now that it was clear why Lulu had left, Izzie was starting to wonder why she'd come back.

Lulu had informed her family she had met a changeling and a wizard during her travels, but she hadn't gotten any further into it. Attempting to save Lulu from being the center of attention any longer, Izzie answered for herself. "Hi, Timmy." It always threw people off balance when you intentionally messed up their name. "My name is Isadore, but everybody calls me Izzie. I'm a midwizard."

Before she could get any further, the royal family's eldest child gasped, leaping out of her chair. "*You're* the midwizard? What are you doing here with *her*?" Jandor pointed accusingly at Lulu. "You're supposed to be here with *me*!"

"Woah woah woah," Izzie said before Lulu could respond to the accusation. "I'm not here *for* anybody. I was on my way here already when I met your sister. She was kind enough to accompany me here, where I will be serving the people of Pwise for the next six years."

"*No*," the princess responded emphatically. "You're here to serve *me* for the next six years."

Izzie wasn't a big arguer, especially not with somebody she had just met. Even more so when she was a guest in that princess's palace. But she wasn't going to stand for these lies. "That's not how being a midwizard works. I've been writing back and forth with Dr. Rodnaj... Oh fuck."

An evil smile spread across Jandor's face. "Midwizards," she said coolly, "are so gullible. 'Oh please, honored one, my community desperately needs the help of a talented and powerful midwizard such as yourself,'" she continued mockingly. "Whatever. I have documented proof of you committing to help me, so we'll come up with a plan for you to help me after dinner."

"The hells she will!" the only sister Izzie hadn't heard from yet, Mmeme, burst out. "You're not getting any advantage the rest of us don't get!" From there, the situation devolved into chaos.

"I've been trying for thirty years; I get first priority!"

"If it hasn't worked by now, you're never getting the throne—she belongs to me!"

"I was so close last year; I have the best chances of success."

"Success? I eat success for breakfast! With skim milk."

"You haven't been drinking enough of that skim milk if you ask me..."

"Are you fat shaming me?!"

"If the flipper fits!"

"Mom loves me the most."

"Well Dad loves me the most!"

"The hells he does, bitch."

"Who you calling bitch, skank?"

"I'm not the one who porked Lulu's betrothed..."

"I told you that in confidence!"

"Well maybe you shouldn't have told everybody my betrothed is gay!"

"He *is* gay!"

"No, he's bi! It's very different."

"Nobody cares about your boyfriend's sexuality; he's never going to be king anyway."

"Neither is yours, infertile Myrtle!"

"We're all infertile, that's the whole reason we're here."

"I'm just biding my time. I'll wear that crown one day and you'll be banished from the Palace."

"Over my dead body!"

"Gladly!"

"I'm the oldest and it's my birthright."

"Birthright schmirthright, I'm the prettiest."

"And the sluttiest…"

"Now you're slut shaming me?!"

"If the peni—"

"ENOUGH!" the king slammed his fist against the table. During the argument between the four sisters, neither the king, the queen, nor any of the betrothed had said a word. Clearly an argument breaking out at the dinner table wasn't new territory for any of them. Izzie was appalled at the vitriol they were spewing at each other. She couldn't even follow who said what, but nobody was blameless. Even Lulu, who never had a cruel word to say, sank to their level.

"My youngest daughter is finally home, and I will not have her homecoming marred by your petty fighting and jealousy." He turned to Izzie. "Isadore, welcome to our home. I apologize for my daughters. Being a royal child can be stressful, but it does not excuse their behavior." Each one of them received a pointed look. "Thank you for coming to Water Fae Territory to serve our people. As you know, the situation is dire. In spite of our long lives, our numbers are dwindling yearly. The population of Pwise was double its current size when my grandfather became king one hundred and fifty years ago. We've tried and failed hundreds of methods to improve our birth rates. My physicians tell me our fertility rate is down to five percent, a significant drop from just a few decades ago. You will not be forced to serve any of my daughters, but know that any help you can contribute to our community will be appreciated and rewarded. Girls, would you please apologize to our guest?"

Izzie looked at her feet awkwardly while the princesses mumbled half-hearted apologies. The midwizard was busy thinking about the king's remarks. The physicians were saying only five percent of fae could get pregnant? Down from the twenty percent she'd learned about in school only fifteen years prior? *Just like the giants and the changelings*, she realized. *Why is pregnancy getting harder for Cosconians? Shouldn't there be enough Maternal Magic to go around?*

"Not only that," the king continued, "but there have been strange rumors going around. Rumors that a war is coming."

"War?" Izzie asked, even though she had heard the same thing. "Why would there be a war?"

Tidor shook his head. "I'm not sure. But each year there are more border disputes, more fights, and rising tensions between the races. But if there is to be a war, the water fae will not take it lying down."

Was there really something to these rumors? Why would a war break out? Between whom?

Silence followed the king's words, nobody wanting to restart the conversation after the heated argument. Only Timu looked pleased as he took a second portion of dinner. Finally, somebody broke the silence. "I'm Pyke, by the way. I'm not a midwizard or anything; I just met these two at an inn in Ajabu and decided to tag along. I'm a changeling," she added, morphing into her natural form.

The queen gasped in surprise. "How many forms do you have?"

"Four," Pyke lied easily. "My natural form, water fae, human, and halfling." Izzie didn't blame her for concealing her Apex status, especially from the queen, who was revealing herself to be a very stereotypical evil mother. She also wasn't surprised the changeling didn't mention her ability to morph into a mermaid, the sworn enemy of the water fae.

"Father, thank you for welcoming me back into the Palace," said Lulu. "Let's catch up later, but I think my companions are exhausted from our journey. May we be excused?"

"Of course, dear. Thelonius," the king addressed the captain of his guard. "Take my daughter and her *protected* guests back to her suite." He glared at Jandor when he said this, ensuring she wouldn't attempt to steal Izzie into her service. "Luxor, why don't we convene for dinner tomorrow night so we can figure out how to integrate you back into court life?"

At this comment, the queen sneered and couldn't help herself from getting in a parting shot. "That is, if you don't run away again before then." The rest of her daughters chuckled while the king gave his wife a withering stare.

Izzie had completely forgotten about the spurned ex-fiancé at the table until he stood up at the same time as Lulu when she tried to depart.

"I will accompany you to your bedchamber, madam," he said with saccharine kindness.

"The fuck you will, Timu. I'm not sure how you didn't get the message from me leaving the entire Palace for years while you gallivanted around with my sister and gods know who else. We are done. Over. Finished. Do I need to keep saying it to get it through your tiny brain?"

The mele didn't even look fazed by her uncharacteristically harsh yet definitive words. He just smiled and sat back down, blowing Lulu a kiss.

Izzie shuddered and leaned over to Pyke to whisper in her ear. "That guy gives me the serious creeps. I can see why Lulu would rather give up her entire royal heritage just to be rid of him."

Pyke giggled in response to her comment. "Yeah, my ex-boyfriend is chasing me across Cosconia after he knocked me up, and I still think I'd take him over this douche-canoe."

Izzie cocked her head, confused. "What the hells is a douche-canoe? And why do I feel like I've heard it before?"

Pyke nervously glanced at the bag under her chair. Izzie groaned and lightly kicked the bag with her foot. "Would you stop teaching my friends insults nobody else understands?"

"You got it, dipstick." Izzie figured that was another insult, so she ignored it.

"Daddy, could you please *please* annul the engagement? You know he's disgusting," Lulu pleaded, regardless of her fiancé's presence.

The king turned red and looked over at the queen. Izzie could tell this was not the first time Lulu had asked this, and she suspected the two parties may have different opinions on the matter.

"We will talk about it tomorrow, with a little more privacy. And without your," his complexion turned slightly green at the next word, "*betrothed* here to listen. Thelonius, if you would." The king gestured toward the captain of his guard, who moved toward the door to wait for the three freles. It was the same hunky dreamboat who had first welcomed them. He led them through the winding passageways of the second highest ring of the palace, where it appeared most of the royal living quarters were.

Izzie was astounded when she entered the fae princess's room. Instead of an outer wall, there was a rippling, translucent cascade of water, glowing a vibrant green. She tried to reach her hand through it, but it was completely solid. *This water magic is amazing.* Pyke stood next to her, marveling at the grandeur of the room. They were in the main portion of the room, which was full of fountains and water features, with a few couches and chairs scattered around for lounging. As the two of them looked around, they realized Lulu had disappeared.

Pyke wandered around the room, opening different doors until she discovered where the princess had gone. She followed a trail of discarded clothing to a closed door, where the sounds of passionate lovemaking could be heard. Strewn among Lulu's clothes and belongings were parts of the royal uniform worn by the king's royal guard.

Pyke and Izzie looked at each other with knowing smiles.

"I thought all the rumors about court intrigue among the fae were overblown, but the king's youngest daughter consorting with the captain of his guard is *classic* fae drama," the changeling said.

Izzie laughed at her comment. "We actually had plays at home inspired by the convoluted relationships among fae royals, and I'm pretty sure I've seen this one already. Maybe we should get out of here?"

Izzie laid down on the most comfortable bed she'd ever felt in her life. Somehow, the fae had managed to enchant a small sleeping pad and fill it with water, making it feel like she was lying on a gentle ocean current. But she was wide awake, thoughts filling her mind. Thoughts of love. Thoughts of loss.

* * *

60 years before the Twelve Race War
Mithor, Elf Territory

"Come on Donrel, just one more drink!" Isadore begged.

"I can't keep up with you two lovebirds," Donrel slurred. "It's no fair, you wizards can drink way more than I can."

Isadore sipped her Jerdalin wine. "I'm pretty sure I can drink both of you under the table."

"I think I'm tapping out too, dear," Syrel said, enunciating each word in the way one does when drunk and trying to pretend one isn't. His arm hung lazily over Izzie's shoulder. This was how most of their nights in Mithor, their home for the past four years, went. Donrel, an archer in the small Elven Guard, spent his days training and hunting while Isadore and Syrel did research.

Though it was but a small border town, Mithor contained the largest library in Elf Territory. The librarian, who was the oldest elf in Cosconia and also Donrel's grandfather, provided the couple with guidance and tutelage. He had firsthand knowledge of much of Cosconia's long history, and he had a special interest in longevity.

"I juth love you both so much and you're the beth couple and I want you to get married and have lots of kids and come visit me and we can all be friends forever and all live happily ever after,"

Donrel said drunkenly, trying his best to maintain his composure. "Did I mention I love you both so much?"

Isadore laughed heartily. "You did mention that, Donnie. This is the time of night when you're so drunk you get overly emotional, so I think it is time for you to go to bed."

"You juth want to get rids of me so you can two can fuuuuuck," he mocked.

Syrel shrugged and winked at Isadore. "You are not wrong."

She flicked the back of his ear. "Stop winking at me! And I'm pretty sure if we had sex tonight, I would be taking advantage of you. There is no way you can give consent in this state."

"I swear to Cactus I'm not drunk that." He paused. "Not that drunk."

"Busted!" Donrel shouted, sending the trio into fits of drunken laughter. Isadore was the most sober of the group, but that wasn't saying much.

"Sure, you're not drunk but you forgot the name of the wizard god? It's Cect."

"Tomato, potato," Syrel retorted, and a second later he was slumped on the ground, snoring loudly. Isadore kissed his head and grabbed a blanket from their shared bed to put over him. She wasn't carrying him to bed, so he'd sleep on the floor that night.

"Donrel, are you going to sleep over—" Before she could finish, she realized the elf was also asleep. *These two.* She rolled her eyes.

The next morning, Isadore awoke to Syrel making breakfast and Donrel already gone to work.

"Morning, darling," he said. Somehow, he never seemed to get hungover, which was not a gift Isadore possessed.

"G'morning," she mumbled. She rubbed her eyes and forced herself to get out of bed and take a sip of the coffee Syrel had set out for her. "Are we headed back to the library today?"

Syrel nodded eagerly. "We're getting close, Isadore. I can feel it. I had a stroke of inspiration last night."

"Oh?" Isadore raised her eyebrows. "You could barely remember your own name last night."

He waved her off. "Yeah, yeah. Anyway. We're thinking about this the wrong way. We're not going to find a spell or an incantation or a curse to help with our problems."

"What other choice do we have? Magic would be the only way to make me fertile, and the same goes for giving you an Affinity."

He grinned his toothiest grin. "A ritual circle."

CHAPTER NINE

The Ritual

---

*The War changed everybody, myself most of all.
I can't help but wonder—would it have
happened without that damned ritual? But at
the same time, could we have made this
progress without it?*

—*Isadore the Red*

---

38 years before the Twelve Race War
Cosc River Water Palace, Water Fae Territory

Izzie woke up feeling intensely lonely. She missed him. She missed him *so much*. She rarely allowed herself to think about him, but that night, the memories came pouring back. She thought about his smile, which split across his face like a lightning strike. She remembered his hair, black as night. She reminisced on the way conversation flowed so easily with him.

She'd really thought they'd had it all figured out. After years of research, talking with some of the oldest and wisest beings in all of Cosconia, living among the elves for decades, they had finally developed a ritual circle that should have solved both of their problems. It should have worked. If only...

A knock on the door roused her from memories, and she got up to answer it, wiping tears away from her face.

"Hi Lulu," she sniveled, trying to conceal the fact she'd just been crying. "Seems like you had a fun night!" Izzie gently elbowed the fae princess in the ribs. "Now that you're with Captain Sexy, is Timu single?"

Lulu's face dropped at that question. "Izzie, he—"

Izzie immediately cut her off, laughing raucously. "Obviously I'm kidding. I almost boiled his blood right there at the dinner table." Izzie immediately regretted mentioning her blood magic in the context of hurting somebody, but the princess didn't seem to notice.

"Oh thank the gods. I can't lose another friend to his insipid charms."

Izzie felt a flush of warm contentment sweep through her at being referred to as a friend by the fae even though they had only known each other for a short time. This was what Izzie had been missing these years on the road. Since Syrel died, there was nobody in her life she could trust. Nobody she could lean on when she was feeling down. She needed friends. Confidants. Izzie pulled the princess into a tight hug, which she returned in kind.

"I'm here to ask you for a favor. A big one. But you have to promise me that if you don't want to do it, you'll tell me. You're allowed to say no—I'm not like Jandor."

"I'll do it," Izzie responded immediately.

"I haven't even told you what it is yet!" Lulu protested.

"It's pretty obvious. You want my help getting pregnant with Thelonius."

The princess blushed, indicating to Izzie she was spot on. Izzie grinned. "I thought so. My answer stands. You took me in, treated me with kindness, and guided me to your ancestral home. You're one of the kindest people I've ever met in my life, and kindness always deserves to be rewarded. My grandma told me to use my power to do good for those who deserve it." She left out the part about doing ill to those who don't.

"Th-that's extremely nice of you, Izzie, but how can you even say I'm kind after seeing the way my sisters and I acted last night? Or the way I talk to Timu?" There was acid in her voice even mentioning the name of her betrothed.

"Well first off, I don't think anybody should be held responsible for what they say in an argument with family. They know how to anger us like nobody else. Secondly, you could have cursed that idiot's name by every god in the heavens and devil in the hells and it still wouldn't have been enough."

Lulu laughed, amused by the side of the midwizard she hadn't seen much of yet. "Then I have one other favor to ask. Will you go with me when I speak to my dad about it tonight?"

"Of course I will," Izzie answered. She wasn't worried about being in any danger, as the king seemed benevolent and wouldn't ever lift a finger toward his favorite daughter. She assumed the same protection would extend to her guests.

"Thank you, Isadore. From the bottom of my heart, thank you. I don't know how I will ever repay you."

"Midwizards don't need payment for their help. I wouldn't accept it even if you offered."

The pair set off to find Pyke and let her know the two of them would be attending dinner with the king and queen that night, and they advised her to find something fun to do in the Palace. She informed them she had an idea, and darted away with a mischievous smile on her face.

"I don't like that look..." Izzie lamented. "That girl is trouble when she wants to be."

Lulu laughed, seemingly unperturbed by the amount of trouble the changeling could cause in an afternoon. After this detour, Lulu took Izzie to her royal closet and let her pick out anything she wanted. Izzie rarely ever changed out of her enchanted midwizard robes that stayed white no matter how much blood or bodily fluid she got on them, but she figured it couldn't hurt to dress up for a change. She picked out one of the few dresses that wasn't blue—an amethyst gown with long sleeves that cascaded like a purple waterfall down her legs. Using a reflecting pond in Lulu's room, Izzie examined herself. She usually didn't consider herself to be particularly attractive, but something about this dress... *Of course*, she realized. *More fae magic.* She knew the fae could enchant their clothes with a touch of water magic to give off an aura of beauty, an enchantment Lulu never needed, as the frele would be breathtaking in a potato sack.

After some primping and preening by both parties, and an afternoon spent in mindless chatter and court gossip, dinnertime arrived. Lulu let Izzie know Thelonius would already be at dinner, being the captain of the king's guard, so the two of them would go alone. They made their way back up the elevwater to the dining chamber of the Palace, where the king and queen awaited them.

"Hi, Daddy!" Lulu squealed, wrapping the burly water fae in her arms. She turned to her mother, a small frele by fae standards. "Mother," she said curtly.

No love lost between those two, Izzie thought to herself.

"Thank you for having us for dinner, Daddy! I'm surprised Mom didn't invite you-know-who..." Lulu mumbled.

"As a matter of fact, I *did* invite your betrothed. He's running a bit behind, but I'm sure he'll be here soon," her mother responded acidly.

Lulu didn't respond, simply rolling her eyes and gesturing for Izzie to sit down. The meal was served shortly thereafter, a delicious platter of fish prepared in ways Izzie had never even heard of. Conversation was casual, mostly consisting of Lulu filling her parents in on what had happened over the past years since she'd left. Unfortunately, she eventually had to discuss the matter at hand.

"Father. Mother. I have something I need to tell you. I will not marry Timu, eve—"

"Unacceptable!" Her mother cut her off.

Before she could continue, the king stepped in, speaking softly. "Let her finish, Nuptia."

"Thank you, Daddy. I will not marry Timu. He's lying, philandering orc shit and I won't spend another moment with him. Instead, I would like your permission to marry Thelonius." Lulu looked nervously over at the guard captain, who stepped forward from in front of the door.

"Unacceptable!" This time, her father was the one who cut in. The king looked furious. His pallid complexion glowed bright red with ire.

The queen, never missing a chance to get a jab in at her husband, stepped in. "Let her finish, Tidor," she said, a sardonic smile plastered across her face.

"Sir, if I may," came a timid voice Izzie had yet to hear. She whirled around to see it was Thelonius speaking. The fae mele was wearing the typical armor of a fae warrior. A thin, aquamarine steel chest plate covered his torso, while his arms and legs were wrapped in leather coverings, dyed blue. His soft voice did not match his frame at all, as his muscles bulged through the leather clothing. *No wonder this guy is the king's guard captain; he's jacked as hells,* Izzie mused. His curly hair was closely cropped to his head in the military style. His skin was the dark shade of freshly set ink, and his amethyst eyes stood out to Izzie, as they were almost the exact same color as her dress.

"I've served you faithfully since the day you became king. I have stood by your side through uprisings and political infighting. I have protected you and your family like they were my own. But, sir, I love your daughter more than I love any creature in Cosconia. Her smile brings joy to my darkest days. Her kindness is only paralleled by her beauty. If you'd allow it, I would step down as captain of your guard and marry your daughter. You are still my king, so if you say no, I will leave Pwise and exile myself."

"Thelonius, wait," protested Lulu. "You can't leave if he says no. We can't be apart again."

"I'm sorry, my darling. I took a vow when I became the captain of your father's guard, to serve him above all, and I won't violate that vow."

Lulu nodded, not seeming surprised by his words. "I don't like it, but I respect it. You are a mele of your word. That's what I love about you."

The king, to his credit, had listened to his captain's words quietly and attentively. His wife was still sneering, living for the drama of her husband having to rebuke his beloved daughter. After a long silence in which the tension in the room was palpable, the king finally spoke.

"I'm sorry, daughter. You know the law. The princess is required to attempt to produce an heir with her betrothed for a minimum of ten years, a law you've already violated. A violation punishable by death, I'll remind you," he said firmly. He continued, this time in a more sympathetic tone. "There is a reason we chose Timu for you. He comes from a powerful family, and his line is fertile. I know he can be... difficult at times." The king looked pained by each word that left his pale mouth. "But it is what must be done."

He turned his attention to his captain. "Thelonius, I have never questioned your unwavering support to me and my family. You are well aware the punishment for consorting with a member of the royal family is death. I'm willing to overlook this... indiscretion—if you vow to never speak to my daughter again and take an oath of celibacy for the remainder of your days."

The captain immediately responded, "Yes, sir," at the same time his lover screamed, "Daddy you can't!"

Izzie was shocked. She knew in fae culture, which was plagued by infertility, it was considered the harshest punishment to condemn somebody to celibacy. The king had seemed so kind and magnanimous previously, but now she questioned her earlier conclusions. *Lulu has always been on his good side*, Izzie suddenly thought. *I'd hate to see his bad side.* The queen continued to look pleased by how the situation was developing.

An idea suddenly popped into Izzie's head. An absolutely batshit crazy idea, as her bag would probably tell her. It was a huge risk, but hells—Izzie was nothing if not a risk-taker. What was life without a little gambling?

"What if I could vow Luxor and Thelonius would produce an heir within a year?"

It was like the air had been sucked out of the room. Izzie instantly regretted saying anything. How could she possibly promise conception in a race notorious for their infertility? They were living in a land where pregnancy got harder every day. She considered taking it back, but Izzie was not the kind of person to second-guess herself. When she made a decision, even if it was a poor one, she stuck with it. *That's probably why I'm a lonely bachelorette still pining over a mele I lost decades ago,* she chuckled inwardly. For the first time since the conversation had started, the queen actually looked shocked. She was no longer reveling in the misery of others.

Eventually, the king nodded his head slowly. "Six months. If Luxor and..." he gnashed his teeth, struggling to get the words out, "my captain can conceive in six months, they have my blessing." Izzie wasn't surprised. He had a midwizard's sworn word that she could help continue the family line, which would certainly trump any other obligations Lulu had.

The fae squealed with delight, running over to stand on her tiptoes to hug her father, who looked taller and more imposing than ever after his decree. He didn't react to his daughter's display of emotion. After kissing her father on the cheek, Lulu walked over to grab Thelonius's hand. Her confidence and excitement gave Izzie a small glimmer of hope, though her chances of accomplishing her vow, in six months no less, were daunting.

Thelonius, however, wasn't celebrating. He asked the question in the back of everybody's minds. "And if we can't?"

"Execution. For all three of you." His tone left no room for argument.

It wasn't the first time Izzie had risked it all for fertility, except this time it wasn't her own.

* * *

64 years before the Twelve Race War
The Central Wasteland

They had finally figured it out. Years they had spent studying the secrets of Cosconia—fertility, Affinities, and power being the areas of focus. They had spent time among wizards scattered throughout the land. They had visited the dwarves in their halls of stone and the halflings in their underhill homes. They had stopped at every library they could find. Their longest and final stop had been Mithor, where the guidance of Donrel's grandfather and the extensive library proved invaluable.

Decades after their chance meeting in Gifldor, Isadore and Syrel walked hand-in-hand through the brutal Wasteland. They had to be as far away from the nearest civilization as possible, since they didn't know what the ramifications of the ritual would be. All her life, she had grown up hearing one thing about the Wasteland: It was completely incompatible with life. There were no permanent settlements, and even the amount of wildlife was extremely limited compared to the rest of Cosconia. The Wasteland was the geographic center of the continent. The Cosc River formed a natural boundary to the north and west of the Wasteland, while the southern border was the Iron Mountains, home to most of the dwarven population of Cosconia. There was no definitive eastern border of the Wasteland, but barren terrain eventually gave way to grassy plains that extended to the sea. These plains were considered part of Human Territory, though most humans lived in giant metropolises close to the Discovery Ocean, where the first inhabitants of Cosconia had discovered the new land.

"Isadore, can I say something?"

She pecked him on the cheek. "Of course, my darling."

Syrel returned her peck with a deep kiss, hands on her waist. His tongue slid across her lips in a teasing way, and his hands ventured to her back. He pulled her in close, and she felt all her cares slip away. His mouth moved from her lips to her neck and from her neck to her shoulder, which he knew would make her melt with desire.

"Didn't you have something to say?" she mumbled.

"It can wait," he answered, though the sound was muffled by his face being pressed against her skin. He slid his hand into her robes, and his soft lips moved to her chest.

"Syrel! We're completely out in the open!"

He pulled his face back from her chest and glanced around the barren Wasteland. "Who's going to see us? The tumbleweeds?"

Isadore thought for a moment. "Good point." She grinned and ripped his shirt off. She meant to just *take* his shirt off, but she was so riled up it actually tore. "Oops."

In a dramatic flourish, Syrel ripped his pants off.

"That was so fucking hot," she gushed. Isadore slipped out of her own robes and jumped into Syrel's toned arms.

Even though they'd made love thousands of times before, this time felt special. Momentous. When they were finished, they stayed lying on the dusty ground.

"What was it you wanted to say to me?" she asked breathlessly, still dizzy from their passionate encounter.

He smiled. That smile still melted her heart after all these years. "I love you. And I know we've said it a million times by now, but just in case anything happens..."

Isadore cut him off, playfully smacking him on the back of the head. "Come on. We've run through it a thousand times. The theory is good. Our tests have all been perfect. It's foolproof."

"I love your confidence, and I agree. But I still need to tell you. You're it. You're all I've ever wanted, and all I' ever needed. I love the way you stick your tongue out when you're super focused. I love the way you giggle at jokes about poop." Right on cue, Isadore giggled. "You have made me a better wizard, a better mele, and you've improved my life in about a billion different ways. Not only that, but you're a badass, powerful wizard. I love you, Isadore. If you forget everything else, remember that."

Isadore beamed at his compliments, in spite of his ominous final words. "Okay, fine, if we're going to be sappy then I'll be sappy. Syrel, my life was empty before you walked up to me in the library that fateful day. I should have known when I found a fellow lover of history it was meant to be, but you've proven in countless different ways why you're perfect for me. I know our ritual will be successful, and you'll join me in living a long, happy life. I also..." At this, Isadore started to tear up. "All I've ever wanted was to be a mom. When we met, I had written that dream off as a young wizard's fantasy. But you... you reignited it. Not only did you keep the dream alive, you also helped figure out a way to achieve it. I'm nothing without you. No matter what happens today, know that I will be by your side through it all. I love you, Syrel."

He pulled her into another deep kiss before they got up and continued walking. *Damn. I'll never get sick of that.* The happy couple continued their foray into the Wasteland. They had ventured out from the safety and comfort of Mithor days before. They had no specific destination in mind because the Wasteland remained uncharted, but they knew you couldn't be too safe when delving into new and dangerous magic.

"Whelp... this seems like as good of a place as any. You ready?"

Her paramour nodded and unslung his bag from his back. He'd cast some sort of spell on it that expanded the amount of space inside. *I've gotta get me one of those*, Isadore thought to herself for the hundredth time. The first thing he took out was a set of twelve large stones to be set in a circle, each twelve feet away from its neighbor. Throughout their research, the number twelve had popped up countless times as being a significant and sacred number throughout Cosconian history. The first water fae to cross the Discovery Ocean and arrive in the land came aboard twelve ships. There were twelve races settled in the land. There were twelve peaks in the Iron Mountains the dwarves called home.

They hadn't found any accounts of another wizard being born without an Affinity, but there *were* stories of wizards who obtained new Affinities. Some were stolen from other wizards— though this only seemed possible for a blood wizard—and others were created with dark magic, but there were examples of Affinities being *shared* between wizards. It was only natural Isadore might share her blood Affinity with Syrel.

Each stone was inscribed with runes, written in their own blood, packed with lore related to fertility and blood magic Affinity. The *Sangrila* had proven to be invaluable for their research, so much so that Isadore had hoped they'd find a similar book for another Affinity, which she'd heard existed, but they hadn't stumbled across one. Many of the runes were in the old languages of their races of origin, from a time prior to when the common tongue, Fingol, was adopted. Most of their time over the past decades had been spent unearthing these secrets and compiling them into their notebooks. Once they felt like they had ascertained enough information from each race, they had set out to apply their knowledge of magic to create a ritual that would fix their respective problems. There was only so much testing they could do without actually setting up the ritual circle, but they were certain that what they had developed would work. The goal of the ritual was simple, yet profound: share her blood magic Affinity with Syrel and grant her fertility in the process.

Isadore pulled out the wand she loved so much. When her great-grandmother, a famous blood mage herself, had disappeared, she hadn't taken her pure cherry wood wand with her. Instead, Isadore had found it in her room on page thirty-three of the *Sangrila,* the ancient blood magic guidebook her great-grandmother had given her years before.

After Syrel set out the twelve stones, Isadore used her wand to connect each stone to every other stone with a glowing thread of blood magic. This was to represent the interconnectedness of life in their nation. The next step was to inscribe each of their bodies with several powerful spells using an ink created with their blood by a wizard with an alchemy Affinity. Syrel used his wand and the ink to write multiple spells regarding fertility, childbearing, labor, and delivery across Isadore's arms and legs. He finished by writing *Forever Mine* in small letters across her forearm. Isadore repeated the process on him, writing spells about blood magic and Affinities across Syrel's body. She mirrored her own tattoo on his shoulder, writing *Mine Forever* in slightly larger letters than her own temporary tattoo. Their shared motto.

Just like that, it was time to start. Nearly half of their lives they'd spent studying, traveling, learning, and developing this ritual, and it was finally here. Isadore tried not to be too hopeful, but she knew it was going to work. It *had to* work. Mostly for her lover's sake. She could survive without an offspring—even when the pain of her infertility felt like its own loss—but Syrel had to find his Affinity. How could he ever be a true wizard without one?

They had both memorized the words to the ritual through hours of practice. It would only take about two hours, but they couldn't miss a single line. Everything had to go perfectly. Isadore stood behind the rock at the top of the circle and faced Syrel, who stood at the bottom of the circle. Counting down with his fingers, he winked at her. *He* would *do the thing I hate the most right before we start this ritual.* When he got to one, the ritual began. Immediately after, the stones began to glow with an eerie red light, exactly as they expected.

Over the next hour, the threads between the stones began to disappear one by one. When a glowing stone lost its last thread, it returned to its previously dull state, leaving a small remnant of the inscribed runes. They had anticipated this would happen, as Isadore and Syrel were absorbing the very magic they created as they continued their chant. After the first hour, the runes on their bodies started to light up as they were activated. Ninety minutes in and all but one rock, filled with script in the ancient tongue of the changelings, began to flicker. *This is it*, Isadore thought. *Once this stone deactivates, we'll be on the home stretch.*

However, the stone didn't stop glowing. Instead, everything went haywire. Random stones started to rapidly flash between their previous bright red and a deathly black. She thought about stopping the ritual, but, reading her thoughts, Syrel shook his head. *He must know something I don't.* Isadore continued the words she knew by heart as the threads between the rocks started to reignite. Random connections were formed and broken. *It's not working. I must have messed something up. We have to stop now.*

All of a sudden, the runes inscribed on her body stopped glowing. Strangely, Syrel's runes glowed even more brightly when hers stopped. She continued to chant as blood began to pour out of his nose.

"Syrel!" she screamed, interrupting the ritual. The moment she stopped, a ring of fire blasted up from the stones, obscuring her view of the most important person in her life. The heat was so intense it blew Isadore back several feet, where she collapsed to the ground and briefly lost consciousness.

When she came to, the world around her looked completely different. The Wasteland was already barren, but now the earth was scorched and black as far as she could see. Cracks stretched out from the ritual circle, which was the only part of the surrounding area that wasn't black with ash. Oddly enough, there appeared to be one small, green stalk sprouting from the ground, but Isadore paid it no mind. Her wand had disappeared. She was desperately thirsty, like she'd been unconscious for days.

There was no sign of Syrel besides his burnt robes lying in a smoldering pile where he had just stood. *No*, Isadore panicked. *No no no no. He can't be gone.* She whirled around, but in the flat land, she could see for miles. He was nowhere to be seen. She ran over to pick up his robes, which crumbled to ash the moment she touched them.

I stopped the ritual too early, Isadore realized. *He told me not to stop, but I didn't listen. I killed him.*

Isadore started running and didn't stop until she collapsed in exhaustion many days later.

CHAPTER TEN

Infertile Crescent

Fertility is not something you conquer. Rather maddeningly, there's no straight line between effort and reward.

—Michelle Obama

---

37 years before the Twelve Race War
Cosc River Water Palace, Water Fae Territory

Izzie sat down with Thelonius and Lulu the morning after she'd made her foolhardy vow to the king. She'd brought Pyke along for good measure, as she figured the more insight she had into the situation, the better. Just as she was about to start brainstorming a plan, an attendant ran into the room.

"Ma'am," she huffed. "I am sorry to interrupt, but I just heard some news that I think you should know. Timu is dead. One of the guards found him floating outside the Palace this morning."

Lulu looked stunned, but she clearly couldn't even bring herself to feel a sense of sadness for the loss of her ex-fiance. Izzie thought she may have even seen the corner of Thelonius's lips twitch up, but that may have just been her imagination.

"What happened?" the princess inquired.

"We're not sure… but it was pretty gruesome. He was full of holes, almost like he'd been… gored? The court physician had never seen these kinds of injuries. He thought they might be from… a minotaur. But obviously that's impossible."

Thelonius perked up at this, not expecting to hear his rival had died in such an unprecedented way. "A minotaur? How is that possible? How would it get into the Palace?"

The attendant shook her head, not having any more information on the matter. After Lulu asked her to get a few more details and inform her when the funeral would be, the attendant left. The second the door closed, Izzie and Lulu both turned to Pyke, who turned a bright scarlet color. Izzie noted it made her beautiful eyes pop even more.

"You didn't," Izzie stated accusingly. Pyke didn't respond.

Lulu gasped. "You didn't!" The changeling continued to remain silent, but gave a very slight nod.

"Okay, somebody's gonna have to fill me in here," Thelonius said as the two freles continued to stare at the changeling with wide eyes.

"Well," Pyke started. "I heard through rumors in the court that the princess's betrothed was invited to their private dinner by the queen, and I knew Lulu was planning to reveal your illicit affair to the king, and he would be the last person you'd want there. So I shifted to my water fae form and he started hitting on me. I asked if he wanted to walk around the Palace for a bit." She turned her attention directly to Lulu. "I do not know how you could stand to be around that creep for more than a minute. He is—well, was—the grossest, crassest, most vile individual I have ever come across, and I've been in all twelve territories." Thelonius cocked his head at that, his mind obviously putting together the implication, but he remained silent. "Anyway. He tried to force himself on me. I told him to stop. I was just trying to keep him away from the dinner but... I lost control. I couldn't stand the thought of letting him do that to anybody ever again. I morphed into my minotaur form and... well, I think you can all imagine the rest."

Lulu laughed. "I'm imagining it right now!" She calmed a bit. "I'm sorry for laughing. Are you okay Pyke?"

Izzie remained slack-jawed, reminding herself that the changeling, whom she now considered a friend, was powerful and slightly unstable. Thelonius still didn't say anything, but he had the decency to look a little nauseated.

Pyke nodded. "I'm fine. He didn't get anywhere with me. That asshole didn't know who he was messing with."

"Good riddance," said Lulu. "I will not feel bad for that schoolboy bitch. Thank you for doing me, and the entire world, a favor."

"Schoolboy bitch?" Thelonius asked, seeming surprised by his lover's phrasing.

"I may have been responsible for teaching her that one," Izzie's bag said from the floor at their feet. At this point, Izzie just thought it was funny.

"It did!" Lulu said gleefully. "It also taught me dipstick, asshat, twatwaffle, thund..."

"Okay, Princess, why don't we save some for later!" the bag interrupted. Izzie looked on in shock, as she'd never seen *it* be the one to curtail inappropriate comments.

Pyke finally relaxed her shoulders and sagged forward. "Oh gods, I thought you'd be upset. You're really not mad?"

"Mad?! Girl, I'm thinking about organizing a parade in your honor." She turned to Thelonius. "This whole thing has me feeling horny. Should we start trying to complete Izzie's vow now?"

Pyke chuckled, and Lulu cocked her head.

"Oh, I thought you were making a pun. You know, horny? Because Timu got gored?"

At this, the entire gathered crew devolved into cackling laughter.

After the laughter died down, Thelonius grabbed Lulu's hand and started toward the bedroom until Izzie grabbed both of their wrists. "Woah woah woah you two. Keep it in your pants. We're going to do this the right way. Has nonstop fornication worked so far?" They both look abashed. "Didn't think so. We're going to start with a little physiology lesson. I'll keep it as simple as I can." Izzie reached into her bag so she could pull out a large piece of parchment to use in her lesson. She was just about to close the bag when she realized it hadn't made a comment. She couldn't remember a time when she'd escaped without at least some sort of insult or commentary.

"What's wrong with you?" Izzie whispered. "Are you sick?" Could magical bags get sick?

"I don't want to rock the boat here. Just a quick comment for the folks at home: Listen up here. You might learn a little something. Don't put the book away just yet."

"Okay that might be one of your most cryptic messages yet. Who's at home? What book? Are you writing a book?"

In the least surprising turn of events, the bag returned to insulting her. "Yeah, I'm writing a book. I'm going to call it 'How Having Bad Hair Won't Stop You From Being a Good Midwizard.' It's fourteen hundred pages."

Izzie ran her fingers through her silver hair. Admittedly, it was extremely frizzy right now, but she never had time to tame it. She knew she could do it with a spell, but she cared more about her craft than her appearance. The red streak wouldn't cooperate anyway. "That was *particularly* cruel but... also maybe a compliment there at the end? Are you getting more mature?" Somehow, the bag made a sound that was almost a scoff as she closed it.

"Okay, sorry for the interruption. I'm going to give you a little background information here so I can explain my plan to you. Water fae are humanoid creatures. The word 'humanoid' originates..." Izzie trailed off. She couldn't get distracted with a semantics lecture, as much as her know-it-all brain wanted to. "Nevermind. All humanoid freles have a relatively similar physiology. That would include wizards, giants, dwarves, changelings, elves, orcs, halflings, and, of course, humans. They all have a uterus, which is a big muscular organ in the pelvis that, under the right circumstances, can grow a baby. Every moon cycle, which is around thirty days, the uterus prepares itself for a pregnancy. Every month, this inside part of the uterus grows wayyy thicker and full of blood vessels." Izzie wasn't sure how this knowledge was obtained by ancient midwizards and blood mages, but she suspected it wasn't pretty. Most of the history of midwizardry wasn't.

"When a frele and a mele have sex, a part of each of them comes together to form a clump of tissue. We don't know much about what happens there. What we *do* know is that this has to happen when the inside of the uterus is at its thickest. This tissue sticks in the uterus, and eventually grows into a fetus, then a baby. If that doesn't happen, the lining of the uterus has to go somewhere. That's called a period—when a frele bleeds for a week or so to get rid of that inside of the uterus. Also known as the worst week of every month for most people." Lulu and Pyke vigorously nodded in agreement, though Izzie wouldn't tell them her secret. Ever since the ritual in the Wasteland, she hadn't had a single period. Sure, it was great not having to deal with the cramps and the bleeding, but she knew it was also part of the reason she couldn't get pregnant. She would take the periods in a heartbeat if it meant she could get pregnant. "Then the whole process restarts."

Izzie checked in with her audience to see if they were still with her. She could go on all day about this topic, as it was her greatest passion in life. It still always made her think about the fact that she couldn't conceive. She couldn't even figure out what part of it went wrong for her. She'd used her blood magic to explore her own body, but she couldn't come up with any answers as to why her body refused to get pregnant. She had even tried to *give* herself a period one time, and that had gone south real fast. She had nearly burnt herself out using blood magic on herself. She had grieved this loss for a long time, but it still hurt.

"Is everybody following so far?"

Thelonius was the first to ask a question. "Is the..." He struggled to even say the word. Izzie rolled her eyes, but culturally, it was very taboo for fae meles to discuss frele issues.

"Is the period painful? When the body gets rid of the inside of the uterus?"

All three freles immediately confirmed that it did, in fact, hurt. Like a bitch. Thelonius winced. "I think maybe freles are tougher than we give them credit for."

Lulu kissed him on the cheek. She was somehow even more bubbly than usual, which was saying something for the cheerful fae. "You bet your ass we are, babe. That's why you better not mess with us."

Izzie smiled at the exchange. These two deserved it. She continued with her plan. "This is just a theory, but I think the fae problem is that their bodies run so efficiently they don't send enough blood to the uterus throughout the moon cycle, so they never build up the lining of the uterus. They can have sex as much as they want, but if the uterus isn't ready, it will never happen. My plan is to change that. Other midwizards have experimented with this, but none have the blood magic power I have." After twelve years of using her blood magic for the giants and the changelings, she'd grown notably stronger. The Skill level of most of her blood magic spells had increased significantly since she graduated. "The plan starts on the last day of your next period, Lulu."

The gorgeous fae princess interrupted her. "That should be today!" She wrapped her arm around Thelonius's. "It's fate! I'm ready to start if you are."

He kissed her on the forehead. "I was ready the day I met you. Let's do it."

Lulu addressed Izzie. "I think I get what your plan is. Let's start now."

Izzie set her wand on Lulu's abdomen and channeled her blood magic. As predicted, the lining of the uterus was as thin as papyrus. Izzie spent several minutes using her *sangimovi* spell to circulate blood throughout the body with a focus on getting as much to the uterus as possible. Nothing visibly happened, but Izzie knew it would be a long process. "How do you feel, Lulu?"

"Fantastic!" she exclaimed cheerfully. "My abdomen feels a little warm, but—" she doubled over in pain. "Okay... maybe a little crampy. But nothing I can't handle!"

Izzie continued this process every six hours for a week. After a few days, the progress was noticeable. The lining of Lulu's uterus continued to thicken at a rapid pace. The toll it took on the princess, however, was also noticeable. Her pale skin became almost translucent after each session, and it took longer and longer for her to return to baseline. The cramping was so intense Lulu couldn't leave her bed for most of the day. Her hair started falling out. She told Izzie privately she was partially using the cramping as an excuse, as her energy levels were so drained she didn't think she could get out of bed if she wanted to. Even when Izzie suggested they take a break, Lulu insisted they continue. *Note to self*, Izzie didn't say out loud. *Fertility treatments are* extremely *hard on the patient.*

About two weeks after Lulu's last period, Izzie conducted her final session of blood magic. Izzie had to admit that performing this service wasn't completely selfless—the more she did it, the more control she developed over her blood magic, which improved her Skill and even helped hone her Intent. The lining of the girl's uterus was thick and full of healthy blood vessels. She told the couple it was time, and there was only one thing they could do now: hope and pray to the gods, whom Izzie barely believed in anyway.

Two weeks passed after Lulu and Thelonius had officially attempted to conceive with Izzie's new system. She had no illusions it would work the first time around, but she was happy with the results of her experiment. She had set the couple up for success, and the rest was up to fate. One of two things would happen at this point. It was right around the time Lulu should have another period, which would indicate she was not pregnant, and they would be left with five more cycles until the king's deadline. The problem was, fae cycles were very irregular—though the absence of bleeding could indicate a pregnancy, it could also just be a normal variation.

A week went by, and Lulu reported no changes—no bleeding, but also no new symptoms. Most humanoid freles started experiencing pregnancy symptoms three to six weeks after conception, but it could also be months before anything happened. Unfortunately, Lulu continued to experience the same lack of energy she had during the weeks of blood magic, so she was still nearly bedridden. Izzie suspected there was an emotional component to this, as she was extremely discouraged by the lack of progress.

Two, then three months passed with no changes. Izzie kept a large supply of wheat and barley seeds in her bag because they could be used as a form of pregnancy test. She didn't know how it worked, but something about the pregnancy made the seeds grow when the pregnant frele urinated on them. Every few weeks, Izzie pulled out more seeds and gave Lulu a pregnancy test, and every month it failed. She was hesitant to use the *majalir* after what had happened the time before.

When five months had passed, Izzie truly started to panic. The feeling that she could die soon was tangible. *Am I the only midwizard who somehow constantly seems to be in life-or-death scenarios? I know Dalfa is struggling too, but at least her own life doesn't seem to be in danger. I have to write to her soon, it's been too long.* She checked in on the princess daily, because if Lulu didn't have a cycle during this time, it would be too late to conceive within the timeline.

Much to the dismay of everybody involved, there was still no change in the status quo. Lulu remained drained of energy, and Izzie was terrified she'd pushed the frele too far. Her internal dialogue ran rampant with doubt and guilt. *Why did I continue when it was draining her dry of her very life force? Did I do irreversible damage? Will she ever get out of bed again? Who am I to try experimental treatments? Who am I to make vows I don't know I can keep?*

A knock on her door came from an attendant who informed her the king would be visiting his daughter in thirty minutes. *This is it*, she thought to herself. She checked the last set of wheat and barley seeds one more time, but they remained seeds. *There's only one option left at this point.* She grabbed her bag so she could pull out the *majalir*, consequences be damned.

"Do you not remember what happened last time you used that godsforsaken thing?" her bag asked her. Izzie was startled by the fear she could hear in its voice. She'd never seen her bag exhibit any emotions other than… ridicule, she supposed, though that wasn't really an emotion. *It's definitely growing and changing*, Izzie realized.

"I know, I know. You don't have to tell me twice. But what other choice do I have?"

"You could just kill the king," the bag suggested unhelpfully.

"We both know that while I probably *could*, I would never. Not only would it probably start a war, that's just not who I am. I'd rather die than take somebody else's life." *Again*, she thought darkly, Syrel's winking face still burned into her mind. She packed up the *majalir* and headed to Lulu's chambers. The king was already there when she arrived.

He looked distraught. He sat waiting impatiently for Izzie to show up. His hand rested on his daughter's shoulder. Thelonius sat by her bedside, holding her hand.

"Midwizard, please tell me you have been successful and I won't be forced to put my beloved daughter and my most loyal guard to death." Izzie noted he didn't seem too concerned with *her* death.

"Thank you for your time, sir." Her previous interactions with the king had all been informal, but there was no acting casual here. It was strictly business. "Unfortunately, all of my tests have been negative so far. But I do have one other tool I can use to see if she's pregnant. It's a bit of midwizardry magic that will show the inside of her abdomen, and it will confirm whether or not she is pregnant."

"Proceed," was all the formerly friendly fae in front of her said.

Izzie pulled out the ancient magical device and explained to Lulu how it was going to work. She didn't tell any of them about the possible side effects, like the images she and Pyke had seen in the crystal the last time she'd used it. She didn't plan to spend any more time on the ultrasound than necessary—last time she'd had to spend several precious minutes examining each part of Pyke's changeling baby, whereas all she had to do this time was confirm there was something inside the fae's uterus.

She instructed the king and the couple to look closely at the *majalir*, and she placed her wand on the frele's belly. *Moment of truth*, Izzie thought.

"*Vibro ultrasonorium.*" The second she placed her wand on the fae's belly, one thing was very clear.

Lulu had conceived in the nick of time, during their last treatment session. Izzie looked at the fae princess, who was trying to make sense of what she saw. Izzie grinned. There must have been a little Maternal Magic at work after all. "Congrats, future Queen Luxor. You're going to be a mom!"

Lulu, Thelonius, and Izzie all simultaneously looked at the king, who still hadn't broken his doleful expression. He stayed silent for a moment longer before the corners of his mouth practically reached his ears in the most genuine smile Izzie had ever seen.

"We've got a wedding and a coronation to plan!" he screamed. His water powers surged, and a warm mist filled the room.

Her feelings of ecstasy were dashed as quickly as they started. Even though Izzie had taken her wand off the fae's abdomen, she hadn't yet put the *majalir* away, getting distracted by the king's proclamation. Just like last time, several images flashed across the screen.

The first was the hooded figure she'd seen before, except this time, the feeling was different. She couldn't explain why, but somehow it felt... closer. And more malicious. Was this really Pyke's baby daddy? Or somebody even more evil?

Again, like the previous time she'd used the device, images of war flew across the screen. Dwarves digging trenches. Humans slaughtering everybody in sight. A giant beast, dwelling just beneath the water. Then the same impossible metal structure as before, with Izzie inside.

Finally, a fae coronation. Izzie looked at the happy couple and soon-to-be grandfather, who continued to celebrate. *They didn't see any of that*, Izzie realized.

Lulu paused her celebration, noting Izzie's terrified expression. "What's wrong, Izzie? Is everything okay with the baby?"

Izzie forcibly replaced the horror on her face with fake happiness. "Yes, the baby looks great. I was just so scared before, I'm having a hard time switching my mindset," she lied. "Let's start planning that wedding, yeah?"

* * *

Izzie,

I'm nearing my breaking point. I ended my orc rotation early because I simply couldn't do it anymore. I was sad to leave Kurai behind, but he said he would see me again. I thought perhaps my time with the minotaurs would be easier, but I was wrong. Dead wrong. The mothers have no problems, but the minotaur babies just aren't getting enough milk, and they are dying at an unprecedented rate. How can we prevent this? How can we save them?

Anyway, I hope you're doing well. You mentioned in your last letter you've been in Water Fae Territory for the past few months. I can't imagine how hard it is treating freles with infertility when you've struggled so much with your own.

I have to be honest with you, Izzie. I don't know how much longer I can do this. I'm not cut out for it like you. I can't stand the constant death and heartbreak.

Have you heard about these war rumors? Kurai said something awful is brewing, and I'm starting to believe him. Even the minotaurs seem to be gearing up for battle. But why? Isn't there already enough death in Cosconia?

Dalfa

CHAPTER ELEVEN

The Coronation

I was a princess made of ashes; there is nothing left of me to burn. Now it's time for a queen to rise.

—*Laura Sebastian*

---

37 years before the Twelve Race War
Pwise, Water Fae Territory

Izzie sat next to Pyke in the front row of the coronation ceremony. The changeling was now visibly pregnant, but had still not exhibited any signs of labor. By her own estimates, she was about eighteen months at this point. Izzie wasn't surprised—she knew changeling pregnancies were variable in length, and often reflected the gestational period of the form the changeling was in at the time of conception. Since that would be a wizard, she figured it would probably take around two years, the average length of a wizard pregnancy. Pyke had spent most of the past year lounging around the Palace and getting herself wrapped up in the drama and intrigue of the fae court. She hadn't left its safety and protection, and Izzie didn't blame her. She herself had not ventured out too much, though that would change after the coronation. The two had grown quite close living together in the beautiful architectural marvel, and Izzie knew she would miss her.

Love was in the air, as water fae couples everywhere kissed and laughed and danced. Izzie ran her hand over the tattoo on her forearm, a jagged scar splitting the two words in half. *Forever Mine.* After the failed ritual that had taken the life of the only mele she ever had or ever would love, the rest of the magic script had disappeared, but those words remained. No matter how hard she scrubbed, the words wouldn't even lighten. Something about the process had emblazoned the words on her skin forever. She felt a deep pang of sadness, separate from the low-level melancholy that ruled her days and haunted her nights. She loved Lulu with all her heart. She only wanted what was best for the kind fae princess, and she was so happy for her. But at the same time, she couldn't help but be jealous. The frele would have every single thing Izzie wanted. A loving husband. A healthy baby. Youthful beauty. A supportive family. *I could have had that too*, she lamented. *If I hadn't fucked everything up and killed my soulmate.*

The ceremony was taking place on a floating platform on the Cosc River. Most of the water fae in attendance floated or swam around the platform, but Izzie and Pyke were given seats of honor due to their involvement in the events earlier that day. As was tradition, the coronation ceremony, which was also the wedding of the newly crowned king and queen, took place the day the heir was born. Izzie thought this was a pretty unfair tradition, as these were seemingly the three most important events in Lulu's life and she had to do them all in one day. Not only that, but she also knew it took significantly more than a few hours to recover from giving birth, but she didn't doubt the soon-to-be queen's fortitude. *Everybody thinks the hard part is having the baby, but they don't realize that the postpartum time is just as difficult—if not moreso.*

The delivery had gone without a hitch. The only difficult part of fae pregnancy was the conception—it was smooth sailing from there. Lulu was in labor for just shy of sixty hours, which was very standard for fae. Izzie hadn't even had to use her blood magic, as the delivery was nearly bloodless and the baby came out kicking and screaming. His name would be revealed in a few moments.

Just as Izzie smiled, thinking about the uncomplicated vaginal delivery, the makeshift curtain in front of them began to open to the uproarious applause and water spouts of the audience. Lulu walked out in the regal attire of a fae queen, babe in arms. Accompanied by her husband, who was helping to support her while she walked to the front of the stage, Lulu held the screaming baby boy above her head.

"Simba," Izzie's bag said with awe.

"Is that your guess for the baby's name?" Izzie asked.

"I really wish you understood my references," it complained. "Maybe in your next life."

The couple was breathtaking.

"I present to you for the first time, the heir to Water Fae Territory, my son," Lulu shouted. The applause continued to increase. Her words drifted to the audience in water bubbles generated by fae at the sides of the stage. Streams of water shot all over the place, a common show of enthusiasm by water fae.

"My son, Doren." The lovely postpartum mother looked at Izzie and winked.

Pushing down the negative feelings that bubbled up at the memory of Syrel winking to her right before their ritual, Izzie registered what the princess had said. Doren, inspired by the last four letters in "Isadore." Lulu had named the baby after her. Fat tears started to roll down her face. She looked at the changeling next to her, who was also sobbing. She recognized it must be hard for Pyke to see the healthy dynamic shared between Lulu and Thelonius when she was still terrified of what would happen if her baby's father ever found her.

As Lulu handed the baby off to an attendant, which appeared to be physically and emotionally painful for the new mother, the rest of the royal family paraded onto the stage. Queen Nuptia and her eldest daughter, Jandor, both looked as sour as ever, but the rest of the family was visibly happy for the new parents. Nobody smiled brighter than Doren's grandfather.

The king set a hand each on the shoulders of the bride and groom. This simple action elicited further cheers from the crowd, who quickly quieted down to hear Tidor's words.

"Fifty years I've waited for this day. Being your king has been the greatest honor of my life, and I will continue to serve the fae until I take my dying breath. But nothing brings me more joy than to pass the title of king to a mele who has served me faithfully for decades." He turned to address the powerful warrior who was about to become his son-in-law. "Thelonius, you may remember this, but I was not happy when I found out you were sleeping with my daughter." He paused to allow the crowd's laughter to die down. "However, I will be the first to admit I was dead wrong. Who better to take not only the hand of my daughter, but also the scepter of my kingdom, than the one mele whose loyalty I could never question? Who else could I feel confident would serve the kingdom than the mele who has already dedicated his life to serving? Son, you have made my daughter happier than I've ever seen her. My only regret is the time I missed with her, but I look forward to many more years with my children, and now, my grandson."

He turned his attention to his daughter, wiping away tears. "My darling Luxor. I still remember the day you were born like it was yesterday. You were a daddy's girl from the moment you entered this world. You were born to be a queen. You were born to be a mother. I don't need to wish you luck, because a fae as strong as you doesn't need luck. You will rule this kingdom with a benevolence never before seen in Cosconia. You will raise Doren into the kind of mele all meles will aspire to be. You are beauty and you are grace. I love you, Lulu."

Izzie knew the couple had exchanged vows privately shortly after Doren was born, so there wouldn't be any further fanfare. The king continued. "By the power vested in me by... well, me, I now pronounce you King Thelonius and Queen Luxor. Husband and wife. You may now kiss the bride!"

With that, Thelonius wrapped his strong arms around his bride's waist and pulled her into a sloppy kiss. The crowd went absolutely ballistic at this, and explosions of vibrantly colored water started going off everywhere. The kiss continued, and Izzie could practically see the joy radiating off the couple. She knew that as soon as the official pronouncement was made, the party would start. It would be a night of drunken debauchery for everybody... but not her. She was sick of living in the Palace and only focusing on one patient, even if that one patient was one of her dearest friends. She wanted to be out in the community, so she had made contact with a doctor in Pwise—a real one this time—so she could help other members of the fae community like she had done for Lulu.

Just as she was about to sneak away, Pyke tugged on her sleeve. "Izzie. He's here."

Before Pyke could even complete her sentence, Izzie watched the former queen explode on the stage. Nuptia was dead in an instant. For a moment, the entire crowd was silent. Izzie would recognize the blood boiling curse anywhere. *Sangracala*. She had never used it because of how deadly and awful it was, but she had learned a lot about blood magic with Syrel over the years, so she knew how terrible it could be.

"Pyke, you have to run. Get out right now. He's here for you."

"Not a chance. This is my mess. I have to help." Just as she started to transform into her wizard form, which would be her most powerful, Thelonius went the way of Nuptia and exploded in seconds, leaving Lulu to be a single mother just minutes after she became the queen of Water Fae Territory. Izzie watched as pieces of Lulu's dead husband rained down on the stage. The former king reacted quickly and put a water bubble around the entire platform, protecting all the members of the royal family. Everybody else on the stage reinforced the barrier created by the king. Izzie knew spells wouldn't make it through the water barrier, but it was easy to breach and she knew the wizard would soon be here. *Thank goodness Doren is already back in the Palace.*

Izzie went into action mode. This was like a midwizarding emergency—if she didn't act quickly, more would die. One of Lulu's sisters shrieked and pointed at a hooded figure approaching the water barrier, flying through the air. His gaze was focused only on Lulu, ignoring all of the commotion around him. As he got closer, the clear water barrier began to turn crimson red.

Nesbreth was about to breach the barrier. They had to act *fast*. Izzie looked to Lulu, who was draped over her dead husband. She wasn't going to be of any help with this counterstrike.

"Okay everybody, we can mourn later. But right now we have to deal with him. According to Pyke, Nesbreth is a powerful wizard who may have a blood Affinity." Izzie shuddered. As far as she knew, there weren't any other wizards in Cosconia with a blood Affinity. It felt like something truly evil was happening here. Izzie laid out the plan for the remaining members of the royal family: Jandor, Imelda, Mmeme, the former king, and his guard—absent their captain. Thelonius would have had the power to appoint a new captain of the guard after becoming king, but that was no longer possible, leaving the eleven other members of the king's guard without a captain. Still, they were powerful water fae warriors who could hold their own in a battle, or so Izzie thought.

The plan immediately fell apart when the water barrier dropped and all of the guards dropped to the ground. Izzie recognized the effects of the *bajasangra* spell—the same one she'd used to escape Pyke during their first meeting—which would sap blood away from the victim's head and make them pass out. With the proper Intent, it could easily be cast on multiple people. The remaining members of the king's guard would be unconscious for only a few minutes, but they didn't have a few minutes. Unfortunately, they were supposed to act as the first line of defense while Izzie and the others launched offensive spells.

"King Tidor! Cover me!" A thick water barrier appeared in front of her that would briefly protect her from any of the wizard's spells. She still didn't know where Pyke was, and she was starting to think that instead of having a master plan, the changeling had just taken off. *I know I told her to do that, but now I'm starting to regret not having all hands on deck.* Wand in hand, Izzie tried casting *bajasangra* on the dark wizard, but he easily blocked it with the *cudrado* spell. She followed quickly with *cabesangra*, which would have the opposite effect—sending all the blood to the head, which would cause a blinding headache and temporarily immobilize the foe. Again, he blocked it.

Izzie was starting to panic. While she knew she had enough power to get *herself* out of the situation, that would mean abandoning everybody else. Water fae were powerful, but their water magic was no match for this wizard. None here had seen any combat in their lifetime of peace, and it showed. Most of the attendees of the ceremony had already dove far beneath the water, out of range of any of Nesbreth's spells. *Think, Izzie. How can you save as many of the fae as possible and still make it out of here alive?* A part of her considered just leaving the rest to their fate, but she wasn't that kind of wizard. Sure, she'd dedicated her life to healing people, not defending them in a battle, but at the end of the day it wasn't all that different. There was more than one way to heal. *I have to focus here.* A plan was forming in her head, but it would only work if she had more support.

Izzie took a deep breath and decided to fight fire with fire. For years, she'd only used her blood Affinity for healing. But she also studied the *Sangrila* every single day, and she'd learned a thing or two about the kind of offensive magic blood wizards of yore had used. Still, she knew once she did that, she could lose all credibility as a midwizard, so she would save the blood magic as an option of last resort. She had another idea.

"Quick! Everybody put a bubble around their heads!" She realized Lulu was completely lost in her own world of grief, so she quickly cast a spell to put a bubble around the grieving fae's head.

She didn't wait long enough to confirm that the fae remaining above the water had followed her order. Using the *burbujum* spell to protect her own ears, she shouted, "*Ultrasonorium enfocarte!*" A powerful burst of sound flew from her wand directly to the dark wizard. She had been working on this one for a while—a modification of the skill she used for ultrasound that could also be used offensively. It created a burst of sound so intense it would knock the target unconscious for a short time. Sure enough, the hooded wizard put his hands over his ears and started dropping from the air to the platform on which they all stood. Since ultrasound magic wasn't her Affinity—she didn't even know what Affinity it would fall under—it required a high level of Skill, which her practice doing ultrasounds had given her. Izzie's Intent had never been stronger than in this do-or-die situation, and hopefully it would buy them enough time to permanently disable Nesbreth. She was worried that if she kept going at this rate, she would burn out, and there was nothing worse for a wizard than burnout.

Izzie motioned for the king and those around him to drop their air bubbles. In a stroke of good luck, the guards were just starting to wake up. "King Tidor—quick, send a message to all the fae who have taken shelter underwater. We need everybody on the surface." The wizard was still unconscious on the ground, hood covering his face. She had to immobilize him and chain him up so she could bring him back to Wizard Territory to face a tribunal of his peers.

One by one, fae started appearing at the top of the water at the order of their king. Wait, was he still king? Izzie wasn't exactly sure how the succession rules worked now that he had handed off the crown to his successor, who lay dead at their feet. About a hundred fae were now at the surface, and between them and the king's guard and his remaining daughters, Izzie thought there were enough people to finish this off.

"Everybody! I need you to use your water magic to create a thick bubble of water around the dark wizard. Hold it for as long as you can!" The former king was the first one to start, and shortly thereafter, dozens of rivulets of water streamed toward Nesbreth. A bubble of water formed around him, only about an inch or two thick at first. Izzie kept a close eye on the unconscious wizard, who was starting to stir. "Keep it up! As much water as you can!" Having received Tidor's message, more and more fae were arriving at the surface and joining their comrades. As the wizard seemed like he was going to get up, Izzie pointed her wand at the water bubble, nearly a foot thick now, and screamed at the top of her lungs. "*Glaciartus!*" It was a spell Izzie used commonly in her daily life, but usually just to make ice when a patient had a fever. This time, the bubble of water imprisoning the wizard turned to solid ice. She could see he was awake now, but there was no way he could get any spells through the ice. The fae continued to shoot water at it, and Nesbreth's prison grew by the second. She wished she had an ice Affinity right about now, as the spell took what was left of her energy. She wouldn't be able to cast any more spells without burning out.

Izzie's original idea had been to keep him inside this ice prison and have some water fae help transport him back to Wizard Territory, but she had to admit it was not a foolproof plan. One false move and he'd break out and go on a killing spree. She turned around to quickly survey the scene. Nuptia and Thelonius lay in disfigured, melted piles. Thousands of fae at the surface continued to utilize their water magic. Lulu had finally risen from her position at her dead husband's side to assess the situation. She marched toward the ice prison.

"Lulu! Wai—" Izzie was cut off when a disturbance in the water of the Cosc River surrounding the platform distracted her.

It looked like a mountain was rising out of the water. The tip of something breached the surface, water pouring off it. After a few seconds, Izzie realized what it was. Or, more accurately, who.

"No... It can't be," Izzie whispered.

The head of the changeling, now in giant form, lifted from the water. Pyke's face was unrecognizable since Izzie had never seen her in giant form, but this was no ordinary giant. As Pyke continued to rise from the water, Izzie realized she must be standing on the bottom. *It's at least fifty feet deep here*, she thought to herself. Soon, the changeling's entire head, neck, and shoulders were out of the water, meaning she had changed to a size of nearly eighty feet, larger than any giant Izzie had ever seen or even heard of.

A massive hand emerged from the water. The hand had to be at least eight feet across. Izzie tried to get the giantess's attention, but to no avail. The large hand grabbed the ice prison, which was two feet thick by Izzie's estimation. Pyke squeezed, and the ice exploded into millions of tiny shards. The wizard looked like a bug in the enormous changeling's hand. He looked as shocked as the rest of them.

A deep voice rumbled through the entire town. "LEAVE. ME. AND. MY. BABY." Pyke shook him violently with each word. "ALONE!" The changeling cocked back her arm, intending to throw the wizard. This brought him right next to the platform. During the vigorous shaking, the wizard's hood fell off, giving Izzie and everybody present a clear view of his face.

Izzie looked at the wizard, confused. "Syrel?"

The dark wizard looked directly into her eyes. The changeling giantess then threw Izzie's lost love far beyond the horizon.

* * *

63 years before the Twelve Race War
Wastetown, Northwest Wasteland

"Another one," Isadore slurred. The bartender looked at her skeptically.

"I'm sorry ma'am, but I'm not sure I can continue to serve you."

"I'm a wibard. A wirzid. A zwizard. Damn it, a wizard. I can handle my al—" she burped. "Alcohol."

"Clearly," the bartender rolled his eyes. "How about I get you a room and you get some sleep?"

Isadore, suddenly feeling far less drunk than she actually was, slid her wand out of her robes and surreptitiously cast a spell. "*Quitojogre*," she whispered. She completely lacked Skill or Intent with the spell, but her Affinity was enough to make it happen. The bartender gasped, dropping the mug he was cleaning. This was a spell she'd learned while traveling with... It hurt too much to even think about him. It drained the blood from somebody's eyes, rendering them temporarily blind. If it wasn't reversed after a few minutes, the effect would no longer be temporary.

"If you ever want to see again," she said, her voice shaky but harsh, "you'll give me another drink."

"Y-y-yes ma'am," he stuttered. "Right away, ma'am." He blindly felt around for a mug and stumbled over to the barrel. The mug overflowed as ale poured out of the mug over his hand. He shakily handed it to her.

"Thank you, kind sir. *Regrasangra*." She cast the spell to reverse the damage. Isadore drained the mug in one go. Her vision blurred even further than it already was.

Everything after Syrel died during the ritual was fuzzy. She'd wandered around the Wasteland for weeks, barely eating or drinking. By the time she stumbled into Wastetown, she was on death's doorstep. She'd nursed herself back to physical health with ale and meaningless sex. It wasn't like she had to worry about getting pregnant.

Wastetown was the only integrated town in Cosconia. It was also the only permanent civilization in the Wasteland, though it barely extended a few hundred yards beyond the river. Sitting on the Wasteland side of the bank of the Cosc River, where it made its sharp turn toward the Southern Ocean, the town was a waypoint for anybody traveling along the river or traversing Cosconia. It was also the dirtiest, most depraved place Isadore had ever been. Changeling prostitutes wandered the streets, offering to turn into new races. There were more taverns than houses. The only permanent residents were the ones giving you ale or charging you for sex.

Isadore had been here for three months already. She got drunk at a different tavern every night, making her rounds to avoid exactly the kind of situation she was in now, in which a bartender thought she was overserved. She briefly thought to herself how embarrassing it was to be refused a drink in a town in which basically all there was to do was drink, but she pushed it away. Just like she'd pushed away all her thoughts since the failed ritual. She had no plans for the future anymore. She couldn't get pregnant. Syrel was gone. Life was meaningless.

She stumbled out of the bar and threw up in the street. Nobody even gave her a second look, as this sight was all too common in the transitory town. As she walked down the alley to get to the inn she'd called home for a month, she ran directly into an orc. He had a broad chest, rippling with muscles. He wore no armor, as was customary for an orc, save his helmet, which had a sigil on it: some white lines and an eyeball.

"Hey pretty lady." He roughly pushed her back, holding onto her shoulders. "I don't see too many wizard changelings. How about we make a little magic?"

"You wanna see some magic?" Isadore pointed her wand directly at his heart. "*Frijangre.*"

The orc dropped to the grimy street as all of the blood in his heart froze. Isadore kept walking, not turning back to assess the orc's fate. He'd probably die. She didn't care. What was one more death? She'd already killed the only mele she'd ever love.

CHAPTER TWELVE

The Little Mermaids

But a mermaid has no tears, and therefore she suffers so much more.

—Hans Christian Anderson

---

36 years before the Twelve Race War
Mermaid Territory

The last few hours had passed Izzie by in a haze. When she had seen that Nesbreth was actually Syrel, she had shut down. It didn't help that she had expended so much of her energy on the fight against her former partner, which gave her very conflicted feelings. *Could that really have been him?* Izzie pondered. The only thing that had been left of him was his burnt robes. She had watched him die during the ritual. Izzie paused for a moment. *That's not* technically *true is it?* She realized. She hadn't *watched* him die. That huge wall of fire had risen from the stones and knocked her out. She'd thought she was only out for a few seconds, but was she really unconscious long enough that he could have run away? *Would* he have run away from her? He had just finished telling her how much he loved her, so there was no way he would have abandoned her. *Right?* And where had he been all these years? Was he really the same wizard Pyke had a relationship with? And a *baby* with? And the blood magic he'd used... Was that all the same blood magic they'd learned together? Was she responsible for all of this? There were far too many questions to answer right now.

After Pyke had tossed Syrel deep into the Wasteland, she had reverted back to her changeling form, unconscious. Lulu, shaking out of her daze, had snapped into queen mode. She insisted Pyke and Izzie leave Pwise, and Water Fae Territory altogether, for their safety, but also the safety of her people and her baby. Enlisting her father and sisters, the water fae created an air bubble and put the midwizard and changeling inside.

"I'm sending you into Mermaid Territory. The merfolk are our sworn enemies, so you have to tell them you're seeking refuge from us—they have been known to assist our enemies in the past. Use the code word 'Lork.' My people thank both of you for saving our kingdom. Now please, you must go. Pwise will be going into full defense mode, and we'll keep most of the fae under the water or in the Palace." Lulu hesitated, her grieving interior pushing through her queenly exterior. "I may have lost my husband, but I only had a husband in the first place because of you. Doren and I will see both of you again. I promise. Now go," the new water fae queen had said before pushing them into the Cosc River. Izzie wasn't sure if Lulu had heard her identify Syrel, whom she would know all about from the stories Izzie had told her about him over the past year.

Izzie thought of her brief time visiting the merfolk with Syrel. The memories of her time traveling through Cosconia with him were always painful, but now they gave her conflicting feelings. If he hadn't really died during their ritual, why hadn't he ever come looking for her? Could he not find her? She hadn't really kept a low profile over the years aside from referring to herself as Izzie instead of Isadore, which wouldn't take a genius to figure out, though she really hadn't gotten out much during midwizardry school.

A thought struck Izzie like a bolt of lightning. Syrel used powerful blood magic spells with ease. The ritual must have worked! He *had* to have gained a blood magic Affinity to cast those spells. For a moment, Izzie considered the ramifications of this news. If the ritual had worked for him, maybe... But no. It wasn't possible. In the two years between the ritual and midwizardry school, she had gone through a... phase. Her bag called it her "ho days." Needless to say, if she was fertile, she would know it by now. There were too many questions right now, and not enough answers. She had to focus on the matter at hand.

She and Pyke were deep under the water, moving south with the current toward Mermaid Territory. The Cosc River originated from a spring deep within the Jerdalin Forest, which was occupied by the elves. It flowed westward through the heart of Cosconia. Near the middle of the continent, the river took a sharp curve southward. Pwise sat on the banks of the widest part of the river, just south of the curve. After that, it was considerably deeper in its southern portion, making it ideal for merfolk. Izzie could feel the bubble sinking as the current carried it south.

Izzie was interrupted in her silent musings by a moan from the changeling next to her. Pyke had stayed in her natural form after collapsing from the effort of the battle. Izzie couldn't imagine how much energy and power it had taken for her to turn into the impossibly massive giant, but she was surprised she was rousing after only a few hours. As her gold-flecked eyes fluttered open, Izzie could see the fatigue deep within them. The changeling moaned, hands clutching her stomach.

Izzie placed her hand on the girl's shoulder and shook it. "Pyke? Are you with me? Are you okay? How are you feeling, Pyke?" Izzie had learned in midwizardry school that using somebody's name was the most effective way to rouse them, as one's own name was ingrained deeply into one's subconscious.

The changeling slowly opened her eyes. "W-where are we? What... what happened?" *Thank goodness she's okay.* Izzie had been starting to wonder what would happen if Pyke never woke up at all.

"Shhh," Izzie hushed her. "Everything is okay. Do you remember any of what happened?" Izzie used her wand to cast the *brillos* spell to light up the small bubble. The light had started to fade as they gradually descended toward the riverbed. In an ominous last word before they left, King Tidor had told her she didn't need to worry about finding the merfolk—the mermaids would find them.

Pyke slowly sat up, rubbing her stunning eyes. "Well... I remember when Nesbreth showed up at the wedding. It's almost like I could sense him. It was... it was the first time I felt the baby move." *Now that is interesting,* Izzie thought. *I assumed that her pregnancy would be about two years, but usually fetal movement can be felt about halfway through a pregnancy. It's likely just a coincidence she felt him move when Nes... Syrel showed up, but maybe she has even longer to go than I thought.*

"Then what?" Izzie prodded.

"At first I froze. I couldn't face him again. But then I got the idea about becoming a giant. So I dove to the bottom of the river so I could morph into giant form without him knowing."

"How did you become so tall? I thought changelings still had to be the general size and shape of the race they could morph into?"

"... I don't know. I've never done it before." She looked down at her belly. "I think he gave me the strength to do it."

Izzie wasn't sure about that, as pregnancy usually *took away* more strength than it gave, but she didn't have an explanation for it either. *Must be another example of Maternal Magic.*

Pyke continued. "When I got my head out of the water, I saw he was inside the ice bubble. I meant to just grab it, but my grasp was too powerful. It shattered in my hand. I could easily have crushed him. Even a wizard of his strength couldn't have survived it. But I couldn't do it." She looked at her belly again. "I couldn't kill his father."

Izzie winced, knowing there was even more to the child's father than Pyke realized. *More than I realized too.* "Do you remember anything else?" She hoped the girl didn't remember Izzie saying Syrel's name before she tossed him.

Pyke looked pensive for a moment. "I thought I hear—" the changeling doubled over in pain, wrapping her arms around her bulging abdomen. She groaned in pain for fifteen seconds, then relaxed.

Izzie didn't have to ask what it was. She'd seen that exact look a thousand times. A contraction. Based on her estimate of the changeling's due date, it was far too early for her to be going into labor.

"Okay, Pyke, just breathe. That was a contraction. I think it's a little early for him to come, but it could just be false labor from all the stress you just went through."

The changeling frele looked horrified. "He can't come now. I know it's too early. I can feel it. You have to do something."

Izzie didn't respond immediately. Trapped in an air bubble drifting into the depths of Mermaid Territory was quite possibly the absolute *worst* place to have a baby. She knew once early labor started, it was hard to slow it down. She pulled out her trusty bag to rifle through it and see if there was anything that might help. She whispered just as she opened it, "Don't say a word about what happened back there. I don't need to stress her out any more than she already is."

"Fine," it "whispered" back, though it, like Izzie, really only had one volume—loud. "But I knew you were sister wives all along."

"We're not sister wives, cut that shit out! Do you have anything in here that can help stop labor?"

"Even *I* know that's impossible."

"Fine, at least give me some wat—" A torrent of water splashed directly into her face. *Should have seen that coming.* She used the sleeve of her robe to dry off her face. "We're already underwater, you lunatic! How about in a cup this time, please?"

"Ahh, why didn't you say so? One 'cup' of water, coming right up!"

"Wait. Why are you saying it like that? Please, no funny business right now. I'm already shaken up enough as it is." Thankfully, it didn't seem like there were any tricks this time as she reached in and pulled out a large mug of water. She looked closer at the mug. *That little bastard.* It was the mug she'd gotten in Dwarf Territory when she and Syrel got into a beer chugging contest with some dwarves in a tavern. This was her trophy for winning.

"Seriously? Brat. I've half a mind to stitch you closed." She tightly tied the bag before it could respond again.

She handed her prized mug to Pyke, who took it with trembling hands. *Turning into that unprecedentedly large giant must have really taken it out of her. No wonder she's going into preterm labor.* In midwizardry school, they considered anybody who was having their baby at about the expected time to be "term," while anybody who was earlier than that was considered to be "preterm." It wasn't an exact science since typical pregnancy lengths were just estimates, but in a situation like this, she was worried it was months, or even years too early for the changeling to deliver. Before she could finish her water, the changeling was hit with another contraction. Izzie guessed it had been about ten minutes since her last one, which was good since she wouldn't really consider it to be real labor until they were every five minutes.

"That's right, hon, just breathe through it. You're doing great." As the contraction passed, Izzie helped lay the changeling on her side. The bubble they were in wasn't quite large enough for an adult to lay down flat, but Pyke naturally curled herself into the fetal position.

The midwizard surveyed her surroundings. The light from her spell only extended about fifteen feet in any direction, and the view through the bubble was distorted. They were currently in a massive seaweed forest, which Izzie knew from some old maps was on the outskirts of Mermaid Territory. Anything past that, however, was uncharted territory.

Pyke started to stir again, a new contraction beginning. *That was definitely less than ten minutes*, Izzie thought. *I've gotta do something for her, but first we need to get out of this bubble and onto dry land.* She was worried Syrel was going to come back, which was why they were staying underwater—it was likely the last place he'd think to look. Lulu had also been worried there may be fae who were angry about the events of the day who would seek retribution, but there was no chance they would follow into Mermaid Territory.

"Keep breathing, Pyke; everything is going to be okay. This kiddo is just excited to meet his mama, but we need to tell him to stay inside a little longer."

Before she could come up with any more ideas, dark shapes began to appear outside their bubble. Even though it was exactly who they were coming to find, Izzie was still scared. Little was known about mermaids, but they could be vicious, and they defended their territory fiercely.

Of all the races that populated Cosconia, the least was known about blood sprites and merfolk due to the isolationist policies of the two races. While Izzie knew merpeople could survive on land for about as long as a human could survive under the water—only a few minutes naturally, but longer with magic supplementation—they rarely appeared out of the water. A few wizards and changelings throughout history had visited and spent time among the merfolk to chronicle their history and study the structure of their society, but much of this information was limited and outdated. Merpeople could live in the ocean surrounding the continent, but it was far more dangerous than the calm waters of the Cosc River.

Straying from the typical patriarchal structure of many Cosconian societies, merfolk society was ruled by freles. Prior to graduating from midwizardry school, Izzie had written her dissertation on the relationship between patriarchal societies and childbearing. Izzie considered herself to be a frelinist, or one who supported the equal rights of freles and meles within society. It did not mean, as she had to point out several times, that she thought freles were superior. Frelinism was all about equality.

The main point of her thesis was that societies were founded on the subjugation of the childbearing sex, which was almost always freles. This led to a more "dominant" sex, the very idea of which made Izzie nauseated. One of the strongest rationales supporting her argument was that merfolk society, in which meles bore offspring, was a matriarchal society. There were many theories Izzie had posited to explain this. The most obvious was that the childbearing sex naturally tended to spend time out of society during the labor, delivery, and postpartum period. Izzie had argued in her thesis that while this may have been the case currently, *everybody* deserved some time apart from society.

She proposed everybody be given a three-month break every two years. It could be used for raising a child, traveling Cosconia, writing a novel, or just to rest. This would level the playing field so that freles were never barred from advancement in society because they would be "gone too much" trying to raise their child.

The second point Izzie had argued against was that a patriarchal society was natural since meles were born stronger than freles. In her mind, this was just ridiculous. Giantesses were larger than giants. Frele blood sprites were famously stronger than meles. And she, along with Pyke, had just kicked her ex-boyfriend's ass. Their ex-boyfriend's ass? *This situation is way too messy.*

The final argument in her dissertation was, in her mind, the most obvious one. Society literally *could not continue* without childbearing freles—or, in the case of the merfolk, meles. If, one day, all the freles in Cosconia decided they were done reproducing until they achieved equality, life would cease to exist. Izzie fully believed it was an individual choice to reproduce and she respected those who didn't want to, or in her case couldn't, have children, but producing offspring was still the backbone of society. In her opinion, childbearing freles, or meles, should be put on a pedestal in society, not relegated to the background.

Though she believed all freles should have the same right as meles, that didn't mean she supported the structure of merfolk society, where meles were essentially just livestock for breeding. Izzie knew from her studies all mermen were oviparous, meaning they laid eggs, called meggs in this case, instead of giving live birth. The meggs took about three months to hatch, but during this period they were extremely fragile and susceptible to attack. Though there were far fewer predators in the freshwater Cosc River than in the saltwater ocean, there were still many beasts who would happily make a meal of the meggs. Merfolk were born looking exactly like fish, and over time each would mature into a merperson, with a fishlike tail and humanoid torso and head. The sex of a merperson wasn't even known until they developed fully into their adult form, at which point they would go down one of two paths. Mermen were raised into egg-laying warriors, meaning their entire lives were dedicated to laying and protecting meggs. Mermaids would enter society like normal to do anything they wanted with their lives—practically the opposite of the intensely patriarchal minotaur society.

A muffled voice drifted through the dark water into the bubble. "Who goes there?"

Izzie could just barely make out the creature. Starting right below the belly button, brown skin gradually progressed into scales. Where the legs should have been was a long, powerful tail, swishing slowly through the water as the mermaid floated in place. Starting just above the scales, small shells covered the entirety of the mermaid's torso and breasts. It almost looked to Izzie like chain mail. The mermaid had long, red hair that drifted in the waves. She was baring her sharp teeth at the unexpected guests and brandishing a golden trident.

"We come as refugees from Water Fae Territory. My friend here needs help, and I know any enemy of the fae is a friend of mine. I have a code word. It's 'Lork,' if that means anything to you."

"Who told you to say that?" hissed the mermaid. Two similar figures coalesced behind her.

Might as well tell the truth, Izzie figured. "Queen Luxor," she started, not sure exactly how *much* of the truth she wanted to tell. "There has been a... change in leadership."

Surprisingly, the mermaid seemed to know more about the fae royal court than she expected. "Lulu is in charge now? What happened to Queen Nuptia?"

Izzie figured the death of their foe's queen would be good news. "Yes, Lulu is queen. Nuptia is dead. Please, my friend here needs help. Can you escort us to the surface?"

"The surface is strictly off limits, what with war on the horizon," the mermaid retorted.

There it is again, Izzie mused. *Why does everybody seem to think there's some big war brewing?* Although it did seem the tension between races was increasing, and the declining birth rates and atrocious maternal mortality could be putting everybody on edge. Just like it was destroying Dalfa. Izzie felt guilty about how little she was writing to her friend. The letter she'd written in Water Fae Territory had been the first in years, in spite of Dalfa's consistent communication—she hadn't even had time to read her friend's last letter, which still sat in her bag. The constant rumors, however, were starting to worry her.

Izzie didn't have a chance to respond as the three mermaids swam in synchrony ahead of the bubble, creating a current to drag the bubble along with it. They showed no reaction when

Pyke cried out again with a contraction, this time only six minutes after the last one.

Izzie realized she wasn't getting any help from the merfolk. She would have to take matters into her own hands. After her fertility treatment for Lulu had proved successful, it had given her some new ideas about how to use her blood magic for other purposes. What better time to try a new technique than when trapped in a floating bubble surrounded by mermaids after fighting for your life against your ex-lover? *To help* his *ex-lover, no less.*

"Pyke, I'm going to try something here. I'll be fully honest with you—I've never used my magic like this before. But necessity is the mother of invention—that's what Professor Seres taught me."

"I trust you," the changeling said quietly. Izzie had far too many secrets to feel like she'd earned that trust, but she appreciated it nonetheless. Taking that as consent, Izzie put her hand on Pyke's abdomen. She had used enough magic in the fight outside of her Affinity to exhaust her, but it had been a few hours, so she was mostly recovered at this point. After her success with Lulu's conception, she had been enlisted by many other fae in the Palace for assistance. She had gladly accepted, for two reasons. The first was she truly wanted to help every frele in Cosconia, regardless of race or affiliation. The second, more selfish reason was that it refined her blood magic in a significant way. She felt more powerful every day. Though she was still committed to only using her blood magic for good, she knew, in the back of her mind, that she would be a force to be reckoned with if she so chose.

Immediately upon channeling her blood magic into Pyke's bloodstream, she could identify the problem. Nobody knew how changeling physiology worked, but Izzie could see the side effects plain as day. Naturally, when she had morphed into a giant, everything had grown—including her blood volume. Izzie postulated that when she'd turned back into her natural changeling form, the amount of blood was slightly higher than it was prior to the shift. The growing uterus, which required more and more blood circulating to it every day of the pregnancy, was drawing in nearly all the extra blood at the moment. This must have been causing signals that made her body think it was in labor, similar to how an infection could send a person into preterm labor. *Damn it; I wish I knew more about how all this worked. I feel like I'm just scratching the surface, like there's so much my eyes can't see.* Izzie shook off her frustration and continued her examination.

She could feel another contraction coming on as the uterus began to draw in even more blood. Izzie initiated her novel technique. *Dematrisangra.* She'd invented the spell to move blood away from the uterus while working with the water fae. Slowly, she started to divert blood away from the uterus. This was a careful dance, as she knew taking too much blood away would prevent the growing fetus from getting oxygen. As the contraction reached its peak, she spread the excess blood to the rest of Pyke's body, since she knew sending it all to one place would cause its own set of problems.

She watched Pyke breathe through the contraction. It might have been her imagination, but she felt like the changeling looked *slightly* less uncomfortable. The mermaids still carried the bubble ever forward into the depths. It was now or never. After the contraction faded, Izzie continued the same task of gently diverting blood away from the uterus. She sent most of it to Pyke's extremities, thinking it was possible they would need to fight again soon, though she certainly hoped not. The next contraction came ten minutes later, which made Izzie extremely optimistic.

"That one... wasn't so bad," Pyke breathed. "But my arms and legs are killing me. They feel super... heavy? Is that normal?"

Izzie cursed under her breath. She must have distributed it poorly, so she wasn't surprised the diversion was having unintended consequences.

"I think it's a side effect of what I'm doing. I'm sorry—I am kind of figuring this out as I go. Just give me a few more minutes." Izzie continued her work, this time trying to distribute the blood she steered away from the uterus into the heart, lungs, and brain. Messing with the brain was dicey, but she thought it also might give her the boost she needed to recover fully from the battle.

"Wow, Izzie, I feel amazing!" Pyke said immediately before passing out. Izzie grimaced. *Maybe I overdid it a little bit on that one. But good to know a little extra blood to the brain might give somebody a mental boost—as long as I don't overdo it.* The changeling was out for only a few minutes before coming to. Izzie gave her some more water and had her rest for a bit.

"Ugh, I feel terrible. What's happening to me?"

"This is what happens when you're a blood magic test subject. Thank you for trusting me—if I ever have to do this again, I promise it'll be better. How are the contractions?"

"Actually... I think they're gone! You did it! Izzie, you saved him."

"I think we should hold off on any conclusions until we figure out what's going on here." Just as Izzie finished speaking, the bubble came to rest on the floor of the deep river. Based on the limited amount of light coming through, Izzie estimated they were about 150 feet down. The mermaid with whom she had spoken earlier faced them again.

Her muffled voice came through the bubble again. "Can you give yourself an air bubble?"

Izzie nodded. It was essential all midwizards knew the *burbujum* spell to help them breathe underwater, so she cast it on herself and Pyke. It created a form-fitting air bubble around the face that allowed the user to see, hear, and breathe underwater. She had no idea how it worked, but somehow the air was continuously renewed. It also helped the user to resist their natural buoyancy in water, so they could stay on the bottom and swim around as needed. *I love magic, even when it makes absolutely no sense.* She gave a thumbs up to the mermaid, who used her trident to pop the bubble they'd called home for the past several hours.

The mermaid, clearly the leader of the trio, swam in front of her. There was a thick wall of seaweed behind her. Izzie hadn't noticed before, but the mosaic of shells that were somehow stuck to the mermaid's entire body were glowing, giving off a natural, warm light. Similar to the glow of the water fae Palace. She supposed this was what passed for clothing among mermaids. The frele was beautiful in a terrifying sort of way. Her eyes were small and beady, the exact opposite of a changeling's. Unlike the striking colors of Pyke's eyes, the mermaid's eyes were nearly all black, surrounded by a small rim of green. The mouth was smaller than that of a human, and razor sharp teeth glowed in the light of the shell armor. She spoke again, her voice no longer muffled by the large air bubble.

"My name is Baztia. You can call me Baz. You are a friend of Queen Luxor?"

Izzie paused. Lulu had told them the mermaids were the enemy, which was a well known fact among fae-kind, but she had also given a code word. The mermaids hadn't immediately killed them, which was theoretically a good sign. The way the mermaid talked about Lulu was almost... friendly? Something in Izzie's gut told her to tell the truth, but she was hesitant.

Before she had a chance to answer, Pyke spoke up. "Yes. Close friends. She named her baby after Izzie here." *Whelp, I guess we're telling the truth, the full truth, and nothing but the truth, as my bag would say*, Izzie mused.

"I'm Pyke by the way. She told us to come to Mermaid Territory with that code word. What does it mean?"

Baz grinned. "Greetings, friends of the fae. Welcome to Lork."

* * *

Hello,

I'm quitting midwizardry. I had two weeks straight in Minotaur Territory without a single baby surviving. It broke me. There's an inn by the beach where every room is its own secluded cave. I just need to be alone. It's hard for me not to blame myself for the deaths of so many. I feel like a murderer. I have nightmares every night. Are you struggling as much as I am? Are freles and babies not dying on your watch like they are on mine? I constantly find myself wishing I had your blood Affinity so I could have been a better midwizard.

You might not hear from me for a while.

Farewell.

CHAPTER THIRTEEN

Sea Monsters Inc.

There is a silence where hath been no sound,

There is a silence where no sound may be,

In the cold grave, under the deep, deep sea…

—Thomas Hood

---

36 years before the Twelve Race War
Lork, Mermaid Territory

"This," Baz said, parting the wall of seaweed, "is our home." Izzie was flabbergasted by what she saw. Spreading out in every direction was the most breathtaking city she had ever seen. Even though the deep river had previously been almost too dark to see more than a few feet, a soft glow from bioluminescent coral illuminated the city. There were houses and buildings as far as the eye could see, made from a variety of materials. Many were made of coral, others of seashell, a few from seabed clay, and a sprawling complex at the far end of the city was made of gleaming pearl, which reflected the light in a dazzling display of color. Mermaids darted between buildings, swirling and swimming through the flowing currents.

"What the..." Pyke muttered under her breath. "When I visited Mermaid Territory last time—" She hesitated when she realized she had just revealed herself to have the ability to take mermaid form, but she soldiered on. "Last time I was here, there was, like, nothing? Just a few scattered dwellings at the bottom of the river?"

"That's just what we want you to think." The mermaid winked. *Why does everybody in Cosconia love winking so much?*

Before she could continue, Izzie asked the question burning in her mind. "I'm sorry, but I thought the fae and the merfolk were sworn enemies? Trapped in an endless turf... well, surf war?"

"You have your friend Lulu to thank for that. Did she ever tell you where she was for the years she disappeared from the Palace?"

"Come to think of it—" Pyke thought for a moment. "No, it never came up. I guess we probably should have asked."

"Yes," Baz retorted smugly, "you probably should have. But if she trusted you enough to tell you about Lork, then you have our full trust as well. Come, swim with me while I tell you a tale." The mermaid and her two companions led the pair through the city, slowing down for their awkward part-swimming, part-walking on the riverbed.

"Where you are right now is the spot where the Cosc River meets the Southern Ocean. It's brackish water—part salt, part fresh. The perfect environment for mermaids. This city is thousands of years old, though it's grown significantly since its founding." Izzie marveled at a trio of mermaids sparring with their tridents. The way they could move under the water was astounding. Baz continued. "Merfolk have kept their affairs separate from landfolk. For centuries, there was nobody even dwelling in this land you call Cosconia. At least, as far as we could tell—our scouts can only see so far when they pop above the water, but civilizations tend to spring up near water. We roamed the entirety of the Cosc River, from the now-named Discovery Ocean to the Southern Ocean, where we are now. Then one day, the water fae showed up. They believed themselves to be the first ones to arrive in Cosconia, though we had already called this land home for centuries. Years of skirmishes over the river led to the Mermassacre, or as I believe *your* historians call it, the Water Wars."

Izzie nodded along, having learned about this in midwizardry school. She hadn't realized that, unsurprisingly, the version she had been taught was a little different—*History is told by the victors*, she supposed. She'd been taught that the mermaids were evil aggressors who targeted freles and children, and that they should be avoided at all costs.

"The water fae came into our territory and murdered our leaders in warm blood. Of course, we fought back to defend our territory, which led to years of war. Eventually, a tentative 'peace' was reached and we were banished to this small corner of the river, with the fae claiming the rest. Their superior water magic made them unbeatable foes. Ever since then, there has been a deep-seated enmity between our races. Until Princ... Queen Luxor came around.

"To her credit, she was well-versed in mermaid history and knew the real story of the Mermassacre. When she ran away from the fae, she showed up waving a black pearl in the air—a traditional mermish peace offering. As you may have noticed, I'm a sentry. My job is to keep everybody out so they don't know how far our society has progressed since we adopted our isolationist policy. It's not a hard job, as the only ones who occasionally wander into our territory are the fae, and they are scared enough of us that it isn't hard to keep them away. But when Lulu came bearing the black pearl, I knew it was above my pay grade, so I brought her to our leaders. Long story short, she brokered a peace between our races. It makes sense: We have to live in the water, and they have to live near it, so we are natural allies. Unfortunately, she knew her parents—or, more specifically, her mother—would never go for it. Fae grow up hearing tales about the wicked merfolk, which is why peace always seemed so unattainable. However, and this might be news to you, there have been rumors of a war starting. Not just any war—the war to end all wars."

It wasn't news to Izzie, who kept hearing the same rumors, but this was the first she was hearing of it being the "war to end all wars." She wasn't sure what the basis was, but she was a little afraid it would become a self-fulfilling prophecy. The mermaid continued. "Lulu promised us that when she became queen, she would make the alliance official. Any aggression between our kind would be punished swiftly and severely."

Pyke interrupted. "Wait a second, how did she know she would become queen? She has three older sisters, all of whom were just as likely to become queen and continue the hatred between your kinds."

Baz shrugged, her shell armor rippling as her shoulders moved. "No idea. There were a lot of meetings I wasn't privy to, but she must have said something that convinced the leadership it was worth it. I guess there was really no downside to believing her? If she was right, we had everything to gain. If she was wrong, things would stay the same."

Izzie supposed that could be true, but she suspected there was something deeper at play here. She'd have to check back in with the fae next time she saw her… if she ever saw her again.

She also wondered why Lulu had never mentioned it to her, but figured she probably would have told her after the coronation. Izzie shuddered thinking about how much of a disaster that day had been.

Their journey had taken them all the way to the far edge of the city, where the massive structure constructed of glowing pearlescent material stood. Izzie and Pyke stood slack-jawed, taking in the wonder of the luminescent edifice. It was constructed as a dome, and Izzie could tell it was open at the top by the movement going in and out of the dome.

"What is this place?" Pyke marveled.

"Ahh yes, we've finally arrived. This is the Mursery."

At that moment, it clicked for Izzie. She was wondering why she hadn't seen a single merman while they were walking throughout Lork. *They must just keep them all here*, she realized. While Izzie was all for the empowerment of freles, she certainly didn't support keeping all the meles stuck in this Mursery, which was admittedly an apt name.

"Why did you bring us here?" Pyke asked.

Baz looked slightly reticent before she spoke, but plowed ahead. "Queen Lulu sent us a message a few months ago. She didn't even mention the pregnancy or the coronation. All she said was that she was eventually going to send a midwizard here to help us with our... problem." Izzie had informed Lulu of her plans to head to Mermaid Territory when was done with the fae, but she'd had no idea the queen had passed the message on to the merfolk.

Izzie had a bad feeling about this. She knew the number one threat facing the meggs guarded by the mermen were aquatic beasts who would gladly make a snack of them. As far as she had learned in midwizardry school, the merfolk settlements were mainly in the fresh water of the Cosc River, which had its fair share of terrifying creatures, but the size of the river naturally limited how large anything could grow. This position on the border of the salty sea and the river opened them up to attacks from both sides.

"Why would you possibly make your Mursery here? Why not deeper into the river where the saltwater creatures can't reach?"

Baz led them inside the dome. It felt like being inside a giant clamshell. Mermen darted to and fro, tending to meggs and tiny merfolk.

"Something about the brackish water here nurtures babies that are far stronger and healthier than in freshwater or saltwater alone. We call it Maternal Magic. Over the years, we've conducted several studies and found that the most economical option is to lay the meggs here, even accounting for the losses"

Izzie gulped. "The losses?"

Before Baz could respond, a pulse vibrated through the water. Four more followed in quick succession. Some sort of signal. Immediately, dozens of mermen started pouring out of the opening at the top of the Mursery.

"*Oh Miton.* Here she comes," Baz said, backing up toward the city.

They watched the horror unfold above them as a creature emerged from the deep. Izzie had never seen anything like it. Its body undulated as it slowly swam toward the waiting line of mermen, who floated at the ready, tridents wielded. She estimated the monster to be around fifty feet long, half of which was the powerful tail that propelled it forward. The rest of it looked almost like the pictures of dragons one could find in any children's fairytale book, even though Izzie was confident nothing like that had ever existed... until now. Its body was covered in scales, which looked oddly similar to those of the merfolk, except each scale was the size of her torso. She could make out several humps on its back, and though it was difficult to tell in the murky water at the edge of the city, it appeared to be pitch black in color. A large dorsal fin jutted straight upward. Eight flipper-like fins extended from its scaly body, slicing through the water like daggers. The monster's neck was long and thin, jutting upward at a sharp angle from its body.

Just as it reached the battalion of mermen, its mouth opened to reveal a long, flickering tongue, reaching out past rows of jagged teeth. Its maw was just like that of a shark. In the blink of an eye, the beast ripped one merman's head completely off. His body dropped to the ocean floor in a bloody heap, clouding the water with a haze of green blood. One of his comrades took the opportunity to stab a trident into its neck, but the prongs looked like seaweed hitting the scales, as the trident crumbled without piercing the beast's flesh.

"Aren't you going to do anything?" Izzie asked, horrified by the indifference of Baz and her companions, who floated next to her, watching with pained expressions.

"There's nothing we can do. She wants the meggs. Sometimes if the guards distract her enough or make her angry, she'll decide it's not worth it for now and then leave. Other times she'll blitz right through and scoop up thousands of them."

Each merman laid upwards of ten meggs, but still— thousands of them could represent the offspring of hundreds of mermaids. That was a devastating amount to lose in one fell swoop, even by Cosconian standards. There was no way anything that large could exist in the Cosc River, so the benefits of this location must truly be astounding to outweigh the risks.

"Why is there a hole on top of the dome? Why don't you just bury the meggs or something?" Pyke squeaked through tears, which were visible through her air bubble. The monster briefly disappeared from sight, giving Izzie hope the attack was over, but not before its tail whipped out behind it and slammed into the chest of another merman, who went tumbling through the water like a rag doll, dead. The rest of the mermen swam away, resigned to their fate.

"They need the light from above, as well as the water flow. They'll never hatch unless we leave them in the open. We used to be able to protect the meggs better, but over the past couple decades, it has become more and more difficult. It's almost like the Maternal Magic is fading."

There it was again. This couldn't be a coincidence. Giants, changelings, water fae, and now mermaids. Each with worsening pregnancy outcomes over the years. Something awful was happening in Cosconia, and Izzie was smack dab in the middle of it.

"We call her Lursa," Baz continued. "She's only been around for about thirty years, but the devastation she's caused has been... horrific. Thankfully, after they're born, the babies are able to swim away and hide under the sand or in crevices too small for her head, so they're safe... usually." As she spoke, the monster shot into the dome, making a beeline for the meggs.

Izzie felt ill at the sight. She'd seen the demise of hundreds of mothers and babies. Maybe even thousands by this point. But there was something about the scene before her, the merfolk helpless as a terrifying monster pillaged their meggs and slashed the future population of Lork in a matter of seconds. She had to do something.

She patted the pocket of her robe, thankful her wand hadn't floated out. She didn't mind pulling out her deadliest blood magic to slay this foul beast, and she decided to take a page out of her former soulmate's book. With maximum Intent, Izzie shouted "*Sangricala,*" the new spell feeling particularly powerful on her tongue.

But the monster didn't swim away screaming in pain like she expected. Instead, she turned around to find the most awful scene she'd ever witnessed. Her spell must have bounced off Lursa's chitinous scales and rebounded into a bed of meggs. Hundreds of them disappeared into boiling bubbles. In the blink of an eye, all those lives snuffed out by her own hand. Not only was she no longer able to save her patients—now she was actively responsible for their demise.

It was too much. It was all too much. She couldn't take it anymore. All of a sudden, the past decades all came crashing down on her. Watching Sydyr die. The images in the *majalir*. Running from Pyke. The attack at the coronation. Seeing Syrel again. And death. *So. Much. Death.* Dalfa was right. She couldn't do this either. Izzie started to panic. This land... it must be cursed. How could the outcomes for moms and babies be *so* awful? And somehow getting worse?

The giant babies getting stuck, causing their giantess mothers to die. The gruesome changeling birth defects. The look on the face of a water fae as each new month passed without any success getting pregnant. She had learned in midwizardry school that pregnancy and childbirth could be dangerous for both mother and baby, but the things she'd seen since she'd graduated were just... devastating. Mortality rates double, triple what midwizards before her had observed in the community. Intrusive thoughts continued to assault her as she spiraled further. She felt like she couldn't breathe.

What was happening in Cosconia? Was it her? Was she just a terrible midwizard? Was she the root of the constant death and devastation that took place around her? *Oh gods, I can't breathe.* Izzie felt the crushing pressure of the water around her. A thin layer of magical air between breathing and drowning. *If I was going to die, couldn't it have been with Syr...* She stopped, realizing she was so used to dwelling on Syrel's death, but that was no longer the truth. *Even the love of my life faked his own death to get away from me. Am I just a blight on this land?* Izzie was completely unaware of her surroundings, not realizing Pyke and Baz were shouting her name, tugging on the sleeves of her robes, trying to drag her back into the city.

She couldn't do it anymore. She *wouldn't* do it anymore. Maybe Cosconia was better off without her. Maybe Pyke and Baz and Lulu and Syrel and Skygyr and Donrel and every person she'd ever met was better off without her. Why had she even gone to midwizardry school in the first place? Because of Vera? Out of some selfish, misguided attempt to make up for the fact that she couldn't get pregnant? That she thought she had killed her own partner? What kind of sick person went into healthcare for themselves instead of for others? She'd spent decades traveling the continent, learning about every form of magic she could just so she could have a godsforsaken *baby*? She couldn't be a mom. She'd never cared for anything but herself. *Besides Syrel,* she thought darkly, *and look how* that *turned out.* A thought crossed her mind, connecting the failed ritual with Syrel and the current state of pregnancy in Cosconia, but she quickly swept it away, not willing to go down that path. She didn't feel herself being dragged away from the mursery.

Izzie was having a full scale panic attack. She couldn't breathe. She could barely think straight. The water pressure weighed on her like an anchor, dragging her down. She was done. She couldn't watch another mom hold her dead baby in her hands. She couldn't watch another mele kiss his dying partner on the forehead. She couldn't stand the thought of another Cosconian baby, growing up without a mother or father. She couldn't stomach the fact that she would never get a chance to raise a child. Teach them their first spell. Travel the world with them. What was even the point of living?

Izzie became faintly aware of her surroundings. She was on the silty floor of the river. She was moving, being dragged. She focused her vision, finally seeing what was in front of her.

Lursa. The monster was swimming directly toward them. Directly toward her. *If I'm going out, I'm doing it on my own terms. Not hers.* This monster had caused so much destruction. Izzie channeled every ounce of power and magic she had in her body. She channeled years of pent up rage. Decades of emptiness she had felt without a child. Years of sorrow and mourning. Affinity, Skill, and Intent, all bundled up into one of the most powerful spells she could cast, which she'd need if she wanted any chance of stopping the monster. It occurred to her Lursa was barely any more of a monster than *she* was, but she'd have to come to terms with that later. She pointed her wand directly at the monster and shouted, "*Frijangre!*" at the top of her lungs. Then everything went dark.

* * *

Izzie floated. Not in water, but in empty space. She couldn't feel anything. Everything was dark. It was warm. Almost like she was in the womb. *I died*, she realized. *I died, and I'm being reincarnated.* Sparilist evangelists said every soul would be reincarnated in the next life, as a different race, based on their actions in this life. She realized that wasn't good for her—she'd be reincarnated as an orc warrior from the lowliest clan, or a merman guard back in Lursa's path. She wondered if she would be able to remember anything once she was born, or if she would just be a blank slate. She hoped she wouldn't remember. It would be nice to get a break from the intrusive thoughts for a while.

* * *

63 years before the Twelve Race War
Wastetown, Northwest Wasteland

Isadore sat on a small bench in Wastetown with her head in her hands. It was early in the morning, and the decrepit town was quiet. Like her, most of its inhabitants were probably nursing hangovers. Since she couldn't sleep, she had decided to go for a short walk, but she felt too nauseated to be on her feet, so she had retired to the small open area that passed for a park in Wastetown, though it didn't even contain a single blade of grass. The smell of vomit hung thick on the air, which wasn't doing Izzie's stomach any favors.

Tears streamed down her face. Grief overwhelmed her. All she could think about was Syrel. How much she missed him. How much she needed him. How stupid she'd been for even doing the damn ritual in the first place. The sadness she felt was almost tangible, like she was being squeezed by a giant. She replayed the events of that day over and over in her head. *How did it go so wrong? We had every aspect planned in excruciating detail.* She kept telling herself that further dwelling on it was not helping, but she couldn't stop.

"Isadore?"

She looked up at the sound of her name, surprised to hear it said out loud. She had barely told another soul in Wastetown her name, ashamed at her current state.

"Vera?"

"It really is you! I can't believe this."

Isadore hadn't seen the human female in years. Her belly was massive, and she looked adorably pregnant.

"Vera, how are you?" She pointed at her old friend's abdomen. "Busy, apparently!"

Vera laughed. "You got that right!"

Isadore gestured to their surroundings. "What are you doing in this dump?"

"I could ask you the same thing!" She pointed to her pregnant belly. "It's kind of a long story. I've been a sex worker here in Wastetown for a while, but we're headed out tomorrow," she patted her belly.

"Are you safe?" Isadore had no problem with her friend being a sex worker, but she knew many freles, especially in Wastetown, were forced into prostitution.

Vera waved her off. "Oh yeah, completely my choice! It's great money."

Isadore grinned. "Where are you going? Back to Cico?" Isadore and Syrel had met the female while they were in Human Territory during their travels.

She shook her head. "Nope. I'm headed to Gifldor."

"Wizard Territory?" she asked, confused. "Why would you be going there?"

"I got pregnant last year and I almost died. I lost the baby. It was traumatizing. This time, I'm taking matters into my own hands. We're going to the Midwizardry Institute of Gifldor."

Isadore was vaguely familiar with midwizardry, but she never really understood it. You either got pregnant and had the baby, or you didn't. *Like her.* Why get somebody else involved? What could a midwizard do?

"Do you really think they'll be able to help you?"

Vera shrugged. "If they can't, nobody can."

Isadore couldn't blame the human for doing everything possible to save herself and her baby.

"What about you, Isadore? You and Syrel gonna be popping out a little one any time soon? Where is he anyway? When you two were in Cico, you were attached at the hip."

"He's dead," she answered without emotion. "I killed him."

CHAPTER FOURTEEN

Halls of Stone

What sort of gods make rats and plagues and dwarfs?

—George R.R. Martin

---

36 years before the Twelve Race War
Gamdo, Dwarf Territory

The clang of hammer against metal jarred Izzie from a fitful sleep. As she slowly opened her eyes, she became aware of the cold stone she lay upon. Just a few moments after she woke up, she turned over and vomited. Her throat felt raw, indicating this probably wasn't the first time she'd thrown up. The cacophony continued as she wiped her mouth with the sleeve of her robe. She had no idea where she was, but she wasn't concerned with figuring it out. Izzie was just going to roll over and go back to sleep.

"Ummm hello? Earth to Isadore? Are we ever gonna talk about what happened?" came a muffled voice from the foot of the stone bed. *That is the last thing I want to deal with right now*, Izzie groaned internally.

"I don't know what happened, and I don't care. Just let me sleep."

Before she could drift back off to dream world, she was assaulted with a deluge of freezing water. She gasped from the cold and launched herself out of the bed, sputtering and cursing.

"What the hells did you do that for, shitbag?"

"While that is an admittedly clever insult for a bag, we need to talk. What's the last thing you remember?"

Izzie thought hard about what had happened. After the coronation, she'd learned a new blood magic trick to slow down early labor, which was a handy tool to have in her arsenal. Then they'd met the mermaids and learned about the alliance with the fae, which was shocking. Then... Izzie suddenly gasped, remembering the monster swimming right toward her. That was the last thing she'd remembered. *Or... wait. I remember... floating? But not in water? Where was I?*

"All I remember is that monster coming to steal the meggs and killing a bunch of mermen. My spell rebounded off it and decimated those meggs, and then she was trying to attack me." She decided not to mention the floating part, because she didn't want to sound crazy. Well, any crazier than it was to be defending herself to a talking purse.

"Don't worry, I don't think you're crazy. Besides, we're all a little mad here."

Did I say that out loud without realizing it?

"You're probably wondering right now if you said you were crazy out loud—you didn't."

Can this thing read my—

"Now you're thinking 'can this thing read my mind?'"

"Okay what the hells is going on here? You have a lot of powers that I can't explain, but there's no way you can read my mind." *Right?*

166

"Nah, not yet. We've had this conversation three times already; you've been drifting in and out of consciousness for a few hours now. Though I didn't waterboard you last time, so maybe this one will stick. But I *have* lived on your side for a few decades now, so I do usually know what you're thinking. You talk to yourself a lot."

"Point taken, but if you ever dump water on me like that again, I'm dismantling you thread by thread. I know a spell for it."

"Oh nooo, I'm trembling with fear. If you did that, my consciousness would just jump into some other inanimate object. Maybe your wand..."

"Stay away from my wand! Do you know what happened? And where the hells are we?"

"Now those are two very different questions. To answer the first one: yes." The bag didn't say anything else.

"Uh okay... Can you please tell me?"

"Oh yes of course! So I think you had a moderate-to-severe panic attack. Which isn't unreasonable, given the shit you've seen and been through. But you were clearly freaking the fuck out."

It was all coming back to Izzie. Being personally responsible for the demise of those meggs had broken something inside her. She'd just seen so much death over the years—and caused a fair amount of it too. The world just seemed so...

"Alright there, cowgirl, I'm gonna cut ya off right there. You're not gonna go spiraling on me again. So you were panicking, and I think you'd lost all awareness of your surroundings. That sea monster, Lursa, was coming straight toward you. You used the *frijangre* spell, which I haven't seen you use in a looong time."

Izzie thought back to the last time she remembered using it. She'd frozen the blood of some random orc in an alleyway in Wastetown, not caring if he lived or died.

"Did it work? Did I stop it?"

"No idea, shrug."

"Did... did you just say 'shrug' instead of doing it?"

"I'm a bag! I don't have any shoulders; sometimes I have to improvise." Izzie started to laugh, but the ache in her throat stopped her. It still felt completely raw.

"Okay, then what happened?"

"You looked like you were thinking about doing something foolish. So I scooped you up."

"You... scooped me up? How?"

"When I sensed something wasn't right with you, I opened up my mouth and sucked you right off. I mean, in."

There's gotta be a better way to say that, was her first thought. But it was all coming back to her. She had been panicking and spiraling out of control. She supposed the floating feeling was when she was inside the bag. Must be some kind of weird void or something in there.

"So then..." She looked around at the small room she was in. There was a small lantern burning in the corner, and nothing else in the room besides the stone slab she figured was supposed to pass for a bed. Her legs were hanging off the end of the short slab. "Where are we now?"

"While you were inside me..." The bag paused as if desperately fighting the urge to make a joke, but in a rare turn of events, it resisted. "I propelled us up toward the surface as fast as possible. I'm not sure how long somebody can stay alive inside me. When we got to the top, I ralphed you up somewhere on the beach of the Southern Ocean. You were unconscious when I spit you out, and you just laid there for days. It was... really scary."

Izzie paused for a moment before breaking out into a wide smile. "Awww you actually care about me, you old sap!"

"Yeah yeah so I do. You did create me after all, Dr. Frankenstein."

"Doctor who?"

"No, he's different. He'd need a blue phone booth to get here."

"A blue... whatever, I'm not playing this game right now. Did somebody rescue us?"

"You'll see soon. Now we're in Dwarf Territory. Ready to learn all about dwarf pregnancies?!"

"I barely learned anything about fae *or* mermaid pregnancies!"

"I think Lulu would beg to differ. She's queen now because of you."

"Wait!" shouted Izzie, startling herself with the outburst. "What about Pyke? What happened to her?"

"Sorry, Iz. I don't know about that one. I was so focused on saving your dumb ass. But I trust she can fend for herself."

She respected the decision. *You can't save everybody all the time*, she reminded herself. The midwizard motto, even if she could barely bring herself to believe it. She also continued to marvel at the maturity her bag was showing—not only in saving her, but also in the way it spoke about her accomplishments. It was almost... sweet?

"Y'know, all this time, I've just been referring to you as my bag, but I think we've become close enough that I consider you a friend. I feel like I should name you."

"*You* should name *me*? If anything, I think I should be naming *you*. I've always thought Isadore was a little stuffy anyway. How about Tracy?"

"That's a terrible name! I would much rather change it to something fun and sexy like Eowyn or Celaena."

"Gross; I think maybe you're more of a Britta."

"Hmmm... that one's not too bad actually. Or maybe Ke—wait a second! How did we get on the topic of changing *my* name? I have a name already. We're giving *you* a name!"

"Alright, fine. How about Baggin' Tens?"

"Does that mean something gross?"

"Definitely."

"Next."

"Bagger Vance?"

"For some reason 'Vance' gives me the 'ick,' as you always say. Try again."

"Bilbo Baggins?"

"I actually really like that one!"

"Nah, doesn't work. It's copyrighted."

"Copy what?"

"Baggie Smalls?"

Izzie thought for a moment. Strangely enough, it fit perfectly. "Baggie Smalls it is! Now, Baggie Smalls, you have to help me escape from here."

"Escape? Now why would you want to do that?" a voice said from the stone doorway. A voice Izzie would recognize anywhere.

"*Dalfa*? What in the twelve hells are you doing here?!" She jumped off the stone slab and sprinted into her old friend's arms. They collided with the force of a charging minotaur. Tears erupted from Izzie's eyes. "I was so worried about you after your last letter." The freles continued their emotional embrace. "I'm so sorry I didn't write back. Life has been... tough."

"You're telling me," Dalfa croaked. "You have no idea how happy I am to see you awake."

"Why are you here? How did you find me?"

"Remember how I told you I was going to be on my own for a while? Well, the easiest place to do that from Minotaur Territory is the beaches south of Gamdo, so I've been staying here for the last month. I spend a lot of time walking up and down the beach, thinking. Imagine my surprise when I stumble across my former best friend lying half-dead on the banks of the Cosc?"

Izzie tried to ignore the phrase "former best friend," but she had to admit it hurt. Dalfa had every right, since Izzie's correspondence had been spotty at best, even though it was clear from the frele's letters she was struggling.

"I already filled her in on the details," Baggie said.

Izzie groaned. "What did you tell her?"

"I think I was able to parse out the truth from the downright absurd lies," Dalfa chuckled.

"Aw, so you didn't really believe Izzie had a threesome with a merman and a blood sprite?"

"Not a chance. Just like I didn't believe an eighty-foot changeling threw Izzie's ex-boyfriend halfway across Cosconia."

Izzie's face turned red. "Well... that one is true."

Dalfa laughed again, but Izzie didn't join her.

"You're being serious?"

She nodded and launched into a brief summary of what had happened over the past few years, pausing occasionally for Dalfa to react to some of the wilder scenarios Izzie had found herself in.

"Wow. That's a lot to process. Most of what your bag told me was actually true. Speaking of the bag..."

Izzie pressed her palm against her forehead. "Sentience charm gone wrong. *Very* wrong."

"Hey! I thought we were best friends!" Baggie Smalls responded, offended.

171

"So I've been replaced with a sassy purse? That's a new low, even for me," Dalfa said, but her face indicated she was teasing.

"That's enough about me." A distinct grumble came from the bag. "Enough about *us*," she corrected. "How are you doing? Are you really done being a midwizard?" She'd finally read Dalfa's letter shortly after waking up.

"I think you should hear what our hosts have to say before I get into that."

Before she was able to ask for an explanation, a knock sounded at the door, and in stepped a trio of dwarves, one frele and two meles, though it was difficult to tell them apart. Dwarves were known for their thick, luscious beards, and unlike humans or wizards, both sexes displayed their facial hair proudly. They were even born with tiny little beards, which was unusual but adorable. They all stood at around four feet tall, which was considerably smaller than Izzie's six foot frame, but nearly a whole foot taller than a halfling. One of the meles was obviously the oldest, with wrinkled skin and a white beard that fell in knots all the way down to his feet. The frele, who had guided the older mele into the room in a granddaughterly sort of way, had bright red hair, and her beard was demurely braided and only extended to her waist. Her companion, who Izzie guessed was her twin brother by the way their smiles mirrored each other's, had dark hair and a wild, frizzy beard that barely went past his shoulders. One of the other defining characteristics of dwarves was their bulbous noses, a trait that the three in front of her did not lack.

The older dwarf spoke first, his voice shaky. "Greetings, honored midwizards. I am Pythe, Gamdo's physician." Izzie internally cringed at the name, which sounded similar enough to Pyke that she couldn't help but wonder about the changeling's fate. She stuffed those thoughts down since there was nothing she could do about it now. She knew the frele could handle herself.

"These are my grandchildren, Lago and Drago." He pointed at the redheaded frele holding his hand first, and then the black-haired mele next. We have had the privilege to speak with your friend at length. If I may be so bold, how did you end up in such a debilitated condition on the shore of the Southern Ocean? We very rarely see wizards this far south, much less midwizards."

Izzie wasn't sure how much she should tell them. It would take hours to recount everything that had happened in the past few months, and she barely remembered what had happened at the bottom of the Cosc River. She decided to give them an abbreviated version of the truth. "I have been traveling around Cosconia working with each of the different races in our great land, learning about their pregnancies and deliveries. I was headed toward Dwarf Territory when I got... waylaid on the Cosc River." Dalfa gave her a sidelong glance but didn't say anything.

"By mermaids?" Drago asked excitedly. "Or water fae?!"

His sister lightly smacked the back of his head. "Would you let the frele talk, Drago?"

The dwarf blushed but didn't say anything more.

"That's pretty much it. I don't want to get into the details right now, but since I was heading here anyway, I'm ready to get started."

The elderly dwarf smiled at this, though it looked pained. "We are very lucky to have you. We dwarves are doing our best to rapidly increase our population, and as you likely know, this is extremely difficult for us."

"Of course. I can't imagine how hard it is for all of dwarfkind."

Like those of changelings, dwarf pregnancies were far more dangerous for the baby than the mother. Unlike giant babies, who got stuck because they were too large, dwarf babies often couldn't survive outside the womb since they were too small. The medical term for it was growth restriction. A wizard baby was born weighing, on average, between six and ten pounds— similar to many other humanoid races. One would think a dwarf, being about two-thirds the size of a wizard, would have a baby between four and seven pounds, and in an ideal circumstance, they would. However, growth restriction could lead to dwarven babies being born weighing only one to two pounds, which was rarely compatible with life.

A tiny dwarf baby had a host of issues—they couldn't stay warm (which was especially hard in the cold mountain halls they occupied), they couldn't feed well, and they often passed after just a few days of life. Izzie wasn't sure what was worse: a changeling baby who never took a breath, or a dwarf baby who held on for a few days but couldn't make it. *Or the complete inability to have a baby in the first place. I think that one is the worst of all.*

"It is very difficult for our people, and it only seems to be getting worse."

There it was again. Since she'd started traveling through Cosconia and delivering babies, every race she encountered had told a similar version of the same story. Things had historically been difficult for pregnant freles and babies in Cosconia, but over the past few decades, it had gotten demonstrably worse. Maternal, fetal, and neonatal mortality were rapidly increasing, with no relief in sight.

"That seems to be a common theme. Do you have any idea why that might be?"

Pythe shook his head. "I've conducted many of my own studies and tried several different methods to increase the size of our babies, but none have been successful. Being the town's doctor, I've been delivering babies for decades. It used to feel magical, and now it just feels like we're fighting against nature. And losing. I used to believe in Maternal Magic, but... I'm not so sure I do anymore."

It was the second time he had mentioned increasing the dwarf population, and she was afraid she knew why. "Are the dwarves preparing for war?"

"Unfortunately, yes. We have been trying to avoid it, but we must. We can't be the only race left out of the battle for the Wasteland."

Izzie froze. She looked at Dalfa, who was intently starting at her own feet. *That* was new information.

"The Wasteland? Why would you want to fight over the *Wasteland*?"

This time, Lago butted in. "You haven't heard? I would think *you* of all people would know about it." This earned her a retaliatory smack in the back of her head from her brother.

"I don't think it's common knowledge yet, sis. Dwarves were the ones to discover it, after all."

"Can I tell her, Papa?" Lago inquired. "Please, can I tell her? Drago got to tell the other one!"

The old dwarf sagely nodded his head. "She must know."

From there, the red-haired dwarf launched into a tale that made Izzie increasingly uneasy as it went on. "So, as you probably know, the Wasteland is completely empty except for a few nomadic groups who wander through, mostly humans. They can't survive there long, since it's completely incompatible with life. No water, scorching hot days and frigid nights, and unpredictable storms. Most dwarves will never enter the Wasteland in their lives, but there are some who must travel through for trade. Our kind produce weapons and other stone and metal goods sold throughout all of Cosconia, since they're of better quality than anybody else can make. You see, the reason weapons crafted by dwarves are so much better than—"

"Lago," Pythe interrupted. "How about you focus on the story, and we can tell the nice frele all about dwarven craftsmanship later?"

Lago blushed. "Sorry. I tend to get hyperfixated. Anyway, a while back, a group of dwarf merchants were traveling through the heart of the Wasteland to deliver goods to Elf Territory, when they stumbled across a small group of humans. They had set up a temporary camp around a circle of twelve ancient stones, carved with runes in the old languages of each of the twelve races of Cosconia. In the middle of the stone circle was a towering Baobab tree—you know the one? They call it the Mother Tree. Usually they're only found in the Jerdalin Forest, but..."

The sound of the dwarf's voice faded as horror overtook Izzie. Suddenly, she was back in the Wasteland. Standing next to a circle of twelve stones, carved with runes. Surrounded by land that was scorched and parched. But in the middle of those stones was a small sapling. She had noticed it then, decades ago, but had paid it no mind in her panic over Syrel's death. After that, she'd spiraled so far out of control she never thought about it again. How had she ignored it? The Wasteland was completely incapable of supporting life, yet she'd run away from a sign of life that had sprouted up in a matter of hours. Izzie's stomach sank as she thought about the implications of this. A word snapped her out of her internal dialogue.

"Wait, what did you just say?"

"I said one of the humans who lived under the tree had a baby there. It was the first ever recorded birth inside the Wasteland. And apparently, both mom and baby were completely healthy."

"Completely healthy? No signs of preeclampsia?" she asked, shocked to hear the human wasn't affected by the most common pregnancy ailment for their race.

"Never heard of it, but hopefully you can teach me later! I love learning about medical stuff from my Papa. Keep in mind, this is all secondhand information from the dwarf merchants, who are notorious for fabricating details to tell grandiose stories. But over the years, more and more reports came in of humans having babies in the Wasteland. So now, everybody wants a piece of the pie. War is brewing over who gets control of the land, since rumor has it, it's the best place in Cosconia to have a healthy pregnancy and delivery."

Izzie had so many questions, but she asked the most burning one first. "So why isn't everybody fighting over it already?"

"Very astute question, Izzie." Pythe answered this time. "There have been a few skirmishes here and there, but large-scale war has yet to break out. The first reason is that the vast majority of the Wasteland is still incompatible with life. It's extremely difficult to obtain water and there is no infrastructure to support civilization there, even if it *is* easier to have a baby. The second reason, and I believe the more important one, is this: nobody wants to fight until they're sure they can win. Each race rightly believes that a few more years, or even decades, of freles and babies dying is preferable to their entire race being wiped out in a losing war effort. I can only imagine the plotting and scheming going on behind closed doors throughout all of Cosconia."

Izzie felt nauseated. The world started spinning around her.

"Could you excuse me for a moment?" She quickly exited the small room; she didn't know where she was going, but she had to get out of there. She ducked through narrow stone corridors, getting strange looks from the dwarves she passed. It felt like everybody was staring at her. Judging her. It was like they all knew. They knew war was coming, and it was all her fault.

A dark thought occurred to her, and the second it entered her mind, she knew it was the truth. The ritual she and Syrel had created was intended to grant her fertility. She'd tried to harness the mysterious Maternal Magic for herself. Instead, it had backfired and granted the land fertility, rendering her forever incapable of having children. It seemed that now, anybody who entered the land would be granted fertility and health. This could change everything, change the entire trajectory of Cosconia's future. A society that didn't have to dedicate resources to preserving the life of mother and baby throughout a pregnancy, as well as one that could continuously grow its population, could lead to countless scientific and technological breakthroughs. She couldn't blame anybody for wanting to lay claim to the land.

For years, she'd been hearing rumors of a brewing war, but she could never figure out *why*. Now she knew. *She* started this war. Thousands were going to die. Maybe tens of thousands. All because of her.

She wouldn't let herself spiral out of control. She was stronger than that. But she knew this was her fault. Izzie made a commitment to herself, right then and there, as she finally exited the stony tunnels and took a deep breath of clean mountain air. Though many deaths were already on her conscience, and there were countless more to come, she would dedicate every fiber of her being, every waking moment, every thought, every move, and every action to doing the one thing that truly mattered: bringing life into this world and preserving it at any cost. She made an oath to herself to do no harm. Never again would she use her power to harm another living being. *Even if it killed her.*

Dalfa caught up to Izzie sobbing in the harsh light of day.

"Izzie, do you realize what this means for us? Cosconia won't even *need* midwizards if this land is what the dwarves are saying it is. Can you imagine it? Healthy pregnancies and deliveries for everybody?"

If she was being honest with herself, she *couldn't* imagine it. For decades, pregnancy and danger had been practically interchangeable. She'd seen more freles and babies pass than she could count. The thought of a place where that *didn't* happen seemed to be too good to be true.

"But at what cost?" she hiccuped. "Thousands, tens of thousands of lives lost fighting over it?"

Her friend's face fell. "It's completely different, Izzie. The lives lost will be soldiers willingly sacrificing their lives to benefit their race for the future."

Izzie couldn't believe what she was hearing. "Dalfa, are you hearing yourself? You *want* Cosconia to go to war?"

Her friend backed off her enthusiasm a titch. "Of course I don't *want* war. But doesn't the end justify the means?" Before Izzie could protest, she continued. "Have you been living in a different Cosconia than I have? I watched halfling litters die in their parents arms, too many to even hold. I cared for orc freles as they bled out, telling their orphaned children they loved them. I watched minotaurs drain themselves dry attempting to breastfeed their babies to no avail. You heard what Pythe said. Cosconia is *sick*. And it's nearly destroyed me. To be honest, I don't know how it hasn't destroyed you."

She attempted to explain it *had* nearly destroyed her, but Dalfa continued her tirade. Izzie was shocked at how jaded her friend had become.

"Pregnancy is not a choice for our society, Izzie. It's a necessity. Cosconia can't continue without pregnancy, and Maternal Magic is dead and buried, like thousands of mothers and their babies. Everywhere but the Wasteland. Why *wouldn't* we fight for it?"

"But why fight?" Izzie finally got a word in. "Why not settle it peacefully?"

"What world are you living in, Izzie? Have you ever heard an elf talk about their hatred for orcs? Or a giant tell you how disgusted they are by changelings? Did you forget about the increasing number of border disputes and fights between races? You think everybody is just going to hold hands and sing Sparilist hymns and settle down side by side? Are you delusional?" she spat.

Izzie winced at her friend's harsh words, but she couldn't deny them. Dalfa was right. Cosconia *was* sick, and a peaceful resolution seemed impossible. The races had been living separately for centuries; how could they be expected to settle down harmoniously?

"So what? We just accept that thousands are going to die in a bloody war?"

"Do you have any other ideas?" Dalfa asked, and it seemed like she genuinely hoped Izzie had another idea. But she didn't. She shook her head.

"I didn't think so," Dalfa said, her harsh tone cooling. "But Izzie, we're wizards. Don't think about this in terms of decades; think about the distant future. Sure, there may be a war. And it may be a bloody one. But all wars end. A victor will emerge. A treaty will be signed. Eventually, the war will be over, and we'll be left with a beautiful land flowing with Maternal Magic."

"We're not *just* wizards, Dalfa. We're *midwizards*. We've dedicated ourselves to saving lives, not taking them."

"And what better way to save lives than to give all Cosconians access to Maternal Magic?"

Though she didn't want to admit it, Izzie saw the logic in Dalfa's conclusions. She was probably right. Now that Cosconians knew about the fertile land, war was likely inevitable. But that didn't mean she had to accept it.

"I don't understand you, Dalfa. Every letter you sent me lamented the loss of life. How can you be so cavalier about it now?"

"Not all of us can impregnate fae queens and save giant prophets with our blood magic," she said acidly. "You can only watch so many innocent lives fade into nothing until you have to turn off your emotions altogether."

Izzie recoiled. "So that's what you've done? You've turned off your emotions?"

"I've turned off my weakness. My focus is securing Cosconia's future. You can keep trying to prevent the inevitable, but I'm going to start preparing for a new era."

She's right. War is coming. I have to accept it and get out of the way until it's over. Peace is impossible. The ends justify the means. This is the only way Cosconia will move forward. War is inev...

Those aren't my thoughts, Izzie realized.

"Dalfa... did you just use your mind magic to try to convince me to accept the war?"

Dalfa didn't look at all ashamed. "I don't want you to stand in the way of what must happen, and I'll do what it takes to ensure a healthy future for our land."

Izzie was flabbergasted. Partially at her friend's brazen attempt at influencing her mind, but mostly at the sheer *power* of her mind magic. They'd practiced magic with each other in midwizardry school, but this was on an entirely different level. She knew how hard it was to use mind magic spells on another wizard, and Dalfa had almost successfully changed Izzie's entire way of thinking. It was as impressive as it was terrifying.

"Stay the hells out of my mind! What kind of friend would do that?"

"Friend?" Dalfa scoffed. "How can you even call yourself my friend? You barely answered my letters. You show up here and start fighting with me. And you fail to understand that the only way out of this mess is through it."

"I feel sorry for you that you think peace is impossible," Izzie shot back.

"You'll see." Dalfa backed away. "Everybody will see."

CHAPTER FIFTEEN

Hi Ho, Hi Ho, It's to the NICU We Go

"We are all weak most of the time," she said finally. "Look at the baby. Born to his mother, he learns how to eat from her, how to walk, talk, hunt, run. He does not invent new ways. He just continues with the old. This is how we all come to the world."

—Yaa Gyasi

---

24 years before the Twelve Race War
Gamdo, Dwarf Territory

The isolation of the dwarven mining colonies was exactly what Izzie needed. Without the consistent setting of the sun to mark the passage of time, a day melted into a week, which quickly became a month, and before she knew it, years were passing without her notice. Dalfa hadn't returned since their argument, which Izzie was fine with. She felt like she didn't even know the frele anymore, and she was scared of Dalfa's ability to influence her mind.

She tried as hard as she could to stay away from any discussion of war, but it was a losing effort. It was all anybody could talk about. Every day, she heard a new rumor about the war. Some were relatively banal: The minotaurs had been sharpening their horns. The halflings were practicing battle formations. Others were more ominous: Giants were being spotted further south every day. There was movement in the southeast, in Blood Sprite Territory.

So Izzie buried herself in her work. She realized this was what she always did—immersed herself so fully in a task she couldn't think about anything else. If she'd spent the last twelve years dwelling on the fact that her failed ritual had done something to the land that was now setting Cosconia up for the bloodiest war it had ever seen, she'd have gone crazy. So she would just keep working. It was the reason she'd gone to midwizardry school in the first place—to escape from the pain she had when she thought she'd killed Syrel. Maybe if she saved enough freles and enough babies, she could balance the scales for all the evil she'd caused in the world.

Like she did every day, Izzie wondered where Syrel was right now. She had realized some time before that Pyke had tossed him toward the Wasteland, probably several miles in. *Good*, she thought. *He can return to the scene of the crime. I hope he dies out there... No, I don't. That's not true at all. He must have had a good reason for not coming to find me. Twelve hells, I wish I could see him again.* She wasn't even sure what she would do when she saw him. Slap him? Kiss him? Kill him? All of the above?

"Isadore, you have to stop spiraling. Focus on the task at hand," she admonished herself sternly under her breath. She'd spent the last twelve years doing exactly what she would have done in Dwarf Territory if her time after midwizardry school had progressed like she'd expected, except she never took a break.

She would sleep for a few hours, and then work for thirty, sometimes forty, hours straight. Her focus was singular: save as many babies as possible.

She used her blood magic nonstop. It was relatively easy, but it required constant attention. Before her arrival, dwarf mothers would take their tiny babies home and try everything they could to save them. They usually failed. So Izzie helped them set up a nursery. Per her guidance, they'd excavated a large cave underneath the forge, which kept the room warm—at least by dwarf standards. Izzie still shivered when she walked in, but it was far less cold than the rest of the bleak mountain halls. The nursery was a simple room, but Izzie had specifically requested "cribs" be carved into the floor. They certainly weren't as nice as the intricately carved wooden cribs used by the elves—they were just depressions cut into the floor, and Izzie filled them with straw and old clothes to wrap the babies in. Instead of taking the babies home, the dwarf freles delivered and then immediately brought them to Izzie's nursery. She called them her NICU babies: Newborns in Izzie's Created Uterus. It was silly, but she felt like this room acted as a second uterus for the babies, nurturing them and protecting them until they could survive in the outside world.

Prior to her unceremonious arrival in Gamdo, Izzie's blood magic—and the rest of her magic, for that matter—had grown significantly in power with constant use. Now, it had grown to the next level: She could use it on multiple living beings at once. Before, she'd basically had full control over one person's blood, but nothing more. Now, she could control the bloodstreams of multiple NICU babies. From reading the *Sangrila* her great-grandmother had left her, she wasn't sure any other wizard had been able to accomplish this task, but she supposed it was easier when the recipients were only one or two pounds.

The main cause of death for the dwarf babies was either freezing, or what midwizards referred to as failure to thrive. Basically, they were just too small to survive. Izzie's blood magic changed both of those things. She essentially circulated their blood around their bodies ten times faster than their tiny little hearts could do on their own. Not only did this keep them plenty warm enough for survival, but it also accelerated their growth. The most difficult part was keeping up with feeding, since they required ten times the normal amount of sustenance, but the dwarf mothers were dutiful and committed, as mothers almost always were. This process allowed the babies to grow from their birth weights of one or two pounds to the appropriate weight of five or six pounds in just a matter of days.

Izzie's routine was consistent. There were always at least twenty or thiry NICU babies at any given time, and she was increasing the number she could control at once by the day. At this point, she could keep twenty-five babies alive at once. Dwarf mothers would bring their babies in, and as soon as Izzie determined one of the babies under her care could survive without her blood-magic-induced growth and temperature maintenance, she'd discharge the baby to go home with its mother. The pregnant and newly postpartum freles came from all over Dwarf Territory, not just Gamdo, so there was never any shortage of patients. Some of the babies still died in their mother's arms waiting for her care, which was why she pushed herself harder and harder every day. Any time she slept, or ate, or even had a conversation, it would break her concentration and the NICU babies would suffer. So she barely slept. Or ate. Or had conversations. She knew this wasn't sustainable, and it certainly wasn't a viable alternative to fighting over the Wasteland, but the more she thought about her fight with Dalfa, the more she knew she needed to come up with a better solution.

As she'd noticed many times before, the mortality rate was going up. There was a clear increase in the number of growth-restricted babies born now compared to how many there had been twelve years before.

Lago frequently came by to bring her food, check on her, or encourage her to sleep. Even after twelve years, the girl's enthusiasm did not wane. She loved taking care of the freles and their babies, so she was happy to be around Izzie. Sometimes she sat near Izzie and observed her for hours at a time, taking notes and observing her behavior. Izzie had tried to tell her time and again the only reason she herself could be a midwizard was because of her blood magic, but the frele wasn't discouraged.

"Good morning, Izzie!" the dwarf girl said cheerily, walking into the nursery with a plate of food that would most likely go uneaten. Her red hair, which matched the crimson streak in Izzie's own sweat-soaked hair, was pointing in all directions. Izzie didn't respond. She usually didn't. Partially, she wasn't trying to make any more friends. All of her friends ended up dead, missing, or in some kind of danger. But mostly, she wanted to stay focused. Any lapse in concentration could be the difference between life and death.

Lago was undeterred, as always. "I brought you some haggis. I hope you eat it today; it's extra tasty!" Izzie continued to focus on her task. Like usual, Lago settled into her spot observing Izzie. She really was a sweet frele, but didn't she have anything better to do?

One of the NICU babies under her care was ready. The dwarf baby's mother was already in the room breastfeeding her. Izzie pointed at her, and Lago nodded, understanding the message. At least she was helpful for this part of the job. The dwarf got up and walked over to the breastfeeding mother, tapped her on the shoulder, and whispered a few words in her ear, careful not to let any of the other mothers hear. The dwarf mother gathered up her baby and made her way between the stone cribs that housed the rest of the NICU babies. She stopped by Izzie on the way out the door.

Though Izzie made it clear she was not interested in hearing words of gratitude or thank-yous, every dwarf mother still stopped by on their way out the door.

"I do not have words to express how grateful I am to you, Madam Midwizard. You saved my baby, and I will never forget you." She pulled a small bag out of her robe that jangled as she pushed it toward Izzie. At first, Izzie had rejected these gifts. She wasn't in it for the money. She barely even had a use for money. But Lago had explained that it was considered a grave offense to reject freely proffered gold in dwarven society, as this was a resource that dwarves held on to even more tightly than their smithing tools. She nodded in gratitude to the dwarf and sent her on her way, tossing the gold into the bag at her side. This venture had actually been shockingly lucrative for her.

"More money, more problems, that's what I always say!" Every time she put money inside Baggie Smalls, it made a comment she didn't understand. She still had no idea where it learned all of these odd words and phrases that were not native to Cosconia, but she had long stopped questioning anything it did.

"Well, I've got plenty of money and plenty of problems," she whispered to it, not wanting Lago to hear she was willing to talk to the bag but not the dwarf.

"Can I teach you a new term?" Baggie Smalls asked her.

Izzie was shocked. "You never ask permission. I don't know if I should be excited or scared." She didn't even think twice about how strange it was her bag, who never left her side, would know things she didn't.

"Hmm... Excited! The term is 'nurse.'"

"Like a nursery?"

"Exactly! Except a nursery is a place, and a nurse is a person."

"Okay? So what's a nurse?" Izzie was getting frustrated at having her attention pulled away from the task at hand.

"Basically somebody who does all of the work of helping people without any of the credit."

"I'm not sure I understand."

"So you know how you've been focusing on keeping the babies alive?"

"No," she retorted sarcastically. "I completely forgot about the one task that has singularly consumed my focus for a decade."

"Exactly. But who cleans the cribs? Who brings the babies in and out? Who consoles the grieving mothers? Who brings you food? Who keeps track of everybody coming in and out of here?"

Izzie looked guiltily at Lago, who was in the middle of cleaning and resetting the crib of the NICU dwarf who had just vacated the room. She was softly humming to herself, unaware of Izzie's conversation with her bag. *Have I ever even said thank you?*

"Lago," Izzie called, doing her best to focus on the conversation while continuing her blood magic. The dwarf bounced over, ever present smile plastered across her face.

"What's up?"

She glanced at the bag, who seemed to give a grunt of encouragement. *I think I'm anthropomorphizing this bag far too much.*

"How would you like to be a nurse?"

"I would love to!"

"I haven't even told you what it is," Izzie said blankly.

"I trust you," Lago answered. "If you think it will help, I'll do whatever."

Izzie nearly cried. After falling out of contact with Pyke, finding out about Syrel faking his own death, and having her fight with Dalfa, she thought she would never trust anybody ever again. But here was Lago, offering her unconditional support.

"Besides," the dwarf continued. "Baggie already told me what a nurse was."

Izzie laughed. "Of course it did. So you're interested?"

"Interested? Being a nurse sounds like the best job in the world! I get to help mothers and babies every day? And be by your side through it all?"

"Yes, but it can be a difficult and thankless job."

"As long as I'm helping, that's okay."

The midwizard wasn't usually a big hugger, but she pulled the dwarf into a deep embrace. It was awkward since Lago barely came up to her chest, but it felt good to be accepted. Maybe she finally had a friend she wouldn't lose.

"Oh! By the way, I meant to tell you," Lago produced a letter from her backpack. "This came for you!"

Izzie,

I'm sorry it's been so long since I've reached out. I've been traveling around Cosconia discussing the current situation with many leaders and important folks. Most agree with me that war is inevitable and the benefit is worth the cost. I hope you've changed your way of thinking and you can accept that the night is darkest before the dawn. Trust me; if I thought the fertile Wasteland could be settled peacefully, I would do whatever it took to make that happen. But it can't. The racial tension in Cosconia is too high, which is only exacerbated by the constant loss of freles and babies.

I'm currently in Orc Territory. My old friend, Kurai, thinks he has a way to drastically reduce the death toll of this war, but he needs your blood magic. I won't be sticking around since I have much to do and little time, but I think you're going to want to come here. I'm working on my mind magic skills every single day.

Maybe one day, after the war is over, we'll be able to see eye to eye again. Maybe not. I'll never forget the times we had together.

Dalfa

* * *

After months of effort, with the assistance of Lago, Drago, Pythe, Baggie, and many hours spent studying the *Sangrila*, Izzie finally finished the nursery. They had developed a system of runes to carve into the walls of the dwarven nursery. Izzie hadn't used any runes since the failed ritual, but she had researched their use for years with Syrel. These runes would hold her blood magic in continuous circulation to support the NICU babies after her departure. She knew she couldn't leave Gamdo until there was a sustainable solution that didn't require her constant presence. She wasn't sure how long the runes would last, but it would hopefully buy the tiny NICU dwarves more time than they would normally have.

Izzie could have stayed in the tunnels of Dwarf Territory forever, isolated from the rest of Cosconia, but if this Kurai truly had a way to reduce the number of lives lost in the war, she had to hear him out. From everything Dalfa had told her, he seemed like a kind and level-headed soldier who had been tirelessly working his way up the ranks. While her relationship with Dalfa had soured, she still trusted her old friend's judgment. If she thought the orc could help, Izzie believed her. She was willing to try anything to reduce the death toll of the war she was responsible for.

So she would head to Orc Territory, but not before stopping in the Wasteland to see if she could confirm any of the rumors for herself. For years, she hadn't been sure if she was ready to return to the place where everything fell apart, but she had to see it for herself.

Originally, she planned to go by herself. However, Lago's skills as a nurse had proven to be so helpful she couldn't imagine life without the dwarf by her side. She was still reluctant to let her in after losing so many loved ones over the years, but Lago was never deterred.

They'd been walking for ten days, and Lago had estimated the journey would take them about three weeks. The dwarf frele didn't stop talking for nearly the entire journey to the Wasteland, not caring whether Izzie was participating in the conversation. She would tell stories that seemed to last for hours, with no encouragement from her travel companion.

"So," the dwarf said, rapidly switching from complaining about her brother to a more serious topic. "Y'know how I was watching you and taking notes while you took care of the NICU babies for all those years?"

Izzie grunted. Like she could forget.

"I did some math to see if I could figure out the impact you made on the dwarf population. Wanna hear what I came up with?"

Izzie had to admit, this piqued her interest. She never really thought about her work in terms of statistics. Usually the numbers were bleak anyway. She answered with a hesitant nod of her head.

"Okay, so it took two years to carve out the nursery, and I didn't really watch you before that, so we're just going to do the math based on the last ten years. When I first started watching you, you could control five babies at a time with your magic. You were able to increase that number by about two every year, which is how you ended up at twenty-five. That's an average of fifteen babies at a time over a decade. You with me so far?" Izzie nodded again. Math wasn't her strong suit, but it was simple enough. Her power had grown at a much faster rate than she'd realized.

"Great! On average, it took four days to get a baby to the size where you could hand it off to its mother and it would survive without your blood magic. Sometimes it took two days, sometimes it took six—"

Izzie cut her off. "Yes, Lago, I know how averages work."

Lago had the good sense to look embarrassed before she continued. "So if you took care of an average of fifteen at a time for four days over ten years..." she looked down at her notepad, tapping each number and ensuring that the math was correct. "You saved at least thirteen thousand, six hundred and fifty dwarf babies over that time!"

Izzie stopped in her tracks. "Thirteen thousand babies? That can't be right. Do the math again."

"It's right! I swear! I did the math, like, fifty times."

Tears welled in Izzie's eyes. She'd really done that? *She* had saved that many lives? Izzie dropped to her knees, thick tears dropping onto the dry ground of the Wasteland they traversed. She had really made a difference. She had committed to bringing life into this world and preserving it at any cost... and she had truly honored that commitment. It felt good. It was the first time she'd felt *good* since before she found out there was going to be a deadly war over a land she'd created. The feeling inspired her. *Maybe I can offset the losses by single-handedly saving lives until I drop.* She stood up, looking at the dwarf in a new light.

A thought crossed her mind. "How many couldn't be saved?"

Lago shook her head. "I don't know. I didn't do that math. I don't think that's what you should focus on. Thirteen thousand babies, Izzie! *That* is what you should be focusing on."

"Thank you, Lago," she said softly, trying not to think about all the lives lost. "I needed that. You have no idea how much I needed that."

"Actually, I think I do. I watched you for many, many hours, Izzie. Don't get me wrong—you're doing amazing work. You're saving more lives than maybe anybody in Cosconian history. But at what cost? You're running yourself ragged. You look like you've aged a century in the past decade." Izzie inspected her hands, which were far more brittle than they had been just a few years prior. "You're gonna crash, and you're gonna crash hard. This trip couldn't have come at a better time, because we had to get you out of there. You're only one wizard."

"That's where you're wrong, young padawan."

"Pada-what?"

"I don't know; my bag calls me that all the time. I don't know what it means, but it sounds cool. Anyway. I'm not just one wizard."

"Yes, you are!" Lago insisted.

"No, I'm absolutely not."

"Then what are you?" she asked, taking the bait.

"I'm a motherfucking midwizard."

* * *

24 years before the Twelve Race War
Gravipar, Central Wasteland

Once Izzie arrived in Gravipar, which was what Cosconians were calling the site of the ritual she had performed with Syrel all those years ago, she ventured to the tree in the center of town. The nomads of the area were calling it the Mother Tree. There were dozens of hastily built shanties and shacks. The construction of each different edifice reflected the builder. A roof over a hole dug into the ground had been constructed by a dwarf. This was only possible now that the packed dirt surrounding the stone circle had softened and was even showing some signs of life, with the few blades of green grass poking through. A hut with perfect wooden craftsmanship naturally belonged to the elves. The one that used a hodgepodge of material was, of course, by the humans, who stole a little bit from every culture. There was even one she would have to crawl into, belonging to the halflings she'd seen skittering about.

Lago had explained there were no permanent residents of Gravipar, but all of the races who were sending delegations to study the land had built temporary lodging. The lack of water was still a problem, as one could only stay for as long as one had a water supply. The days were painfully hot in the Wasteland, and the nights were bitterly cold. It didn't make sense to Izzie, but it was another reason nobody could live here. She idly wondered if she would see Syrel here, but it had been many years since Pyke had unceremoniously tossed him in this direction.

A voice from behind her called her name, but Izzie instantly knew it wasn't Syrel. She whirled around to see a water fae standing in front of her.

"*Mmeme?*" Izzie asked, shocked. "What in the twelve hells are *you* doing here?"

"Good to see you too," she mumbled. "I'm here on *Queen* Luxor's behalf." The way she said her sister's name was overly formal, and Izzie guessed she might be a little salty *she* wasn't the one being called queen.

"Are you studying the effects of the land here too?"

At this, the girl lit up, almost seeming to glow in the twilight. "I'm not just studying it; I'm *living* it." She patted her belly. "I'm pregnant!"

Izzie was flabbergasted. "*YOU* are *pregnant?* Hadn't you been trying for almost twenty years back in Pwise without success?"

The water fae beamed. "Yep. I was here a couple months ago with my betrothed—just for a week—doing some research, and a little while after we got home, I found out I was expecting! Isn't it amazing?"

She had no idea how lucky she was. For as long as she could remember, Izzie had wanted nothing more than to get pregnant, and Mmeme was able to do it after a few days here? It made her wonder if she'd be able to conceive in this new magical land, but she knew in her gut it wouldn't work for her. She wasn't sure *how* she knew, but she knew.

"Yeah, really amazing!" Izzie tried to feign excitement, but she didn't think she was doing a very good job. "So why are you back here?"

The fae lowered her voice. "Between you and me, I think we've got a plan for how to make this place habitable. We've teamed up with the dwarves. With their expert excavation and tunneling skills and our water magic, we're going to create a channel. Directly here from the Cosc River. Once there's water, we're going to turn the Wasteland into paradise."

"But what about the war? Won't providing water make it livable for everybody? It will be a bloodbath!"

"The queen has a plan for peace. It's going to blow everybody away."

"Do you really think you can make a channel? It has to be a hundred miles to the Cosc River."

"One hundred and twenty, to be exact."

"That will take an eternity, even with the help of the dwarves."

"Work is already underway. We should be done in about twenty-four years."

Could Lulu really have a plan for peace? Izzie wondered. If anybody could, it was her. She had already brokered a peace agreement with the mermaids, so why not with everybody else? Izzie felt something strange, deep inside her. It almost felt like it was bubbling up within her. An extremely foreign feeling. Izzie felt... *hope.* For the first time since finding out about this very land, she felt hope. Instead of war, could there be peace? Twelve races living in harmony again, like Cosconia of old?

Peace in Gravipar would change *everything*. Izzie could imagine it now. Twelve races, living together in harmony. Humans who didn't seize and die from eclampsia. Orcs not bleeding out. Changeling babies born happy and healthy. Fertile fae like Mmeme. It would mean the ritual actually led to harmony instead of division. Peace instead of war. Love instead of hate. Maternal Magic returning. *This* was the kind of Cosconia Izzie wanted to live in.

Peace in Gravipar would also mean maybe she *wasn't* a monster. All her work delivering babies and saving lives wouldn't be for naught. For years, Izzie had worried every baby she saved would be another body thrown at a bloody war. Instead, Lulu's peace could mean the babies she delivered would be the ones to lead Cosconia into a new and prosperous age. Maybe Kurai's plan could be combined with Lulu's, and Izzie could be the one to facilitate a peaceful future.

CHAPTER SIXTEEN

Letters From an Orcish Prison

And deep in their dark hearts the Orcs loathed the Master whom they served in fear, the maker only of their misery.

—J.R.R. Tolkien

---

24 years before the Twelve Race War
Ungledor, Orc Territory

The moment Izzie and Lago stepped foot off the bridge crossing from the North Wasteland into Orc Territory, they were ambushed. Her bag, which contained her wand, was immediately ripped away from her. She knew her attackers couldn't open it because of the enchantments she'd put on it, but she watched them throw it into some sort of sack she worried had magic that would prevent Baggie from acting on its own. She could do magic without her wand, of course, but it made it harder to focus the magic. It also made the magic weaker.

The second thing the ambushers did was shove a cloth in her mouth that would make speaking impossible. Again, she could do magic without speaking, but it would be weaker still. Next

199

came a blindfold and a bag over her head. She assumed it was orcs who were attacking her since she was now officially in their territory, but they didn't say a word. They didn't even make a sound, which was eerie, since a quiet orc was like an ugly fae.

Izzie tried to think scientifically about what was happening to her, even though she was absolutely terrified. Orcs were notorious for their brutality. And this was no random attack—they were careful and coordinated. They knew she was a midwizard, and they clearly even knew about her bag, which was extra concerning. They were able to neutralize her in little more than a heartbeat. *Dalfa betrayed me*, she realized.

After the bag went over her head, her wrists and her ankles were roughly bound by thick cords of rope. She could already feel her skin chafing. It had barely been ten seconds since they were jumped, and already she was essentially powerless. Izzie was most worried for her companion. She knew she'd be able to figure a way out of this; she just needed to get her head right. But poor Lago didn't have any blood magic. She didn't have a wizard's constitution. These orcs could, and probably would, kill her without a second thought. And Izzie was *not* about to let anybody else die on her account. She had made a promise to herself, and she wasn't going to break it. Just as she was about to channel her blood magic, she lost consciousness when a blow to the head dropped her to the ground.

When she finally blinked awake, she heard a guttural shout. She still couldn't see anything, and the ropes around her wrists and ankles had been exchanged for metal shackles. The gag remained in her mouth.

"War is in the air!" an orc voice shouted to a chorus of cheers. He took a big whiff of the air, heavy with the stink of what Izzie figured had to be a massive gathering of orcs based on the sound and the smell. "Can't ye smell it?" he called to the congregation, which was met with a raucous round of chest pounding and whooping.

The blindfold was ripped off, and Izzie squinted at the sudden blinding light. A massive orc loomed above her. Appearing to be slightly shorter but practically twice as wide as Izzie, a crooked smile was plastered across his face. His dark blue skin seemed almost taut over the rippling muscles of his bare chest. He had five white lines across his chest, radiating from an eyeball painted in the center of his torso. *Why does that look familiar to me?* Izzie wondered. Slung over his broad shoulders was a battle axe, dripping with blood, which looked like it weighed as much as she did. A headless orc lay at his feet.

Izzie swiveled her head around to take in her surroundings. She was flat on the floor of an elevated wooden platform, which towered above the heads of the thousands of orcs surrounding it. There were orcs in every direction. Behind her stood four soldiers in full armor, each one holding a gleaming, golden metal chain attached to one of her limbs. The same white lines radiating from an eyeball were painted on each of their breastplates. She'd never seen an orc in full armor before, as they were known for charging into battle with naught but a weapon and their inherent bloodlust. Only the ones guarding her wore armor.

"'Ello poppet," the hulking orc said in a falsely sweet voice. "Name's Kurai. S'pose ye could call me the boss around here."

So Dalfa did betray me. I knew a benevolent orc warrior was too good to be true. They must have organized this to capture me. Izzie was filled with anger toward her former friend. Though she couldn't speak, she focused directly on the white line painted on his chest that crossed directly over his heart. She knew she could stop it with a blood magic spell with enough Intent. Her commitment to never taking another life didn't apply when her own was on the line, right? *Paracorzra*—she invoked her blood magic, using the most effective heart-stopping spell she knew.

Kurai burst into harsh laughter. "What's this? I feel a bit o' tingle in m' chest! I think this here wizard's trying to stop m' heart!" He laughed harder, causing the rest of the gathered orcs to join in the chorus of gruff laughter. It grated on Izzie's ears. *Why isn't it working?* Izzie thought frantically. *It should be working.* Did she not have enough Skill? If she couldn't use her magic, then she really was in trouble. And if she couldn't save herself, then she definitely couldn't save Lago.

"Bet yer wonderin' why yer cursed blood sorcery won't work!" He pointed at the chains that were attached to her wrists and ankles. "Lyonium." He grinned. "'At'll stop your blood magic right in its tracks."

Izzie would've vomited if the gag wouldn't send it right back down her throat. She'd thought lyonium was a myth. Evidently, she was mistaken. Lyonium was an ancient metal that could stop blood magic because of how it was made—by literally melting a blood sprite and infusing it into pure gold. To get this much must have cost a fortune... and thousands of blood sprite lives.

Most considered blood sprites to be the "twelfth race" of Cosconia, since the least was known about them. They lived in the treacherous marshes of southeast Cosconia, where no race dared to tread. Even in midwizardry school, it only took a few days to cover every known fact about blood sprites, since so little had ever been confirmed. Rumors abounded, however. Rumors that they could kill with just a look. That they could remove all the blood from your body with a word. That they reproduced by splitting themselves in half. Izzie wasn't sure if any of it was true, but one thing was for sure: They, like Izzie, could use blood magic. Apparently they could inhibit it as well. *But they'd have to give their lives for it*, she realized darkly.

The beastly Kurai, who she assumed was the chieftain based on her knowledge of orcish social structure, ripped the gag out of her mouth.

"S'a pleasure to see you again, Isadore."

Izzie was confused. She reexamined the orc, but she couldn't make out any features she recognized.

"I ain't surprised ye don't remember. Ye looked like ye'd drunk more than an orc after a glorious battle." At this, several orcs in the front row lifted their mugs of ale toward him. "We ran into each other in a lovely little place called Wastetown. Ye tried to kill me."

Izzie's heart sank as she remembered the encounter. She had stumbled out of the bar blind drunk and ran directly into an orc. A massive orc with the exact same eyeball sigil that adorned every orc around her. In her months-long binge after she'd lost Syrel, she had done a lot of things she would come to regret. Including freezing an orc's heart without a second thought.

"*You*," she whispered. "*You're alive.*"

"Right-o, girl. I was but a foot soldier then, drinking me life away in Wastetown. I almost died that day, but the chieftain of the Ungledor orcs dragged me from that alley and revived me. He told me I owed him my life, and from that day forward, I worked my way up through his army." He kicked the headless body lying at his feet. "Thanks again, Chief."

"What do you want with me?" she spat, venom in her words.

"Yer pal Dalfa is a real nice frele. She told me allll about you and yer blood sorcery. It weren't hard to guess ye were the bitch who tried to stop me heart. It was too easy to convince yer friend to tell me everything about ye. I've been planning my revenge ever since, but not before ye help out the orcs a bit."

"I wouldn't help you if my life depended on it. I'd rather die."

"Oh that'll come. But not yet. War's a-coming, poppet. Preparations must be made." His voice switched from casual cruelty to a more formal tone, sounding more like a leader. "Our population has thinned with the recent clashes with other clans, but that is no more. We are banding together with the other five orc factions to create the largest army Cosconia has ever seen. We need soldiers. As many soldiers as we can create."

Izzie's entire body went numb. *The orc factions banding together?* That was unprecedented. She had studied some of Cosconia's history before she started midwizardry school, and the orcs had been warring with each other for as long as history was recorded. Sure, there were plenty of times when two clans would team up to take on a fae town encroaching on their territory or to savage a roving band of elves, but the tribes would eventually turn on each other. All six of the factions coming together was... impossible.

"W-w-why? Why are you banding together?" she stuttered, but she already knew the answer. The same reason the dwarves were producing weapons at an unprecedented rate. The same reason the fae and mermaids had teamed up. Was there any way Lulu could stop this war and create peace? Her hope for peace had dissipated the moment she realized Dalfa had betrayed her and that Kurai wasn't an ally, but rather a wicked monster.

Kurai ignored her question. "We still have many years to prepare, but the time draws near. The orcs will prevail. And we can't do that without creating the largest army this land has ever seen. And we can't do *that* without ye."

The answer to Izzie's next question confirmed her suspicions and eliminated any thought that there would ever be peace. "Who are you going to war against?"

"Everyone," the orc smiled, and again the orcs surrounding the platform whooped and hollered.

"Where's my friend?" she asked, her voice trembling.

"Show her the wee one!" the chieftain shouted, and a group of orcs in front of the platform parted to reveal a small form on the ground. Lago, cuts and bruises covering her innocent face, looked up at her. The terror in her eyes tugged at Izzie's heart.

"Izzie! Help me!" she cried, but an orc backhanded her across the face. Izzie winced at the violent reaction.

An orc called out from the crowd. "Dwarf is back on the menu, boys!"

"Lago! I promise I'll get you out of here!" Izzie shouted, and she meant it.

"Awww, the lass thinks the wizard is gonna save her!" Kurai shouted, and then kicked Izzie in the gut with his heavy boot. It took all of the energy left in her weakened body not to cry out, but she wouldn't give him the satisfaction. "Here's how it's going to work. Yer going to help me raise an army. If ye don't, I'll kill the dwarf. If ye try to escape, I'll kill the dwarf. If ye so much as utter one curse toward one of my soldiers, I'll kill the dwarf. Once ye've completed that job to my satisfaction, *then* I'll release the dwarf."

"And then what will you do with me?" she asked through gritted teeth, her stomach throbbing from the kick.

"Then ye'll have my permission to die."

* * *

14 years before the Twelve Race War
Ungledor, Orc Territory

Izzie's guards dragged her back to her cell after another long day of delivering orc babies. Sometimes they only took her back here to sleep once a week, taking advantage of a wizard's ability to forgo sleep for long periods of time. Using her magic day in and day out without respite had her dangerously close to burnout.

Burnout was one of the worst afflictions that could happen to a wizard. Nobody knew exactly *how* it happened. It seemed to affect some more than others. She was already starting to feel some of the symptoms of burnout: fevers, nausea, fatigue, and anxiety. If a wizard fully burnt out, they would be completely incapable of using their magic. Sometimes it lasted a day; sometimes it lasted years. Izzie was terrified Kurai would force her to use so much magic she would burn out forever.

The smell from the waste bucket in the corner of her cell permeated every moment she spent in the tiny underground prison. The orc guards would only swap it out once every few weeks, otherwise leaving it to overflow onto the cold dirt floor. Izzie positioned herself so her nose was as far away from the bucket of her own waste as possible, trying to gain a temporary reprieve from the stench. A plate of raw meat sat untouched on the ground. She could barely see it since her cell had no windows, the only light coming from a torch down the hallway. Even though it was the only time she was allowed to eat or sleep, she still dreaded coming back to this godsforsaken cell. The only mercy her captors had shown was not locking her up with the general population in the underground prison. The sound of fighting and brawling was near constant.

Izzie munched on stale bread, harder than the chains that bound her, while she thought yet again about how to escape. It had already been years, and yet she still had no idea how to get herself and Lago out of captivity. She had only seen the dwarf once since their imprisonment, when she demanded to see proof that she was alive. It didn't appear the dwarf was being treated any better than she was.

Before she could do any plotting, she drifted off to sleep. Nightmares assaulted her instantly. One moment, she was languishing in an orc prison; the next, she was standing in the middle of the Wasteland. Twelve stones surrounded her, each speaking in a tongue of old. She could make out the language of the changelings, speaking louder than the rest of the stones, but she couldn't understand a word of it. A tree towered over her, each of the leaves a baby from a different race. The leaves started falling. All of a sudden, halfling and dwarf and human babies alike fell from the tree and hit the ground. Izzie tried to catch as many as she could, but they kept slipping through her grasp. The stones continued their chants as they morphed into distinct shapes.

"Why did you let my husband die?" Lulu asked, her body covered in burns. "Why didn't you protect him?"

Izzie spun around so she wouldn't have to face the fae widow. She came face to face with Lago.

"Izzie, just let me die. Save yourself."

Another figure appeared, one she hadn't seen in decades. A wizard.

"Remember me, Izzie? You know what you did." *No*, Izzie thought. *It wasn't like that...*

Her brother's tiny face popped into existence next.

"It wasn't my fault Mom died, Iz. Why did you have to blame me?"

"No!" she shouted, spinning around again. This time, it was Pyke.

"You left me," the changeling said just before she collapsed into a puddle of water.

"I'm sorry, Pyke; I'm re—" She was cut off as another ghost confronted her. Izzie looked up, surveying the giantess. *Sydyr.*

"You let me die, Isadore. Why couldn't you save me?"

"I tried! I swear, I tried..." She trailed off as Sydyr turned into the colossal tree above her.

"They're all coming here, Izzie. To claim the land you created."

"I'm sorry..." she squeaked, her voice weak. "I didn't know..."

Izzie was yanked from sleep when a calloused hand yanked her up by her hair. Her eyes shot open to reveal a hideous face mere inches from her.

"My favorite prisoner, sleeping on the job, I see?" Even though the sight of Kurai filled her with dread, it was still better than facing the ghosts of her past in her nightmares. His rancid breath invaded her nostrils, and she had to fight the urge to gag.

"Time to get back to work, poppet," the chieftain whispered in her ear, his breath hot on her skin. Before he could pull his face away, Izzie spat directly into his eyes. Kurai smiled and wiped away the saliva. The orc's massive hand was the last thing she saw before it cracked across her face.

* * *

63 years before the Twelve Race War
Wastetown, Northwest Wasteland

After Isadore had given the pregnant Vera a carefully curated version of the past few years, the human had taken her back to her lodging in Wastetown. They talked all day, and then all night. Thankfully, the human female didn't blame Isadore for Syrel's death, as she knew from their time together how focused he had been on finding his Affinity regardless of the potential consequences.

Vera had been a security guard at the Cico Library, so Syrel and Isadore had run into her nearly every day. Their relationship had developed over the time spent in Human Territory, and the human reminded Isadore of better times. They told stories about her dead ex, and it felt like the first time since Syrel's death that Isadore had smiled. They laughed and cried as they both told stories about some of the horrors they had encountered over the years.

"Can I come with you?" Isadore finally worked up the courage to ask.

"To Gifldor?

She nodded. It was difficult for Isadore to imagine returning to the place her mother had died. The place the father she barely remembered had abandoned them. The place she had met Syrel. But she had nowhere else to go, and she wanted to just live out the rest of her days in quiet peace. She had given up on her goal of starting a family after Syrel's death and the failed ritual, but she couldn't, for lack of a better word, waste her life away in Wastetown.

"I don't think you need my permission to go home! But the answer is yes, of course! I think having a wizard by my side would make this a much better journey."

The pair set off the next day. They would follow the Cosc River east, skirting around Orc Territory, and travel up to Gifldor once they reached the border of Elf Territory. It took them nearly a month, but eventually they arrived at the outskirts of Wizard Territory.

"Can we take a break?" Vera asked breathlessly. The pregnant human had been requiring more and more time to rest. In spite of all her fertility research, Isadore knew remarkably little about pregnancy itself, but she assumed it was normal to have a little shortness of breath near the end of pregnancy. There was a baby kicking her lungs, after all. The human was eight months along, about a month shy of her expected delivery date.

"Are you feeling okay?"

"I just feel—" She paused for a few seconds; "like I can't—" Another pause; "catch my breath."

Vera's breathing was heavy and labored. Isadore felt helpless. "Is there anything I can do?"

"Just," she huffed, growing notably more short of breath, "let me rest."

"Is this anything like what happened last pregnancy?" Isadore asked, scared to know the answer.

Vera only nodded, too out of breath to answer.

Isadore attempted to use her blood magic to assess the situation, but she didn't even know where to start. She mostly only knew offensive spells, so she pulled out the *Sangrila*. One of the first few pages described the *vitalagra* spell, which would reveal the status of a living being's blood. Harnessing every ounce of Intent she could muster, she cast *vitalagra*.

Vera's blood gave off an overwhelming sense of intensity. Isadore had no idea how to interpret the effects of the spell, but something seemed horribly wrong. Did the human have too much blood? It almost seemed like the blood was trying to burst forth from her body like a dam about to break.

The human female started to twitch. First her fingers, then her whole arm, and before long, her entire body was shaking.

"Vera! What's happening? Is it the baby?" Isadore shouted, but Vera couldn't respond.

Isadore desperately tried to help her. *Sangrimovi. Regrasangra. Dejasangra. Fortangra.* She attempted every blood magic spell in her arsenal, but nothing worked. Vera continued to shake uncontrollably.

After a few minutes, the shaking stopped. And so did her breathing. Isadore let out a wail so loud it could have been heard in Blood Sprite Territory. She screamed again. And she didn't stop screaming until her voice no longer worked. Her pregnant friend lay dead at her feet, only a day's journey from the midwizardry institute.

Isadore made a decision right then and there. She was done being Isadore, the failure. She had failed to get pregnant. She had failed Syrel. She had failed the ritual. She had failed Vera. She had failed everybody she ever knew.

So she was going to reinvent herself. She would continue her journey to Gifldor and become somebody who helped those around her instead of failing them. It was time to use her blood magic for good. She had accepted she would never become a mother. She would never feel the kick of a child in her womb. She would never give birth. But she could help other freles. Maybe if she worked hard enough, she could save the next Vera.

She was going to be Izzie the midwizard.

CHAPTER SEVENTEEN

Baby Factory

Abuse is a more effective form of captivity than a cell will ever be.

—Brandon Sanderson

---

14 years before the Twelve Race War
Ungledor, Orc Territory

Izzie got to the next patient, who had delivered a baby a few minutes prior. She looked at it before it was whisked away. Surprisingly, the baby was pretty cute. The light blue skin brought out the color of the bright, beady yellow eyes. The little mele was covered in wrinkles, looking like he was accidentally given skin three sizes too big. He wasn't screaming or crying as he lay peacefully on his mom's chest. In short order, a warrior came to collect the baby. The new mom didn't say a word, but Izzie could see the hurt in her eyes. It didn't matter how little a community valued life or how important war was; taking a baby away from its mother *always* hurt. However, she had seen what happened when freles refused to give up their babies. It wasn't pretty.

"Hey," Izzie whispered to the orc frele as she watched her baby be taken away, likely the last time she would ever see him. "Are you doing okay?"

"I am here to do my duty for the tribe. War is coming. The orcs will prevail." This was the party line every single orc gave her. She had seen this exact same look in the eyes of thousands of orc freles over the years, and she'd gotten the same response.

"How is the bleeding?" she asked the orcish attendant, likely a frele who couldn't get pregnant. Izzie had a soft spot for these attendants, but maybe they were the lucky ones.

"Bad. Very bad."

It had been ten years since she was taken. Ten long, grueling years. A decade wasn't long considering the lengthy lifespan of a wizard, but it still felt like an eternity. Izzie dragged herself to the next mat. She was in the large hall where she had first been displayed in front of the orcs after being taken prisoner. Hundreds of straw mats, soaked in the blood of their previous occupants, lay spread a few feet apart. Most of them were occupied by laboring orcs.

After Kurai made his declaration of war, he had turned the entire city of Ungledor into a baby factory. Even though it was sick and twisted, she had to admit he had done a phenomenal job of turning his society into a machine dedicated to nothing but producing soldiers.

Kurai had completely disassembled the family structures of everybody in Ungledore. Marriages were dissolved. Children were taken from their homes. The freles were divided into groups. Each week, a new group of them reported to the meeting hall to be impregnated by meles carefully chosen by Kurai. There was a group of a couple thousand of the largest, strongest, meanest meles responsible for this task, from what she could tell, with the rest of the meles being charged with training and preparing for war. Izzie had to watch as each week, a new group showed up to be impregnated. She had no idea what would have been going through their minds as they walked into the massive edifice, just to be impregnated by an orc warrior they'd never met. She saw Kurai frequently, making her suspect he would be fathering many warriors in the new generation.

All the freles were required to give birth here, but Izzie didn't think it was only because she was there. There was no way she could take care of that many patients. As soon as the baby was delivered, it was carried off by some orc grunt to be raised as a warrior, if it was a mele, or a breeder, if it was a frele. The ones who didn't get pregnant were added to the next group, and if they weren't successful after the second time, they were reassigned to another role to prepare for the war. From a utilitarian perspective, it was ruthlessly efficient.

Izzie couldn't believe she was still here ten years later. But what choice did she have? She wasn't hurting anybody directly by being here—technically, she was still sticking to her commitment to only preserve life. About a quarter of frele orcs died during childbirth, or so she had learned in midwizardry school. In the beginning of her imprisonment, an orcish doctor had told her that it was currently more than a third. As with all of the other races she'd encountered since midwizardry school, the mortality had increased in recent decades. Kurai was well aware of how deadly pregnancy was for his charges, but since he treated them as expendable, it was just a numbers game.

She wasn't sure she could go much longer before she was completely burnt out. Already, she could feel her powers waning. She was constantly feverish and anxious, struggling to make it through the day.

Izzie sighed deeply as she examined the freshly postpartum orc. She was pretty sure she knew where this was going. Nearly all the deaths that happened during orcish childbirth were due to excess bleeding, or postpartum hemorrhage. Orcs had a very unique physiology, in that they carried nearly double the blood volume of a human or wizard of a similar size. This meant all of their blood vessels were massive, making it easy to deliver oxygen and vital nutrients to their tissues—specifically their muscles, which was why it was easy for an orc to become a massive powerhouse of muscle. Izzie had noticed it seemed like the stronger an orc was, the less blood must go to their head, because so many of them were dumb brutes. Kurai, who was built like a fortress but was also a cunning mastermind, was a notable exception to this rule. Which made him extra intimidating.

This benefit of orc physiology, which enabled them to become muscular war machines, was often their downfall during childbirth, just like it was during war. When an orc was wounded during war, lacerated blood vessels bled like waterfalls. One slash of a sword through a bicep, which wouldn't be a mortal injury for most races, could easily slay an orc, who would bleed out in minutes. This debilitating weakness was exactly why Kurai wanted to build up their numbers as much as possible. He was going to throw as many soldiers as possible at the opposing armies.

Similar to the equal distribution of sexes, another trait common to all races (at least all the ones Izzie knew about) was bleeding after delivering a baby. To Izzie, it seemed like a terrible quirk of evolution that delivering a baby always led to losing your most valuable resource. It felt especially terrible looking at the frele orc in front of her.

She was sitting in a pool of her own blood. Izzie didn't think there was anything she could do to save the orc, but as she had done thousands of times over the years, she set her hand on the orc in front of her and channeled her blood magic. Naturally, she was allowed to use her blood magic for the benefit of the tribe. Even if she'd wanted to forfeit Lago's life and slay everybody around her, she couldn't. At any given moment, she had an escort of twelve orcs stationed around her. She was chained up, though not with lyonium, as the rare metal would inhibit her healing blood magic. Four of them were ready with lyonium chains and four of them had lyonium-tipped swords poised, ready to relieve her of her head if she made any false moves. The remaining four faced outward in each direction, making sure outside help wouldn't be possible. They weren't taking any chances, and that was why Izzie hadn't made an escape attempt. She had brainstormed a million ways to get out and save Lago, but she always came up empty.

Assessing the circulatory system of the orc who had just delivered, Izzie suspected the prognosis was bleak. She cast *vitalagra*, assessing the orc's status. Her blood pressure, which was a good marker of how much blood somebody had remaining, was dangerously low. Izzie systematically tried to constrict each of the blood vessels in the orc's uterus so she would stop hemorrhaging, but it was too late. She could slow the bleeding, but the orcish frele had already lost too much. She tried the *dematrisangra* spell, which had helped Pyke avoid preterm labor, to move the blood away from the uterus, but she'd already lost too much.

"She's gone." The orcish attendant checked her pulse and confirmed the patient was dead. Izzie's blood magic, which had continued to grow significantly stronger despite her imprisonment, saved the majority of orcish freles she could get her hands on, but she couldn't save everybody. By this point, she was completely numb to death.

"I'm sorry. Please mark it in the log and remove the body."

A hush fell across the normally cacophonous birthing hall. That could only mean one thing. Izzie tried to focus on doing her job, but somebody yanked one of the chains attached to her leg and she collapsed to the ground.

"Another dead frele?" Kurai roared as he sniffed the patient she'd just lost. Izzie tried to stand up, but he pressed his dirty boot against her calf. "Aren't ye here to *save* my people?"

"Like I tell you every time"—she pushed out her words through gritted teeth—"I can't save them all. The Maternal Magic—" Her words cut off as the chieftain dug his boot into her leg, causing her to shriek in agony.

"Pah! Don't talk to me about yer made-up fairy tales."

The orc roughly pulled her to her feet and shoved her into the dead orc until they were face to face.

"Is this what ye want? Are ye secretly killing off my loyal subjects?"

"I'm not, I swear," Izzie sobbed, tears cascading down onto the patient she couldn't save. "Please, I'm doing everything I can. I can't save them all." They had been through this song and dance before. Even though Izzie was saving every orcish frele she could, she still lost patients every day. Once in a while, Kurai would storm in and demand answers on why she didn't save everybody. She knew what was coming next. Kurai knocked her to the floor and picked up a lyonium chain.

"Yer lucky I need more soldiers; otherwise I'd toss ye in the body pits with all the freles you've killed." Izzie didn't feel lucky as she heard the chain drag across the floor. Every nerve in her back tingled as she anticipated the blow. Scars crisscrossed her back from their prior encounters.

"Maybe next time ye will try a little harder."

An ear-piercing scream shattered the quiet hall as the golden chain connected with Izzie's back. She knew he was holding back, because if he hit her with his full might, it would shatter her spine. He was careful to make sure it would be exquisitely painful but not cause any long-term damage. It felt like a million fires danced across the tender skin of her back.

"Reports say ye have lost twelve of my subjects this week. What do ye say to a lash for every one of 'em?"

Izzie's vision went black as she heard the orc's words. He'd never hit her more than two or three times, since she usually couldn't maintain consciousness past the third one. Twelve lashes... *He was going to kill her.*

Yet even though she was a prisoner, even though she carried the guilt and pain of her past, even though a war was brewing over a land she had created... she wasn't ready to die. Something told her she had more to accomplish. That Cosconia still needed her, and she needed it. Izzie cringed as the monstrous orc lifted the chain yet again, ready to weather the blow.

"STOP!" a voice rang out as Izzie cowered on the floor, waiting for the blow that never came. She looked up as a beautifully plump orc, holding a baby Izzie had just delivered, charged toward her. Her round face, stunning in its postpartum glow, glistened with tears. The frele draped herself across Izzie's tender back, protecting her from Kurai's fury.

"She's trying to help us; can't you see?"

The warlord set down the lyonium chain, a wry smile crossing his face. "Well ain't ye cute, trying to save the midwizard. 'Spose yer effort shouldn't be in vain—I'll let ye and the babe take the punishment this time."

"NO!" the orc and Izzie shouted simultaneously. Before Izzie could protest further, the frele continued. "I don't think you want to do that," she said coldly, all emotion having left her voice. "He's yours."

The orc looked confused for a moment, but then understanding seemed to pass over him. "Well I'll be damned. Wh—"

A torrent of water washed over the orcish warlord, knocking him from his feet. Before his guard could respond, random objects started raining down from the ceiling. Izzie watched in confusion as books, mugs, clothes—her clothes—fell from above. Water continued to gush directly at Kurai, who was incapacitated by the deluge. Izzie tried to focus on the roof above her, but a panicked scream interrupted her. Another scream followed in quick succession, and the room quickly devolved into incessant shrieking. Mice, thousands of them, scurried every which way. Guards fell as dozens of mice bit their feet.

As the screaming continued, the water stopped, and Lago landed on top of Kurai with a thud, Baggie Smalls draped over her shoulder. The orc's body went limp as he fell into unconsciousness. Izzie hadn't had time to process the dwarf's appearance when she heard a voice call to her from near the hall's entrance. A voice she would recognize anywhere. A voice that still echoed in her dreams. Syrel.

"Let's go!" he shouted, brandishing his wand at any orc who hadn't fallen victim to the water, the unidentified flying objects, or the mice. She hadn't seen anybody enter the hall, but he had somehow broken through the barriers.

Lago gave Izzie a quick nod, kicked Kurai once in the face for good measure, and darted after Syrel. Izzie started to follow when a hand grabbed her ankle and tripped her. Thinking it was Kurai, she lifted her leg to stomp on the hand until she realized it belonged to the orc frele who had just intervened on her behalf. Izzie pulled back her foot just in time.

"You have to take me with you!"

Izzie was momentarily paralyzed with indecision, fully aware escaping would be much more difficult with a frele and a baby. Her indecision didn't last long, however, as she knew the frele would face certain death when Kurai roused.

"Okay! Just follow me and don't look back!"

Following Lago and Syrel, she pulled the orc, babe in arms, out the back entrance of the breeding hall.

"All the other exits are sealed," Syrel said as he slammed the door behind him. "*Reinforza.*" He cast the spell on the door to strengthen it.

"The doors won't hold for long. We have to get out of Ungledore as fast as we can."

"Lago! Do you have my wand?"

The dwarf slid the wand out of Baggie and tossed it to her. She pointed it at each member of the party in turn, casting *altasangra* but holding back some of her Intent. The spell would reduce the weight of their blood, allowing each of them to run significantly faster. If she cast it too powerfully, they would each simply float into the air. Piggybacking off her spell, Syrel cast *fortangra*, which would protect them if they got hit with a curse. Izzie didn't think there were any wizards here, but it was possible Dalfa was still lurking around Orc Territory.

Spells cast, the group was able to practically fly out of Ungledore and not look back.

* * *

20 years before the Twelve Race War
Jubox, Changeling Territory

Dalfa drummed her fingers against her leg while she waited for the king and queen. As it did frequently, her mind drifted to Izzie. It had been years since there had been any communication between them. She wanted to reach out. But her old friend just didn't *get* it.

She hadn't seen the horrors Dalfa had. An orcish frele, lying in a pool of her own blood as she looked at her baby for the first and last time. A minotaur helpless to prevent their own child from starving. A changeling holding yet another stillborn fetus. She shuddered at the thought. *So much death. So much pain.*

But Gravipar was the *future*. Maternal Magic billowing forth in the shade of the Mother Tree, protecting every frele and child, no matter their race. No matter their religion. No matter their history.

Dalfa, unlike Izzie, was never interested in having children. Her mother was a midwizard, so Dalfa was well aware of how hard pregnancy was in Cosconia. Why risk her own life for somebody who didn't even exist yet? *Especially* now that pregnancy outcomes were getting demonstrably worse.

She knew there would be a war for Gravipar. She knew it would probably be one of the most horrific wars Cosconia had ever seen, and she understood Izzie's fear. If there was a way to settle the land peacefully, Dalfa would be the first in line to make it happen. The *last* thing she wanted was more death. But in a land divided along racial lines for centuries, a peaceful solution was impossible.

But she was practical, and she could put her emotions aside. The amount of death she'd seen had forced her to learn how to bury her emotions deeper than the Discovery Ocean. If tens of thousands had to die in a war to save hundreds of thousands, wasn't it worth it? The math was simple. *How can I make Izzie understand?*

"Midwizard," King Mamut addressed her as he walked into the room, hand in hand with his bride. "What brings you to Jubox?"

"I'm traveling throughout all of Cosconia to inform leaders of the magical land of Gravipar."

Queen Luva looked at her skeptically. "We're familiar. Are the rumors true? Is there really a new source of Maternal Magic?"

Dalfa was surprised at how much the king and queen knew, but they were both Apex Changelings after all. She shouldn't underestimate their power. "Yes. And from my initial studies, it seems better than we could even imagine."

"The changelings want no part of this new land. Even *if* it is as magical as you say, every Cosconian will want a piece. The fight over the land will be protracted and bloody," the king stated. "We are a peaceful people."

"Besides," the queen added, finishing her husband's thought. "The other races of Cosconia already don't trust changelings. We were targeted unfairly in the War for Cosconia, and I anticipate this would be no different."

"But you've seen the changeling stillbirth rate go up. How can you just sit idly by and watch? Do you not care about your citizens?" The volume of her voice started to increase.

"We accepted this meeting because we respect midwizards and what they do for our community, but we will not be criticized in our own home," the king shouted angrily.

She'd figured this would be the response, but she had to try first. She didn't mention she no longer considered herself a midwizard.

"*Iquinto*," she uttered, and a blank look crossed over the faces of both the king and the queen. While Izzie had honed her blood magic over the years, Dalfa's mind Affinity had grown significantly. Using the *Mentala*, a book passed down in her family from generation to generation, she'd discovered her mental magic was much more powerful in times of great emotion. This was why she had deliberately antagonized the king and queen.

The *iquinto* spell wasn't powerful enough to completely control somebody's actions—though she hoped to be able to use that type of spell some day—but it could significantly influence their way of thinking.

You want to lead your people to Gravipar and save hundreds of future generations of changelings, she spoke into their minds. Dalfa found that people were much more susceptible to her influence when she framed her "suggestions" in a positive light. "*Desiquinto*," she said, reversing the effects of the spell.

The king blinked a few times before speaking again. "We will take your council into consideration. You are dismissed."

Dalfa smiled. The future of Cosconia was bright. *But the night is always darkest before dawn.*

CHAPTER EIGHTEEN

On The Road Again

The pain of parting is nothing to the joy of meeting again.

—Charles Dickens

---

14 years before the Twelve Race War
Ungledor, Orc Territory

The *altasangra* spell wore off shortly after they'd left Ungledore, and the diverse crew was now close to Elf Territory. As soon they crossed the border into safety, Izzie fell into Syrel as he wrapped his strong arms around her. He'd held her like this so many times, but she'd forgotten what it felt like after all these years without him. A tear dropped from her eye onto his strong shoulder. Then another. Soon, the tears were flowing. For several minutes, she cried in his arms. She knew Lago, and a newly postpartum orc and her baby, were there too, but she didn't care. She wept for the years she'd spent as a prisoner. She wept for the orcs she couldn't save. She wept for the orcs she could. She wept for the lashes across her back. She wept for Lago, also a prisoner for a decade.

Forcibly stopping the tears, she pulled away from Syrel's embrace, balled her right hand into a fist, and started pounding on his chest with all her might. Her left hand soon followed. She rained blows down on him as she screamed.

"You motherfucker! Where did you go? You left me! For decades, you left me behind! I thought you were dead. I cried myself to sleep so many nights for you! I drank myself stupid over your death." He stood there and accepted her beating as tears began pouring down her cheeks again. "Why didn't you find me? I needed you! I *needed you*, Syrel. I still need you but I hate you. Why didn't you come find me?" she sobbed, the words and tears both an endless flood.

"We were in this together, Syrel. You and me. You told me you loved me. I thought you died that day, and I couldn't live without you. Did those words you told me before the ritual mean anything? I thought you were dead for so long, and then you show up one day? Knock up a changeling and then try to kill her? *Kill* my friend's mother and husband? And then you disappear again? You truly are sick."

Izzie dropped her arms, even though she had decades worth of pent up rage. "And you don't even *try* to find me?"

"Isadore," he said, gently, interrupting her. The sound of her name on his tongue felt familiar, though she barely used that name anymore. "I deserve all that and more. We have so much to talk about. You don't even know the half of it. But we're still close to Orc Territory, and they're going to be coming after you. We have to get out of here." He glanced at the orc. "All of us. Even the... unexpected extras."

Izzie realized that, of course, he hadn't planned to take the large orc with them.

"What's your name?" Izzie asked the orcish frele who had defended her against Kurai.

Her voice trembled with fear. "Arkan," she responded. "Please don't make me go back there. He'll take my baby." Izzie looked closely at the baby, who was sleeping peacefully on his mother's chest, in spite of the hectic surroundings. She remembered what the scared frele had told Kurai in her moment of boldness, and the baby's features were unmistakable.

"Arkan. This is…"

She nodded her head. "He was there when my group came in. He spotted me and wanted me for himself. I don't want to think about it anymore. It's just me and him."

Izzie didn't push her to discuss it any further, but internally she was panicking. They'd just inadvertently kidnapped Kurai's baby. She shuddered to think about what would have happened to both of them after Arkan had tried to defend Izzie.

She grabbed Baggie Smalls from Lago's shoulder now that the situation had calmed slightly. She pulled it tightly to her chest.

"Alright, alright. You're suffocating me."

"You don't need to breathe," she said, rolling her eyes, grateful for some normalcy.

"Metaphorically. But I missed you too. I'm glad you're safe, Iz."

"Hate to break up this reunion, but we've gotta get going," interrupted Syrel.

"Alright, can it, Casanova. Aren't you gonna tell her how we saved her?"

"We?" Izzie asked, confused.

"Come on," Syrel urged. "Let's talk as we walk." They were on the Wasteland side of the river, headed east along the waterway.

"Where are we going?" asked Arkan nervously.

"Elf Territory," Syrel informed her.

The orc stopped abruptly. "No way. We can't go there. I'm an *orc*. With the war chieftain's baby in my arms, no less. They'll kill me. I'll take my chances with Kurai." She started walking toward the bridge, but Syrel grabbed her arm.

"No they won't. I promise."

Arkan turned to look at Izzie. "Should I trust him?"

"He's the most trustworthy mele I know." Izzie's voice dripped with sarcasm. "But unfortunately, I don't think any of us have a choice."

She turned to address Syrel. "The next words out of your mouth better be an explanation of what the twelve hells happened over the last fifty years."

"Oh just a quick fifty year recap? That should be nice and easy." He smirked.

Izzie glared at him. "I've got nowhere else to be. Let's hear it."

Syrel sighed and then launched into his tale. "After the ritual broke down, the last thing I heard was you screaming my name before I lost consciousness. When I woke up, I heard a voice speaking in a tongue I barely recognized. Spyridian. The ancient tongue of the blood sprites. I barely knew any, but from the time we spent observing Blood Sprite Territory and studying their language, I recognized a few words: blood. Magic. Ritual. Wizard." Izzie had only seen a blood sprite twice before. Once was observation from afar, and once was an accidental up-close encounter. Blood sprites were about a foot tall, almost like a human shrunk down to a minuscule size with two pairs of near-translucent blood red wings on their back. Izzie recalled the ethereal glow they had to them, almost like they were a trick of the wind. When their wings beat rapidly to keep them in place, the color of the wings made it seem like they floated in a cloud of blood.

"I tried to speak to them in Fingol, and I was worried they were going to take you." He directed his comment at Izzie. "I kept hearing them say 'blood' and 'wizard,' so naturally I was concerned they were after you. In hindsight, I realize now this was a bad idea, but I thought it would be best to make it seem like you were dead. So I cast the *parcemort* spell on you." He cringed away like Izzie would attack him.

She shook with rage. "You. What."

He subtly walked a bit further away from her. "You know blood sprites hate blood wizards! They would have taken you and killed you. I convinced them I was the one they wanted."

In theory, she knew he was right. But the spell explained why she woke up feeling like death—*parcemort* would bring somebody to within an inch of death, making them seem dead to the outside observer. The problem was, about half the time, the spell turned illusion into reality and really did kill its victim. Syrel had risked her life to save it, according to him.

"I'm going to choose to believe that was the right decision. Carry on."

"Once I convinced them you were dead, they took me instead."

"Took you where?" Lago asked, getting invested in the story.

"Blood Sprite Territory."

Arkan perked up at this. "Kurai sent a massive orc delegation there a while back. They were never heard from again. What was it like? Did they torture you?"

Syrel's silence seemed to be answer enough. "It was many years before I escaped. I traversed the canyon and arrived in Human Territory. I tried to look for Vera but nobody knew where she was."

"She's dead."

"What?" he gasped. "How? She was so young, so full of life!"

"Eclampsia. Pregnancy complication. She's actually the reason I went into midwizardry."

"Now this story I want to hear!" Lago chimed in.

"I wouldn't mind hearing that one too," Syrel added.

"I'm not the one on trial here," Izzie deadpanned.

"Pleeeeease," Lago pleaded. "Is being your own personal nurse not good enough to get your life story? Or a quick decade of imprisonment?"

Izzie winced. Neither of them had addressed the unicorn in the room, which was the torture and horrors they'd both faced over the years. The middle of the escape was certainly not the time to start processing, but Izzie was impressed Lago could already *joke* about it. *Gods she is such a genuinely good frele. I don't think I've ever respected anybody so much.*

"There isn't much to it. After Syrel 'died,'" she put her fingers up to indicate air quotes, "I lost it. I wandered aimlessly through the Wasteland, barely surviving. I settled in Wastetown, where I made... a lot of bad choices. Suffice it to say I had a complete and total breakdown—mentally, physically, and emotionally. I was at rock bottom when I ran into Vera, who was about seven months pregnant. She was headed to Gifldor to seek help from the midwizards." Izzie wiped a tear away and continued. "We almost made it. We were so close. But out of nowhere, she started shaking. I tried to use my blood magic, but I had no idea how to heal with it. I watched her die in front of me. I know now it was an eclamptic seizure, a common occurrence for human females. It happens when their blood pressure gets too high, I think. If I had the Skill then that I do now, I could have saved her in my sleep."

Lago strolled closer to her and pulled her into a side hug while they walked. Providing comfort was one of the dwarf's greatest skills.

"Anyway. I decided at that moment I was done hurting people. I was done putting myself or anybody else at risk. Remember, I thought I killed Syrel. I thought it was my fault."

"Of course it wasn't your fault," Syrel interjected. "It was a complex and novel magical ritual. It could have gone wrong a million different ways. You were perfect."

She glared at him. "A little too late."

Baggie Smalls spoke up. "Can we pass the talking stick back to Syrel? I want to get to my part in the story!"

"Well I spent a lot of time in Cico. Too much time. Hiding. Recovering. Regrouping. Trying to figure out what went wrong in the ritual. Planning my next steps."

"Why didn't you try to find me?" Izzie asked the burning question.

"I thought you'd hate me for failing the ritual."

Izzie exploded. "Hate you for failing the ritual? You *knew* I would be content if it was just the two of us. You *knew* I had accepted I would never have a child. That's orc shit."

"I know. I know! I wasn't thinking right. By the time I finally decided to come find you, the trail was too cold. I went to Mithor to see Donrel, but he hadn't heard from you either. Eventually, I decided to go back to Gifldor. I asked around if anybody had heard about you being back, but nobody knew anything. I was terrified the blood sprites would somehow try to find me again, so I changed my name to Nesbreth, my grandfather's name. I got a job at the Wizarding Institute of Gifldor."

"Where we met," Izzie said quietly.

He nodded. "It made me feel connected to you, somehow. My plan was to lay low and start my life over."

"And then you met Pyke," Izzie stated.

"And then I met Pyke. It was nothing like our romance, Isadore, but it felt comfortable. Safe. It wasn't what I wanted—I wanted you—but it's what I thought I needed."

Izzie cut him off. "Let's skip the intimate details of your little tryst, yeah?"

"Fair enough." He grimaced. "One day, she disappeared. She was just gone. Not a letter, a goodbye, nothing. I had no idea what to do. I looked everywhere and there wasn't a single sign of her. In a last-ditch effort, I got suspicious that maybe she was pregnant. We... weren't always particularly careful. I started asking around the midwizardry school, and I finally got some answers. I wish I'd asked about you there, Isadore, but it never crossed my mind. I spoke to a Professor Seres, who told me the one I was looking for was in Orc Territory."

Izzie laughed out loud. "She duped you! She deliberately threw you off the trail to protect Pyke." Izzie was surprised by the development since, according to Pyke, the changeling had been quite forceful with the professor. *But she still protected the frele in need. She's a better midwizard than I'll ever be.*

Syrel grunted. "I know that now. But what else could I do? It was the only lead I had. Trust me, I didn't want to go hang out with a bunch of stinking orcs..." he trailed off when he remembered his audience. He gave Arkan a shaky grin. "Sorry about that. But you'll understand after the next part."

"I can't imagine an explanation that would make me forgive you for attacking the coronation and killing Thelonius and Nuptia," Izzie added.

"Kurai told me the fae queen was going to kill you at the coronation."

That shut Izzie up. *So the coronation attack had nothing to do with Pyke at all? He wasn't hunting her down?* "I don't understand."

"When I got to Orc Territory, I asked every orc I could find if they knew anything about somebody named Pyke. Naturally, everybody laughed me off. Until I ran into an orc named Kurai, who showed me this letter." He pulled a crumpled up piece of parchment out of his pocket.

Dear Dalfa,

I'm sorry to hear how difficult it's been for you. My blood magic does help, but there's only so much I can do. Is it just me, or is pregnancy getting more dangerous in Cosconia? Sometimes I wish it was just the two of us back in our little apartment, cramming for a final exam.

I'm so glad you've made a friend in Orc Territory! I've had the opposite experience. Can you believe a pregnant changeling (who was apparently pretending to be a wizard in Gifldor??) forced me to use my majalir on her? Her name is Pyke. At first I thought she was totally crazy, but turns out she was on the run from her deranged ex. Since I know a thing or two about that, we actually ended up bonding. We're headed to Water Fae Territory next; hopefully things are a little better there.

Sincerely,

Izzie

Izzie recognized her own handwriting. It was one of the letters she had sent Dalfa during her early days on the road, and somehow it had ended up in Kurai's grimy hands.

Syrel continued his tale. "I knew instantly it had to be you. To be honest, once I read that, I completely forgot about Pyke. I had to find you. Kurai told me that Dalfa, who had since departed Orc Territory, got another letter a few months later. One that said the water fae were holding you hostage, and the new king and queen were going to execute you after the coronation."

"The first letter is mine, but I never said anything about hostages or executions," Izzie exclaimed.

"Again, I know that now. But he already had one letter from you; who was I to say there wasn't a second? In hindsight, I wish I had asked to see it, but I was too excited and terrified to think straight. I got tunnel vision. I had to protect you, no matter the cost."

"Excited?" Lago asked skeptically.

"It was the first confirmation I had that the light of my life was still alive."

Izzie had to stop herself from feeling all warm and mushy at his words. He was a *murderer*. It was good to know he *wasn't* trying to kill his pregnant ex, but he had still committed a heinous and unprovoked attack.

"I had a complete meltdown. I almost went into some sort of fugue state. I barely remember my actions. I was dead set on finding and freeing you. I got to Water Fae Territory as quickly as I could, only to find the coronation already in progress. I thought you'd be dead if I didn't stop it, so I knew I had to shut it down. No matter the cost. I would protect you no matter the cost."

It was hard for Izzie to be mad at him when she knew she probably would have done the same thing in his position. If she had heard Syrel was still alive but on the verge of execution? There was no telling what she would be capable of in that situation. She wanted to hate him, but she also loved knowing she had an unyielding protector.

"So you murdered two water fae in cold blood based on one orc's testimony?" Izzie shot back.

"Is that more orc slander I sense in your tone?" Arkan asked. Before she could respond, the orc continued. "Because I completely agree. Fuck orcs, and fuck Kurai." She was briefly taken aback by Arkan's strong language, but she'd been through an ordeal even more harrowing than Izzie and Lago's, and she had a baby to take care of. Her abuser's baby no less. During the long walk, she had alternated between breastfeeding her new baby and consoling him to sleep. Izzie looked at the orc in a new light. Her thick curves were lovely, and Izzie was surprised how beautiful she was—orcs weren't known for their aesthetics. A few hours postpartum and she was a gorgeous sight to behold.

"Trust me, it was the biggest mistake I've ever made. Well, the second biggest. The first was performing that damn ritual in the first place." He shuddered. "Their faces... they haunt me. I can't imagine how awful it must have been for Queen Luxor. I found out about the baby afterward. Trust me, nothing you can say will make me feel any worse than I already do." Izzie doubted that, but she wouldn't push it. He obviously wasn't faking this level of emotion.

"It's difficult for me to talk about it." Syrel dropped to his knees and violently wretched. He broke down into heaving sobs. Lago, ever the caretaker, stood next to him and comforted him. She held his hair, now long and scraggly, out of his way as he hurled. It took several minutes for him to regain his composure.

"It's okay," Lago said gently, rubbing his back. "Tell us what happened next."

"I was singularly focused on finding Izzie. When I saw her, safe and sound and defending the fae *from me*, I knew I had colossally screwed up. But all I could think about was how happy I was that you were alive and safe. When you looked into my eyes... When you said my name... For a moment, it felt like everything was going to work out. And then I was flying across the Wasteland."

"Wait wait wait. What did I miss here? Why were you flying across the Wasteland? How did you escape?" Arkan spoke up again.

"Oh I didn't escape. Pyke transformed into a giantess and tossed me about ten miles."

"And you didn't die?!" Lago practically shouted.

Izzie thought she saw a shadow cross Syrel's face, but it passed quickly. "Thankfully wizards are pretty hardy."

Arkan started laughing. "She *tossed* you?" Her laughter was infectious, and suddenly Lago and Izzie started chuckling too. "After turning into a *giant*?" Something about the incredulous tone of her voice made Izzie laugh even harder. "Damn, that bitch *really* hates you."

At that, Izzie lost it. She had to stop walking, laughter overcoming her, which spread to Lago and Arkan, who couldn't seem to help themselves either. Even Syrel's heaving sobs turned into hiccuping laughter. Izzie couldn't imagine how ridiculous they looked: two wizards, a dwarf, and an orc—with a baby—in the outskirts of the Jerdalin Forest, laughing uncontrollably. Lago fell to the soft dirt, gasping for breath at the absurdity of the situation.

Finally, after several minutes of raucous laughter, the motley crew was able to rein themselves in when Izzie's bag tuned into the conversation. Syrel was able to pull himself together and regain the casual confidence she was used to.

"Can we get to my part already?"

Izzie slung the bag to her front so she could address it directly. "What do you mean?"

"Remember all those mice you used to give me? Like a few hundred pages ago?"

"I remember the mice, but what pages are you talking about?"

"Not important. Well, when you got your dumb ass kidnapped by some brutish orc, I got to work. You know that old robe of Syrel's you keep inside me?"

Syrel looked at her with the adorable smirk she'd seen a thousand times. *How can I still be so attracted to him after everything he just told me? He's a* monster.

"You kept my robe?"

She ignored him. "Okay, Baggie, how about you have some chill? That was our secret!"

"Oops. Not anymore. Anyway. I trained the mice to seek out the scent of the robe. I wrote the same message hundreds of times and sent each mouse out with a note tied to their back."

"And it worked," concluded Syrel. "I got the message while I was back in Mithor, recovering. It took me a few months to plan the escape. It would have been completely impossible without Lago."

"It was nothing really," Lago said.

"How? I had a million different plans in my head, but they kept me under constant surveillance."

"Well, their jail cells are designed to hold orcs, not dwarves. It took a while"—she gestured down at her gaunt frame—"but eventually I was small enough to squeeze through the bars. A message from Baggie told me right where it was, and it was easy from there. I climbed to the ceiling of the delivery room, and the bag had enough water stored in it to... What did you call it?"

"Waterboard," Baggie Smalls answered helpfully.

"Yeah. Waterboard that orc psychopath." Izzie guessed it was the same water the bag had consumed when rescuing her from Lursa.

"I knew the mice would cause enough of a panic to distract everybody long enough for Syrel to sneak in and rescue you," Lago continued.

"How did you get all the way through Orc Territory and into the center of town?" Izzie asked, baffled.

"I have my ways." He smiled mysteriously.

"What about Pyke?" Izzie asked suddenly. "Have you heard any word of her whereabouts?"

Syrel shook his head sadly. "Unfortunately, no. I wish I had. I would love to apologize to her and explain everything. Do you think—"

"I'm gonna cut you off right there, buddy. I'm not getting in the middle of your baby-mama drama. I'm your ex-girlfriend after all."

Syrel turned so red that Izzie thought for a moment she'd accidentally cast a blood magic spell on him.

"Fair enough. So is there any hope of removing that 'ex' some day?"

"Fat chance."

"I rescued you from the clutches of the evil orc warlord!"

"Okay first off, I'm not some damsel in distress. And it seems more like *Lago* rescued me. Second, and I feel like I shouldn't have to say this, you disappeared for thirty years, reappeared, went on a murderous rampage, disappeared for *another* ten years, and then you're going to show up here and try to win me back?"

"Yep, that's pretty much the plan!" He grinned his stupid squinty-eyed grin that had convinced her to go against her better judgment too many times before. *Not this time.*

Izzie rolled her eyes.

"OoOoO lovers to enemies, way to flip that ol' trope on its head you two!" her bag said in a singsong voice.

"Wh—" Syrel began, but Izzie stopped him. "Trust me—it's better not to engage."

Syrel sighed. "I have so much more to say to you, Izzie. I don't expect you to listen."

"Good, because I'm not planning on it," Izzie retorted, but she knew it wasn't true. They had too much history. And if what he'd said about doing it all to protect her was true... how could she blame him? She felt so conflicted. On one hand, she wanted to hate him for all he'd done. Disappearing, chasing Pyke, killing Thelonius, abandoning her. On the other hand, this was *Syrel.* Not a day had gone by in the past thirty years she didn't think about him. He was her first and only love. She'd listened quietly to his story, just watching him. Remembering the way his jaw clenched when he was upset. How his right eye twitched when he focused. She'd practically forgotten the sound of his voice, forgotten the way it made her feel, forgotten the way his name tasted on her tongue, but it all came rushing back to her the moment he spoke.

"Wait, so what happened after you landed in the Wasteland?" Izzie finally said.

Arkan guffawed again at the thought, but she was able to maintain her composure.

"As soon as I could walk again, I looked for you. I knew I wouldn't be welcome back into Water Fae Territory with open arms, but I hired a few changeling scouts from Wastetown to see if there was any word of you. All of the reports said you disappeared the day of the coronation. I lost you again."

Before he could continue, a hulking figure emerged from the dark wood, barreling toward their party. Izzie didn't even have a chance to react before the figure was upon her. In the blink of an eye, she was tumbling to the ground.

*   *   *

62 years before the Twelve Race War
Gifldor, Wizard Territory

"I'm sorry, Ms. Izzie, but we're not accepting any more applicants at this time. The new year starts tomorrow, and we only allow two students per year due to our limited resources. You'll have to apply for next year's class," the headmistress said. She was seated behind an ornate wooden desk in her office at the Midwizardry Institute of Gifldor. The famous MIG. Midwizardry had been around forever, but in spite of Cosconia's dire pregnancy situation, there were very few midwizards, since there was so little anybody could do to help.

After Vera died and she made her decision to be a midwizard, she had trekked directly here. She hadn't even stopped at her mother's grave. She was already in enough pain. Izzie had managed to secure a meeting with the school's headmistress, but it hadn't gone how she'd intended.

"Please, Headmistress Magala. You don't understand. I've spent years studying conception and fertility. I probably know more about pregnancy than most of the midwizards here." She was being haughty, but it was true. After years of research for her own fertility, she had accidentally learned a great deal about midwizardry.

"I understand where you're coming from, Izzie, but I'm afraid there are rules and protocols in place for a reason, and I can't make exceptions. If I made an exception for you, I'd have to make one for everybody."

Izzie thought that was orcshit logic, but she'd known she might encounter resistance. She'd have to use her trump card. She knew an Affinity for blood magic would show the headmistress she could perform healing spells better than anybody else in the school. Over the years, she had learned many spells that could be used to harm somebody, but she'd also picked up a few that could be repurposed for healing. She didn't know many, but she knew two that would help her make her point.

Desperate times called for desperate measures. Izzie pulled a large knife out of her robe's pocket. The headmistress immediately reached for her wand, but hesitated when she saw what Izzie was doing. Izzie took the knife and cut a deep slice into her own left arm, extending from the crook of her elbow to her wrist. It slashed right between the words *Forever* and *Mine* tattooed on her forearm. Blood poured from the wound, as Izzie had purposely hit two major blood vessels. The headmistress shrieked, but clapped her hand over her mouth when she saw what happened.

Izzie exchanged the knife for her wand. It was a replacement she'd gotten the day before, chosen specifically for her goal of being a midwizard. She pointed it at her arm and uttered a spell. "*Dejasangra.*" Immediately, the blood stopped flowing. But Izzie wasn't done yet. She was here to make a point.

"*Regrasangra.*"

All the blood pooled on the floor and flowing from her body returned to her arm. The deep gash remained open, but no blood flowed from it any longer. It could be dangerous to perform blood magic in yourself, but a few small spells wouldn't burn her out. *I hope.* Both Izzie and the headmistress were quiet for a long while.

"Welcome to the Midwizardry Institute of Gifldor. Classes start tomorrow."

CHAPTER NINETEEN

The Elf, The Mithor, The Legend

---

*Elves are wonderful. They provoke wonder.
Elves are marvellous. They cause marvels. Elves
are fantastic. They create fantasies. Elves are
glamorous. They project glamour. Elves are
enchanting. They weave enchantment. Elves are
terrific. They beget terror. No one ever said
elves are nice. Elves are bad.*

—Terry Pratchett

---

14 years before the Twelve Race War
Mithor, Elf Territory

"Donrel!" Izzie squealed. "You're gonna crush me! I'm not as young as I once was!" The broad elf wrapped her up in a bear hug as they crashed through the underbrush.

"Donnie!" she squealed. "Let me up!"

"No way, babe. I'm not letting you go and disappear on me for another thirty years. No way, no how."

Izzie laughed, delighted by the presence of her old friend. The unlikely trio of Donrel, Izzie, and Syrel had spent decades together. Exploring the Jerdalin Forest, studying Cosconian history, taking lessons from Donrel's grandfather, sparring, drinking, fighting, laughing, and doing life together. And drinking. Lots of drinking.

He helped her to her feet and then pulled her into another embrace. "It's so good to see you, Iz," he whispered into her ear.

At this, her laughter gave way to tears. Here she was, *finally*, with somebody who truly knew her. Thoughts of all the relationships she'd developed over the years crashed into her head. Syrel and his disappearance and betrayal. Pyke coercing her into using ultrasound magic. Lulu and all the intricacies of court life and infertility. Even Lago, whose kidnapping and capture she was responsible for. Each relationship was wrought with complexity and heartache. But not this one. Her friendship with Donrel had always been so... *pure*. No romantic entanglements, no betrayals, no fakeness. Just pure, unadulterated friendship. And she'd left him.

"You don't... hate me?"

Donrel backed away from the embrace and put a hand to his chest, feigning indignation. "Hate you? Isadore, how could I ever *hate* you? You're my best friend!"

"But we abandoned you..."

"Eh, what's a few decades between friends? Besides," he continued, wrapping one arm around Syrel and one arm around her. "Syrel explained the whole story. I get it. I'm just happy my two best friends are back together!"

At this, both of them pulled away from the elf's embrace. "The fuck we are!" Izzie scoffed at the same time Syrel said, "It's complicated..."

Izzie glared at both of them, who looked at each other with conspiratorial grins.

"We'll see about that!" Donrel said, laughing. Before Izzie could protest, he continued. "Syrel, you told me there would be a dwarf, which I wasn't crazy about in the first place. But you never told me you'd be bringing one of those disgusting monsters in here. Much less two of them." He pointed with disgust at Arkan and her baby.

"See!" Arkan cried. "I knew I wouldn't be allowed in here! I never should have come with you; I was better off with Kurai." She spun around on her heels and started marching back the way they came from. Izzie ran after her and stopped her before she could wander off too far.

"Come on, Donrel. Not only is she a terrified new mom, but she's also a badass who stood up to the orc warlord for me, and she is under my protection. Got it?"

As they spoke, a retinue of soldiers came jogging up.

"Sir," one of the guards huffed. He was as slight as Donrel was broad, and his squeaky voice the exact opposite of Donrel's baritone. "How many times do we have to tell you not to run off without your guard? These are dangerous times, and you know we live right on the border of—ORC! At arms!"

The rest of the soldiers raised their bows and pointed them at Arkan. Izzie immediately lifted her wand and pointed it at the guard who had just shouted the command.

"If you harm a single hair..." she trailed off, looking at the bald orc and reconsidering. "If you harm her, I'll boil every drop of blood in your body." The poor orc was shaking. Sensing her mother's distress, the baby started wailing.

"At ease, soldiers," Donrel said cautiously, trying to deescalate the situation. "All of them, including the orcs, are under my protection." Izzie could hear the disgust in his voice.

"Yes sir, General Donrel, sir!"

Izzie cocked her head and looked at her old friend. "*General?* That's quite the promotion!"

Donrel grinned. "You've been gone for a while, Iz. I've really worked my way up the ranks." He gestured toward the group of twelve soldiers, six freles and six meles, who had reluctantly lowered their bows. "This is my personal guard, which is one of the many perks of the job."

Then he walked over to the squeaky voiced elf.

"And this," he said proudly, kissing him square on the lips, "is Werna. The best perk of the job. The captain of my guard, and more importantly, my current boyfriend."

Werna flicked the back of Donrel's pointed ear. "Current? Really? Who else would want to date somebody with such a big target on his back? Even if he is cute as hells."

"Was that a fat joke? I'll have you sent straight to the gallows!"

"Speaking of being hung..."

Syrel cleared his throat, reminding the cute couple there were others present.

"Anyway." Donrel pulled away from his boyfriend, who squeezed his hand as they separated. "I'm so glad you're here, Isadore. We could really use your help."

As they walked through Mithor, one thing was instantly apparent to Izzie. It was impossible to miss. Everybody was pregnant. And not like *"Oh, it seems like everybody is pregnant these days, I'm the only one missing out."* Izzie had pretty much felt *that* her entire life. More like the population of Mithor was at least ten times larger than it was the last time she'd been here, and all of the population growth was due almost exclusively to pregnant freles.

Izzie had never seen so many in one place. There had to be thousands. Sitting near fountains, climbing up into treehouses, chatting in the center of town. She noted that they were all *visibly* pregnant, bursting at the seams.

"Are you in heaven right now?" Lago asked her, eyes appearing lost in a dreamlike state. "Because I certainly am!"

She had completely forgotten how much Lago loved her role as a nurse and thrived on helping others, and apparently even an imprisonment at the hands of a deranged orc couldn't dampen her spirits. *Y'know what,* mused Izzie, *I'm not going to dampen her spirits either. The last thing I want is to become a jaded old midwizard who says shit like "back in my day" or "you should choose a different path, you don't know the kind of horrors I've seen."* Granted, Lago probably *didn't* know how bleak it was to take care of freles these days, but she should follow her dreams regardless. The dwarf, like her, must have been traumatized from the time they'd both spent imprisoned, but they had to put on a brave face.

"Lago, I think you're going to have to make a career switch."

"What do you mean?"

"Well, you were an incredible NICU nurse. I think now you'll have to be a..."

"Labor and delivery nurse!" Baggie exclaimed. "The best and worst job in the world."

"I'll do it! I'll do anything to help."

Arkan, feeling left out, volunteered her own help. "What can I do?"

Izzie thought about it for a moment. "How about you be my personal assistant?"

"Assistant midwizard? How hard could it be?" Arkan responded.

"Assistant *to* the midwizard," Izzie corrected her.

"Why do you think there are so many pregnant elves here?" Lago asked innocently.

Izzie had a bad feeling about it. "Like most other races in Cosconia, the elves have a pregnancy complication specific to their race. As you probably know, they live extremely long lives—sometimes even as long as a wizard. Unfortunately, what is usually a blessing for the fair folk is a curse for their pregnancies. Here's one of the first things you should know about pregnancy: The concept of predicting when a baby will come is more of an art than a science. Each race has their own gestational period, or length of time they stay pregnant. When the baby is ready to come out, we consider that 'full term.' A dwarf, for example, is considered full term seven months after their last period.

"An elf is considered full term when three years, or thirty-six months, have passed since the start of their pregnancy. It's bad to go into labor too early..." Izzie trailed off when the thought of preterm labor immediately sent her mind to Pyke. She knew the powerful changeling had likely long since had her baby—*Syrel's* baby. *Twelve hells*, she realized. *The kid is probably almost a teenager. It's been twenty years since I saw Pyke.* And she still wasn't sure she was ready to face her, knowing what she knew now.

"So going into labor too early is bad, but so is going into labor too late?" Arkan asked.

Izzie nodded. "We call it a 'postterm pregnancy.' Just like the elves live very long lives, their pregnancies sometimes go far too long. Sadly, the more postterm the pregnancy gets, the more likely both mom and baby are to pass. The baby will keep growing and sapping all of mom's life force, and sometimes they just never go into labor. They die before ever even giving birth."

"We're here!" Donrel interrupted their conversation. He had walked hand in hand with Werna, bantering and giggling the whole way. Izzie was thrilled for the elf. He'd always been a hopeless romantic, but his dedication to the military—which was barely ever needed until now—had always gotten in the way of his dating endeavors. She wasn't sure how exactly it would work with the whole different rank and bodyguard dynamic, but if anybody could make it happen, it was Donrel. He was the most committed friend she had ever had, and it already seemed like Werna was different from any of the brief relationships he'd had before.

"The war committee is waiting for us."

"War committee?" Syrel asked. "I thought elven cities like Mithor were led by a governor?"

"Things have changed around here with the upcoming war," Donrel said over his shoulder as the crew climbed into his treehouse. "The governor of Delriv, the capital city, was the leader of all Elf Territory. A few years back, he stepped down as leader and installed the military as temporary leaders of the elves."

Syrel put two and two together. "Wait. Does that mean...?"

As they entered the large open room inside Donrel's home, the three armor-clad elves who were present knelt at the sight of their leader.

"That's right!" Donrel grinned. "I'm the head honcho now." He grabbed his boyfriend's hand. "That's also why nobody can say shit about me dating a subordinate."

"This is the only time in the relationship that he's on top," Werna whispered to Izzie, who could barely contain her laughter. It was a little difficult for Izzie to conceptualize her old friend as a general and leader of the elves since he had been at the bottom of the ladder when they'd met, but he was always the type of elf others gravitated toward. He had an easygoing charisma that made others want to follow.

"These are my captains. Brimir"—he pointed at a frele with stunning black skin and hair braided down her back—"is in charge of the archers. We both started as common bow-elves many moons ago. She's the most badass archer you'll ever meet, and I trust her with my life." He then gestured toward an elf who was much older than anybody else in the room. Izzie knew that for an elf to appear old, they had to have been around for at least 500 years. "This is my great-uncle Smise. He's in charge of logistics. He's been serving the elven military for much longer than I've been alive, so anything you need taken care of, he's your mele. Finally"—he indicated a slight elven frele with hair cropped close to her head on the sides and long on top, an unusual style for an elf—"we have Anaro, who is our field general and infantry leader. Don't fuck with Anaro." Her cold smile made Izzie extremely uncomfortable.

"First order of business," Donrel declared, instantly turning from the happy-go-lucky elf in love to the bonafide general of one of the strongest races in Cosconia. "This is Arkan. She just had a baby. I want her given the same treatment that my own wife and baby would be given. If... y'know." At his words, an elf who must have been an assistant to Smise, the logistics coordinator, appeared and whisked Arkan and her baby away.

"As you all know, Cosconia is on the brink of war. Our experts predict the water fae and dwarves will complete their channel within the next ten to fifteen years, and then the Wasteland will be officially livable. Allegedly, the fae are developing a peace treaty to be extended to each race, but I suspect it's a ruse. Even if not, there is no way the orcs will agree to a peace treaty. That being said, we must prepare for war."

"Why, Donrel? Why not just continue to live in peace in the Jerdalin Forest? Your borders are protected; the source of the

Cosc River is literally in Delriv, so you'll always have fresh water... Why not just stay out of it?" Izzie pleaded.

He grunted. "I had the same thought. Until our physicians showed me this." He produced a set of meticulously created charts and graphs on papyrus, which she knew was produced right here in the Jerdalin Forest. "Iz, you've been traveling around Cosconia delivering babies and taking care of pregnant freles for a few decades now, right?"

She answered hesitantly. "... Yes, I have. And a few pregnant meles, after my time in Mermaid Territory."

Donrel cocked his head at this, apparently not knowing anything about merfolk reproduction. "Sure. Have you noticed any strange trends happening since you started?"

Izzie knew exactly what he was talking about. Pregnancy outcomes were getting demonstrably worse since she'd set out from midwizardry school nearly forty years prior. She had learned in midwizardry school that labor and delivery could be dangerous, but at this point it seemed downright fatal.

"Yes," she responded quietly. "Freles and babies are dying at a much higher rate than they were before. And it seems to be getting worse."

Everybody in the room grimaced at that, Syrel most of all. It must have been the first time he was hearing this news. *I wonder if he's worried about his own child.*

Donrel continued. "Exactly. Our physicians noticed the same thing. Thankfully, they keep detailed records, so we were able to go back and study the trends over the past two hundred years. I know you are aware of this Izzie, but for everybody else in the room"—he looked at Syrel, who was probably the only person who didn't know this information—"elven pregnancies are often complicated by something the midwizards call postterm gestation, meaning they stay pregnant too long and eventually mom and baby both perish if she doesn't go into labor. We found that, for elves, the mortality rate of pregnancy consistently stayed around ten percent for many decades. A tragic number, but at least it was stable. Until..." He pointed at a line in one of the charts on the table they all sat around. "Until exactly fifty years ago. For some reason, it started getting far worse. Mortality rates catapulted up. On average, the mortality rate increased by about another five percent every decade."

Izzie gasped at the staggering number. Before she could make the calculation in her head, Lago spoke up.

"That would mean... that would mean that the mortality rate now is thirty-five percent."

Donrel sighed before going on. "I wish that were true. It seems to be accelerating more recently. We're up to forty percent now, with no sign of it slowing down."

Izzie felt almost relieved to finally have confirmation of her theory—pregnancy in Cosconia was growing significantly more dangerous. She'd observed it in every single race she'd visited. *Hells*, she realized, *even the merman eggs were being taken by that monster at a much more alarming rate than before.* But forty percent? Nearly half of all elven freles were dying, along with their babies, during pregnancy?

Izzie thought further about the timeline, studying the graphs splayed out in front of her. Fifty years ago. Mortality started increasing fifty years ago, just a little before she started midwizardry school. Fifty years... *Oh fuck.* The realization hit Izzie like a thunderclap. *No. No no no no.* How had she not realized this before?

It was exactly fifty years before that she and Syrel had performed the ritual. The ritual that apparently created a land that gifted fertility and improved pregnancy outcomes for anybody who resided there. An overwhelming source of

Maternal Magic. And the ritual must have leached it from the rest of Cosconia. The timing lined up perfectly. Fifty years ago, the ritual was performed, and something happened that made the Wasteland the only place in Cosconia where pregnancy was safe. And now, mortality was through the roof in the rest of Cosconia. So not only did she create the land that the entire world was about to go to war over...

It's my fault. All of it. Sydyr's death. The changeling birth defects. Lursa's attacks. The NICU babies. The bleeding orcs. All of it. For so long, Izzie had put every ounce of energy she could muster into saving mothers and babies, yet they only needed to be saved in the first place *because of her*. Her vision started to blur. She felt like the walls were closing in around her. Like she was back in that fetid cell she called home for ten years. Izzie's mind went to Dalfa, who would never forgive her when she found out *Izzie* was the reason maternal mortality was unacceptably high.

She was still staring down at the charts, everybody else in the room silent. Looking at her. Waiting for her response. *I'm a monster. A murderer. This is all my fault.*

Before her thoughts could spiral any further out of control, she felt a warm hand on her leg. Syrel. She turned to look at him. He had the same sadness in his eyes she'd noticed the very first time they met, except this time it persisted for longer than a moment. That same look had passed over him from time to time in the years they spent together, but it was such a happy time, there had rarely been a reason for sadness. She could tell he'd had the same realization she did. And he knew that she had a tendency to spiral into a cascade of negative thoughts if left unchecked.

"Later," he whispered. "Be strong now, and we'll mourn later. I know you can do this, Isadore. You're the strongest wizard I've ever known."

Damn him, she thought. Even after everything, a part of her still loved him deep down. A big part. She couldn't deny it, no matter how hard she tried. She had never *stopped* loving him, and that wouldn't change. They had done so much life together. Created so many memories. Laughed until their throats hurt. *But he's wicked*, a voice inside her said. *He's done so much evil.*

So have you, a different voice said. *You're just as bad as he is.* She looked at Syrel again, who wiped a tear from her eye with his thumb.

"I'm sorry, everybody," she said at last. "I'm just really passionate about maternal health, and the thought of pregnancy and delivery being so deadly is hard for me to bear."

Everybody in the room nodded, but they didn't understand. Izzie knew they could never understand. To her chagrin, the only one who could truly understand was the one who'd been on the other side of that damned ritual. The one sitting right next to her. The one she loved. The one she hated. The one who had committed unspeakable acts. The one who had rescued her from Kurai.

Donrel spoke at last, breaking the sober atmosphere of the room. "So that's why staking our claim on the land is absolutely crucial. Our race won't survive without it. I still hope Queen Luxor's plan for peace works, but we need that land. Which brings me to the reason you're here."

Izzie knew what he was going to say before the words left his mouth. He was hoping she could use her blood magic to induce labor for the thousands of pregnant elves in Mithor.

"Can you help all of our pregnant freles? They've been gathering here for months, ever since Syrel got the message you were in Kurai's captivity and made the plan to get you out. It must have been destiny he was already here and could bring you with him. You're our only hope."

"I can't do it, Donrel. I'm sorry. I already spent years forcibly helping build an orc army, I'm pretty sure I did the same thing for the dwarves, and now I'm supposed to do the same for the elves?"

"So you can help our enemies but not us?" Anaro snapped, her tone cruel.

Donrel slammed his fist on the table. "Bite your tongue, *Captain*. Isadore has saved more lives than you could even count. Say one more negative thing about my friend and I'll have you back on the front lines."

Izzie knew Donrel had a temper, and she was thankful she wasn't on the receiving end of his ire, even if she felt guilty she was responsible for much more *death* than life.

"I understand your hesitation, Izzie. I really do. But we can't go on like this. Our population is dwindling. If we can't have control of the fertile Wasteland, the future of the entire elven race is in danger."

"My *evening* is in danger!" Baggie Smalls said from Izzie's lap.

Every eye in the room turned to her. Before she could defend herself, it continued. "Where is my super suit?!"

Donrel spoke before Baggie could continue its nonsense. "Do I even want to know?"

Izzie shook her head. "I promise you do not."

"Is it done?"

"There's no way to tell, but usually after a comment or two it'll settle down."

"Okay... moving on. Isadore, I'm sorry to ask this of you, but the elven race is on the line."

"Won't you be sending them off to die anyway? Will they even be old enough when the war starts? Nobody knows when it's coming! Couldn't it start tomorrow for all we know?"

"Not without a water supply."

"And you think the fae and the dwarves are just going to give it to you?"

"I think we will do whatever is necessary to protect our race."

"You do realize everybody has the same plan, right? The orcs, the fae, the dwarves, the humans... It's going to be a bloodbath, Donrel."

He nodded sadly. "I know. But I have a duty to protect my people, Izzie. Not only to protect them now, but to protect our future as a race. I'm asking you, as a friend, if you'll help."

"Don't pull that card with me. Don't you dare."

He put his hands up in defense. "You're right. That's not fair. Then I'm asking you as a leader."

"I can't, Donrel."

"It's your choice, Izzie, but only you can help us. Only you have the power to save the lives of the pregnant freles gathered in Mithor. I just want you to think about it."

Izzie hesitated, and then relented. "Fine. I'll think about it." She got up to leave the room, Syrel in tow. A voice stopped her before she could climb out of the treehouse.

"Is there anything I can do to help?"

She'd practically forgotten Lago was still here. Izzie thought for a moment. She didn't want to give the frele some meaningless, banal task, but there wasn't much she could do without magic.

"I want you to start making a list. Of every pregnant frele in Mithor, and how far along they are. Get as many as you can."

"Yes ma'am!" the dwarf shot off to start her task. When they got to the bottom of the ladder, they saw Donrel following them.

"Can I at least show you to your lodging?"

He led them along a path through Mithor, which had changed significantly. There were small houses everywhere, and not just in the trees as was typical of an elven town. Everywhere she looked, there were pregnant freles. Some had the beautiful glow of pregnancy. Others looked desperately ill. She knew that meant they had been pregnant for far too long, and the baby was sucking their life force right out. It was probably too late for them.

As they walked, the surroundings began to look familiar. Donrel stopped in front of an old tree.

Syrel pointed out the obvious. "This is our house."

Donrel smiled, though there was clearly hurt in his eyes. *He must be pretty upset I'm not willing to help.*

"I kept it empty for you. In case you ever came back."

Izzie almost broke down, but she was able to keep it together, bolstered by the strength of her oldest friend and... whatever Syrel was to her now.

"Thank you, Donrel. I promise whatever I decide, you will always be my best friend."

He hugged her. "I know. I trust your judgment. Now I'm sure you both could use a little rest." He looked up at the treehouse. "Uhhh, I guess I didn't think about... Are you two... How is...?"

"I'm sure our old bed will still fit us!" Syrel suggested.

Izzie gave him a withering look. "In your dreams." Izzie wanted to send him away, but she couldn't stand the thought of being alone that night. "Donrel, can you have somebody bring a separate bed?"

After Donrel departed, Izzie laid down in her bed, which she had positioned as far from Syrel's as the small treehouse would allow. When she closed her eyes, Kurai's face appeared. She clenched her fists and tried to shake the image away, but she couldn't. Her back ached where he'd hit her. Her mind drifted to Lago, who must be feeling the same.

"Hey," Syrel whispered. "You up?"

"I'm not sure if I'm ever going to sleep again."

"Can I tell you something?"

"I've never once heard you hold your tongue, so I suspect my answer is meaningless."

She practically heard his grin from across the dark room. "You know me so well. And you're right; I'm going to tell you no matter what, because you need to hear it. It's not your fault, Izzie."

She immediately started to protest, but he wouldn't let her. "It's not your fault," he said more emphatically, his voice breaking as he spoke. "It's not your fault."

Tears started to stream down Izzie's face. It wasn't true. It *was* her fault. Both of their faults, really. She was glad he wasn't trying to pretend like it didn't happen. Decades they'd spent roaming around Cosconia—for what? So she could have a baby and he could do some extra magic? Why did their whims matter in the face of the lives of thousands?

"Izzie, there's no way we could have known. We did our due diligence. We studied for years. We read every text there was about fertility. This is completely unprecedented. Nobody could have predicted this."

"And?" she snapped. "It still happened, didn't it? We literally sucked the life out of Cosconia."

"Accidentally!"

"Who cares! And if that wasn't bad enough, we started a fucking war!"

"Izzie, we did not start a war. Throughout all of Cosconia's history, there have been wars. If it wasn't this, it would have been something else."

Damn his logical thinking and relentless optimism and cute butt. She was having a hard time reconciling the Syrel she knew with the one who had murdered Thelonius at the coronation. At the same time, the thought of him being willing to risk anything and everything to protect her was more comforting than she cared to admit.

"I guess, but you and I both know this is going to be the bloodiest war Cosconia has ever seen."

"I'm choosing to have hope for the future. Izzie, look on the bright side: We created a land bursting with potential. Just like you told me on the walk over here. Fae are getting pregnant overnight, reports from the humans say that their rates of perc..."

"Precum," Baggie Smalls filled in.

"Preeclampsia," Izzie corrected firmly.

"Yeah, that. It barely exists in Gravipar. Think of the possibilities!"

It was similar to Dalfa's way of thinking, which was more utilitarian than she was comfortable with. It was going to get worse before it got better, but maybe it *would* get better. These kinds of conversations were exactly what she missed about Syrel, even if she wasn't sure she could ever forgive him.

The war was inevitable, unless Lulu could somehow get everybody to agree to a treaty, which she doubted. She knew the orcs would be a massive threat, as she'd seen firsthand how large their army was growing. She wasn't interested in building an army, but that wasn't her problem. She didn't get to decide which freles to help and which ones not to. It was her *duty* as a midwizard to help. She'd committed to saving as many lives as she could, and she was going to honor that commitment. As she thought, she heard Syrel get up from his bed and drag it next to hers.

"I have to help them, don't I?" she said after a long silence.

He reached over from his bed, now next to hers, and grabbed her hand. He squeezed it and didn't let go. Neither of them said anything else. Izzie fell asleep with her hand in his, just like she used to.

* * *

14 years before the Twelve Race War
Rotoplas, Giant Territory

"I have no doubts the giants can win a war against the small races," Skygyr said slowly. "But at great cost."

"Aren't you already paying a great cost? Watching your freles and babies die at unprecedented rates?" Dalfa countered. After spending some time in Jubox, she had ventured to Giant Territory to accomplish her goal of convincing every race that fighting for Gravipar would be worth it.

The more she traveled around Cosconia, the more obvious it became that peace wouldn't be an option. Decades of rising racial tensions were at a boiling point, and no amount of mental magic could convince Cosconians otherwise. The *Mentala*, the most important tome a mind mage could get their hands on, stated it was nearly impossible to assert enough control over somebody's mind to get them to do something completely antithetical to their nature. Instead, it was much easier to twist somebody's existing desires to her own whims.

"Careful, midwizard. I have great respect for your kind, and I agreed to see you because I wouldn't be here today if it weren't for a midwizard, but only *I* know what is best for giantkind."

Dalfa didn't want to go here, but she knew it would be effective. Back when they corresponded frequently, Izzie had described Skygyr's birth in great detail in one of her letters.

"Is this really what your mother would want? Did Sydyr die to let you watch the rest of Cosconia bask in Maternal Magic while the giants stay isolated in their mountains?"

Skygyr slammed her fist on the table, sending her enormous mug of ale flying. "Do not profess to know anything of my mother or her wishes." It was exactly the kind of emotional display that would make the giantess susceptible to her spell.

"*Abrido*," she said, under her breath so Skygyr wouldn't hear. The mind Affinity spell would open the giantess to the power of suggestion. Dalfa had used it on hundreds of giants over the last few years in Rotoplas, spreading far and wide the idea of fighting over Gravipar. Giants were particularly resistant to mind magic, so these years had helped her grow her power more than she ever though possible.

"I'm sorry," Dalfa said. "But I truly think your mother would want you to find a way to stake your claim in Gravipar."

Slowly, the giant nodded her head. "Yes. I suppose my mother would want me to ensure the future of our race."

CHAPTER TWENTY

Postterm Gestation

When you're pregnant, you can think of nothing but having your own body to yourself again, yet after having given birth you realize that the biggest part of you is now somehow external, subject to all sorts of dangers and disappearance, so you spend the rest of your life trying to figure out how to keep it close enough for comfort.

—Jodi Picoult

---

2 years before the Twelve Race War
Mithor, Elf Territory

"Hey, boss, I'd like to get your thoughts on a patient in the next group," said Lago after escorting out the most recent patient who had started to feel contractions. It usually took a few hours of channeling blood magic to induce labor. "She says she's exactly four years along, but she looks surprisingly healthy. Donrel says she gets the VIE treatment because she's Werna's sister—she just got here from a small town deep in the forest. They said it took a long time to get word to her."

Izzie smiled, thinking of the couple. She'd watched their relationship grow strong over the many years since she'd arrived in Elf Territory, the two somehow making the whole general/bodyguard thing work. Izzie had come to deeply love Werna after she'd seen how happy he made her old friend.

"Of course. Bring her in."

Izzie was a pro at induction of labor by this point. For twelve years, she'd helped elven freles who didn't go into labor on their own. Lago had yet again proven to be an excellent nurse, triaging the ones who needed it the most and bringing them to the front of the line. The dwarf worked tirelessly to organize the freles who continuously poured into Mithor to see the midwizard. They'd discovered that any elf who was pregnant for more than four years was, unfortunately, almost always beyond saving. The baby would have drained too much of their life force.

If Izzie caught them in time, however, she would have great success. Essentially, she did the opposite of what she had done to stop Pyke's preterm labor. She channeled her magic to *increase* blood flow to the uterus, using the *matrisangra* spell she'd developed, which would in turn lead to contractions. She had to be careful not to send too much of the elves' dark green blood to the uterus; otherwise, the risk of bleeding was too great. She had learned that the hard way. Once the elves were in labor, things were smooth sailing from there. The labors were long, just like the pregnancies, but mostly uncomplicated. Lago would be there with them every step of the way.

The babies she'd delivered at the beginning of her time in Mithor were already being trained for the military, Donrel having decided that ten was old enough to start training. He swore he wouldn't send anybody to war before they turned fifteen, but she was skeptical. She tried to stay out of politics and stick to medicine.

The population of Mithor continued to swell, partially due to the arrival of pregnant elves and the subsequent arrival of their babies, but also because, it being a border town, the army was amassing there.

"Hi Izzie; I'm Lorna. Werna's sister," she introduced herself. Her voice was weak, her words stilted. Lago may have oversold her level of health. "Thank you for agreeing to see me."

"Of course. Werna is practically family to me, so that makes you family. You've been pregnant for four years now?"

The girl grimaced. "It might be closer to four and a half. Can you get this damn baby out of me?"

Izzie laughed, but internally she was worried. Most freles were ready to be done with pregnancy by the end, but this pregnancy was literally draining the life out of Lorna.

"I can certainly try." Inducing labor in somebody who had been pregnant for almost five years might be too much even for her.

She still had her blood magic extended to several other elves still in the room, but she had enough Intent to continue focusing on them while giving a little extra attention to Lorna. The moment she assessed her circulatory system, Izzie knew it was much more dire than they had realized. The elf's heart beat weakly, and there was so little blood flow to her uterus that it almost felt cold. *This is going to be a doozy.*

It was much harder to use blood magic on multiple adult-sized elves compared to her NICU babies, but her power continued to grow. Now she could use her magic on at least twenty adult patients at once. She reflected on her level of power when she had left midwizardry school. Present Izzie could kick past Izzie's ass. Handily. And she'd already been halfway decent at blood magic when she'd started midwizardry school. After nearly fifty years of traveling and practicing, she could practically do it in her sleep. She could feel the power coursing through her. She was still committed to only using her power for good, and she actually felt like she was making a difference in Elf Territory.

Unlike her time with the dwarves, in which she worked herself to the bone to assuage her guilt, or her imprisonment with the orcs, during which she was forced to work with minimal respite, Izzie had a great work-life balance here. During her time in Orc Territory, she had feared she would face the most deadly affliction a midwizard could encounter: burnout. Here, however, Syrel had convinced her that in order to be the best midwizard she could be, she had to focus on herself sometimes, and she'd taken the advice to heart.

Over the next several hours, Izzie slowly attempted to create more blood flow to Lorna's uterus without compromising the rest of her organs. One by one, the rest of the patients she had been taking care of started having contractions, and Lago led them away to the luxurious birthing springs, where they would deliver their pointy-eared babies. There were enough elven attendants to take care of them once labor had started.

Now Izzie could put all her energy into helping Donrel's future sister-in-law. The pair had gotten engaged three years ago, and the wedding planning was well underway. She needed to make sure Lorna could be present for the big day. Usually Izzie was able to go home by sunset, but that had passed hours before. Lago, as always, stayed faithfully by her side, holding the elf's hand and whispering reassuring messages into her ear.

Izzie panicked when she felt the elf's heartbeat slow down. That was an ominous sign. She poured every ounce of Skill she had into her blood magic, refusing to give up. If this were any other patient, she likely would have called it quits by now. Had she tried this when she first started in Elf Territory, she wouldn't have had the Skill to do it. She tried to hide her fear for the elf's life, but Lorna must have picked up on it.

"It's okay," Lorna murmured. "We're not going to make it, are we? I knew it was a possibility. Thank you for trying." Her voice shook as she spoke.

"I'm not giving up yet," Izzie stated through gritted teeth. More hours passed as she circulated the elf's blood over and over, trying in vain to force her heart to beat strongly enough to get enough blood to the uterus. The sun peeked through the window as it rose. Had she really been at this all night? She was no stranger to all-nighters, but it certainly didn't fit into her new goal of work-life balance.

Eventually, the elf doubled over in pain, grabbing her stomach. A look of horror crawled across her face. Izzie looked at Lago, who smiled.

"Oh gods what is it? Am I dying?"

"Nope." Lago grinned. "You're in labor."

* * *

"How am I supposed to know you won't go back to Pyke the moment you see her again?" Izzie asked Syrel, her anxiety getting the better of her.

"Izzie, you have to understand. I thought you were long gone. Pyke was never anything but a replacement for you."

"I'm sure you never mentioned that to her." Izzie rolled her eyes. Even though it made her sympathize with Pyke, it also made her feel like she actually was special to him.

"I didn't, but a part of me feels like she always knew she didn't have all of me. Maybe that's why she left. She doesn't want to see me, and I respect that. If I ever see her again, I'll do whatever I can to support her baby and apologize profusely for how everything went down, but I have no romantic interest in her. The moment I saw you again, I only had one thought."

"And what thought would that be?"

"I have to win her back."

Izzie had to admit to herself his overwhelming desire to protect her and be with her was attractive. She actually believed he had no romantic interest in Pyke. He barely ever brought her up, but he frequently wondered aloud how his son was doing. She knew he desperately wanted to meet his child, but he couldn't face him or Pyke after what had happened at the coronation.

"And how did you plan on doing that?

"Would you believe me if I said I thought my charm and wit would do the trick? Not to mention how pretty I am." He fluttered his long eyelashes.

She tried to conceal a chuckle. "Would I believe you *thought* that? Without a doubt. But you had to know it was a bit more complicated than that." As always, he was able to quell her anxiety. It was hard to stay mad at the person who could make you laugh in the middle of an argument.

Izzie's relationship with Syrel over the past twelve years had been... complicated. After spending that first night in Mithor together, they'd decided to live separately while they figured things out. Well, *she'd* decided that—if it were up to him, they would have just picked up right where they'd left off. As tempting as it was, she couldn't do it. Even though they had so much good history together, there was plenty of bad history too.

"But you agree? You think I'm really pretty?"

"Pretty obnoxious," Baggie mumbled. Syrel looked like he would rise to the bait, but he thought better of it.

"Syrel," she started.

"Yes, darling?"

"Don't call me that!" She tried to conceal her smile. "I'm serious; I have something to say. I've been thinking about this for quite some time now."

"Oh? Do tell!"

"I'm not going to like this, am I?" the bag muttered again. She ignored it even though it was right.

"I forgive you," she stated simply.

"... For what? Not that there isn't plenty to forgive, but specifically?"

"All of it. I'm sick of holding on to negative feelings. You've apologized a thousand times. You were kidnapped by blood sprites. Pyke ran away from you. You don't have an Affinity. I sometimes pretend like I've had it far worse, but your life wasn't a walk in the park after that damned ritual. You saved me from Kurai, and you've been nothing but respectful of my boundaries over the past few years. But none of those are the reason I am forgiving you."

It had taken a long time for Izzie to come to terms with this. She and Syrel had had many late night conversations, processing the myriad of emotions they both felt.

"I'm forgiving you because I think we're the same. We've both done a lot of evil. We're responsible for the loss of Maternal Magic in Cosconia—"

Syrel attempted to cut her off, never willing to let her blame herself for the result of the ritual, but she wouldn't let him. "I'm rambling anyway. Here is what it comes down to: You and I are both good wizards who have done bad things. But we're both trying to be better. So I can't blame you any more than I can blame myself, and I'm doing my best not to do that either. So I forgive you."

Izzie felt like a weight lifted off her chest. Somehow, forgiving Syrel felt like forgiving herself. For the first time, she felt like she could focus on the future instead of dwelling on her past. She didn't know what the future held. She still loved him—there was no doubt about it. He was her soulmate.

But that didn't mean they were right for each other. Sometimes history with a partner was good, but there might be *too* much history here. She worried they would never get back to where they were before the ritual. *Maybe that's okay? Maybe we can start fresh?* She shook the thoughts off. Countless times, she had weighed the pros and cons of throwing caution to the wind and giving a relationship a shot, but there just weren't enough pros.

Syrel sniffed, holding back tears. They were silent for a long time. Finally, he thanked her in a barely audible voice.

"You have no idea how much I needed that, Isadore. For so long, I've hated myself because I thought you hated me. And Pyke hated me. And Donrel hated me. And Vera hated me."

"You're starting to sound like me with all those anxiety thoughts!"

"Besides, I'm sure Pyke still hates you," Baggie added.

He hiccuped, halfway between a cry and a laugh. "Just... thank you. Maybe one day I can forgive myself."

Again, silence overtook them. But a comfortable silence, one only possible with somebody you've connected to on every level possible.

"What are you thinking about?" Syrel asked her after several minutes of silence.

"You," she answered simply, not finding any reason to lie to him. They'd both committed to radical honesty with each other, no matter the cost.

"All good things?"

"Yes, Syrel, I'm thinking all good things about the love of my life who disappeared for decades and then murdered a bunch of fae after impregnating an Apex Changeling, who then came to his ex for help." She rolled her eyes.

Baggie Smalls piped up from under the bed. "Thanks for the SparkNotes version of the story so far!"

They both knew better than to engage.

"So I'm the love of your life, eh?" He grinned. He had this frustrating optimism about him that almost seemed to ignore everything negative she said and focus on the good. It was one of his best and most annoying traits.

She sighed. "Unfortunately, yes. Which is why I've chosen to be celibate."

"You certainly didn't seem very celibate last night," he retorted, winking at her in spite of her known hatred for the practice.

"That was *one* moment of weakness!"

"If I recall correctly, it was more like three moments of weakness."

Syrel climbed out of bed and started making her coffee, just the way she liked it. Izzie had learned to separate love and sex with Syrel. She loved him, and she also loved sleeping with him. She knew she couldn't be in a relationship with him, since it meant facing the reality of his child with Pyke, the future of Cosconia and their role in the war, and her infertility. But a wizard had needs, and he satisfied those needs *quite* adequately.

"Can I have one more moment of weakness?"

* * *

62 years before the Twelve Race War
Gifldor, Wizard Territory

Izzie was nervous about the first day of classes. The wound on her arm throbbed. The bold move to get into midwizardry school had paid off, but now she was paying the consequences.

"Congratulations to the three of you on gaining acceptance to the MIG. Over the next twelve years, you'll learn the intricacies of pregnancy, labor, and delivery for all twelve races of Cosconia," Professor Williams began. "Being a midwizard is the most difficult and most rewarding endeavor you will ever undertake. You'll experience the highest highs and the lowest lows. You'll be there for the best moment of somebody's life, and also the worst. You'll bring life into this world, but you'll also watch some of those very same lives fade away. You'll walk side by side with freles—or swim side by side with mermen, if you ever venture far enough south—during the most difficult time in their lives. Pregnancy in Cosconia is dangerous, but many freles will still choose to take the risk. You're there to lower that risk as much as possible.

"I will be fully honest with you," the halfling professor continued. Sitting down, Izzie was at just about eye level with the frele. "There will be times you are powerless. Here at the MIG, we will teach you how to deal with orcish bleeding, minotaur breastfeeding, and halfling litters. Sometimes, you'll arrive in the nick of time to save a human from developing eclampsia. Other times, you'll have to watch, powerless, as a giant baby gets stuck on the way out." Izzie shuddered, imagining how terrifying it would be to handle a giantess's baby getting stuck.

"Don't get discouraged. Use the pain as fuel. Invent ways to care for pregnant freles. Find new ways to use your Affinity. Hone your Skill. Never give less than one hundred percent

Intent. Follow in the footsteps of your forebears and leave your mark on Cosconia forever." Professor Williams distributed blank stacks of parchment to the three students in the class. "Here's your assignment: Each of you is to write a ten-page essay on what midwizardry means to you. No other rules. You won't be graded on content—I just want to know where you're coming from so I can teach you better." The professor walked out of the room.

The frele next to her leaned over to start a conversation. She was much smaller than Izzie, and far prettier. Stripes of black and white layered her hair, like the most beautiful salt and pepper pattern. Compared to Izzie's larger build, her classmate was slight. But her size did nothing to diminish the emotion on her face. Izzie could tell this was a frele who wore her emotions on her sleeve, which she respected.

"That was quite the speech." She extended her hand to Izzie. "I'm Dalfa, mind mage. My mom was a midwizard, so I'm following in her footsteps."

"Nice to meet you, Dalfa. I'm Isad—Izzie," she corrected, remembering the name change that came with reinventing herself. "I have a blood Affinity."

"Woah," both of her classmates said simultaneously. Without warning, the classmate who hadn't introduced herself yet stood up. Sweat glistened on her face.

"A blood mage and a legacy mental mage? I can't do this. I'm out of my depth. I should have listened to my dad and taken that job as a beast tamer." Those were the last words Izzie ever heard out of the frele, who walked out of the classroom and never returned.

"Well, I guess it's just me and you now, Isad-Izzie," Dalfa joked.

I think I'm going to like her.

CHAPTER TWENTY-ONE

Wedding Before War

A wedding? I love weddings! Drinks all around!

—*Captain Jack Sparrow*

---

31 days before the Twelve Race War
Mithor, Elf Territory

"Come on! We're going to be late!"

"I'm almost ready!"

"Izzie, you're not even dressed."

"It's going to take me two seconds." Izzie pointed her wand at her head and used her favorite spell. *"Derchallo!"* It was one of the first spells any frele wizard learned, and it was especially useful for her, since it turned her wavy hair straight. She scrambled around her treehouse, throwing robes this way and that to find the right one.

"You know you have to wear white, right?" Syrel added helpfully.

"Cect, that's right," Izzie cursed. She found a dress buried at the bottom of her chest and threw it on. The flowing white dress draped to just above her ankles. She didn't want to trip when

272

dancing the night away. The bodice was snug and lacy. The skirt was a mix of buttery soft fabric overlaid with tulle. When she twirled in a circle, it spun out from her waist to rise and fall like churning ocean waves.

"How do I look?"

Syrel looked at her but didn't say anything. She couldn't make out the expression in his eyes.

"Um, hello? Is it that bad? You can't even come up with a single compliment?"

"No no no," he answered hurriedly. "It's just… Izzie, you look… I can't find the right words. Breathtaking. Stunning. Gorgeous. Sexy. None of these even do justice to your beauty. I can't imagine anybody in Cosconia is more attracted to anybody else than I am to you. Holy Cect."

Izzie blushed deeply, embarrassed by his verbosity. "Knock it off, Syrel!"

"I really mean it, Izzie. I'll stop saying it out loud if you want, but not a day goes by I don't think about how lucky I am that you would even give me the time of day."

She decided to accept the compliment. "Thank you, Syrel. But that sounds an awful lot like *boyfriend* talk, and if you'll remember correctly, we're just *friends*!" Izzie felt conflicted daily about her relationship with Syrel. She loved the strong, protective, wild side of him, but it also scared her.

"I thought you agreeing to be my date today meant I had a chance!" he protested.

"I very clearly told you that we are going as friends—besides, we're also going with Lago and Arkan, who should be here any moment."

"Oh they've been waiting outside the treehouse for fifteen minutes; we're all waiting on you."

"WHAT! Why didn't you stop me from dilly-dallying?!"

"It seems more like lollygagging to me, but I suppose that's neither here nor there," Baggie Smalls commented.

"Okay, I'm ready! I certainly hope this wedding goes better than the last one I attended," she joked.

Syrel winced but didn't say anything.

"Too soon?"

"No, I deserve it," he called up, climbing out of the treehouse before her. "Good evening ladies! You both look lovely, as always."

Lago politely thanked Syrel while Arkan shoved him playfully. They both loved him, partially because he was their savior from Kurai's captivity, but also simply because of who he was. *Everybody* loved him. He had an easy way about him that just made him fun to be around. He remembered everybody's name. He always asked about something personal, even if it was a tiny detail they'd mentioned in passing.

"How's Sintu?"

Arkan lit up at the mention of her son. "He's great—fourteen this year! Some of the elves have been teaching him archery. He's going to be the best orcish archer in Cosconian history, I think."

"Wouldn't he be the *only* orcish archer in Cosconian history?" Baggie asked condescendingly.

"Knock it off, BS. I bet he is, especially if he gets his mother's strength! Lago, how is Blist?" Syrel brushed off the bag's comments.

An angry look passed over her face, but Izzie quickly realized it was only mock fury.

"Taller than me," she harrumphed. "I knew this day would happen, but so soon? It felt like only yesterday I was holding him in my arms." About five years prior, Lago had become extremely attached to one of her patients. She had been pregnant for just shy of four years, and while she was able to successfully get into labor, she passed during the process. Thankfully, her baby had survived, but without a mother to raise him. Blist's father had tragically passed in a border dispute with the orcs, so Lago channeled her maternal instincts and adopted the baby. It was pretty unusual seeing a dwarf raise an elven baby, but she'd seen stranger things. Lago and Arkan lived together and raised their family in what was maybe the most multicultural family in Cosconia. Izzie dreamed of a day when, after this war was over, all of Cosconia looked that way.

"Oh my gods, Izzie, your dress is to die for!" Lago said, then looked at Syrel, seeming to realize she could have chosen her words a little more carefully.

"Okay, ladies, can we please go?" Syrel pointed at the empty town around them. "We're the only ones who aren't there yet."

The quartet rushed through town toward the Center Tree, which was already surrounded by a sea of white. Contrary to weddings in human culture, which Izzie had read about in the smutty novels she loved so much, the entire crowd wore white while the marrying couple wore green. Just as the elves were one with the forest, they wore green to symbolize becoming one with each other. Izzie, Syrel, Arkan, and Lago slid into the crowd, only drawing a few quizzical looks. Most of the population of Mithor knew them, or at least knew *of* them by now. Izzie made brief eye contact with Lorna, who sat near the front. The look they exchanged was full of emotion.

"See!" Izzie whispered to Syrel. "We didn't miss a thing!"

Just as they settled into their seats, the lovely couple made their appearance. Donrel was clad in full ceremonial war regalia, the green of the sleek armor matching the forest around them. He stood in front of the Center Tree, the holy tree around which all elven communities were established. He had one hand on the tree, and one holding his groom's hand. They looked an unlikely duo, Donrel thick and broad, Werna slight and slender, but Izzie knew firsthand they made it work. Despite his diminutive looks, Werna was a fierce bodyguard and fighter. Syrel, seated next to her, muttered something, and she shushed him, but he just looked at her and smiled, putting his warm hand on her knee. She let it linger for a few moments before subtly shifting so it would fall off. She instantly regretted it, her leg tingling where he'd been touching her moments ago.

Donrel began to speak, his voice somehow amplified so it echoed off the trees around them. Izzie turned to Syrel, who was barely restraining a goofy grin. He must have been casting a voice amplification spell under his breath.

"Just a little idea I had. Donrel loved it." *Ugh, he really* is *thoughtful, isn't he?*

"Werna, I remember the first time we met. After I was promoted to captain, you were assigned as my guard. My first thought was, 'How is this scrawny little fella going to defend me from anything? He's half my size!'" The crowd laughed. "But what you lack in size, you make up for in every other category. Our very first border patrol together, you jumped in front of me and took an arrow for me."

Werna briefly broke contact with Donrel to rub his shoulder. "It still hurts sometimes!"

Donrel smiled softly and continued. "You have so much heart. You love hard and party harder. You support me in all that I do, even when I'm acting the fool. I could spend forever looking into your sexy gray eyes. Hundreds of times I've tried to force you to stop being in my guard and become a captain, but you always tell me you were put on this continent to be my guardian. I am nothing without you, Werna."

Izzie wiped tears away from her eyes. Nearly everybody around had tears in their eyes, including Syrel, who may have been crying harder than anybody else.

Izzie elbowed him in the ribs. "Softie!" He laughed and hiccuped at the same time, and she grabbed his hand and held it. *Friends can hold hands, right?*

Werna's turn was next. "Donrel, you may have seen me for the first time when you became captain, but I noticed you long before that. And not just because you're double the size of the rest of us." Again, the crowd broke out into laughter, loving the repartee between their leader and his soon-to-be husband. "You are a natural-born leader. People follow you not because they have to, but because they want to. Don't be fooled—I may have saved you from an arrow that day, but you're the one who saved me, Donrel. I am happier every day I get to spend with you. I'm not sure what the future holds for us. But I do know one thing. You're it for me. You're all I need. I love you." Werna's words were reminiscent of the ones Syrel had said to her before the ritual. Deep within her, she felt something awaken.

The pair kissed the Center Tree, kissed each other deeply, and kissed the tree again in typical elven custom. Music burst forth from the trees around them as several elves with harps and lyres emerged. Elven weddings were more of a party for the community than a celebration of the wedded couple, as elves were a relatively private people. The vows were about the most sappiness you could get out of them.

Izzie and Syrel were lost in a sea of dancing. Attendants with booze began circulating through the crowd. She threw back her first goblet of wine in one gulp. Thankfully, her hardy wizard's constitution made her relatively tolerant of alcohol, so it would take at least four or five cups until she felt a buzz. Since her spiral in Wastetown, she still tried to be cautious with her alcohol use.

The night passed in a joyful blur of dancing. Izzie laughed as Syrel bent down to dance with Lago while she took a round with Arkan. Donrel and Werna floated throughout the crowd, dancing with each other, kissing, and grabbing others to have a dance with them. She laughed and cried while she danced with Donrel, so happy for him but also scared he was preparing to lead an army to war. He and his new husband were not holding back on the wine, and she was happy they could let loose.

It was deep into the night when she shared another dance with Syrel. She'd since gained and lost a buzz, wanting to be sober by the time she went to bed so she didn't wake up with a hangover. There were still labors to induce and babies to deliver. He wrapped his strong arms around her waist as she draped hers over his shoulders. Their faces were only a few inches apart. He smiled softly at her.

"Isadore, can I say something to you?"

She knew exactly what he was going to say. She'd been expecting it all night. She shook her head. "No, Syrel. Because I'm going to say something. I've been dragging you along for too long. It's not fair of me to leave you on the hook for this long, wondering if we're ever getting together."

"That's not true!" he countered. "You've made it very clear where we stand."

She flicked his ear. "Don't interrupt me, punk. I've *said* it wasn't going to work out, but I also still come knocking on your door several times a week. I flirt with you all the time. I asked you to be my wedding date. And do you know why I've done all that?"

He hesitated and then shook his head, not wanting to interrupt her again. She unwrapped her arms from around his shoulders and put her hands on his cheeks, fingers wrapping behind his head, and pulled him into a deep kiss. She held her lips on his as the music continued. "It's because I am hopelessly in love with you. I loved you the moment I saw you in the library. I loved you the years we spent traveling the world together. I loved you when you disappeared in the Wasteland. I loved you when I started midwizardry school. Hells, I even loved you when I saw you at the coronation."

Syrel's lip trembled a bit, but he listened to her with rapt attention.

"It's taken me a long time to come to terms with everything that's happened to us, but I'm done being cautious. I suspect the twelve hells are about to open up on Cosconia, and I can't spend another day without you by my side. Seeing Donrel and Werna commit to each other tonight finally made me see that I've been stubborn. I am so comfortable with you. It's the only time I can fully be myself. You understand the guilt I'm ridden with. You constantly reassure me. You know about my infertility, and you've never been anything other than supportive."

His arms flexed around her waist, pulling her in closer until her lips were just a breath away from his.

"You're it, Syrel. I love you."

Their lips met, and they kissed for a long time. The world melted away around them. By the time they separated from each other, nobody else was left in the clearing in front of the Center Tree. There was no more music. The lanterns had gone dim. But for the first time in a long time, Izzie felt at peace.

"Oh by the way, what was it you were going to tell me?" Izzie figured he had been planning on professing his love for her for the millionth time.

"It was nothing. Let's talk about it in the morning."

"Are you sure it was nothing? We're committed to being honest with each other now, remember?"

Sadness crossed his face. Izzie started to panic. Was she wrong? Was he not going to profess his love? Maybe he was about to tell her he was done with her. Maybe...

"Isadore, pull yourself out of it. This has nothing to do with me and you. I've been waiting for you to tell me that for decades. I *have* never, *could* never, and *will* never stop loving you. You're it for me too, Izzie. I was so terrified my mistakes would keep us apart forever, and I would never have forgiven myself." He reached down to his pocket and pulled out a letter. "I got this earlier this morning from one of Donrel's messengers. She was too afraid to give it to him on his wedding day." She snatched it out of his hands and read it.

General Donrel,

Please join me for a peace summit in Gravipar forty days hence. Do not bring any armies, and you have my promise of protection. If Isadore the midwizard is in your territory, her presence at the summit would be appreciated. You each will be permitted one guard. Your refusal to participate will be considered a formal declaration of war.

Queen Luxor of the Water Fae

Izzie read the letter over several times. There wasn't much she could take away from it. It was Lulu... no, *Luxor's* handwriting, so she had no doubt as to the authenticity.

"How long did the messenger take to get here?"

"Ten days. We have thirty days until the summit."

"Have you given this to Donrel yet?"

"Of course not. I couldn't ruin his wedding. I knew it could wait one more day."

"Do you think she's serious about peace?"

He shook his head. "I'm truly not sure. Certainly not if I'm there. I don't know if she knows I'm still alive, but you obviously can't mention your relationship with me. I killed her husband."

Izzie grimaced at that, but she had meant what she said. He was forgiven, and she wouldn't hold his past against him any longer. She wasn't even sure how Luxor felt about *her* at this point.

"I have to go."

"I know. Can we just have one night together before you do?"

Izzie grabbed his hand and led him back to her treehouse. *Their* treehouse. They'd spent many nights together over the years, but this was different. The love between them was palpable.

She went to slide her dress off, but he gently grabbed her hand.

"I want to commit this moment to my memory." He gazed at her from head to toe. "Do a twirl for me." He grinned.

Izzie spun, letting go of all her inhibitions.

"Wow," was all he said, and she could tell he meant it. She giggled and twirled again. Syrel imitated her movement, doing his own twirl, though it was much less impressive without a flowy dress. They both giggled, and their lips crashed into each other.

Their kissing escalated in passion.

"Okay," he whispered in her ear breathlessly. "Now it's time to get you out of that dress." He spun her around and started untying the strings in the back. The dress dropped a bit lower with every knot undone, and he kissed lower and lower along her back until the dress fell to the floor.

She turned back around to find all of Syrel's clothes were already missing and she laughed. "Hey! You didn't let me undress *you*!"

"I'm impatient."

"Oh? So you're done with the foreplay?"

He smiled broadly. "I've waited too long for this night." He ran his fingers through her tangled, sweaty hair.

"We've done this plenty of times," she huffed as his hands slid down her back.

"But now you're mine." He kissed her neck then slowly started to crouch down and brought his lips down to her navel. Before he could go any further, she grabbed his chin and pulled him up.

"And you're mine." She pushed him onto her bed. "And I can do anything I want with you." She jumped on top of him, straddling him. "Or to you." Neither of them slept that night, but they didn't feel tired. Finally, after far too long apart, they were together again. In body, mind, and soul. They didn't need vows to know that after that night, they were united together as one. Forever.

* * *

3 months before the Twelve Race War
Cico, Human Territory

Dalfa vomited into the grass. She looked up, thinking she could handle it, and then vomited again. She wiped her mouth with the sleeve of her robe.

"I'm so sorry. I didn't think I would have such an emotional reaction."

"It would be strange if you didn't, midwizard," Jilette said, pulling her by her sleeve away from the graveyard. Outside of Cico, gravestones were lined up in rows that seemed to go on forever. This was a cemetery reserved for human females who died during childbirth. Several mounds of fresh dirt circled the perimeter, indicating recent additions to the graveyard. Instead of leaving the graveyard, Jilette led her to a small garden near the entrance.

"I'm no longer a midwizard. And this is exactly why." She indicated the morbid scene.

"This is also the reason I've chosen to remain childless, in spite of my wishes."

"I don't blame you. I've made the same decision myself."

"So tell me, Dalfa," Jilette said as she ripped a weed from the small patch of dirt. "Why are you here? Why did you request to see this place?"

"Because there's a better way."

"I assume you refer to Gravipar. Nobody knows more about it than the humans, I assure you. Our territory borders the Wasteland, and our females were the first to conceive and deliver there."

"Then you should know better than anybody how necessary this war is!"

"War is never necessary." She paused. "But my husband agrees with you."

"As much as I hate to ever admit this about a mele, he's right. Perhaps *necessary* is the wrong word. *Inevitable* is more like it."

Jilette grunted as she examined a beautiful black flower. "What about the fae's plan for peace?"

"A ruse." Dalfa dismissed the notion. "Imagine it, Jilette. All twelve races of Cosconia, living together peacefully. No more eclamptic seizures. No more frele graveyards. No more orphans. No more widowers."

"You make it seem like peace will come easily."

Dalfa shook her head. "It won't. I wish it would, but it won't." She knelt down next to Jilette, who continued to tend to her garden. Jilette plucked several healthy-looking branches from a flowering plant.

"Why did you do that?" Dalfa asked, already knowing the answer. Using the *abrido* spell to make the human more susceptible to her mind magic, she had set up this entire encounter. Humans with their simple minds responded very well to metaphor.

"For the hydrangea to flourish, it must be pruned to allow for new growth."

"Don't you want that for Cosconia?" Dalfa jumped on the metaphor. "The war will prune the evil from our land, those who can't accept racial harmony, leaving the rest of us to enjoy the benefits of Maternal Magic forever."

She only had one leader left to visit. The most important one. The way things were progressing, it seemed everybody would be content to just prepare for war and sit on their hands, waiting. But what was the point of that? That meant they weren't reaping the benefits of Gravipar, letting more freles and babies die. Dalfa couldn't sit by and watch that happen any longer.

This war needed an inciting event. A catalyst. A way to light a fire under the generals. *A villain.* Dalfa swallowed guiltily. She knew the next step would cost lives. But what were a few lives in the face of eventual peace and harmony in Gravipar? It was time to finally test out the *mentopo* spell.

CHAPTER TWENTY-TWO

A Bid for Peace

Only the dead have seen the end of war.

—*George Santayana*

Day 1 of the Twelve Race War
Gravipar, the Wasteland

Izzie looked up at the tree towering above the gathered leaders who sat in a tentative peace. The Mother Tree had to be at least a hundred feet tall, and by all reports it was growing at an unprecedented rate. The tree was in the middle of a circular plot of land, about a mile in diameter, surrounded by a dry moat. All the temporary settlements had been cleared out by dwarven mining teams. Izzie, Donrel, Werna, and Anaro, who was appointed as Izzie's bodyguard for this meeting, had crossed a long bridge to get to the "island," which wasn't really an island since it wasn't surrounded by water—yet. There were four bridges, seemingly in each of the cardinal directions. Izzie had surmised the plan for this plot of land after she'd seen a massive tunnel at the bottom of the east side of the dry moat. That must have been where the dwarves were tunneling toward the Cosc

River. Once they broke through, water would rush from the distant river through the underground tunnel and fill in the circular channel around Gravipar. She figured the moat was about as deep as the tree was tall. She still had no sense of how close they were to bringing water to this area, and it sounded like nobody else did either.

Izzie could see multiple armies gathered in the distance. Some of them, like the giants, were easy to see. Others, like the halflings, she could barely make out. The crowd of leaders, each with their singular guard, turned as a loud grunt came from the east side of the island. A pair of dwarves, covered in grime and dust, climbed out of the dry moat and ambled over to the waiting summit. They must have just come from the tunnel Izzie had seen on the way in. That would be everybody. She knew the blood sprites would not be in attendance, and the mermaids wouldn't be able to survive on dry land, especially here in the Wasteland. Queen Luxor would likely be speaking on their behalf, assuming their alliance still stood.

Each of the gathered leaders kept a healthy distance from one another. Nobody made any aggressive movements, but everybody was on their guard.

Queen Luxor whispered into a bubble, used her water magic to send it toward her camp, and began speaking. Izzie still thought she was gorgeous, but her left cheek was completely disfigured by what looked like a terrible burn. Izzie felt nauseated as she realized it was likely from her husband exploding right in front of her. The skin was raw and red. It looked exquisitely painful.

"Thank you all for responding to my invitation. I think you know why we're here. This land, Gravipar as it seems to have been named, grants fertility and protection to pregnant freles and newborns. Birth rates among the small groups who have lived here show near negligible rates of maternal or newborn losses. Conversely, Cosconian freles, mermen, and their babies are dying at unprecedented rates everywhere else. We all desire the same thing—protection for the futures of our races. A war would compromise that very goal, which is why I hope to propose a peace treaty. I'd like to start with introductions. As you likely know, I am Queen Luxor of the water fae, and this is my son Doren. He is also here representing the merfolk, with whom the fae have a formal alliance."

Izzie looked at the young fae who carried her name. Her quick math revealed he'd be about thirty-six by now. Had it really been that long since the disastrous coronation and wedding? Since Syrel killed the boy's father? He had his father's dark skin tone, looking much more like Thelonius than his fair-skinned mother. His hair hung in long dreads down his back.

Kurai stood to her left. Her throat filled with bile at the sight of him. She thought back to the torture she'd endured at his hands. The years forced to work against her will. Even though she'd mostly processed the traumatic time in the years since her escape, seeing him here brought back many unpleasant memories. The scars on her back burned at the sight of him.

"Oi, the name's Kurai. Supreme orc war chieftain. Good to see some familiar faces." He tilted his head toward Izzie, a crooked grin across his face. She shuddered internally, but kept her stony visage. She wouldn't give him the satisfaction of seeing how afraid she was. A lyonium chain dangled from his belt, stained with blood. *Her blood.*

A few yards away from Kurai was the largest giantess she'd ever seen. She towered over her companion. She had to be thirty-five, maybe forty feet tall. The giant she'd brought with her was at least ten feet shorter.

Her voice rumbled the ground. "I am Skygyr, leader of the rock giants of the Frost Mountains. I come seeking peace for my people and access to this holy land."

Holy Cect. Skygyr! Sydyr's daughter. The chosen one from the prophecy. The baby *she'd* delivered fifty years prior. The prophecy certainly wasn't wrong about how enormous she'd be. There was no way the giantess knew who she was, but she was extremely happy to see one of her first patients alive and well.

The introductions kept moving. The minotaurs were next. It had been quite a long time since she'd last seen a minotaur, and they were even more frightening than she remembered. The one who spoke had a humanoid body with thick black hair matted over rippling muscles. The only clothing he wore was a loincloth wrapped around his waist. He loomed large over the halfling a few yards away, and she estimated he was at least nine feet tall. A bright golden ring was looped through his nose, and his curved horns were wider than her arm span. They looked like they'd been filed to sharp points. Though she hadn't had a chance to work with them in a midwizarding capacity, she knew why they were here. Minotaur babies relied on their mothers' milk to sustain them for years, but in Cosconia, breastfeeding was wildly difficult for minotaur mothers. When their milk dried up, their babies would starve. They would love to occupy this land as much as anybody else.

"I am Labrite, herd leader. This is the leader of my army, Vido. We do not desire bloodshed, but we will not be made fools of. We will lay our rightful claim to this land."

Izzie could feel the tension building with each subsequent introduction. Next were the halflings, who she was surprised to even see here, but she supposed they would likely have the advantage of numbers. Halflings produced multiple babies at once, referred to as a litter. It wasn't uncommon for a halfling to have triplets or even quadruplets. Unfortunately, the more babies inside at one time, the more dangerous it was. Eventually, the halfling frele's body couldn't take the pressure and weight of all the babies inside her, and it would lead to her demise.

A squeaky voice spoke next. "I'm Hortho, and this is my brother Portho. We are peaceful folk, but we can't keep watching our freles die. We are small, but we are mighty."

Izzie introduced herself next. "My name is Isadore. I am a midwizard, but I am not here on behalf of wizardkind."

Queen Luxor interjected. "The wizards have rejected my invitation to the peace summit, but they have also stated they will not lay claim to Gravipar."

Izzie nodded succinctly. *How does Queen Luxor know more about the wizard community than I do? I guess maybe I am kind of here on behalf of wizardkind.* She wondered where Dalfa, the only other wizard with as much interest in Gravipar as her, was. Knowing how intelligent her former friend was, Izzie worried she was working toward her own goals in the background. "I am here as a healer to facilitate peace."

Kurai looked at her hungrily, and Queen Luxor had the appearance of what looked like pity on her face. Donrel introduced himself and Werna next, but he purposely left out the fact that the captain of his guard was also his new husband. They hadn't even gotten to go on a honeymoon, having set off for this summit the day after their wedding.

The humans were next. A man with stunning skin the color of the moonless sky stood in metal armor. No other race had armor so extensive. Elves wore light leather armor, orcs wore practically nothing, and everybody else relied on their natural constitution, magic, or some mix of leather and metal armor to defend themselves. But humans, with their naturally weak bodies and lack of magical abilities, needed more.

"Thank you for gathering us here, Queen Luxor. I am Eko, leader of the humans of Cosconia. This is my wife and second-in-command, Jilette. We are very interested to hear your offering of peace. We have lived closer to the Wasteland than anybody, and we feel as if this territory rightfully belongs to us."

Following the human delegation were the changelings, both in their natural amorphous forms.

"I am King Mamut, Apex Changeling and longtime ruler of Changeling Territory. This is my wife, Queen Luva, the only other Apex Changeling in Cosconia. We are no longer willing to sit back and watch the devastating loss of our next generation. If there can be no peace, there will be war." *Apparently they don't know about Pyke yet.*

Finally, they had come full circle to the dwarves who had appeared last. She recognized one of them, and she was surprised to see Lago's brother.

"I am Drago, a delegate of our leader, who couldn't be here today as he is working hard on finishing the channel to bring water to the Wasteland. As you may have surmised by now, the dwarves have also entered into a formal alliance with the fae and merfolk, so we hope you'll hear our plea for peace." Interestingly, he didn't introduce his companion, a mele dwarf who looked similar to Lago, with bright red hair and beard.

That concluded the introductions. During a brief silence, Queen Luxor quietly colluded with her son. Izzie had no idea what would happen next. They all seemed to be looking to the queen, waiting for her next words. What she was about to say could be the difference between lasting peace and imminent war. Between harmonious coexistence and tragic bloodshed. Between life and death.

Izzie felt a rumble underneath her feet. She looked around, and after a moment, it seemed others noticed it too. In an explosion of sound, water rushed through the tunnel Drago and his companion had recently emerged from. Though she couldn't see the water yet, she could hear it rapidly filling the circular moat. That answered her previous question on how close they were to bringing water to Gravipar.

At the sound of water, the dwarves looked horrified. "What have you done?" Drago asked, aghast. "Our people were still in there! There must have been thousands of dwarves in that tunnel!"

Queen Luxor spoke, her voice suddenly sounding strange and twisted. But also oddly familiar. "Our alliance with the dwarves has officially ended." She addressed Drago directly. "Thank you for your help; we couldn't have tunneled from the Cosc without your hard work."

She turned to face the rest of the gathered leaders, all of whom appeared too stunned to speak. Even Kurai, brutal as he was, looked surprised.

"Consider this my formal claim on Gravipar as official property of the water fae." Izzie watched as the water rose higher in the moat. Mermaid warriors began appearing at the surface, tridents held high out of the water. "We have this island surrounded. I will grant safe passage to anybody who wants to leave. Take your army and go home. Just in case you think about trying anything cute—" Queen Luxor gestured to the water, which was now reaching the brim of the moat. A dorsal fin the size of a minotaur emerged from the water. There was a thick rope around the fin, a merman on either side holding each end.

"This is Lursa. She will kill anybody who threatens me. If you try to return to Gravipar, you will meet the same fate as the dwarves."

Suddenly, a flurry of activity erupted. First, the changeling queen morphed into a familiar water fae. *Pyke.* She produced a dagger from behind her back and slit King Mamut's throat, killing him instantly. Somehow even more shocking than the assassination of the changeling leader, the two minotaurs got down onto all fours so the two halfling brothers could hop onto their backs, and the four of them charged toward the closest bridge. Kurai, taking advantage of the commotion, sprinted toward Izzie.

"Time to reclaim my prize," he growled. Before she had a chance to react, Syrel appeared out of nowhere.

"You!" Queen Luxor shouted, voice returning to normal, pointing at Syrel. "You were supposed to be down there!" He pulled Izzie, Donrel, and Werna into an embrace, and with a crack, they apparated away from the island.

In an instant, the two wizards and two elves appeared back in the elven encampment, several miles away from the island. Donrel swiveled his head around and realized his captain was missing.

"Anaro!" he screamed. "We have to go back for her!"

Syrel just shook his head. "I'm sorry, Donrel. Luxor will kill me. It's probably too late for her anyway."

"I'm not leaving her behind!" Donrel gritted his teeth and began to run back toward the island, but Werna grabbed his collar and pulled him back. "No way, babe. It's going to be a bloodbath."

They could only make out a few vague shapes underneath the massive tree. The two giants, still visible from this distance, ran in lumbering steps toward the edge of the island and leapt over the moat. Skygyr, considerably larger than her companion, cleared the moat and landed with a thud that made the ground rumble beneath their feet. She kept running north without looking back. The other giant landed in the water with a splash. They could make out the large shape flailing toward the shore, but from their vantage, they could tell he was doomed. A colossal fin briefly emerged from the water, then disappeared. A second later, the giant disappeared under the water, which immediately turned red with blood.

So this was it. War had arrived. Already there were shocking betrayals and alliances. Queen Luxor had casually slaughtered thousands of dwarves. The halflings and minotaurs must have had a prearranged alliance. She knew minotaurs considered it a grave dishonor to be mounted, so allowing this signified they were taking the war very seriously. There were still no blood sprites, for which Izzie was thankful.

Donrel was softly weeping over the loss of his friend and captain. Syrel intertwined his fingers with Izzie's as they gazed at the island in the distance. Before Izzie could ask how he'd gotten there to save them, he spoke first.

"Pyke was there," he stated simply.

"She took the appearance of the changeling queen, so I suspect Luva was her first victim. I suppose she's the de facto leader of the changelings now. She's probably the only Apex Changeling left in Cosconia."

"There has to be another one out there," Syrel responded confidently.

"How do you know?"

"Just a gut feeling, I guess."

"How did you get to the island anyway? Did you know what was going to happen?"

"You can never be too cautious."

"Also—since when can you apparate? I thought you could only do that with a spatial Affinity!"

"I've been working on my apparition Skill for years. It was never good enough to be practical, but I guess I just needed the right Intent. I don't know if I can do it again without burning out. What do we do now?"

"I'm not a warrior, Syrel. I made a promise I wasn't going to be responsible for anybody else losing their life, and I'm not going to break that promise. So I'll keep doing what I've been doing: healing. And I'm not going to discriminate. I will heal anybody who needs it."

"Then I'm helping you."

"What do you mean? You're not going to fight?"

"If you're going to be wandering around dangerous battlefields trying to heal the injured, you're going to need somebody to protect you."

CHAPTER TWENTY-THREE

Becoming the Monster

Because not all monsters were monsters in the beginning. Some are monsters born of sorrow. Because not all monsters look like monsters. There are some that carry their monstrosity inside.

—Fredrik Backman

---

36 years before the Twelve Race War
Pwise, Water Fae Territory

"By the power vested in me by... well, me, I now pronounce you King Thelonius and Queen Luxor. Husband and wife. You may now kiss the bride!"

It was her favorite feeling in the world. His strong arms wrapped around her waist, pulling her into a sloppy kiss. She squeezed her eyes shut and leaned further into Thelonius, the world around her fading away. Lulu could barely hear the crowd going ballistic, so lost was she in the embrace of her lover. She peeked one eye open to see explosions of deeply hued water exploding in every direction.

This is it, she realized. *This is the best moment of my life. It can't get any better than this.* She had heard countless people say their wedding was the best day of their lives, but she always thought it was orc shit. Even her mother, who she'd never heard say a kind thing, looked back fondly on her own wedding. There were so many details to plan, decisions to make, people to invite. What would they eat? What kind of music did she want? Should she invite Uncle Noj even though she knew he'd get too drunk and make a scene?

None of that mattered as her lips locked with her groom's. Too many years she'd spent away from him, though they were productive years. She felt proud of herself for the tentative peace agreement she'd brokered with the mermaids. She had made new friends, Izzie and Pyke, who were sitting in the front row. They were two of the most incredible people she'd ever met. She had a sense these were friendships that would stand the test of time. And if she was being honest with herself, having a few years away from her mother's manipulative cruelty had been a nice break.

But Thelonius was her soulmate. She couldn't bear the thought of spending another moment without him. They were able to pick up where they'd left off without a hiccup. His devotion to her was unwavering. His gentle kindness reminded her of her father in the best possible way, which made sense given the decades of service Thelonius had dedicated to the king. Even her long fae lifespan wouldn't be enough time to spend with him.

And now they were *parents*. They had brought *life* into this world. Even though it was custom, she hated that just a few short hours after delivering Doren, named after the midwizard who had made all of this possible, she had to leave him behind for the wedding and coronation. Maybe she'd change that when she was queen. It was also completely unfair because she wouldn't even be able to drink that night lest she get Doren drunk with her milk. She and Thelonius had an abundance of big changes they planned to institute, to not only better their own race but also improve relationships between the races like she had with the merfolk. They would raise their son to be kind yet strong, gentle yet passionate, relaxed yet ambitious.

Their kiss lingered on as all her plans for the future ran through her head. Lulu knew that night would be filled with drunken debauchery for all present, but after the official ceremony was over, she was going to slip out, hand in hand with her dream mele, and retire back to the Palace with her son. As the cheers continued in the background, she thought about what a great father Thelonius was going to be. She knew his quiet dedication to her father would be replicated tenfold for their son. He talked every day about teaching him to swim, helping him learn water magic, and showing him the world. Even though *she* was Doren's mother, Thelonius would absolutely be the more nurturing one. And that was what she loved about him.

The newly crowned Queen Luxor finally pulled her mouth off her new husband's, though she could have spent all night kissing him, crowd be damned. She looked deeply into his soft, dark eyes. She grabbed his hands, ready to lift them in the air and turn to the crowd in celebration when her mother exploded into a mess of steam and gore.

Lulu turned toward where her mother had stood a second before and blinked several times, unsure what she was seeing. Was this some sort of sick joke? A nightmare, where the best day of her life turned into the worst one? Screams broke out all around her, but she was still trying to process what she was seeing. None of this made any sense. Who would be attacking her wedding? Her ears were ringing from the explosion. She couldn't hear anything.

She turned back to her husband, sure he would know exactly what to do. He was the captain of the king's guard, after all. Protection was his job. She was able to look into his eyes for a fraction of a second before he stepped in front of her. Then he was gone. She still couldn't hear anything as he silently exploded. Boiling blood and flesh plastered her left cheek, and she silently screamed as she dropped to her knees. She couldn't make sense of anything going on around her. A water bubble appeared around the stage, though she had no idea how.

Lulu looked at the pile of melted flesh that used to be her husband. Her face felt like it was on fire. She could feel skin and blood dripping off it. She was covered in pieces of her husband. Of Doren's father. He would now grow up without a dad. She would be a single mother, trying to run the kingdom and her own house without Thelonius by her side.

Lulu could sense commotion all around her. Somebody was shouting commands. Just as she was about to join the defense, she looked at the disfigured mess of the beautiful mele she was to spend the rest of her life with. Emotion overwhelmed her. She collapsed in a pile, draped over her late husband. Her surroundings faded.

An air bubble appeared around her head, further detaching her from the disaster. She didn't know how it got there, but she didn't care. She was lost in her grief as she lay across the ruins of Thelonius's body, still hot from the spell that took his life. Tears stung her eyes. She felt like the nightmare would never end. Her mother and husband, murdered on the day of her coronation. Her son's birthday.

This heinous act would not go unpunished. Somebody was going to pay. Lulu finally brought herself to pop the air bubble around her head and looked up and to observe what was happening around her. *Whoever did this is going to regret it. They are going to regret the day they were born. They are going to regret* ever *messing with me and my family.* There was a hooded figure trapped in a block of ice on the platform. She couldn't make out who it was. Before she could investigate further, a mountain rose out of the water next to them. Except the mountain... had a head? A giant? Here in Pwise?

And then it clicked. Pyke. Who else could take the form of a giant?

Lulu felt her insides turn to jelly as a booming voice thundered from the giantess, who grabbed the wizard frozen in a block of ice. *How did he get in there?* she wondered.

"LEAVE. ME. AND. MY. BABY. ALONE!" And then something else clicked—it was Pyke's baby daddy. Nesbreth. She knew Pyke was on the run from an evil, powerful wizard, but Lulu had never expected him to attack her here, while she was under fae protection.

Just before the changeling threw the wizard toward the Wasteland, Lulu heard Izzie say something. A name. Syrel. *Why did that name sound familiar?* She shook herself out of the daze she'd been in since Thelonius was killed. Pyke had dropped into the water, unconscious, and Lulu shouted an order for one of her guards to retrieve her body. She was done being the sweet Princess Lulu. It was time for her to be Queen Luxor. Her cheek was screaming in pain, but there was no time for weakness.

"Isadore, you and Pyke have to leave. For your safety and ours. I think that was Nesbreth." She looked to Pyke for confirmation, but the changeling was unconscious. Izzie, usually completely composed, was nonverbal. Her eyes were fixated on Queen Luxor's torched face. "I don't have to tell you how powerful he is. I'm sending you into Mermaid Territory. The merfolk are our sworn enemies, so you have to tell them you're seeking refuge from us—they have been known to assist our enemies in the past. Use the code word 'Lork.' My people thank both of you for saving our kingdom. Now please, you must go. Pwise will be going into full defense mode, and we'll keep most of the fae under the water or in the Palace." Queen Luxor hesitated, her grieving interior pushing through her queenly exterior. "I may have lost my husband, but I only had a husband in the first place because of you. Doren and I will see both of you again. I promise. Now go," the new water fae queen said before pushing them into the Cosc River.

It was a small gamble, but she suspected the duo would be taken to the mermaid leaders, who would know about the truce. She couldn't speak of the truce in front of her people yet. The hatred between their races ran deep. But nobody else would know about the city of Lork, the existence of which the merfolk guarded fiercely. After she'd sent her friends to safety, she dove into the water and made for the Palace. She needed her baby in her arms right then.

When she got there, she was relieved to see he was sleeping peacefully. She was worried part of this plot may have involved an invasion into the Palace, but it was too well protected. She squeezed him to her chest and broke down. Loud, heaving sobs escaped her chest. All of the plans she and Thelonius had had were gone. Doren would never know his father.

Over the next weeks, Queen Luxor replayed the events of her wedding day in her head. Over and over and over. One detail bothered her. What had Izzie said at the end? *Syrel?*

And then it struck her. Syrel. Izzie hadn't revealed too much of her past, especially her time before midwizardry school. But she did mention an ex, somebody she'd spent decades together with. The love of her life. The way she'd talked about him had made Queen Luxor assume he was dead, but that was clearly not the case. *Were they working together? Did Izzie orchestrate this whole plot?*

Years went by, and Queen Luxor couldn't uncover any more information about what had happened. She had confirmed with her contact, Baz, that Izzie and Pyke had successfully arrived in Lork. Unfortunately, after an attack by the monster that terrorized the city, Izzie had disappeared and Pyke had gone home. She hadn't heard from either of them, which practically hurt just as much as losing her husband. She had nobody left in this world. Except her son, who she kept close by her side at all times. He was never allowed to leave the Palace.

* * *

2 years before the Twelve Race War
Lork, Mermaid Territory

For the first time in years, Queen Luxor left the safety of Water Fae Territory. She reflected while she swam deep into the Cosc. Each year that went by, she became angrier. Colder. More jaded. More hateful. And Izzie and Syrel were the target of that rage.

The image of the two of them together was seared into her brain. She had convinced herself this had been their plot all along. For Izzie to find her in Ajabu, embed herself in her life, and eventually take her down. They had started with her husband and her mother, but they were sure to finish the job eventually. She knew exactly why. Izzie wanted her baby. The infertile midwizard talked constantly about her inability to have a baby. The coronation was probably all part of her plot with her boyfriend to steal the baby.

Though she had a kingdom to rule, all she could think about was taking down her husband's murderer. She was slowly passing off more and more royal duties to her son so she could focus on the task of finding and killing Syrel. And maybe Izzie. She hadn't decided on that one yet. He was growing into a wise and benevolent young fae, and eventually she would do away with the old fertility customs that ruled her people and pass off the mantle of leadership to him. Under her guidance, he had overseen the construction of the tunnel between the Cosc River and the newly named Gravipar. They would be heroes to all Cosconians, providing water to all in the fertile land. As long as everybody submitted to fae rule, her son would rule the new land with wisdom and grace. He would be the hero Cosconia needed, and finally the land would be united under one banner.

As she dreamed of the bright future, she arrived in Lork to visit an old friend. They had communicated via messenger over the years, and the changeling acted as a liaison between the water fae and the mermaids. The alliance was official now, but they weren't publicizing it.

The first thing Queen Luxor did after greeting Pyke was to ask for her version of the events of that fateful day she'd lost her mother and husband. Pyke explained that when Nesbreth arrived, she had felt her baby move for the first time and then gone into action mode. She told her how she hoped tossing him halfway across Cosconia had killed him. Queen Luxor doubted that. She told her about Izzie stopping her preterm labor on the way here, to Lork.

"Did she happen to mention she already knew your ex when he arrived?"

Pyke looked confused. "No? How would she have known him?"

"Do you remember her talking about her ex, Syrel? The one who died? The one who she was still in love with?"

"Yes..." Pyke answered hesitantly.

"Nesbreth is Syrel. Syrel is Nesbreth. They were working together all along. She was lying to you when she said she didn't know him. She never told you that, did she?"

Queen Luxor could see Pyke was at a loss for words, which was exactly her goal. She needed the powerful changeling to be unequivocally on her side for this next part.

"I assume you're aware there's a war brewing above the water? For the Wasteland?"

Pyke nodded, but before she could respond, a merman rushed up and started swimming around Pyke.

"Mom! Who's your new friend?"

"Capino, this is Queen Luxor, leader of the fae, forger of the Water Alliance, and one of my oldest friends."

"Hi, mom's friend! I'm Cap!" The small changeling merman morphed into a water fae and continued swimming in circles.

"It's great to meet you, Capino."

"Bye, Mom! Bye, Queen!" He swam off, leaving both mothers smiling in his wake.

"He seems like he really keeps your hands full! How old is he now?"

"He's thirty, but he still seems so young. Can you believe I was pregnant for almost four more years after I left Pwise?"

"Honestly, no. I can't imagine being pregnant that long. Sounds terrible."

Pyke laughed, happy to be with her old friend again. "It *was* terrible!"

"How many forms does he have now?" she asked conspiratorially.

Pyke looked around to make sure nobody was listening and lowered her voice. "All of them. We tested it on dry land. He was born an Apex Changeling."

"I've never heard of such a thing."

"Me neither. He might be the most powerful changeling ever born. Don't tell anybody about it. We've been hiding out here in Mermaid Territory since shortly after he was born."

"Of course. Your secrets are always safe with me."

"How is Doren?"

"He's wonderful. He has been training under our greatest military minds, and he's currently overseeing the construction of a tunnel between the Cosc River and Gravipar. You'll have to come visit soon. He looks just like his father."

"I'm sor—" Pyke started, but Queen Luxor cut her off.

"No, don't be sorry. You were the victim. But we're both mothers now, Pyke, and we have to protect our children. At all costs. Do you agree?"

"... Of course," Pyke responded hesitantly.

"They're going to come for you. That was their plan all along. Izzie and Syrel could never have children of their own, so they're going to take ours. We have to ensure that never happens. Are you willing to do whatever it takes?"

Pyke looked in the direction her son had just swum off in. She hesitated again, but came around. "Yes."

"Good. I have a plan to peacefully settle Gravipar and get our revenge at the same time."

* * *

41 days before the Twelve Race War
Pwise, Water Fae Territory

"Once the other races have accepted my peace agreement, the water fae will rule Gravipar and I'll be able to protect all my citizens from the type of evil that killed my husband," Queen Luxor told the wizard visitor.

"I was very sorry to hear about your loss. Izzie wrote to me about it," Dalfa responded with sympathy.

"Do not say her name in my presence. She and her deranged lover are the ones who killed my sweet Thelonius and tried to steal my baby."

Queen Luxor rarely mentioned the murder of her mother in the same breath as her husband, as the cruel frele had deserved her fate, unlike the beautiful and kind Thelonius. She sensed skepticism in the wizard's expression, but she didn't care.

"What if I told you I had a way to avenge your husband?"

Queen Luxor had not expected that. She had heard about the former midwizard's visits to other leaders. She claimed war was the only way to save Cosconia. It was nonsensical. Now that the merfolk and the dwarves were on her side, not to mention Lursa, she led the largest multiracial coalition since the anti-changeling alliance during the Great Divide. The other races would accept her peace treaty, or she would force them to. There would be no need for war.

Once peace was instituted and Gravipar was hers to rule, she would have two main priorities. The first would be to peacefully distribute access to Gravipar, with the fae obviously having priority. The second would be to use every resource at her disposal to destroy Syrel. For years, she'd had spies and secret agents searching for him with no success. All her reports indicated he was wily, elusive, and most of all, dangerous. If this wizard had a way to take care of him...

"If it were that easy, I would have done it long ago. How do you plan to kill Syrel?"

The wizard explained her plan, and Queen Luxor listened intently. It made sense, as long as Dalfa was able to do what she claimed she could.

"How do you know you can get him there?"

The wizard tapped her temple. "I have my ways."

I believe you can do what you say you can do, was Lulu's next thought.

"I believe you can do what you say you can do," she said automatically.

"Thank you for your trust in me, Queen."

"And you're sure the tunnel will be empty?"

"Absolutely certain."

"I'll think about it." Queen Luxor wasn't sure how to feel about the wizard's plan. If she really *could* get Syrel into the tunnel, it would be easy. She had to fill the tunnel to isolate Gravipar and put her peace treaty into action.

"*Mentopo.*" A word from the wizard shook Queen Luxor from her thoughts. Out of nowhere, she had a terrible headache.

"What was that?" Queen Luxor asked, squinting from the pain in her head.

"Oh, nothing. Thank you for meeting with me." Dalfa left.

* * *

Day 1 of the Twelve Race War
Gravipar, the Wasteland

Queen Luxor examined the individuals standing around the circle. Izzie was here, but the fae tried to maintain her regal demeanor, not wanting the wizard to have the satisfaction of seeing the pain she was feeling. The pain *she* had caused. The queen couldn't even bring herself to feel bad that her former friend was about to lose her partner. She would still never even feel a fraction of the pain the two of them had caused by murdering Thelonius.

All Luxor had to do was propose her peace agreement. It involved compromises from all sides, but now that she already had the dwarves and the mermaids on her side, it should be easy to get everybody else to agree. Everybody showing up for a peace summit was a good sign.

Drago and a dwarf she didn't recognize climbed out of the dry moat and onto the island. They joined the circle to represent the tenth and final race at the peace summit. *They must have been the last of the dwarves in the tunnel.*

She whispered into a water bubble, giving the signal to flood the tunnel and finish Syrel off once and for all. She introduced herself and called for the rest of those gathered to do the same. One by one, they went around the circle and introduced themselves. It felt like they were in elementary school. Once the dwarves had finished saying their piece, silence filled the air.

She leaned over to whisper to her son. She felt a strange rumble underneath her feet and knew that would be the tunnel filling up. She took a sick satisfaction in knowing Syrel was currently taking his last breath.

"I love you, Doren. This is the start of a new chapter for Cosconia. For us. Instead of war, there will be peace, and we will reign over Gravipar with benevolence." Before she could address the crowd once again, an evil presence overwhelmed her. She couldn't think. She couldn't speak. She tried to fight against it, but whatever it was had burrowed so deep inside her brain she could no longer control it. The sound of rushing water was the last thing she remembered.

CHAPTER TWENTY-FOUR

The War Begins

War is what happens when language fails.

—Margaret Atwood

Day 2 of the Twelve Race War
Elven Encampment

After the failed peace summit, it took everybody a day to recover from the shock of what had just happened. The wholesale slaughter of the very dwarves who had made life in the Wasteland possible with their tunneling was a brutal declaration of war nobody had been prepared for. They all knew it would be a bloody affair, but wiping out thousands of lives with the snap of a finger was particularly bleak.

The sun still hadn't crested on the horizon, but the brutal heat of the day was starting to set in as the elven encampment stirred. Donrel had already set out to conspire with their neighbors to the south, the humans. The two races had always maintained cordial relationships, and it appeared this war would be one of alliances. The halflings and the minotaurs, the water fae and the mermaids.

She lay on her back next to a sleeping Syrel. Their fingers were still intertwined, which was how they'd spent the entire night. Sleeping was one of Syrel's greatest skills, and he hadn't disappointed that night—on the cracked and barren dirt of the Wasteland, on the cusp of battle, he fell asleep the moment his eyes closed and didn't stir for the rest of the night. Izzie knew because she was awake nearly the entire time.

When daylight broke, Izzie woke him up by squeezing his hand and gently kissing his forehead. He smiled before his eyes opened, seeming to forget where they were.

"How do you do it?"

"How do I do what?" he mumbled sleepily.

"How do you sleep like a hibernating giant no matter where you are? Do you not remember where you are?"

He shrugged. "Sleep is my escape. It's the only place I can get away from my thoughts."

Izzie tried not to be jealous, since her sleep was frequently plagued with nightmares. Horrible dreams about miscarriages, infertility, magic rituals, and most recently, war. She knew he wasn't telling the full truth, as they'd discussed their shared penchant for vivid nightmares. She opened up her bag.

"I'll be honest, I for one did *not* see Lulu turning out to be the villain! Pyke... not so surprised."

"Can't you, like, see into the future? How did you not see this coming?" Syrel asked.

"No numbnuts, I can't see into the future—I'm just a bag! I'm more of an omniscient narrator who likes to break the fourth wall with pop culture references."

Izzie tried to resist engaging, but she couldn't do it. "Which wall? Where are the first three walls? What are you narrating?"

"Haven't you ever heard of suspension of disbelief, Iz?"

"Yes, every time I try to ask you where you come up with the crazy shit that you say all the time. Will I ever get any real answers out of you?"

"Maybe in the sequel!"

"Seq—y'know what, forget it. Syrel, what did you call those farseeing thingies you invented?" In his free time, Syrel was always tinkering, trying to come up with the next big technological advancement. A few years back, he'd come up with an enchantment to put on a crystal that granted the user the ability to see far-away objects, and he'd bound them together with iron so you could hold them up to your face. They were brilliant, but you couldn't use them for more than a few minutes without getting a splitting headache.

She looked to him for a response only to realize he'd fallen back asleep. *Brat.*

"Syrel! What are the farseeing crystals called?" She shook him awake again.

"Wh—huh? Testicles," he answered and rolled back over.

She flicked his ear as hard as she could. "You wanna try again?"

The bag answered before he could. "No that sounds right; let me find some testicles to put on your face."

That finally shook Syrel out of his sleepy daze. "Sorry. Spectacles. They're called spectacles."

"Hmmm… that sounds vaguely familiar. I've got a few pairs here, I'll just dump all of them out."

Before she could protest, "spectacles" started spitting out of the bag. The first pair was shaped like the numbers 2-0-0-0, with the middle zeroes being the eye holes. "Ah, Y2K! Now wasn't *that* a crazy year, but those aren't right." The next pair were pink with one blue crystal and one pink one. They looked somewhat like hands extending in either direction. "A little problematic, and still not correct... Here they are!" Baggie Smalls shot out a pair of glasses without any crystal, just what looked like two fuzzy caterpillars on top of the eye holes and a gigantic fake nose. She glared at the bag, still very unsure if it was actually able to see her. Syrel was cracking up at the pile of crazy spectacles sitting on the ground. Finally, it produced the much cruder looking spectacles Syrel had created.

By this time, the sun was starting to illuminate the Wasteland. In spite of the circumstances, it was beautiful. The sun reflected off the shimmering new moat the dwarves had paid for with their lives as the brisk night gave way to a pleasant morning. The effects of the Mother Tree had started to spread, and there were small blades of grass and tiny plants emerging from the cracks in the desert soil. Their camp was about half a mile back from the water, just out of water spear range. Izzie looked at the island through the spectacles, which revealed a flurry of activity. The water fae had already knocked down all the bridges, knowing they would be protected when they swam to their encampment on the other side. She could see the lifeless body of the changeling king Pyke had slain. An orc's body was being pushed into the moat, but she could tell, unfortunately, it wasn't Kurai. The humans must have also made it off the island somehow, since she didn't see any more bodies.

Water fae swarmed all over the island, erecting barricades at the edges, building temporary barracks, and entrenching themselves in the newly claimed Gravipar. She couldn't see Queen Luxor or her son, and she figured they were off the island in the water fae camp, out of the line of fire. *I still can't believe the Lulu I knew and loved would needlessly take so many innocent lives. Something doesn't add up.* Izzie's head was starting to ache, but before she put down the spectacles, she watched a massive boulder crush a water fae patrol standing at the edge of the island. Another one crashed into the water, sending up a tidal wave of water. Izzie set down the spectacles and looked to the sky, where a rain of boulders came from the north. The giants.

The island turned into chaos. Wooden shacks exploded into splinters. Blue blood burst forth from the water fae crushed underneath stones larger than they were. Izzie could hear the shrieks of panic as they responded to the assault. The fae would learn a hard lesson that day—being in the middle of all your enemies was the worst spot on the battlefield, no matter how well you thought you were protected. Some of the fae tried to use their water magic to erect water barriers around the island, but the barrage of boulders kept coming, blitzing right through the walls of water. The few remaining living fae began diving into the water, abandoning their posts. Within a few minutes of the assault starting, it was over. The island was empty, boulders and debris strewn throughout. She knew the giants wouldn't run out of projectiles, as the rocky Wasteland was full of them.

Izzie had worried the Mother Tree would sustain damage during the assault, but it had almost seemed to repel the projectiles. She wasn't sure if that was her imagination, or if the tree had more magical properties than granting fertility to the land.

An idea occurred to Izzie as she stared at the empty island.

"Syrel! Can you apparate me to the giant's camp? Like right now?"

He shook his head sadly. "I wish. Apparition takes a lot out of me since I lack any sort of spatial Affinity. Just doing it once brings me to the edge of burnout."

"Damn it," she cursed. "We have to find Smise." She knew the logistics coordinator for Donrel's army would be the elf for the job. She grabbed Syrel's hand and started to make her way through the camp. Before she could reach the captain's quarters, a voice behind her brought her to a dead stop.

"Izzie, how can we help?"

She whirled around to see a dwarf standing in front of a tent, wearing leather armor three times too big for her. Izzie swore.

"Lago? What the hells are you doing here?! This is an active battlefront!"

She didn't look ashamed for a moment. "I've been watching you heal people for years. I want to help."

"You can't help!" Izzie practically spat. "You don't have blood magic. This place is dangerous. You have to go home, Lago."

The dwarf's expression was steely. "And how do you propose I do *that*? Wander through the Wasteland and hope I don't get murdered like the rest of my people?" Izzie winced. Obviously the frele had heard about what happened. "I've been working with you for years, and nobody is better at healing than you. You know I'm the best nurse in Cosconia."

"You're the only nurse in Cosconia, but I think you'd be the best even if you weren't!" Baggie said.

Why is that damned thing a bully to everybody except Lago?

"Okay," she relented. Lago was right. Though she didn't possess any healing magic, she was calm in a crisis and always extremely helpful to Izzie's healing efforts. "You're right. I could actually use your help. But not yet. I need you to stay in camp and lie low until I'm ready for you."

"And what about me?" Another voice came from the tent, and Arkan walked out. Izzie cursed again.

"Who the hells let you both come with?!"

They looked at each other conspiratorially. "You tell her!" they both whispered simultaneously.

"Tell me what?"

Arkan was the first to speak up. "We told the elves you said we needed to be here, and you demanded they escort us."

Before Izzie could explode at the mischievous pair, Syrel set his hand on her arm, ever the peacemaker.

"They just want to help, Iz. Can you blame them?"

She wanted to protest, but she couldn't. "Fine. But neither of you are to leave this camp until you have my explicit instructions. Promise?"

They both nodded vigorously.

"Wait a second," Izzie added, realizing something. "You didn't bring your children with you, did you?"

"Come on Izzie," Arkan laughed. "We're not crazy. Lorna is watching them."

"Good. I will see to it that both of you make it back to Mithor safe and sound. That's a promise." Izzie briefly considered not making promises she couldn't keep, but she would protect Lago and Arkan even if it cost her life. "But you have to listen to me from now on. I've gotta go, but remember—breaking a promise to a powerful blood wizard would not be wise," she threatened.

Syrel and Izzie continued making their way through camp, and Syrel burst out laughing once the dwarf and orc were out of earshot.

"Your threats are adorable, Isadore."

She scoffed. "I am very threatening! I could kill them with a thought!"

"Sure, and tomorrow Queen Luxor and I will get tea and eat some bonbons together."

"Sarcasm is the poor wizard's wit, Syrel."

"At least I'm *your* poor wizard." He kissed her, and the pair came to a stop when they arrived at Smise's tent. The guards immediately let them in. He looked up from the map he was drawing on the ground, but Izzie gestured for him to continue while she and Syrel listened in. She observed the map, which had a large circle in the middle, representing Gravipar. The elven scouts had run throughout the night to determine where each army was camped out.

They were currently located northeast of the island, while the orcs were their new neighbors to the west. Somewhere past the orcish encampment were the giants, which made sense to Izzie, since the onslaught of boulders had come from the north of the island. The entire western portion of the map was occupied by the changelings and water fae, and to the south of them were the minotaur and halfling armies. The dwarves were regrouping far to the south after the loss of such a large portion of their fighting force.

"Now that the island is empty, we will have to seize the opportunity to move our entire encampment as close to the channel as possible. We need access to fresh water—we only brought enough for a few weeks, and it's too far for a supply line," Smise stated, his voice slow but sure. "That will be our goal for the next week. After this morning's development, we should be able to make it pretty close without any fae on the island. We'll deal with the mermaids when we get there. I suspect the humans camped here"—he pointed to an area just south of their own encampment—"will join us in this endeavor if Donrel is able to formalize an alliance with them." For the next few minutes, his lieutenants asked logistics questions, and they broke the meeting with a solid plan for getting close to the water. Izzie wasn't sure how they would deal with the mermaid problem, much less the Lursa problem, but that wasn't her hill to die on.

"Isadore, Syrel," he greeted tersely. "Donrel isn't here right now. Is there anything I can help you with?" the ancient elf asked her, not even looking up from his map.

"I need you to get me to the giants' camp."

"Absolutely not," he said dismissively. "The only way there is through the heart of the orcish army. We can't take the risk."

"You have to. I need to get to that camp as soon as possible."

"Why? So you can get another one of our captains killed?" he snapped, finally turning to look at her.

Izzie had no response to this, but thankfully Syrel spoke in her defense. "That's not fair, sir. Izzie had nothing to do with that. The only one you should blame for that is Queen Luxor."

"Then can you leave me to my planning so I can figure out how to keep my army alive long enough to take her down?"

"Come on, Izzie. Let's leave the captain to his planning. He has important work to do." Syrel put his hand firmly on the small of her back and guided her out of the tent. "Don't mind him. He's just stressed out. Why don't we just wait for Donrel?"

And that's exactly what Izzie did. She sat in Donrel's tent until he returned from his parlay with the humans, which she assumed had gone well when he returned a few hours later with Eko, the human leader she'd first seen at the peace summit.

"Wow, that was a fast peace treaty," remarked Syrel.

Donrel slapped Eko on the back. "We go way back. We've been communicating back and forth for a few years, in anticipation of a situation exactly like this. He was already on his way here, and I intercepted him outside our camp."

The human leader nodded in agreement. His voice was as deep as a giant's, but much quieter than she expected from the muscled man. "We always expected we would have to defend ourselves from the orcs, but this is much more concerning. The fae are smart, and a partnership with the changelings *and* mermaids is deeply concerning."

"The changelings too?" Izzie asked, surprised.

"Your friend Pyke was clearly in on the plan to disrupt the peace treaty," Donrel responded. "Who do you think came up with that plan?"

Izzie supposed that was true, but it didn't seem quite so simple. She discussed her plan with Donrel and Eko and explained why she needed to get to the giants. To her surprise, they both agreed immediately.

"We will need to send you with protection, but a larger entourage is more likely to attract attention. I can send you with eight of my best elves."

"And I am willing to provide you with eight of my own soldiers, provided the humans can benefit from your idea."

"Absolutely," Izzie agreed quickly.

"You should go tonight. You might be able to sneak around the orcish army unnoticed."

"Thank you. Both of you. And Donrel? Can I ask you one more favor?"

Donrel gave her a wry smile. "Is it about the dwarf and the orc who managed to sneak into my army?"

Izzie laughed. "So you heard?"

"They're hard to miss. I will make sure they are protected."

* * *

Day 2 of the Twelve Race War
Water Fae Encampment

Queen Luxor opened her eyes and examined the space around her. She was inside a tent, her tent, lying on a soft sleeping pad. A familiar changeling sat by her side.

"Lulu? Are you awake?"

The fae queen tried to sit up but then groaned and plopped back down, attempting to lift her hand up to her aching head. She closed her eyes again.

"Get Doren!" the changeling shouted. "Tell him his mother is awake!"

She drifted off again, and this time when she awoke, Doren, Pyke, and several leaders of her army were present.

"Mom? Are you okay?"

This time, the pain in her head didn't keep her from sitting up, so she opened her eyes and tried to respond. "Wh... What happened? Did the peace summit work?"

"Peace?!" Pyke shouted. "You call that a *peace* summit? You... you monster!"

Doren set a hand on Pyke's amorphous arm. "Auntie Pyke. Please, calm down." He turned his attention to his mother. "Mom... what happened out there?"

Queen Luxor searched through her memory, but came up empty. Just staying upright and alert was painful, but she pushed through. "I don't remember much. I remember getting to the island. Introducing myself. Seeing that *bitch* Izzie. The dwarves arrived from the tunnels and I gave the order to flood the tunnel and kill Syrel."

"SYREL?! Syrel was on the island! Why would he have been in the tunnel?" Pyke screamed.

"That was the plan..." She trailed off, trying to focus but finding it increasingly difficult. "She said she would make sure Syrel was there and the tunnel was empty..."

"Who? Who said that, Mom?" her son asked gently.

"We had a plan. She was going to make sure Syrel was in the tunnel when I flooded it. She told me it would be empty." Queen Luxor's head throbbed. She just wanted to sleep. *Why was Pyke so angry?*

319

"And you trusted her?" Pyke said, her voice trembling with rage. "Why would you trust her?"

"I don't know..." She tried to remember what she was thinking, but her memory was fuzzy. "What's going on? Why is everybody so upset?"

"You really don't remember what you did, you lunatic?" Pyke shot off. "Seems pretty convenient if you ask me." This got her a glare from Doren, but he didn't say anything.

"Mom... the tunnel wasn't empty."

Though she barely remembered anything after giving the order to fill the tunnel, she vividly remembered seeing Syrel's face again. It was the first time she had come face to face with her husband's murderer since her coronation.

"Syrel wasn't there," she said airily. "Who was in the tunnel?"

Pyke looked at her skeptically. "You really don't remember?"

Queen Luxor shook her head.

"The dwarves who built the tunnel were still inside," Doren told her.

"That can't be. No... no, it's not possible. There had to have been hundreds of dwarves in that tunnel..."

"Thousands, more like it," Pyke spat. "What happened to our plan? We had a deal. I kill the changeling king and queen so I could take over the leadership of my people. Then I hand control of the army to you and I leave this godsforsaken Wasteland to be with my son."

"Thousands? No, that can't be right. I would never do that."

"Really? Never? Didn't you order me to kill Mamut and Luva? Aren't you actively plotting to kill Izzie and Nesbreth? Or Syrel or whatever the hells his name is. Why would I believe this isn't something you would do?"

"Pyke," Queen Luxor pleaded, tears streaming down her face. "Pyke, you know me."

"Consider our partnership terminated, you monster. The changelings want nothing to do with me *or* you, so good luck getting them on your side. I'm out of here." Pyke stormed off.

"Doren? Is it true? They're all dead?"

Her son nodded his head sadly. "What came over you? Was that part of your secret plan?"

"No!" she shouted, practically jumping off her sleeping pad, but then settling back in when her headache flared up. "No," she said more softly. "I just wanted to avenge your father. I don't feel like myself."

"What do you mean? Who else would you feel like?"

"I don't know..." She trailed off, noticing the movement of her captains. "Wait, what are you doing? What are they doing, Doren?"

Several fae warriors approached the queen with thick cords of rope.

"Stand down!" None of them slowed their approach. "I said stand down! Doren, order them to stand down!"

"I'm sorry, Mom. This is for your own good."

CHAPTER TWENTY-FIVE

A Misguided Attempt

Death begets death begets death.

—Pierce Brown

Day 2 of the Twelve Race War
Orcish Encampment

Izzie, Syrel, and their party had traveled on the outskirts of the orcish encampment through the entire night. It was nearly impossible to go around, as the camp abutted the Cosc River to the north, so the only two options were to go closer to Gravipar's channel or closer to the Cosc river, and they weren't willing to put themselves so close to the mermaids and Lursa.

The entourage, which consisted of the two wizards, eight elves, and eight humans, had been deadly silent throughout the night, using a combination of stealth spells from Syrel and Izzie. Originally, Donrel had insisted he and Werna accompany them, but Izzie had flat out refused the notion. They were both too important to put their lives at risk like this. They'd had some close calls with sentries during the night, but a few well-timed arrows through the brain or daggers from behind took care of them. They were making good time, but the first light of dawn was visible in the sky and they still hadn't cleared the massive orcish army. The movement of giants was visible in the distance, but they had a ways to go.

One of the humans stopped, putting her hand in the air, gesturing for the party to halt. There was a band of ten orcish sentries roaming through the tents and keeping guard. She motioned for her troops to sneak up behind them while the elves nocked their arrows. Syrel pulled his wand out, ready to cast a deadly spell if necessary.

As the leader of the band of humans dropped her hand, five orcs fell to daggers across the throat and four fell to arrows through the center of the skull. The final one turned toward them with an arrow sticking out of his left eyeball and shouted for a fraction of a second before four more arrows found his brain. But it was enough.

Their party broke into a sprint, torches lighting and swords being drawn all around them. Izzie estimated they were 500 yards from the edge of the orcish camp, with about half a mile between the orcish and giant encampments. It was too far.

"Izzie! Run!" the human woman shouted before literally losing her head. They had all been explicitly instructed that the mission was of utmost importance and they needed to get her to Skygyr. Still, it was yet another death on Izzie's conscience. She didn't look back. She knew that ultimately, this plan would save lives. Hundreds of them. But not before it cost a few more. Syrel and a few of the humans charged forward with her, while the elves took a defensive position and nocked arrow after arrow, downing as many of the orcs coming after them as possible. None of them would survive the onslaught. The humans at their sides swung their swords frantically, slaying the orcs standing in their way. But the commotion drew more and more orcs to their position, and eventually they had to stop running. They were surrounded.

Syrel whispered something to the human next to him and then lifted his wand as the orcs closed in on them.

"*Heparangra!*" he yelled, and Izzie didn't have time to cast her own defensive magic before she watched dozens of the orcs surrounding them start to bleed from their eyes, ears, and noses. She knew this blood thinner spell—it was used in the old days to make somebody "bleed out" a disease, though this practice had fallen out of favor. Izzie could probably use it to make any creature bleed out in an instant, but Syrel's control of blood magic Skill was far weaker than hers, not to mention his lack of Affinity. After the spell was cast, the remaining humans brandished their swords and started flailing them about wildly. Usually, it would take at least a few superficial sword hits to kill an orc. However, after Syrel's spell, all it took was a small cut, and the orcs around them collapsed, torrents of blood flowing out of them.

They took the opportunity to charge forward, several more of the humans falling in the melee. It was down to four of them. As she broke into the clearing, hot pain lanced across Izzie's thigh and she stumbled. Before she could even register what had happened, she was over Syrel's shoulder and they were moving again. She was now facing backward, and she watched another of their companions fall. There was no sign of the elves they'd left behind as a rear guard. Thankfully, the orcs didn't have many long range weapons, as the elven folk kept the secrets of fletching closely guarded.

"Go!" the remaining human, a small man with pale skin and dark hair, yelled. "I'll buy you some time!" She watched as he planted his feet in the ground and was quickly swarmed by the pursuing horde of orcs. As promised, they gained a few yards of distance. Izzie thought that at least she and Syrel would survive the encounter when she saw a wide figure emerge from the mass. Kurai.

She didn't expect the massive orc to be so fast, but he quickly outpaced his subordinates, eliminating the advantage the human had paid for with his life. His bloody axe was in his arms as he ran, and he looked her directly in the eye and smiled.

"SYREL! It's Kurai! Drop me and get out of here!"

He didn't respond, but she could feel his legs start to pump faster underneath her. She had no idea where he found the strength.

"Oi, mate, yer lady's got the right idea! I'm taking back what's rightfully mine!"

They slowed down, Syrel's energy starting to fade. The orcish chieftain was within striking distance now. He lifted his axe into the air, ready to bring it down on Izzie's head. Time seemed to crawl to a stop as the axe inched toward her. She wasn't ready to die. There'd been a time when she had embraced death, certain the world would be a better place without her. But this new idea could make up for all the lives lost on her account. There was nothing she could do to help herself, slung over Syrel's back as Kurai gained on them, inch by inch. His blade was a hand's breadth from her face.

Before she could squeeze her eyes shut and accept her fate, a shadow overtook them. A foot, larger than her torso, appeared and kicked Kurai right in the chest. She watched his limp body launch into the air, axe clattering to the ground. He flew through the air, tumbling head over heels, and landed a hundred feet behind them with a thud. Nobody could have survived that fall. *Right?*

Hundreds of giants thundered past, clubs brandished. Syrel kept running toward the giant encampment as the giant army charged the opposite direction, clashing directly with the pursuing orcish horde. Club met flesh as dozens of orcs went the way of Kurai and catapulted through the air from the overwhelming force of the giants' blows. Izzie looked on as some of the orcs turned back, but most of them shifted their focus to the oncoming giants.

Initially, it looked like the giants would slaughter the orcs without so much as a casualty. Orcs were crushed and trampled by the charging giants. Clubs swung to and fro, and it almost looked like it was raining orcs. Izzie felt a sick satisfaction in seeing the devastating slaughter of her former captors. Orcs died by the hundreds. After the attack on the water fae that morning, it seemed as if the giants were going to be a force to be reckoned with in this war, even if their numbers were much lower than the other races.

Their stony skin was naturally resistant to steel, but it could only take so much. The orcs kept coming, and eventually some of the giants started to be overwhelmed. Orcs jumped off the bodies of their dead compatriots, swords brandished, and were able to start landing blows on the vulnerable torsos of the giants. As was often the case in war, the orcs' greatest advantage was their numbers and their willingness to die for the cause. They swarmed the giants, enough of them avoiding the swinging clubs to pull the giants down to the ground, where they were quickly sliced to pieces. One by one, giants began to fall, the earth shaking when they collapsed.

Syrel had slowed to a crawl but was still moving forward. They had officially arrived in the giant encampment. She looked down and saw he was covered in blood, and she panicked, wondering if he'd been injured in the chase. Then she twisted around to look at the back of her leg, where she saw muscle and fat visible in a deep gash. *How much blood have I lost?* she mused as her vision faded to black.

* * *

Day 23 of the Twelve Race War
Giant Encampment

"You are the midwizard," a voice rumbled, rousing Izzie from her dreamless sleep. She tried to force her eyelids open, but they wouldn't move. Her tongue felt heavy, like a wet log inside her mouth. Her leg was on fire. She groaned loudly, trying to make her mouth move and failing miserably.

"Hwth hpd," she mumbled, the words not forming.

"You're okay, Iz," a familiar voice intoned. She felt a hand rest on her uninjured leg. "You're safe. You don't need to say anything. Just rest."

With great effort, she was able to crack open one eye. Syrel sat at her side, hand resting on her leg. He looked haggard. Above her loomed a large presence.

She tried again to speak, this time with more success. "What happened? Where am I?"

"You are in my personal quarters," the deep voice answered. Izzie lifted her head up to examine the giant standing over her. She had to crane her neck to see all the way to the crown of the head she'd delivered.

"You're Skygyr, right?"

"That is correct, midwizard. I understand this isn't the first time we're meeting, though I do not exactly remember the first one." A smile spread across her face, revealing a set of crooked teeth. "I grew up hearing stories about the midwizard who saved my life."

It was rare Izzie got to see the babies she delivered all grown up—even though this one was practically bigger than her the moment she was born. Izzie reflected on the role reversal: The baby she'd taken care of some fifty years before was now taking care of her. It was one of the unique moments when she got to see the long-term effects of her work.

If it weren't for her, Skygyr wouldn't be here, leading her people. From what she had heard over the years, she was a kind and benevolent leader who had ushered in a new era of prosperity and unity for giant-kind.

"Thank you for returning the favor, Skygyr."

"It was not I who saved you. It was him." The giantess pointed her muscled arm at Syrel.

"You healed me?"

"I learned from the best." He winked. "I'm just glad you're okay, my love." He kissed her forehead.

"How long was I out for?"

Syrel grimaced. "Three weeks."

"*Three weeks*?!" Izzie gasped. "Why was I out so long? What happened? Have there been any changes in the war? I must continue with my mission!"

"One thing at a time, Izzie. There's a lot you need to know. The orc weapons must be infused with lyonium, so the injuries they cause aren't responsive to blood magic. That's why it took so long to heal you."

"Lyonium weapons? They'll slaughter anybody they come across! The orcs will cut down every army in their path!"

Both the giantess and the wizard smiled.

"The orcs are not going to be a problem anymore."

"What do you mean?"

Syrel recounted what had happened while she was unconscious. "When the giants saw the orcs chasing us toward their encampment, they thought it was an attack on them, which was why they charged. If they hadn't, we would have never made it out of there alive."

"But before I passed out, it looked like the tide of the battle was shifting. I saw many of the giants start to fall."

Skygyr picked up where Syrel left off. "With their cursed weapons, they would have routed my army in a matter of days. But when the elves saw the orcs charging *toward* us, *away* from them, they immediately mobilized their troops to surprise the orcs from behind. They were caught between two armies and didn't stand a chance. The battle raged for days. Many fell. But by the end, the orcish army had to retreat across the Cosc back toward their territory. I don't know if they'll be back, but it will take them a long time to regroup. And I personally disabled their chieftain."

"That was you?!" Izzie asked, awe present in her voice.

The giantess nodded. "I was at the front of my army, leading my troops into battle. When I saw him chasing you two, I kicked him clear across the Wasteland."

Izzie was in shock. The orcs were already defeated? She knew it wasn't hard to kill an orc, but their numbers were staggering. *I suppose it would be tough for any army to survive being jammed between giants and elves.*

"So how did I survive when I got back here?"

"Your partner didn't leave your side for the entire time. He didn't eat or sleep for three weeks," Skygyr responded.

Syrel blushed. "That's not important. All I could do was stop you from bleeding out until the effects of the lyonium wore off. You'd lost so much blood by the time we arrived here I wasn't sure you were going to make it."

It was then Izzie noticed a long scar on Syrel's arm, similar to the one she had on hers, only much fresher. She examined his pallor closely, and he looked even more pale than she did.

"Did you get injured during our escape too?"

He chuckled nervously. "Uhhh... I had to try something desperate. You lost too much blood, and I could feel your life force fading. Your breathing was shallow, your skin was cold. I knew you needed more blood to survive. So..."

Izzie's eyes widened in horror. "You gave me your own blood? Is that possible? I've never heard of such a thing. You can't have somebody else's blood in your body!"

Syrel shrugged. "Apparently you can. It worked. I could see the color return to your skin immediately after I did it."

Izzie pondered on this concept. Transfusing your blood into somebody else who had lost too much? The possibilities... This opened up so many new doors. How many lives could she save in this war by transferring blood from somebody healthy to an injured warrior?

"Syrel, this might be the greatest medical advancement in history." She turned to Skygyr. With this development, the reason she had come here was even more important. "Skygyr, I need your help."

"I will do anything in my power to aid you, Isadore. Every year on my day of birth celebration, my aunts and uncles would tell the story of my birth. Uncle Grodge still sings your praises. You are a household name in Rotoplas. I wouldn't be here today if it weren't for you. I am just sorry my mother is not here to see it."

Izzie winced thinking about the first patient she'd ever personally lost. "I'm really sorry about your mother. She was as beautiful as she was kind. She would be so proud of you."

The giantess nodded her head, wistfully gazing into the distance. "It was necessary for the prophecy to be fulfilled. Tell me, what is it you desire?"

"Okay, so I had an idea after I watched the attack on the island of Gravipar. There's no way any race will be able to claim the land since it's right in the middle of all the armies, right? It's too susceptible to artillery attacks, like the barrage of boulders your army used to clear out the fae. But what if we used the land for all the sick and wounded during the war? It's centrally located, and we wouldn't discriminate against anybody. I could gather a team of healers to settle on the island and provide healing to all who need it, regardless of race." She gulped. "Even if an orc or a water fae or a changeling needs healing, we would provide it."

Skygyr pondered for a long moment. "And where do my army and I come in?"

"We need your protection. If our enemies know they will face a deadly barrage of boulders from the giants any time they try to attack the island, they might think twice before attacking. It's a risk, but one I think we need to take. It's the only way we might be able to curb the death toll of this war."

Again, Skygyr thought for a long time. "I've never heard of a war with healers who are willing to help their enemies. You'll forgive me if I'm skeptical of this plan. Besides, the bridges have been destroyed; how will you get there?"

Syrel chimed in at that. "Well, with the orcs defeated, at least for now, and an alliance between the humans, elves, and giants—"

Skygyr cut him off. "Alliance is a strong word, wizard. I will do anything in my power to protect Isadore, and by extension I will protect you, but the elves and humans are no friends of the giants. If they take over Gravipar, I do not believe they will welcome us with open arms into the fertile land." Izzie tried her best to hide her surprise at Skygyr's unwillingness to partner with the elves and humans, but she understood. The races of Cosconia had been divided for so long it was impossible to trust anybody.

"Fair enough," Syrel continued. "But would you at least allow us to build a bridge on the northeast side of the island so we can dedicate it to healing?"

"Let me confer with my generals."

* * *

Day 1 of the Twelve Race War
Wastetown, Northwest Wasteland

Dalfa barricaded herself in her room in the Wastetown inn. Her physical body would be completely vulnerable while she activated the *mentopo* spell, so she had to ensure she would be safe. She still felt conflicted about this part of her plan, but what were a few more deaths in the face of all she'd seen? She would bear a guilty conscience for the future of Cosconia. The gathered armies needed a catalyst to spur them into action. Watching Queen Luxor immediately betray her own peace treaty and kill the dwarves who'd built her tunnel was certain to do the job.

Without war there can be no peace, she told herself for the thousandth time. Cosconians were too stubborn, too hardheaded, and too divided to peacefully settle Gravipar. It would be useless to let Queen Luxor's plan for peace play out. Before long, somebody would break the treaty, which would mean even more delay until the freles of Cosconia were free to reap the benefits of the new source of Maternal Magic. The sooner the war started, the sooner it would end. The sooner it ended, the sooner it would be safe to get pregnant and have a baby in Cosconia. She penned a quick letter to Izzie and sent it off.

Dalfa closed her eyes and entered the Headspace. When she had discovered her mental Affinity as a kid—by accidentally hearing the thoughts of a girl she had a crush on—her father had taught her how to enter the Headspace. It wasn't a physical space, but rather the invisible plane that connected all sentient beings. She could envision the threads connecting her to hundreds of her fellow Cosconians, many of whom were gathered in Gravipar.

She followed several bright threads across the hundreds of miles between Wastetown and the Mother Tree to where the peace treaty was about to begin. A deep black thread, brighter than nearly all the other threads, indicating a strong bond, connected her to Kurai. She had gradually lost touch with the orc after she left Orc Territory, especially since so many of his letters seemed to ask more questions about Izzie than her. From what she'd heard, the kind soldier she knew had grown into a power hungry warlord. Though she didn't know if the future held a friendship for the two of them, his role in stoking the flames of war was essential.

The strongest thread, a deep crimson red, connected her to Izzie. In spite of their falling out, the connection remained strong. She mourned the loss of the friendship, but she couldn't make the frele understand *why* this war was necessary. Izzie was too idealistic for her own good.

Invoking the *mentopo* spell she'd previously cast on Queen Luxor, she was able to see through the fae's eyes. She cast her eyes around the circle as each of the leaders introduced themselves. Dalfa only had the Skill to take full control of the queen for a short time, so she had to time this perfectly. The risk of burnout with such a powerful spell was high, but it was a risk she was willing to take. Dalfa pushed all her Intent through the connection and spoke with Queen Luxor's mouth.

"Our alliance with the dwarves has officially ended." Dalfa pushed the words out forcefully. She turned Queen Luxor's head to address the dwarf, and even the simple movement felt like moving through sand. "Thank you for your help; we couldn't have tunneled from the Cosc without your hard work." She knew the false gratitude would infuriate those gathered.

Using Queen Luxor's senses, she could see the water rising in the moat. Time to make the fae queen the villain.

"Consider this my formal claim on Gravipar as official property of the water fae. We have this island surrounded. I will grant safe passage to anybody who wants to leave. Take your army and go home. Just in case you think about trying anything cute—" She lifted Queen Luxor's arm, further sapping her waning energy reserves. "This is Lursa. She will kill anybody who threatens me. If you try to return to Gravipar, you will meet the same fate as the dwarves."

The connection dropped. Pain and fevers racked her body. Her vision swam and her brain felt like it was mired in fog. She collapsed in exhaustion, having no idea what was happening in Gravipar.

CHAPTER TWENTY-SIX

The Beast Returns

---

*Consider the subtleness of the sea; how its most
dreaded creatures glide under water,
unapparent for the most part, and
treacherously hidden beneath the loveliest tints
of azure.*

—*Herman Melville*

Day 46 of the Twelve Race War
Elven Encampment

Izzie opened her bag, knowing it would be full of ideas. "What should I call this place where everybody brings their sick and injured to be healed? A Healorama?

"Dumb. How about the Dildo Emporium?"

"I'm not sure why, but I get the sense that's an inappropriate name. What about Izzie's Healing House?"

"Hmmm... seems a little self-centered. Didn't you already name that dwarf baby shit after yourself?"

"Fair point, but I don't hear you coming up with any better ideas!"

"Maybe the Slut Palace?"

"Okay I know what *that* means; now you're just messing with me."

"Fine, I was trolling you."

"There are no trolls in Cosconia."

"That's what you think. What about Herpes House?"

"I knew this was a bad idea. I'm closing you back up."

"Wait! What if we called it a hospital?"

"A hospital..." Izzie pondered. It was a completely nonsensical word, but for some reason... it seemed to fit. "Yeah. A hospital. I like it. We're building Cosconia's first *hospital*."

Izzie watched humans and giants carry boulders, logs, debris, broken shields, and anything else they could find across the bridge onto the island. Much of it was gear washed up from the dwarven mining expedition. Elves lined the banks of the channel, shooting arrows at any mermaids who dared to show their faces, which was becoming increasingly rare, as they seemed to have learned their lesson after the first few took arrows through the skull. Creatures who couldn't survive on land truly didn't stand a chance in this conflict. At first, fae had lined the opposite bank of the moat and shot a constant barrage of water spears across the island at anybody traversing the bridge, but the giants easily shook off the water, and the human's heavy armor made them resistant. After a short while, they'd retreated, leaving the three temporarily allied races to work in peace.

Izzie felt like everything was too easy. The water fae had left the island immediately after the giants' attack, and they'd barely done anything since. There had been a few minor skirmishes, but besides the battle between the giants, orcs, and elves, everything had been eerily quiet. Nobody knew where the blood sprites were. The orcs were apparently out of the war. Scouts reported the dwarves were still reeling from their losses, and the halflings and minotaurs hadn't engaged anybody in battle. Even the changeling army had been seen retreating further and further from Gravipar. *Even with everything being quiet, the death toll is still in the thousands. Am I so jaded that the deaths of so many living creatures don't faze me?*

Still, it didn't make sense. None of this made sense. Why wasn't Queen Luxor leading her troops into battle after the devastating blow she'd already struck? Why didn't the changelings attack? What the hells were the halflings and minotaurs doing? Izzie was trying not to focus on the negatives, but rather take advantage of their good fortune to build the hospital.

By "build," Izzie really meant they were fortifying the island so they could use it for healing. Every spare item found in the camps of the three races working together on the hospital was piled at the edge of the island so they wouldn't be susceptible to artillery attacks. Izzie had been watching from afar, but she wanted to walk over to the island for the first time since the disastrous peace summit.

"Hey, Syrel, do you want to come and check out our new hospital?"

"What's a hotspital?" he asked, genuinely confused.

"A *hospital*. That's what we're calling the healing building. Well, it won't be much of a building, but maybe someday. Baggie Smalls came up with it."

"And you're sure it doesn't mean something gross or inappropriate?"

"Nope. In fact, I'm pretty sure it probably does. But nothing I know, so hopefully nobody else does either."

Izzie approached the bridge, nervous about going to the artificial island where so many awful things in her life had happened. It was where she had thought she lost Syrel. Where

Queen Luxor had ordered the slaughter of the dwarves. Where the land was blessed with fertility by dooming the rest of Cosconia. But she was going to harness that blessing to the best of her abilities. Though she hadn't tried it, she was guessing—and desperately hoping—the Mother Tree also granted some healing magic in addition to Maternal Magic.

The second she stepped onto the bridge, an ominous feeling washed over her. Like she knew something horrible was about to happen. The same way mothers described their own intuition.

"Syrel," she whispered. "Run. Now."

He didn't move. "But—"

"Fly, you fool!" This time he jumped into action, running across the bridge toward the island. As he escaped, Izzie realized why she was feeling nervous. A massive fin popped out of the water. Lursa.

If I don't take care of this problem right now, Izzie pondered, *we'll never be able to use this island for the hospital. She'll eat anybody who tries to cross.* It was time to take a stand. She didn't even have time to brandish her wand before the fin disappeared and an enormous tail whipped out of the water and slapped down on the bridge, barely missing her, cracking it in half and sending her tumbling through the air.

"*Burbujum!*" she yelled, the air bubble forming around her head a fraction of a second before she hit the water.

Izzie knew the mermaids theoretically had the beast under their control, but she was skeptical a monster like this could be tamed. She was worried she would have to contend with trident-wielding mermaids and Lursa at the same time, but it seemed they were going to let the sea creature take care of her and stay out of the danger zone. She wasn't sure what Queen Luxor had told them about her, but they were keeping a healthy distance. *Good.*

The beast must have dived down to the bottom after slapping the bridge with her tail, as the water was eerily calm as Izzie sank down. The calm was quickly disturbed as she felt rippling in the water approach from underneath her. She used her *brillos* spell to illuminate the dim water around her, and the eerie light revealed the beast swimming directly toward her at full speed. Her plan was to use the same trick she had before and freeze its blood, but a flipper batted the wand out of her hand before she had a chance to cast any spells. *Clever girl*, Izzie marveled. She'd still be able to use her magic, but it wouldn't be as strong without the wand. *If only I had my old wand.* The beast was darting in and out of her range, hesitant after what had happened the time they'd met. She was surprised the sea creature seemed to have learned from their last encounter and was adjusting accordingly. Maybe this wasn't some dumb beast after all. Lursa dragged her handlers behind her, the rope wrapped tightly around her dorsal fin. They didn't seem to have any control at all here.

Izzie decided to level the playing field with a spell she had worked on quite a few times while delivering giant babies, improving her Skill by a reasonable degree. *"Corporus gigantorum!"* Lursa, who was actively charging at her as she cast the spell, used her front flippers to stop herself as she watched her opponent double in size. Then she did it again. *"Corporus gigantorum!"*

Again, Izzie doubled in size. She normally would have never been able to pull off a move like this, but she felt like her Intent was amplified in the shadow of the Mother Tree. She'd never tried this before, and she was worried how much it would take out of her, but there was no way she stood a chance against Lursa, who was evidently more intelligent than she realized, at her normal size. Now, she was about half of the beast's fifty-foot length. She could already feel the backlash of using a non-Affinity spell twice in a row, so she would have to end this fight quickly to avoid burnout. The beast had swum away, perhaps reevaluating her opponent, but Izzie knew she would be back. Sure enough, before Izzie had a chance to react, a tail smacked across her leg.

Izzie let out a scream inside her air bubble that nobody would hear. The beast had landed a blow directly on the injury from the orcish blade that had led to her being out of commission for three weeks. *Did she know where to hit somehow?* As the tail retreated into the murky water, Izzie grabbed onto it with her hands, which had just quadrupled in size. The tail flailed as Lursa swam through the water, trying to get her to let go. *Damn this thing is fast. I have to slow her down somehow or I'm never going to be able to land a spell.* Her wand was likely somewhere at the bottom of the channel, and she'd have to get it if she wanted this battle to end eventually.

"Pesangra!" It was a spell with limited healing utility, but sometimes making blood extremely heavy helped slow down bleeding in a pinch. In this situation, Lursa's newly weighted blood caused her speed to drastically reduce, and she started to sink to the bottom of the channel. The channel paid for in blood by thousands of dwarves.

While the spell did have its intended effect, Izzie's plan backfired when Lursa's tail, now significantly heavier than before, easily launched her off. *Hmm, I may not have thought this through entirely. I just made a fifty-foot sea monster weigh more than a gaggle of giants.* The beast seemed to realize it too, charging at Izzie with all the speed she could muster. They were now on the bed of the moat, which was littered with small corpses. Izzie backed herself against the channel wall as the beast charged. Just before Lursa slammed into her, she cast *vibro ultrasonorium*, using the sound waves to propel herself upward and causing the beast to slam into the hard rock wall. Another wave of exhaustion hit her as she cast the non-Affinity spell, but she'd been practicing with Syrel enough that her Skill could handle it. *For now.* She couldn't risk burnout this early in the war.

Izzie took advantage of the temporary respite brought by the beast being dazed from hitting her head so hard. Thankfully, her wand was still glowing from her *brillos* spell, and she was able to find it resting on the body of a dwarf that had been carried here by the rushing water. She shuddered as she examined the hundreds of bodies littering the bottom of the channel, weighted down by heavy armor and mining equipment. *Is this water still safe to drink?* She wondered idly. Izzie could barely make out the two mermaids at the ends of the ropes around Lursa's dorsal fin, as they seemed to be along for the ride and stayed out of the fight between the two of them. As the creature began to recover from the blow to the head, Izzie examined the rope wrapped around her fin. Scars criss-crossed the massive dorsal fin from where the heavy rope had dug into it, and blood seeped from several different spots. Izzie actually pitied the poor creature.

She wouldn't break her vow to do no harm, but she had an idea that would require her to bend the promise a bit. *All's fair in love and war*, she supposed. In quick succession, she pointed her wand at the two mermaids holding the ropes around Lursa's fin and shouted *"Bajasangra,"* causing blood to rush away from their heads so they would pass out. They fell unconscious into the graveyard of dwarves, the ropes in their hands drifting into the waves. Lursa, realizing she was free, swam to attack again, the effects of Izzie's blood-weighting spell having worn off by now.

Figuring that if it had worked last time, it would probably work this time, Izzie used *frijangre* again as the monster charged at her, and Lursa came to a dead stop as her blood instantly froze.

She had maybe sixty seconds until she would completely run out of energy, which was just about how long the beast would stay frozen, so she quickly swam, grabbed onto the monster's back, and unwrapped the rope digging deeply into her scaled skin. It had caused much more damage than she'd thought. She tossed the rope away as the beast started to stir underneath her, foiling the last part of her plan. Lursa started bucking and contorting to throw the wizard off, but Izzie held onto her fin for dear life. Even though the battle had only been going on for a couple minutes so far, holding on took Izzie's last vestige of energy, and the effects of her enlargement spell wore off. She shrunk back down to her normal size, making holding on to the rampaging beast even harder. Her leg was bleeding again, which was mildly concerning, but she tried to pay it no mind. She felt like she only had enough energy for one more spell before she'd have to recuperate.

"*Pelocer!*" she yelled, mustering every bit of energy left inside her. But instead of pointing the wand at her own leg, she pointed it at Lursa's fin, healing the wounds caused by the mermaids' rope.

The moment the beast's wounds were healed, she stopped bucking. She must have been in so much pain, given her immediate reaction to the healing spell. Izzie let go of her fin and floated a few feet away. Lursa whipped around to face her, and Izzie let go of her wand, letting it float out of reach in a show of peace. The monster stared into her eyes, and she stared back. There was so much emotion in those intelligent eyes. Sadness. Relief. Pain. Fear. Slowly, Lursa backed away into the dark water.

Izzie could see herself in the creature. Just like Izzie had been captured and forced to work against her will in Kurai's captivity, the mermaids and fae were forcing Lursa to act as their enforcer under the water. She couldn't blame the beast for lashing out

342

while in pain—hadn't Izzie done the same thing after she thought she'd lost Syrel? Was Lursa really any more of a monster than Izzie was herself?

Maybe this could be a fresh start for both of them. Izzie was working on leaving her poor choices in the past, facing her own monstrosity and committing to being a positive influence in the world. If she could accept her own past as somebody responsible for so many deaths, couldn't Lursa do the same thing?

* * *

Syrel watched the still water with apprehension. He'd barely made it onto the island when the monster had appeared, destroying the bridge and taking Izzie into the depths. He didn't know why she wanted to face this alone, but he was trying so hard to trust her. Every fiber of his being wanted to jump into the water and save her, but what could he do? He didn't like to admit it, and he wasn't sure she even knew it, but she was far more powerful than he was. And not by a small margin. She had already been stronger than him when they'd reunited, and he had watched her power grow exponentially over the subsequent years. Practicing blood magic day in and day out, essentially without stopping, was making a drastic difference. He had watched her effortlessly use blood magic on multiple individuals at once, which was something not even some of the greatest blood wizards in history could do, based on his studies of blood magic.

He was in awe of her power, especially since she only used it for good. She could kill any enemy with a thought, and yet she had risked her own life to pitch her hospital idea to Skygyr—who was only alive because of her. All so she could help others. He loved her so much, which made it even harder to keep his secret from her, but he couldn't tell her now. Not after everything they'd been through. *After the war*, he promised himself. *I'll tell her after the war.*

He'd worked so hard to help her move past the feeling she was responsible for the war, but he knew it still ate her up inside. How could it not? He felt the same way, but he had to be strong for her. Of course it wasn't her fault. Though she hid it well, he knew how much pain she was burying deep inside her. She blamed herself for so much, when in reality, she was a powerful force for good in Cosconia. She thought she was a scourge to life instead of its greatest protector. Some days, he wanted to grab her face and scream *"You are good! This world is better because of you!"* She wouldn't listen. But they were working on it. Together.

His thoughts were interrupted by a ripple in the water. It had been less than five minutes since she'd gone under the water, but she could be dead by now for all he knew. Dozens of humans, elves, and giants were gathered around the channel, waiting in anticipation. There were no mermaids showing their faces anymore after so many of them had been felled by elven arrows.

The monster's head breached the surface of the water, long tongue flicking past sharp, jagged teeth. Syrel's heart sank when he saw it, but his devastation was quickly replaced with confusion and elation. The beast's head dove back in the water, and its towering dorsal fin appeared, with a beautiful, dripping-wet wizard hanging onto it. A radiant smile was plastered on her face. Lursa kept swimming with Izzie on her back, making a long circle around the entire island. Initially, there was stunned silence all around. Then, led by Skygyr, every creature present burst into applause and cheering as Izzie did a victory lap. The sound of the thunderous applause made Syrel feel like they'd won the war.

344

The frele he hoped to spend the rest of his life with stepped off the sea creature, patting her fin before she disappeared into the deep.

After he picked his jaw up off the ground, he finally spoke. "What the actual fuck just happened?"

She just smiled. The smile he saw in his dreams. The smile that had kept him going all those years he was away. The smile that melted him inside. The smile he hoped he would see every day for the rest of his life. *Gods I love this frele*, he thought to himself.

"Just making some new friends." She shrugged.

* * *

Day 46 of the Twelve Race War
Water Fae Encampment

Queen Luxor idly picked at her restraints, more out of habit than an actual desire to escape. She *hated* being constrained, relegated to the sidelines of the war she'd somehow started, but she didn't trust herself. Her son was officially the acting leader of the water fae army, though the Wasteland had been quiet thus far.

Every time she closed her eyes, she could imagine herself in a dark tunnel, the sound of water rushing in. Helpless as a thundering tide rushed in and snuffed out countless lives. The lives of her *allies*. She had never even had the opportunity to explain her idea for peace. One moment she was listening to her fellow leaders introduce themselves, and the next she was back in her tent.

She'd made Doren explain what happened dozens of times. The pit in her stomach grew every time he reminded her of the death toll. *This isn't how it was supposed to be. There should never have been a war. I had every right to avenge my husband against that maniac Izzie is in love with.*

That wizard had tricked her. But how could she have been so stupid? So gullible? Her father had taught her to *always* trust but verify, and yet she had blindly trusted a wizard she didn't even know. She knew herself well enough to recognize she didn't always think or act rationally when it came to Thelonius's murder, but this was egregious.

Her son entered the tent. She could see the pity in his eyes, which was to be expected when one saw their own mother in chains. The other emotions he exuded were far worse. She could sense his shame, his embarrassment at her actions. Worst of all was the *fear* evident in his eyes. How could she blame him? In his mind, she was a callous murderer, one who was willing to betray her allies. *No better than Syrel.*

Doren still kept her apprised of the happenings of the war, though she'd been stripped of any formal decision-making power.

"I have some bad news. Lursa is no longer under our control."

"The mermaids lost her? She went rogue?"

Her son gulped. "Izzie and Syrel conquered her. I ran over here as soon as I saw Izzie circling the moat on her back."

The former fae queen trembled with rage. How? How were those two still one step ahead of her? "We have to take him out. He's too big a threat to our power." She still spoke about the power like it was hers.

"Mother, please. I want to avenge my father as much as you do, but hasn't this quest for revenge already cost you enough?"

Queen Luxor spoke with a clenched jaw. "He has cost me everything. That's why he has to die." While she still felt gutted by her inconceivable actions against the dwarves, her hatred of Syrel had only intensified after the incident.

Doren shook his head and moved on. They had already had this argument multiple times. "Ruta, one of our more powerful captains, and I have been doing some investigating. I think I figured out what happened during the peace summit."

"Oh?" Queen Luxor perked up. "What have you found?"

"I think you were controlled by a mind mage."

"A mind mage. I didn't think there were any left in Cosconia after the Great Divide."

"Didn't you say the same thing about blood wizards before you met—"

She didn't let him finish. "I am sick of hearing about that frele." Queen Luxor paused. She was putting together the pieces of what happened. "A wizard, a friend of Izzie's, came to see me before the summit."

"Really?" Doren perked up. "What did she say? What was her Affinity?"

Queen Luxor was embarrassed to admit she had never asked. She'd assumed the former midwizard, like Izzie, had an Affinity related to healing. "I'm... not sure. Our whole conversation is a little fuzzy. She told me she had a way to kill Syrel, and I think I tuned everything else out."

"Mom, Ruta was studying wizard Affinities at the Pwise Institute for Higher Learning before the war started. Mind mages prey on you in times of strong emotion. That's probably why she brought up Syrel."

"So you think... maybe I didn't really mean to wipe out the dwarves in the tunnel? I was under some sort of compulsion?"

Doren shook his head, frustrated. "I don't know. But I know you, and I know you would never do something like that."

Queen Luxor choked up with emotion. Doren continued before she could respond. "But I also know you have a blind spot when it comes to Syrel."

She couldn't deny it. Her rage had grown into a flaming ball of fury over the years. He had haunted her nightmares for years, replaced only recently by the faces of scared dwarves drowning in the dark.

"That may be true, but you have no idea how powerful he is." She pointed at her face, indicating the scar left there by the burning flesh of her late husband. "He has to be dealt with."

"How do you suggest we take him out?" he asked, relenting to his mother's wishes.

"Get Pyke in here."

CHAPTER TWENTY-SEVEN

Maternal Magic

The emphasis was on doing everything always for everyone forever to keep the patient alive.

—Samuel Shem

Day 60 of the Twelve Race War
Unity Hospital

"Something is not right, Syrel." Izzie looked over at her partner. She was focused on healing a dagger wound in a dwarf, while he was busy trying to close a gore hole in a changeling's leg. "Why has everything been so quiet?"

"Don't punch a gift horse in the mouth," said her bag, which she typically left open near her in the hospital.

"Okay I've heard you use that phrase before, but last time you said don't count your gift horses before they hatch."

"Yeah I'll admit I have a little trouble with idioms."

"You're all set," she told the dwarf gently, the bleeding now stopped and the wound closed using her *pelocer* spell, which was about as easy as breathing for her these days. Izzie looked at her surroundings. The Mother Tree towered above them, giving

349

much-needed shade that otherwise didn't exist in the Wasteland. The tree seemed to have various magical properties, as errant arrows and boulders didn't even leave a mark on its tough bark. It was still growing, and she suspected the roots now reached the channel surrounding the artificial island, which would likely be a catalyst for even faster growth. After a bit of experimentation, Izzie had confirmed the tree not only granted fertility to those in the land, but close proximity also greatly improved healing. She knew it had to be protected at all costs. At the edges of the island, boulders, shields, debris, felled trees, and a variety of other random objects created a wall about as tall as Izzie, shielding the island's inhabitants from artillery fire.

Izzie had anticipated a constant influx of the wounded and dying, but only a few creatures were brought to the island per day. She suspected many races were still leary of the whole "hospital" concept, and some probably even thought it might be a trap, but there had barely been any fighting after the orcs were slaughtered. There were a few minor clashes every day on the edges of different encampments, which was the reason she had any patients at all, but otherwise, the Wasteland was eerily quiet.

The elves and humans both had left small cohorts of defenders on the island in case it was attacked, and she knew the giants watched from a distance. Lursa, who was now bonded to Izzie in a way she didn't completely understand, patrolled the waters surrounding the island, so Izzie felt completely safe. They'd set a few bridges down so anybody could bring their wounded to the hospital, but they were required to leave their weapons on the other side. All the other races still had to come to the channel to get water for their armies, and Izzie made sure they were safe when they did so.

Lago, who stood on a stone nearby, grunted as she pulled a fifth arrow out of a giant's leg. The Mother Tree's magic enabled the dwarf to use a few minor healing spells, much to her delight. Izzie's theory was the tree was so rich in magic it imbued anybody in its radius with Intent powerful enough to overcome a lack of Skill *and* Affinity, which was previously impossible. Lago may have been the only nurse in Cosconia, but Izzie felt confident that the dedicated and kind frele would be the best nurse anywhere she went. She didn't think the skills would transfer when leaving behind the Mother Tree, but even in the midst of war, Lago was happy doing her part to make a difference for good. The dwarf and Arkan were both integral members of their healing team on the island. Though the magic they could perform was limited, they could remove arrows, bind wounds, hold pressure, and help transport patients. Izzie knew some of the people they healed would still ultimately succumb to their injuries or fall victim to rot, but most everybody left the hospital alive.

She missed delivering babies and taking care of pregnant freles, but she knew this was all a means to an end. Midwizards weren't specifically trained in the art of healing outside of labor and delivery, but she'd been preparing for this for years. Izzie's next patient, a minotaur with an axe wound to the back, stepped in front of her. What would have been a mortal blow was now just a minor inconvenience for the minotaur, who didn't even thank her for her services before running back across the bridge to his own encampment.

"I think they're all *scared*, Iz," Syrel, tying a tourniquet around the leg of an elf who had been stepped on by a giant, finally responded. "They saw what Queen Luxor did to the dwarves. Everybody watched the orcs get slaughtered when crushed between two armies. I think they're all terrified to make a move because they might be the next ones to end up massacred."

"But what about the water fae? Why would Lulu just give up this island so quickly and then go completely silent? Where are the blood sprites? Why have the changelings not made a move?"

Syrel stepped away from his patient and put a hand on Izzie's arm. "War might not be exactly how you thought it was. Maybe you envisioned constant fighting, day and night, nonstop action. But that's just not how it really is. Armies have to be fed and watered. Coordinating attacks is a logistical nightmare. Generals have to figure out a way to maximize their gains and minimize their losses. Besides, we are currently in control of the land everybody wants." The small team of healers, which consisted of Izzie, Syrel, Arkan, and Lago, were the island's only permanent residents.

Izzie wondered why Syrel seemed to know so much about warfare, but he was constantly surprising her with strange knowledge. Perhaps he was right. Maybe all of the armies were terrified of the losses that would ensue if full scale combat broke out. Maybe Queen Luxor was drawing up battle plans. Maybe the changelings had had a change of heart.

Her next patient, a human, walked and sat down in front of her.

"What's your name?"

"Lix." She looked young, maybe early twenties. She was light-skinned, but her complexion looked exceptionally pale. Izzie gave her a once over but didn't see anything obviously wrong. "You don't look injured—how can I help you?"

"I'm not injured, but I feel awful. I can't stop vomiting, I can barely eat or drink. Is there anything you can do to help?"

"Well… that's not exactly what we're here for. This hospital is for those injured in battle." She examined the girl, who put her hands up to her mouth and started to heave. Izzie put a hand on her back and tried to comfort her. "There really isn't anything I can do, but just make sure you drink a lot of water and stay out of the sun." Izzie figured it was just stress or heat exhaustion.

Her next patient, another frele, didn't seem to be acutely injured either. This one was an elf, who leaned in close to whisper to Izzie when she asked what was wrong.

"My boobs are *killing* me." Izzie had to stop herself from rolling her eyes. Here they were pulling arrows out of giants and trying to stop hemorrhages from axe wounds, and this girl was here to talk about her sore boobs? *You're a midwizard,* she reminded herself. A phrase Dalfa frequently used to say occurred to her. *If somebody comes to you with a problem, it's the most important problem to them.* Izzie wondered where her old friend was now that the war *she* wanted was finally here. Probably having a beer somewhere, laughing at Izzie's naivete for thinking Cosconia would end up anywhere else but here.

Izzie dismissed her. "You're probably just on your period."

"It's not that," the elf contested. "I haven't had one in two months."

"Then you'll probably get it soon. Head on back to your camp, stay hydrated, and try to stay out of the sun." Izzie knew her advice wouldn't help the painful breasts, but she had to at least say something.

Lago walked over to the next patient, a halfling.

"Uh, Izzie—I think you should take a look at this patient. She said her stomach hurts. She looks *extremely* bloated."

"Was she wounded in battle?" Izzie asked, feeling ashamed she was hopeful she could treat a *real* problem.

"No, she hasn't been in any fights. She has intense stomach pain that only lasts for about a minute and then goes away, but it comes back every five minutes."

Izzie eyed the halfling, who was currently doubled over in pain, arms wrapped tightly around her abdomen. *That's odd*, Izzie thought to herself. *It almost sounds like...*

"When did you arrive in the Wasteland?"

"I was part of the advance team before the peace summit," she said through gritted teeth, but then relaxed when the pain seemed to pass. "I got here three months ago."

Three months is just long enough..."Can you lie down here for me?" Izzie pulled her wand out of her robe.

"You thinkin' what I'm thinkin'?" Baggie Smalls asked as she pulled out the *majalir*. She gave a small nod, but didn't want to panic the diminutive creature.

She set her wand on the halfling's belly. "*Vibro ultrasonorium.*" Immediately, a fuzzy black and white image appeared on the *majalir*. She could make out a small head inside the halfling's abdomen.

Izzie chuckled slightly. "Well, cong—" Before she could finish, she saw another head in the crystal ball, which was not surprising since halflings usually had multiple babies at once. She had learned all about it in midwizardry school—sometimes halflings would be pregnant with upwards of ten babies, and their bodies just couldn't support it, so neither mother nor any of the babies would make it. Izzie pointed her wand further down, and sure enough, a third and fourth head popped into view. She did a thorough exam to make sure there weren't any more, and then removed the wand so the *majalir* couldn't start showing any unwanted images.

"What's your name, sweetie?"

"M-Makas," she said through the pain, another contraction coming on.

"You're going to be a mother, Makas. You're having quadruplets!"

"No, that's impossible. I was never able to get pregnant before."

"Things are different around here. Don't you know that's what everybody is fighting for? This land is rich with magic that makes getting and staying pregnant much easier and safer than in the rest of Cosconia."

"They didn't tell us nothing. Hortho and Portho just said we were going to war, and now here we are. Wait," the halfling interrupted herself. "Am I gonna die?"

Izzie realized that having four babies would probably be a death sentence for her back home in Hoshir. She hadn't delivered any babies here yet, but she suspected that it would be just fine. She smiled softly and rested her hand on the frele's tiny shoulder. "Not a chance. You're in the hospital now." The halfling gave her a confused look.

"Lago, can you keep an eye on her while she labors? I think it'll still be a few hours yet."

A realization struck Izzie. Nearly all the races of Cosconia were represented here, in the fertile land they were fighting over. And what did soldiers do when they were bored or stressed out?

Fuck, she thought to herself, and then ran off, chasing the human and elf she'd dismissed, who were slowly making their way off the island back toward their respective encampments.

"Can you two come back with me for a second? I just want to check on something."

Two more ultrasounds, two more pregnancies. The elf and the human both were a couple months pregnant. They wouldn't deliver anytime soon since their pregnancies would be significantly longer than the three-month gestation of a halfling, but they were absolutely pregnant. *This war has to end before this place starts drowning in babies.*

Izzie heard a shout and then a small cry. Lago had delivered Makas's first baby, and it seemed like the second one was close. Izzie ran over and lent a hand, coaching the halfling through it.

Before she could help out, Baggie made a comment. "Just like I told you—there's Lago, doing all the work, and you just come waltzing in at the last second and try to steal all the glory." Izzie ignored the comment even though it was partially true.

"You got this, Makas! Give us another push just like before!" The baby slid right out, pink and screaming. The third one followed shortly thereafter. "Congrats again! Another boy!" They handed each baby off to Arkan, who swaddled them in random pieces of discarded fabric she'd accumulated. The midwizard had a moment of panic when she saw feet start to come out of the halfling. *Oh no. This baby is breech. Babies can't come out feet first.* Lago looked at her, terror in her eyes. The dwarf had assisted in many elven baby deliveries, but usually the deliveries weren't the hard parts.

"I got this," Izzie assured the dwarf. The Maternal Magic was strong here. *Everything will be fine,* she reassured herself.

"You gonna use those spoons you used in the first chapter?" her bag asked, but she ignored the quip, wanting to act as quickly as possible. She pulled out the forceps and used two spells in quick succession: *cosarus pecanorum* and *lubricado*, making the delivery tool lubricated and halfling-sized. These forceps were slightly longer, intended to deliver breech babies.

"Okay Makas, go ahead and stop pushing for a minute."

"What's happening? Am I dying?"

"Not on my watch. You've got four babies to take care of. I'm just gonna help out a little, if that's okay with you." The halfling nodded vigorously. Izzie slid the forceps on, feeling them slide into place around the baby's head, like they had with Skygyr all those years ago. "Okay, now give me the best push you possibly can!"

The halfling, who had already pushed out three babies, let out a shrill yell and pushed with all her might. Feeling the baby move, Izzie used the forceps to gently pull while Makas pushed, and like magic, the head popped out. She took the spoons off and threw them back in the bag, who muttered something about the lack of sterilization, which made no sense to her. Izzie examined the baby frele. There were some small bruises on her cheeks, which was very common after using forceps for delivery.

"Are my babies okay? Am I going to bleed to death?" Izzie examined the halfling's postpartum bleeding, which was shockingly light. She took a moment to think about what had just happened. A halfling had had a completely uncomplicated quadruplet pregnancy and delivery, with minimal bleeding, and all four babies and mom had survived.

This place really is magic.

* * *

Day 20 of the Twelve Race War
Wastetown, Northwest Wasteland

Dalfa forced her eyes open. Her mouth felt like it was full of cotton. *Which I would eat right about now with how hungry I am.* Her former midwizard robes, which she'd turned from white to black when she quit, were soiled with urine and feces. It was pitch black in her room, where she'd sequestered herself to harness the *mentopo* spell. From what she'd gathered, everything had worked according to plan. She wouldn't let herself think about what had happened in that tunnel.

She grasped in the dark for her wand and said *"Brillos"* once she found it. Nothing happened besides a flash of heat through her body. *"Brillos,"* she said, more forcefully this time. The room remained dark, and she felt even warmer. *What the hells...*

Dalfa stood up, ignoring the mess, and unbarred the door to her room and walked outside. It was the middle of the night, which meant Wastetown was at its busiest. Whatever was happening in Gravipar didn't slow down the seedy nightlife here. In fact, the town seemed far busier than she'd seen it in the past.

The former midwizard grabbed a passerby.

"Have you heard any updates on the situation in the Wasteland?"

"Situation?" The minotaur grunted. "You mean the biggest war Cosconia has seen in generations?"

"So the war has started?" she asked hopefully, eliciting a strange look from the minotaur.

She nodded her head, horns bobbing up and down. "After what that fae lunatic did? Nobody was going to sit on their haunches after she murdered thousands of dwarves."

Thousands? Dalfa felt a pit grow in her stomach. *I thought there would be no more than a few dozen dwarves in that tunnel, a hundred max. Although I never actually did any investigation to confirm that thought...* As she ruminated, the minotaur wandered away. She wondered what Izzie would think of her if she found out that *she* was the one behind the massacre. It didn't matter. Dalfa knew there was no way around the war. The only way out was through.

"Cereleer." She cast the spell on the departing minotaur. The mind-reading spell was one of the most basic spells a mind mage could use. Unless one was particularly powerful, it gave more of an impression of somebody's thoughts than any specific words

or phrases. Nothing happened. Dalfa sat down on the street, a potent wave of nausea washing over her body.

"Twelve hells," she muttered to nobody. "I burnt myself out."

CHAPTER TWENTY-EIGHT

An Unexpected Visitor

---

*I was delighted to see you again, and forgot for
the moment that all happiness is fleeting.*

—Alexandre Dumas

Day 61 of the Twelve Race War
Unity Hospital

The war started to ramp up the next day. Scouts reported fae
and changelings were clashing at the border between their
encampments, which was surprising since she'd thought they
were allies. *Lulu must be losing control over there.* She could hear
the distant sounds of battle, and when she peaked over the
barrier toward the changeling encampment, she saw what could
only be described as bedlam. Water spears and exploding
bubbles were hurled at giants, minotaurs, halflings, elves, and
humans. The changelings were taking full advantage of their
abilities, and small clashes were taking place everywhere. There
were even water fae fighting other water fae, though Izzie
assumed they were changelings. She couldn't tell the difference
from here, but most changelings, even in their morphed forms,

were recognizable by their eyes. Only the most powerful changelings could completely change their eyes to match those of the race they were morphing into.

After the small battles started, new patients consistently rolled in. Izzie noticed there weren't any fae patients—Queen Luxor must have decreed they weren't allowed to use Izzie's hospital. There had still been no word on the status of the fae leader after she'd massacred the dwarves. Doren seemed to be the one leading the water fae army. Izzie had sent messengers to all of the encampments, including the fae camp, to let them know all wounded were welcome, regardless of race, but she wasn't surprised the fae queen had forbidden it.

To Izzie's surprise, for every injured soldier who came in, there were two newly diagnosed pregnancies or deliveries. She was using her ultrasound and the *majalir* nonstop to let members of every race know they were pregnant. Thankfully, the *majalir* hadn't been showing any unintended horrors, but Izzie supposed that was because they were already *living* the horrors. She saw all the symptoms of early pregnancy: nausea, vomiting, sore breasts, vaginal bleeding, fatigue, brain fog, cramping, back pain... but everybody was healthy. There were no miscarriages. Only the halflings had gestational periods short enough that they were actually delivering, and nearly every one of the deliveries went smoothly. They had recruited even more elves and humans to build temporary lodging on the island for the mothers and babies, not wanting to send them back into camps that could break out into battle at any moment. They had constructed a ramshackle nursery around the Mother Tree, which continued to provide strength and vitality to both mothers and babies after birth. The pregnant freles were sent back to their camps with strict instructions to avoid fighting, even though Izzie knew that was likely impossible.

Syrel and Arkan focused on healing the wounded changelings who continued to come in from the fights with the water fae, and Izzie and Lago delivered halfling litters and let giants, minotaurs, dwarves, and more know that they were pregnant.

Her paramour was currently working on healing a changeling, whose face was buried in the dirt in apparent agony, with a gnarly leg injury. It appeared a sharp spear of water, which some of the powerful fae could create, had nearly severed her leg. Syrel seemed to be having a hard time staunching the bleeding. While his Skill allowed him to practice some blood magic after years training by her side, he still didn't have the natural abilities or the decades of experience she had. She jogged over to help him out.

Before she could produce her wand to start the healing, the changeling morphed into a minotaur, sprung off the ground, and landed on top of Syrel. A horn pierced his shoulder, pinning him to the ground. In a grotesque display, the minotaur tore off her own horn, leaving it inside Syrel's shoulder so he couldn't move his arm. She tore off the other horn, screaming in agony as she did so, and rammed it through his other shoulder.

Izzie's mind went blank as she prepared to kill the deranged changeling, vows be damned. "*Paraco—*" Her spell to stop the changeling's heart was interrupted by the changeling morphing into a blood sprite, hovering above Syrel, and shouting "*Frijangre!*"

A deep chill washed over Izzie's body as she felt her blood freeze. She couldn't finish her own spell, and she was locked in place. The changeling morphed again, turning into a filthy, hideous orc, producing a dagger and holding it to Syrel's throat. During the shift, Izzie briefly saw the changeling's distinctive eyes. Brilliant purple interrupted by streaks of gold in swirling patterns around her iris. *Pyke.*

Arkan attempted to intervene and rip the orc's arm away from Syrel, but a quick morph into a fae followed by a blast of water sent her tumbling away, unconscious. All of this happened in a matter of seconds. The elves guarding the border were running over, bows pointed toward Pyke, who finally spoke.

"Anybody makes another move and I'll open his throat!" In all the forms she took, she had jagged scars on top of her head from ripping off her minotaur horns. Blood streamed down her face, but she didn't even seem to notice. Everybody halted when she threatened the wizard's life.

She turned into a wizard. The form she'd been in when she met Syrel. Nesbreth. Izzie could see him wince, now recognizing who she was.

"You. You monster. You chased me across Cosconia to steal my baby. You slaughtered innocent water fae. You killed Lulu's husband. You're a lunatic. A murderer. You sent me into preterm labor. You have caused me endless suffering, and now I finally take my revenge."

Pyke lifted a wand, evidently one she'd obtained from Lublana's Wandoflust in Gifldor, so it was the real deal. "Do you have anything to say before you take your last breath?"

"I'm sorry."

Izzie watched some of the rage seep out of the changeling, who had apparently not expected that answer. She'd built Syrel up to be such a monster in her head that she probably figured he'd laugh in her face. She had no idea how much Syrel regretted his actions. He didn't talk much about Pyke, but Izzie knew the entire situation still haunted him.

"What did you just say? Are you mocking me?"

"No. You have every right to kill me. I won't fight back. What I did to you, and what I did at the coronation, are the biggest regrets of my life. But that's not who I am anymore."

"You… But… Don't try to manipulate me, monster! I know what kind of wizard you are. You would kill me and my son in a heartbeat if you could."

"It's a boy?" A small smile crossed his face, incongruous with his circumstances. "How is he? Is he healthy?"

"What—stop it right now, Nesbreth. Sorry, *Syrel*." At this, she threw an angry glance at Izzie. "You don't get to hear about him. I shouldn't have let you speak. Now—" She brandished her wand again.

Finally, Izzie's blood had thawed enough that she was able to move her lips enough to speak. She'd been rapidly using her own blood magic internally to counteract the spell. She still couldn't move.

"Pyke," she said weakly. "Pyke, wait."

The changeling turned toward her but didn't drop her wand. "Izzie, I have no qualms with you. I know Lulu thinks you betrayed us, but you were nothing but kind to me. I'm sorry to do this to your lover, but he deserves it."

Izzie shook her head and spoke again, her voice hoarse. "I know. He does. What he did to the queen and to Thelonius was awful. But he wasn't chasing you. He thought the fae were going to kill me. He'll never forgive himself." Pyke looked at her with disbelief. "Haven't we all done terrible things we've come to regret? Didn't our friendship start a little rocky—remember when you forced me to do the ultrasound after threatening my old teacher?"

She could see indecision cross her old friend's face. Nobody said anything for a long moment.

"Don't try to spin this on me, witch!" Tears started to stream down her face. "Lulu says you are both evil to the core. Unforgivable." Izzie could see how confused Pyke was as the changeling stared at Syrel. "She said you'd kill me and my son in a heartbeat. That you're still looking for him. He'll never be safe while you're still alive."

Syrel winced as he tried to sit up a bit, the horns in his shoulders causing him a great deal of pain. "Never. She might be right about me being unforgivable, but I would never hurt you or your son. I came to the coronation to save Izzie, but I was completely misled. I was confused and scared. I'm just happy he's alive. Pyke, I am so sorry for everything that happened between us. But I loved you, and I will never hurt you or your son."

"Yo—you're not going to hurt him?"

"Hurt him?? Never. I'm just happy to hear he's alive after what I put you through. It's not an excuse. What I did was horrific. But I never, *ever* would have hurt you or him."

She looked even more confused. "But Lulu... Lulu said..."

"Can I ask you one question before you kill me?"

The changeling continuously looked back and forth between Izzie and Syrel. "I thought... I just thought..."

"What is his name?"

"H-huh?" she sputtered.

"Your son. What is his name?"

"Capino." Pyke broke down into tears, dropping her wand completely. Izzie saw the elven archers lift up their bows the moment she did so, but Izzie signaled for them to hold off.

"Cap, everybody calls him."

"That's a beautiful name, Pyke." Syrel cried too. "Is he as strong as his mom?"

She sniveled. "Stronger. He was born an Apex."

That's strange. I thought only two Apex Changelings together could create an offspring who was born with the abilities of all twelve races, but I must have been mistaken. Midwizardry school was so long ago I can't keep everything straight. She shook off those thoughts and kept trying to calm Pyke down.

"I think Lulu may have poisoned your mind. Syrel has made many mistakes, just like the rest of us. But he's changed. I promise you—he's changed."

"She... she made me kill the king and queen. I didn't want to. I loved Mamut and Luva. Every changeling did. But she told me my son wouldn't be safe... Now everybody hates me..."

"I'm not sure what's going on with Lulu, but I think she will come to regret her actions one day. You don't have to listen to everything she says. You make your own decisions, Pyke. And I promise you one thing: Not everybody hates you. I certainly don't. You're one of my oldest friend, and I will always love and care for you."

The changeling, still in her wizard form, ran over to Izzie and fell into her arms, weeping. "Oh, Izzie, I've missed you so much. I wish you were there when Cap was born. It was so scary. I've told him all about you. I'm sorry, Izzie. For everything."

Izzie brushed her fingers through the frele's hair as she spoke, doing her best to comfort her. "Shhh, shhh. It's okay. I'm sorry I left you in Lork. I was in a dark place. I should have come to find you."

"I don't even care anymore. I just want my old friend back."

"You have her," Izzie said, now with tears falling down her face.

Pyke pulled away and wiped her eyes. "We have to stop Lulu. She's gone completely mad. I had no idea she was going to do what she did to the dwarves. She isn't even leading her army any longer; that's why things have been so quiet. She sent me here to kill him"—she pointed at Syrel—"but I won't do it. I can't."

"You're right. Stay here with us, Pyke. Help us heal the wounded." Izzie briefly explained the situation of so many frele soldiers getting pregnant from the seemingly nonstop sex that must be happening in the war camps, much to Pyke's delight.

"Maybe I can become a midwizard like you!"

Izzie laughed, thrilled to have her friend back. "I think that sounds like an excellent plan. We have so much to catch up on."

A pained voice spoke out. "Uhhh, little help here?"

Oops. Izzie realized Syrel was still pinned to the ground. She carefully removed the horns and used her blood magic to quickly patch him back up. Thankfully, it didn't seem like there would be any long-term damage.

Pyke addressed Syrel. "I'm not ready to forgive you. But I promise I won't hurt you."

To his credit, Syrel took this gracefully and just nodded.

Everybody on the island had begun to resume their normal activities when a horn sounded in the distance. Izzie looked up, trying to locate where it was coming from. Syrel pointed. Southeast. The horns were coming from the direction of Blood Sprite Territory.

* * *

Day 25 of the Twelve Race War
Wastetown, Northwest Wasteland

Sweat pooled in Dalfa's sickbed. It wasn't worth the effort of getting out of bed to clean the sheets. *How could I clean them without magic anyway? Is this really how non-wizards live?* She was in the throes of severe burnout. Her days were characterized by vomiting and nosebleeds, while she spent her nights tossing and turning with intermittent fevers. It crossed her mind that Izzie was probably the most capable of helping her right now, but she suspected there was no salvaging that friendship.

She had learned in wizarding school how dangerous burnout could be, but she had thought she was too strong to ever experience it herself. She was an adept mind mage, and she rarely had to push herself the way she had with Queen Luxor.

Dalfa replayed the events of the day in her head. Though *mentopo* was an Affinity spell for her, the *Mentala*, her guide for all things mind magic, warned users against it. Taking control of somebody's mind was dangerous and required a great deal of power. Dalfa had figured she had enough Skill to perform it, which she did, but now she was facing the consequences. There was no telling how long the burnout would last.

When the innkeeper had knocked on her door the day before to let her know other guests were complaining of the stench coming from her room, she had asked for a report on the status of the war. He had grunted and informed her matter-of-factly that it was a war—people were dying. What else did she expect? Dalfa rolled over and vomited in a bucket the innkeeper had provided. He hadn't even asked any questions about her condition; he just gave her the bucket and told her to clean up after herself and keep paying.

The decisions she'd made to get to this point continued to plague her. *Without war, there can be no peace*, she reminded herself. The refrain felt flimsier by the day. *Especially* not knowing what was happening in Gravipar.

As she often did, she grounded herself by imagining the future of Cosconia. Freles excited for pregnancy instead of scared. Nurseries full of healthy babies. Bigger dwarf babies and smaller giant ones. *That* was the future Cosconia needed. The future she'd sacrificed her own morality for.

The sound of a gentle tapping on the door roused her from her musings about the future. She pulled a blanket around herself, freezing in spite of her fever, and trudged to the door. She opened it a crack and a letter came flying in the door and repeatedly hit her in the face. *I shouldn't have let Izzie cast the letter finding spell; she was always terrible at non-Affinity magic.* She grabbed the letter and ripped it open, curious what her former friend would write to her in the middle of the war.

Her face fell as her eyes scanned the page. She reread the letter several times before crumpling it up and throwing it on the ground in a fit of rage.

"I'm going to kill that monster!" she screamed to the empty room.

CHAPTER TWENTY-NINE

Blood Sprites

---

*War doesn't determine who's right. War
determines who remains.*

—*R.F. Kuang*

Day 61 of the Twelve Race War
Unity Hospital

The sound of the clash between changelings and water fae
was silenced by the distant calls of the war horn. Even the ever-
present sound of the moaning and weeping of the wounded was
temporarily muted. It seemed as if a hush fell over the entire
battlefield. If the blood sprites were moving toward the
Wasteland en masse, nobody was safe. They had no alliances. No
loyalties. Nobody knew anything about them, other than their
role in the Great Divide, in which history texts depicted them as
vile, bloodthirsty monsters.

Little was known of their power, other than their inborn
ability to use blood magic. Izzie suspected they were far more
powerful at using blood magic than she was, which worried her.
She had no idea if they required Skill and Intent to control their

Affinity, or if they even *had* Affinities. She had also heard their goal was to eliminate any other Cosconian who could use blood magic. That would make her a prime target. Izzie wanted to prepare for their arrival, but she didn't know how. The small creatures could easily fly over the moat, so destroying the bridges wouldn't help. They were too small and nimble to be destroyed by the giant's boulders or Lursa's sharp teeth, and elven arrows likely wouldn't be fast enough to pin them. She and Syrel knew plenty of defensive magic. Pyke, as an Apex Changeling, was *quite* proficient in magic. But still—it was three against what might be an entire army. She just had to hope they would target all of the armies in the Wasteland, not just her and the hospital.

"Pyke, are you with us?"

The changeling nodded her head vigorously. "Capino is safe with my parents back in Jubox, but I'm not going back until I know this war is over."

"Does this mean you made up with your parents?" Izzie recalled Pyke hated her parents, who had barred her from going out on her *spruminga*, the time in a changeling's life when they set out to explore Cosconia and expand their power by touching as many other races as they could. She had eventually spurned their rules and gone on to become the changeling who was now probably the most powerful in the realm.

She grunted. "It's amazing what grandchildren will do to thaw a relationship."

"Are you sure you want to stick around? It's not too late to go home and live out the rest of your days in peace with your son."

"This is why you're a true friend, Izzie. Lulu told me it would be a betrayal to all of Cosconia if I left the war to go home. But yes, I need to see this through. I killed the changeling leaders, so by custom, I'm the leader now. Even if they won't accept me."

"Why won't they accept you?" Syrel asked, seeming genuinely curious.

She glared at him, not quite ready to be on casual conversation terms. "Mamut and Luva were so beloved by changelings that nobody is willing to accept the one who murdered the king and queen as the new leader, even though it's custom. I've tried to flex my power in every way I know how, but they continue to sabotage me at every turn. Besides, they think I'm Queen Luxor's puppet, which wasn't far from the truth. But not anymore." Izzie supposed that explained why the changelings weren't launching any full scale attacks.

"What if you told them the truth?" questioned Syrel.

"Oh that's rich coming from you, lying little—"

"Wait, Pyke. I think he may be onto something, even if it is a bit hypocritical. What if you told them you'd been manipulated and coerced by Lulu? There's no love lost between the fae and the changelings, as you well know. They know what she did to the dwarves. Maybe if you told them you are no longer under her thumb, they would respect you? I think if you are honest with them, and apologize for what you did, they might surprise you."

Pyke seemed to consider this. "I'm not even sure I want to be their leader. I never wanted power."

Izzie remembered that was one of the first things Pyke had told her when they met. She'd laughed at the mere notion she was in Jubox to seize power.

"If not you, then who?"

"There is one sub-Apex changeling in the army. He can morph into eleven races, but not blood sprites. The vacuum in power could create a struggle for the throne."

"That's the last thing they need right now. An internal conflict in the middle of a war is a recipe for slaughter. They need somebody to lead them, Pyke. Be the leader I know you can be."

"But what about all of you? Who will help defend Gravipar from the blood sprites?"

Izzie shook her head. "You worry about the changelings. We'll figure something out."

Pyke morphed into a blood sprite so she could fly off back toward the changeling encampment. Syrel tried to stop her.

"Pyke, can I say one more thing before you go?"

The changeling didn't say anything, but she stopped flying, hovering in the air at eye level.

"There's a vault at Comel's Bank in Gifldor. Number 815. The code to get in is 'Forever Mine.' There's enough gold inside that you and Capino will be set for life. If I don't make it out of here alive, I want you both to have it." He paused for a moment. "Actually, I want you both to have it even if I do survive this. It's the least that I can do."

Pyke didn't say anything else, but hovered in the air for a moment before zooming off. Izzie's hand had instinctively gone to her arm when she heard the password. They were the same words that remained tattooed on her arm, even after the ritual had gone awry. The same ones were mirrored on Syrel's shoulder blade. He hadn't been back to Gifldor since before they'd reunited, and *still* that was his password. She didn't need to say anything. She grabbed him by his shoulders and pulled him in, her lips finding his. They stood there for a long moment, forgetting the world around them. Forgetting the wounded and dying scattered around their makeshift hospital. Forgetting the army of blood sprites charging toward them. Forgetting the murderous fae queen intent on Syrel's demise. Izzie lost herself in his tender embrace, tongue running along the inside of his mouth. She could have stayed like that forever, but he pulled away.

"That was super hot, but you're squeezing my shoulders way too tight, and if you'll recall, there were just minotaur horns stabbed through them."

Izzie blushed and dropped her hands, having completely lost herself in him. She cast a quick healing spell on his shoulders. Night was falling around them, and they had to figure out a plan for the arrival of the blood sprites. She looked to the southeast, but she couldn't see anything yet. That meant they likely had at least a day or so to prepare. She knew they wouldn't be getting any sleep that night.

Izzie burst into a flurry of activity. The first thing she did was send off messengers to Donrel, Eko, and Skygyr, entreating them to send more troops to help protect the island. She even sent one toward the dwarf camp, unsure who the leader was after Queen Luxor had massacred so many of their kind. Next, she ordered the small contingent of elves and humans already on the island, only about fifty of each, to temporarily abandon their defensive posts and assist in finishing the nursery. By this point, there were dozens of halfling babies on the island, all of whom had mothers who did not feel safe bringing their newborns back into an active war zone. The makeshift nursery Izzie had commissioned to be built around the Mother Tree would provide an extra layer of protection for the newborns, though she didn't really think it would be particularly effective against an army of ravenous blood sprites.

It was still dark when the first message returned:

Isadore,

I don't even have enough soldiers to keep my own kind safe. I am sorry.

Respectfully, Drago

P.S. If you know where my sister is, can you please send word?

Lago's *brother* was now the leader of the dwarves? Izzie hadn't even known he was a soldier. She shuddered to think how many in the chain of command must have perished to have somebody so young and inexperienced end up in charge of the army. But if he was anything like his sister, Izzie knew the dwarves were in good hands. As soon as she finished reading the letter, she took off. She found Lago coaching a scared halfling through labor. *Damn those halflings are staying busy over in their camp.*

"Lago! Can I borrow you for a second?"

"Uhhh..." She looked back and forth between Izzie and the halfling, who had a baby sticking halfway out of her. "Kind of in the middle of something, boss!"

"I'm not your boss! And I can see that. Just find me when you finish up, okay?"

"Got it, boss!" Izzie rolled her eyes, but she secretly didn't mind it. She considered the dwarf to be her protege, and Lago's healing skills continued to progress rapidly. She never took a break, but Izzie couldn't blame her—she'd learned from the best.

Izzie checked in on the construction of the nursery, which was coming along nicely. While she oversaw the project, she received rejection letters from the giants, elves, and humans. They all said something similar to Drago—they didn't have enough troops to spare, and they needed to protect their own kind. She was disappointed that even Donrel wouldn't help, but he had already done so much for them. The last time she'd asked for his help, eight of his best troops had ended up dead at the hands of the orcs. She couldn't blame anybody for prioritizing their own interests.

Lago caught up to her while she was checking in on some of the wounded changelings treated that day. Many were still too weak to return to their camps.

"Lago. I got word from your brother. He's now in charge of the dwarf army."

Lago grinned, the corners of her mouth pulling her long red beard upward. "That's m'boy! I always knew my brother was destined for great things."

Izzie was puzzled by her response. She hadn't thought the dwarf would take the news so well.

"You aren't concerned at all?"

"Nah, Drago has always been a natural leader. If my kind are in his hands, I've never felt safer."

"He asked if I would send word if I knew of your whereabouts. What do you want me to write back?"

"Tell him I'm a labor and delivery nurse!"

Izzie smiled softly at her. After the time they'd spent in Mithor, Lago had probably delivered more babies than most midwizards. She was a kind, compassionate, and capable dwarf. Even without true blood magic, she supported her patients and delivered babies with the ease of a practiced midwizard.

"You're damn right you are! I'll send word right away."

Lago returned to her nursing duties. There were still halflings showing up in labor every few hours, which meant the number of babies in the nursery was growing exponentially. The sun was up, and Izzie looked southeast. She squinted her eyes, barely able to make out something in the distance. She couldn't tell what it was. Maybe just a mirage. She opened up her bag to pull out Syrel's spectacles.

"What do you need today? Can I interest you in an egg in these trying times?"

"Why would I want an egg? And where did you even *get* an egg?"

"From the mice, duh."

"Mice don't—" she massaged her temples with her fingers and sighed. *I just can't resist rising to the bait, can I?* "Can you just give me the spectacles?"

"One pair of testicles, *cumming* right up!"

"That one will never get old for you, will it?"

"Nope!" The spectacles came flying out of the bag. "And if you..." Izzie squeezed the bag shut the second it had produced what she needed. She didn't have time for its games right then, even though she usually appreciated the comic relief.

She lifted the device to her eyes and focused on the area in the distance that appeared incongruous with the rest of the horizon. *Here we go.*

"Syrel!" she yelled, and he came running over from a patient he'd been taking care of. "You're going to want to see this."

From this distance, it looked like a swarm of crimson mosquitoes buzzing toward the island. But she knew what it was. Blood sprites. Hundreds of them. Blood sprites had two sets of red wings, so the entire group looked like a haze of blood drifting through the air.

"Do you think any of them will recognize you?" she asked Syrel.

"What do you mean?"

"From the time you spent imprisoned there?" *How could he have forgotten that? Maybe he just blocked it out...*

"Oh, yeah, that. Of course. I doubt it. I was beaten so badly I was probably unrecognizable." Izzie hated thinking about that time in his life, since she felt partially responsible, so she didn't pursue it any further. She wrapped an arm around him, being careful of his injured shoulders this time. He looked slightly uncomfortable with the contact, but it was probably because of the impending disaster. There were no more preparations to be made. All they could do was watch while their enemies drew ever nearer. Izzie knew she could flee, and she and Syrel could get away safely, but she wasn't leaving. This war was her mess, and she would see it through to the end. Besides, there was no way she was abandoning the injured soldiers or the newborn babies on the island.

As the sun rose high into the sky, the swarm drew ever nearer. They had moved all the wounded into the nursery, which was officially complete. It was a motley collection of canvas from tents, discarded shields, and some logs that had likely been carried into the barren Wasteland by one of its rare storms. They'd built up the walls to reach the lowest branches of the Mother Tree, which acted as a natural roof. Izzie and Syrel stood at the entrance to the nursery, while the small group of elves and humans stationed on the island stood nearby at the ready.

When the blood sprites were visible with the naked eye, the swarm stopped moving and settled to the ground. Izzie watched with curiosity as one blood sprite left the pack and flew toward the island. They hovered right at the edge of the moat, but didn't cross. At first, nobody moved. When Syrel took a step forward, the entire swarm lifted off the ground and began buzzing frantically. He immediately stopped and took a step back. When Izzie attempted the same motion, the blood sprites remained deathly still. She took a step forward. And then another. She walked until she stood on the edge of the moat, directly across from the sprite. Dusk had just begun to fall, and a chill hung in the air.

Izzie looked down and saw a ripple in the water. Lursa was nearby, ready to defend her at a moment's notice. She'd developed a special connection with the beast, almost like they could feel each other's emotions.

"Parlay!" the blood sprite called in its guttural voice across the water, shocking Izzie. *Parlay? It wants to talk to a leader?*

"I am the leader here. You can come talk to me."

"I no come there. You come here." Izzie knew most blood sprites didn't use Fingol, the common tongue in Cosconia. They spoke in Spyridian, their native language. Their geographic and cultural separation from the rest of the races made it difficult to learn the language. Izzie felt confident taking on one blood sprite if it came down to it, and if the entire swarm decided to attack, a measly stretch of water wasn't going to protect her. Besides, ancient custom dictated nobody was to be harmed during a parlay. *Do evil blood sprites follow ancient customs?* was her last thought before making up her mind.

She heard Syrel gasp behind her when she stepped into the water, but she knew Lursa's back would be there when she did. Sure enough, it was like stepping onto dry land. Her new friend carried her the short distance across the moat, and she stepped off in front of the sprite.

"Blood wizard," they stated, voice sounding like a mixture between the croak of a bullfrog and the buzz of a fly. It didn't seem like a question, and Izzie saw no use in lying.

"Yes, I am a blood wizard. But I only use my powers for healing."

At the word "healing," the sprite buzzed excitedly. "Heal. We heal. Blood sprite heal."

Izzie realized they must not know what the word meant, so she tried to explain it better. "We are not part of the war. We are here to heal the injured. We only use blood magic for good."

They continued buzzing excitedly... *or angrily?* Izzie couldn't tell which.

"Yes, blood heal. Blood good. No war."

Was Izzie understanding correctly? Were the bloodthirsty maniacs here to... help?

"So you're not here to kill us?"

The buzzing turned from high-pitched to low, perhaps indicating a change in emotion, though Izzie couldn't be sure what emotion it was trying to express.

"No kill. Orc kill. Sprite heal."

She couldn't believe what she was hearing. "Yes, orcs do kill. But they're gone. The giants and elves conquered their army."

The sprite turned frantic. "Orc kill. Orc no gone. Orc come. Sprite heal."

"No," Izzie insisted. "There are no more orcs. Orcs are gone."

At that moment, a blast of horns sounded in the distance, behind the blood sprites. The swarm parted to reveal, far in the distance, thousands of lights. Torches.

"Orc come. Orc make sprite slave. Many years slave. Sprite only want heal, orc want special metal. Orc burn sprite. Orc burn much sprite for metal. Orc evil, orc very bad. Sprite escape orc." Its small hand, sporting a nasty burn scar, pointed toward the rest of the swarm calmly resting on the cracked earth of the Wasteland, which was showing more signs of life every day. "No more sprite left."

Izzie looked at the swarm, horror dawning over her. There were maybe two hundred sprites present. There weren't any recent scouting reports, but Izzie knew at one point there had been tens of thousands of blood sprites. And now their population had been reduced to the two hundred here? Then it all clicked for Izzie.

Kurai had more lyonium than she had thought possible. He'd implied he had a *deal* with the blood sprites, but apparently his orcs had enslaved the peaceful creatures. Somehow, the sprites had escaped, and their former captors were chasing them. Izzie had thought the orcs were out of this war, but it turned out they were just getting started.

"You are safe here. This island"—she gestured at Gravipar behind them—"is for healing. We use our blood magic to heal the wounded."

"Yes, yes, sprite heal. No kill. Sprite love peace. Sprite hate war. Sprite heal. But no heal orc. Sprite hate orc."

Izzie laughed. "You and me both. What is your name?"

"This sprite Flor."

Izzie knew sprites didn't have a traditional concept of gender, so she didn't bother asking. "Nice to meet you Flor. I'm Isadore, but you can call me Izzie. Please, give me a minute to explain everything to my friends, and then the sprites are welcome to join us on the island. This is called a hospital, and we could really use your help."

* * *

Day 25 of the Twelve Race War
Wastetown, the Northwest Wasteland

Dalfa,

I've been thinking about writing this letter for months; I just haven't been able to find the words. I wish our friendship hadn't fallen apart. I miss you. But I guess that's the nature of adult relationships—sometimes you just go down separate paths.

For so long, I wanted to be angry at you for encouraging war instead of trying to stop it. Maybe you were right all along and we never would have been able to prevent this, but couldn't we have tried? We both want the same thing: healthy pregnancies and deliveries for all Cosconians. On that topic, I have a confession.

I created Gravipar. More specifically, Syrel and I created it. I know I never talked much about my time before midwizardry school, but you probably remember me mentioning a ritual I did with my ex (and current boyfriend... you've missed a lot) to get pregnant. Obviously that didn't work, but I found out years later that the ritual, which was done right here in what's now called Gravipar, created the Mother Tree. The very same Mother Tree imbuing the contested land with fertility.

Long after our last encounter, the elves presented me with their findings regarding maternal and infant mortality in Cosconia. Pregnancy got increasingly dangerous after the failed ritual, and I'm afraid the accidental creation of Gravipar led to the tragic state of affairs after we graduated.

I know how much it affected you, and I can assure you it affected me just as much. I wasn't sure if I should tell you any of this, but there's a good chance I won't survive the next few weeks, and I couldn't die with this on my conscience.

I hope you're far away from here and some day we can put this all behind us.

Izzie

CHAPTER THIRTY

War Rages

---

*In love we find out who we want to be; in war
we find out who we are.*

—*Kristin Hannah*

Day 100 of the Twelve Race War
Unity Hospital

After the new orc army arrived, the war turned into exactly
what Izzie had imagined in her worst nightmares. It was
constant chaos. For some reason, it seemed like all the armies
decided to attack at once. She had no idea why. The battles ebbed
and flowed—sometimes the fighting would calm down for a day,
other times the sound of swords clashing and arrows flying
persisted night after night.

Izzie was grateful the armies seemed to respect the hospital
and kept the fighting outside of the channel. Of course, a
terrifying sea monster patrolling the channel and the constant
threat of boulders raining from the sky were, together, a pretty
good deterrent. Now that the mermaids had lost control of Lursa,
they stayed far away from the channel. She suspected they had

returned to Lork, where their meggs would hopefully be safe now that their main predator was gone. Izzie was perfectly fine with one fewer group of enemies to worry about.

Though it had taken some cajoling, the blood sprites had agreed to continue using their healing blood magic even with orcs being brought to the hospital, though they refused to actually work on them. As much as Izzie hated the orcs and everything they stood for, she had vowed to protect *all* life, no exceptions. Most of the orcish soldiers were here against their will anyway. She also suspected part of the reason the hospital remained out of the crossfire was that, besides the fae, all races were sending their injured to the island for healing.

She continued to work side by side with Syrel, who improved his own healing magic Skill every day. He still didn't hold a candle to her, especially because her powers continued to grow as she was able to heal more complex wounds and save most of the patients who were brought to her. Her control over blood was near absolute, and if she focused, she could work on dozens of patients at once now.

Though she had begged Skygyr and Donrel to maintain the alliance that had brought down Kurai and his army, they'd both refused. The night before, the elves had sent a small battalion of their best archers to the giant encampment and rained arrows on the camp for several minutes before they ran off. At least thirty giants had died in the assault, and another twenty or so were brought to the hospital. Blood sprites were busy zooming up and down the rows of prone giants, healing open wounds as Lago and Arkan pulled arrows out.

"Izzie!" somebody shouted, distracting her from healing the few elves who had been too slow and faced the wrath of the giants.

Lying on the ground in front of Lago, who had called her, was Skygyr, with an arrow sticking straight out of her left eye.

"Oh my gods, Skygyr, are you okay? Let's get that arrow out right away."

"Your friend, the elf, will pay for this. The giants will not take this lying down."

"But you're already ly—" Izzie kicked the bag before it could antagonize the giantess.

"Once again, I beg you to just leave this land behind. So much blood has already been shed, and for what? Nobody is any closer to controlling Gravipar."

"I am here for your healing, not your counsel, midwizard. Please, remove the arrow so I can return to my army." It was a distinct change from the benevolent giantess in whose camp she had recovered. *I guess war will do that to you.*

Izzie got to work without saying anything else.

"*Quitojogre*," she said, pointing her wand at the giant's eyeball. This would drain the blood from Skygyr's eye temporarily, making the removal of the arrow safer. She yanked the arrow out, noting that the giantess didn't even change her stony expression when she did. She muttered *regrasangra* and *dejasangra* in quick succession to return the blood to her eye and then stop the bleeding.

"You may never see out of that eye again, but the bleeding has stopped. You'll be okay." The giantess didn't say another word, standing up and lumbering off back toward her encampment. *I hope we still have her protection*, Izzie thought. *Or at least the* illusion *of her protection.*

After Skygyr left, Izzie noticed several blood sprites hovering around a moaning dwarf. *That's odd. I haven't heard reports of any clashes involving the dwarves in a few days. Must be a lingering injury.* She ambled over and surmised what was happening with some quick math. The gestational period for a dwarf was exactly the four months since they'd started arriving.

"Lago! I need you!"

The dwarf came running, and her face lit up when she saw one of her own kind ready to deliver. "Izzie! I've never delivered a dwarf baby before!"

"Well, if you're going to be the best labor and delivery nurse, you'll have to learn how to take care of every race in Cosconia! This one is all you, girl."

Lago's excitement was palpable as they led the dwarf frele to the nursery, already packed with halflings and their babies. It was ironic that even in the middle of a war, having a baby in Gravipar was *still* somehow safer than in the rest of Cosconia. Izzie suspected there would soon be an influx of laboring dwarves coming to the island. They would have to keep moving the makeshift walls of the nursery further away from the tree, giving a modicum of protection to the pregnant and postpartum freles and their newborns.

Izzie held the dwarf's hand as they laid her on the ground and instructed her to start pushing. She had clearly waited until the last minute to come to the island, as her cervix was already fully dilated and she was quite close to delivery. Typically, dwarves didn't have to push for too long since the babies were so small. This one pushed for three hours and finally delivered a chunky baby girl, a tiny beard already present on her button chin. Izzie pointed her wand at the baby and used a spell all midwizards learned on day one of midwizardry school: *plesada*. This was how they ascertained the weight of a baby. This one was five and a half pounds—the largest dwarf baby she'd ever seen. The lack of Maternal Magic usually restricted their growth so much they were born only one or two pounds. This certainly wouldn't be a NICU baby!

Yet again, Izzie marveled at the magic of Gravipar. She couldn't believe how smooth and uncomplicated these pregnancies and deliveries were. It was such a stark contrast to the awful outcomes and complications she had seen over the past fifty years. Thoughts of Dalfa crossed her mind, as nobody would appreciate this magic more than she would. It still pained Izzie to think about their falling out, which she could barely blame Dalfa for. The former midwizard felt her emotions far too deeply, and the mortality in Cosconia had absolutely wrecked her. The mortality Izzie still felt partially responsible. She wondered how her friend would respond to her letter.

The juxtaposition here in Gravipar was so odd—soldiers were dying left and right, falling in battle. But here on the island, pregnant freles and babies were surviving at an unprecedented rate. Izzie wasn't sure how to feel. Mostly, she didn't feel anything, besides cramps in her pelvis as blood began to pool in her undergarments. *Great*, she realized. *As if things couldn't get any worse, I'm on my period.*

* * *

Day 114 of the Twelve Race War
Unity Hospital

"It's like Groundhog Day in this bitch," her bag, who was speaking with more and more human emotion over the years, said.

"Is this one of those times where I ask what you mean, or just ignore you?"

"It means it feels like we're living the same day over and over."

Syrel responded to that. "For once, Douche Bag, I agree with you."

"Hey! I asked you not to call me that!" Baggie Smalls protested.

"It was your mistake teaching me an insult that has the word 'bag' in it. What did you think was gonna happen?!"

"Whatever you Syrup-ass bitch," it grumbled.

"See, your insults mean nothing to me because I have no idea what you're talking about. You can't beat me."

"Sweetheart, I love you, but you do realize you're arguing with a *bag* right now?"

"And losing!" it added helpfully. Izzie closed the bag before the bickering could go any further.

"It's right, Syrel. It *does* feel like we're living the same day over and over." They were lying in a small tent on Gravipar, which they hadn't left for weeks. Donrel was kind enough to at least make sure they had food on the island, and these days their existence was all work and no play. "We wake up, heal dagger wounds, remove arrows, fix crush injuries, deliver some dwarf and halfling babies, listen to the sounds of fighting in the distance, sleep for a couple hours, and then do it all over again."

"What are you suggesting we do about it?" Syrel wrapped his arms around her and pulled her in to his chest as they lay on their sleeping mat. She pressed her face against his warm skin, relishing the few moments they got to be alone together. He kissed the top of her head, and she snuggled in closer. Her body was already pressed against his, yet still she felt like she needed to be closer. She wanted every inch of her touching every inch of him. This was the only comfort she had right now. Thoughts of his past still plagued her occasionally, especially after the confrontation with Pyke, but mostly she was just happy they were together again. She would never let him go.

"What else *can* we do, Iz?"

"I don't know. I'm venting. There's nothing else *to* do. But what if this never ends? What if we really are just in an endless cycle of fighting?"

"Wars always end. There's never been a war in history that didn't end. I know this one seems especially brutal, but isn't that probably what everybody who lives through a war thinks?"

He had a point. She'd never lived during wartime, so she had no frame of reference, but she had to imagine all who lived through one felt similarly.

"You're so wise, Syrel." She pulled away from him just enough so she could tilt her head up and bring her lips to his. He still gave her goosebumps when he kissed her. The kiss lingered, and Izzie felt his hands run through her hair and slowly move down her back. She moved away slightly.

"We can't do this here! We're in the middle of the hospital; we're basically at work right now."

"Well everybody *else* is doing it; why should *we* have to abstain?"

He had a fair point, and she was easily convinced. She returned his hands to her back and picked up right where they'd left off. Izzie's body stayed in the moment, but her mind wandered. Here they were, in the magically fertile land they had accidentally created, in the shadow of the Mother Tree. The land, flowing with Maternal Magic, that was gifting beautiful, healthy, safe pregnancies to everybody in it, whether they wanted it or not. *But not her.* She'd been here with Syrel for long enough that *something* should have happened by now. After the ritual had gone wrong, she'd instinctively known it had forever cursed her to infertility. If she hadn't been already. As Syrel's hands traveled down her body, she couldn't help but lament she was the only one in Gravipar who wouldn't get pregnant.

They woke up a few hours later to shouting. The panicked voice was familiar.

"Isadore! Syrel! Help!" The two wizards quickly dressed and bolted out of their tent to find Donrel holding his unconscious husband. They were both drenched in blood. Izzie didn't panic, even though these were two of her favorite elves in the world. She immediately went into midwizard mode. Years of delivering babies in high-stress, life-or-death situations had prepared her to keep a level head in even the most dire of circumstances.

"Donrel, set him down gently and tell me exactly what happened."

Izzie began her assessment using her blood magic while he spoke.

"It was chaos. I don't know if it was coordinated, or just terrible luck, but everybody attacked."

"What do you mean everybody?" Syrel interjected.

"Everybody," he half shouted, half wailed. "Halflings riding minotaurs. Dwarves, orcs, giants, fae. Maybe changelings, I'm not sure. Even the humans turned on us when they saw the tide of the battle was shifting. The fighting is still going on. I don't think it will end any time soon, but I had to get him here." Izzie was circulating her blood magic through Werna, and the outlook was bleak. "It was a giant. I think their leader. She was targeting me directly, I'm pretty sure. Revenge for our attack on them a few weeks ago. She was stumbling around a little, almost like she couldn't see?"

Izzie nodded, not pulling her attention away from Werna. "Skygyr. She got an arrow through her eye in your assault. I got it out but she's blind in that eye."

Tears were pouring out of Donrel's eyes, but he continued explaining what happened. "We were retreating, trying to regroup. I think she was aiming for me but missed because she couldn't see. Her club slammed directly into his back and he dropped to the ground. Thankfully the rest of my guard was able to distract her while I carried him out. None of them made it."

She almost lost her concentration when he revealed his entire personal guard had died protecting them. That was eleven highly-trained warriors. Gone. Just like that. *When will it end? Is this the final reckoning? Everybody on one battlefield?*

She focused as hard as she could on figuring out where the injury was. There was no internal bleeding. Some severe bruising in his legs and a few broken ribs. But Izzie couldn't find anything else wrong. She circulated a little extra blood to his brain to give him a jolt and wake him up, a trick she had learned while helping Pyke through preterm labor.

Werna's eyes opened slowly. Donrel made to grab his husband, but Syrel held him back so Izzie could continue her work.

"Hey, Werna. It's Izzie. You were attacked by a giant in battle. Are you in pain?"

He seemed to think for a moment, internally doing his own assessment. "My stomach and my ribs are killing me. I think I broke something."

Izzie nodded in agreement. "You have a few broken ribs, but those will heal." She touched one of the worst bruises on his leg, seeing if there were any signs it was still bleeding, but everything seemed stable. "Does that hurt?"

"No, not at all."

He must be in shock, Izzie thought. These bruises should have been exquisitely tender. She poked another one under his knee, this time squeezing a little harder. "How about that?"

He shook his head. "Nope. No pain at all in my legs." Izzie's stomach dropped when she realized what was happening.

"Can you wiggle your foot for me?"

Werna stared at his foot in deep concentration. Izzie could practically see the disconnect between mind and body as he gave the mental command for his foot to move. Nothing. His face scrunched up as he tried harder, but nothing happened.

"What's happening, Izzie? What's going on? What's wrong with his legs?" Donrel asked, breaking past Syrel and collapsing to the ground next to his husband. "I'm here, babe. I'm here. Everything is going to be okay. Izzie is going to fix you. Don't worry. I'm here."

Izzie grimaced at Donrel's promise. She wasn't sure she *was* going to be able to fix him. This wasn't a blood issue, which she could fix easily. Even bones had enough blood supply she was able to fix them when they broke. But nerve issues? There wasn't much she could do about that.

"I'll do my best, but I can't make any promises."

Donrel whipped his head around to face her. "Can't make any promises? Izzie, this is *Werna*. My *husband*. You *have to* fix him."

"Like I said, I will do my best."

"Your best?!" the elf exploded. "You'll do *your best*? You've been here healing everybody else for months. Wicked orcs and bloodthirsty giants. We helped you build this thing, and now you can't heal the only one who matters?"

"Donrel," Syrel said, his tone gentle but firm. "You know how much we care about both of you. You have to let Izzie work. She's going to try to fix him, but only if you allow her to concentrate."

The elf was pacified enough to keep his mouth shut. Izzie didn't blame him for his outburst. Right now, he wasn't her friend, or an elven general. He was a scared husband, worried about the one he loved the most.

She had no idea if she could heal him. All around her, the wounded were starting to pour in. Some humans dropped off a female with a missing leg, and blood sprites buzzed over and immediately started working on her. The process repeated itself with a gored dwarf, an arrow-riddled orc, an elf with a dagger sticking out of his abdomen, and a halfling with an obvious axe wound. If it weren't for the blood sprites' support, they never would have been able to heal all of these creatures. Izzie turned her attention back to Werna and extended her blood magic to him. She focused on his spine. She visualized the blood vessels supplying the nerves that extended to his legs. They were completely crushed, the arteries and veins all sheared. She knew the moment she saw it there was no chance of recovery. Werna would never walk again. She spent a few more minutes completing her examination, but she knew there was nothing she could do, and she had to tell his husband.

She removed her hands from Werna, who had lapsed back into unconsciousness after the brief effect of her blood magic wore off.

"Donrel, we should be thankful he's alive. But—"

"No!" the elf shouted. "No 'but.' Don't say it. You can fix him, Izzie. You're supposed to be the best. You barely tried," he cried. "Keep going. Please."

She shook her head slowly. "I'm sorry, friend. There's nothing I can do. He's paralyzed from the waist down. He'll never be able to walk again."

Donrel broke down into a blubbering mess, draping his body over his newly paraplegic husband.

"This is my fault," he sobbed. "She was aiming for me. I'm sorry, Werna. I'm so sorry. This is all my fault."

Syrel tried to comfort him. "Donrel, of course it's not your fault. This is war. We all knew the risks. Don't do this."

"Please," he sobbed gently. "Please, there has to be something else you can do."

"Come on, Donrel." Syrel said. "I'll help you carry Werna to our tent. You both need to rest."

The elven general collected himself like only a warrior could. "The only thing I can do for him is continue to lead my troops and emerge victorious. I have to go back."

"Donrel, please," Izzie pleaded. "You're going to die out there. You have a target on your back as the leader of the elves. Please, just stay here where it's safe."

"Izzie, are you truly that naive to think this little hospital is going to be protected forever? *This is what we're fighting for.* All of the armies are allowing you to have this for now, but don't you realize the first thing the winner of this war is going to do is wipe you and the rest of the inhabitants of this island off the face of Cosconia?"

She did know that, but there was nothing else she could do. She would spend every waking breath she had left doing good for the world. Her old friend didn't say anything else. Syrel convinced him to at least spend a few hours with his injured husband, and they walked away, whispering back and forth.

CHAPTER THIRTY-ONE

An Indecent Proposal

Love doesn't conquer everything. And whoever
thinks it does is a fool.

—Donna Tartt

Day 100 of the Twelve Race War
Unity Hospital

The battle that continued to rage east of the island was far more brutal than any before it. Having so many armies on the same battlefield created a chaos that resulted in a myriad of gruesome injuries. Izzie noticed that soldiers were dropping off their wounded and then charging right back into the war zone, not spending an extra second in the relative safety of the hospital.

A pair of halflings dropped off a comrade with a clean hole directly through the middle of his abdomen. The work of a fae water spear. She got to work immediately. One of the halflings lingered nearby. Izzie noticed jagged scars on the top of her head.

"... Pyke? Is that you?"

The halfling shifted to a changeling with stunning purple eyes. She ran toward Izzie and embraced her.

"You were right. I just had to be honest with the changelings and they listened. None of us want to be a part of this war, but we can't sit idly by while this bloodshed continues. So we're helping you. It's easy for us to get around the battlefield undetected. When we see somebody wounded, we morph into their race and carry them off."

"Pyke, that's... that's incredible. I was wondering how so many wounded were making it here safely. You're going to save so many lives this way." Izzie marveled at the courage of her friend.

"The credit is with my people. They are the true heroes."

"Pyke, you're a bigger hero than all of us. How are you doing?"

The changeling began to answer, but Izzie interrupted her. "No, how are you *really* doing?"

A look of steely determination crossed her face. "I have a purpose again. I'm going to save as many lives as I can; then I'm going to get the hells out of here and live happily ever after with Cap."

Izzie pulled her oldest friend into an embrace. "You've earned it."

The changeling started to leave, but then stopped herself.

"How are things going with Ne... Syrel?" Just saying his proper name seemed to pain her. "He better be treating you right. I won't kill him for my sake, but I'll certainly kill him for yours."

She grinned. "He's good, Pyke. Thank you for asking. He hasn't stopped working on his healing magic, and he's indispensable to running this hospital. He's been good to me. Very good. I think it's the real deal this time." *Technically*, they weren't engaged or anything like that, but Izzie couldn't see the relationship ending. Not again.

She smiled softly. "There's something I need to tell you about him, Izzie. I've never confirmed it, but I have my suspicions."

"I don't want to know," she said hurriedly. "I trust him, and if there's anything he isn't telling me, I believe he has a good reason for it. So please, for now, just keep it to yourself."

Pyke looked unhappy, but she didn't say anything else. She walked off to return to the battlefield. Syrel sauntered up as Izzie finished working on the injured halfling. He kissed her on the cheek, which elicited a wide smile from her. Even in the midst of a bloody war, his touch still filled her heart with joy. Every single day, she considered just running away together. They could, if they wanted to. They could return to Gifldor, where the rest of wizardkind was staying above the fray. Nobody would bother them. But then she would be leaving behind thousands who could be healed by her blood magic. She would see this thing through to the end.

"Was that Pyke?"

Izzie explained how the changelings were assisting in their healing effort. He didn't seem surprised.

"You already knew?"

He grinned. "I chatted with a few changelings who dropped off an injured fae."

"A fae? I thought Lulu wouldn't allow them to come to our hospital?"

"She won't, but the report I got after I healed her was that Lulu hasn't left her tent in weeks. Doren is leading the army, and he said everybody has the right to be healed. The queen isn't even on the battlefield."

"Good. I hope that means Doren won't lead a charge on Gravipar. I've been constantly worried Lulu was going to attack the hospital."

"I think I have something that might help quell your fears a bit."

"You gonna go kill her ass?" Baggie Smalls piped up from the ground, next to the halfling she'd just healed. "You already killed her husband; might as well finish the job."

Syrel winced and kicked the bag. "That was a low blow."

"Speaking of low blows, when are you two getting married?

"Alright," Izzie interrupted before Syrel could get into it with the bag again. Those two were *not* destined to be friends. "That's enough. What's your plan?"

"Well, it's more like an idea that you, and probably Pyke, will have to enact." Syrel explained his thoughts, which were to send a delegation of changelings to the mermaids in Lork and convince them to join their side. After Queen Luxor's betrayal of the dwarves, he postulated they would be willing to change sides.

"You're brilliant, you know that?"

"Of course I do. That's why you love me."

She rolled her eyes. "Mostly I just love your humility."

"It's one of my many, *many* fantastic qualities."

"And to think, I used to only like you because you were good in the sack..."

Syrel gasped in mock surprise. "Isadore, you saucy minx! You're making me blush!"

"I know for a fact it takes a lot more than that to make you blush, Syrel. You have absolutely no shame."

To Izzie's surprise, he actually *was* blushing. The sounds of battle could still be heard in the distance. She knew this clash was the big one. It would likely last weeks, and they would be run ragged in the meantime. Her flirty conversation with her boyfriend was entirely incongruous with their surroundings. Dying creatures from every race surrounded them. The smell of blood was thick in the air. Yet she could still lose herself in those eyes.

"So, Izzie, I've been thinking."

"That's a first!" she retorted.

"Wow, a classic zinger." He rolled his eyes. "You're starting to sound like Baggie."

"That is the cruelest of all insults!" she playfully smacked the back of his head. "What have you been thinking, my love?"

"Well I've been thinking about you, since you're pretty much all I think about. For a long time, I was just so... lost? I'm not really sure what the right word is. I felt empty, like nothing could fill the void inside me after I lost you. When I saw you again, even though I was in the fist of a spurned changeling-slash-giantess ex-lover, everything clicked back into place. I know it was a long time before we finally got together again, but just knowing you were alive and safe kept me going. That night, at Donrel and Werna's wedding..." he choked up at this part, looking over at the tent in which Werna convalesced. "I couldn't believe I was getting a second chance with you. I didn't deserve it. I still don't. But I won't blow it again. You're everything to me, Isadore. Even in the face of all this pain and suffering, I still can't help but smile when I wake up with you next to me. When I look at you, I know it's all gonna be okay. I can't live without you, my darling."

Syrel bent down to one knee. Izzie's eyes widened with realization. It was a distinctly human custom to get down on one knee to propose marriage, but it had been widely adopted in Cosconia. *No no no. This can't be happening. Not here. Not now. I'm not ready. Do I even truly know him? Pyke thinks he's still keeping secrets from me. He has a changeling kid somewhere out there. Not to mention we're in the middle of a* fucking *war! Surrounded by the dead and the dying. And he's going to ask me to marry him* here? *Of all places?* She barely believed in the concept of a traditional marriage. The environment around them faded as she completely lost herself in his words. She could no longer hear the sounds of battle from the east, drifting over the water. The wounded around them seemed to disappear.

"I love you, Isadore. I've loved you from the moment I saw your adorable, sleepy face stuck to a book all those years ago. I loved you all the years we spent apart. And I love you still more every day. Even when life is uncomfortable, I am always comfortable with you. You're all I need. If Cosconia collapses around us, which it might," he laughed nervously, "I want to be holding your hand when it does. Being with you is simply *easy*, even when it's hard. Your laugh melts me inside. Your touch inspires me, like I could *do* anything, *be* anything. You are the strongest wizard I've ever met—physically, emotionally, mentally, and if I'm being honest, sexually." Tears were already streaming down her face, yet she couldn't help but laugh at this. "I love you, I want you, and I need you. All of you, by my side, forever."

He was really doing this. He was going to pop the question right here, in their makeshift hospital, in the middle of an active war zone. Was he insane? How could she make a lifelong commitment in these circumstances? The logical part of her brain was screaming at her to say no. It wasn't the right time. It wasn't the right place. None of this was happening like it was supposed to.

Syrel pulled something out of his pocket. It was a simple wooden ring with a small, gray stone on top. The ring was a deep cherry color... *No. It couldn't be. It was destroyed...* But there it was. Right in front of her. The wand that was destroyed in the ritual all those years ago. She would recognize it anywhere. Her very first wand. Fashioned into an engagement ring. A thought crossed her mind—hadn't Syrel been kidnapped immediately after he woke up? How did he end up with her wand? *I must be misremembering the details, and it's certainly not the time to open old wounds. I need to let the past stay in the past.*

"Isadore, will you marry me?"

"Yes. Yes! A thousand times yes!" she said without hesitation. It didn't matter the time or the place. It didn't matter if it wasn't happening like it was *supposed to*, whatever that meant. She fought through the tears to continue. "Of course I will marry you, Syrel. You are my light in the darkness. You bring me joy on my hardest days. You pull me out of my spirals. You can make me laugh in a way that brings joy to my very soul. Only you would propose in the middle of a war, but that's what I love about you—tradition and common sense be damned! You are so distinctly *yourself*, and I wouldn't have it any other way. I never, *ever* stopped loving you, and I'm certain I never will." Syrel slid the ring on her finger. It fit perfectly, and she felt a surge of power wash over her. She closely examined her new piece of jewelry. The words *Mine Forever* were engraved on the bottom. She broke down when she saw the same phrase she'd engraved on his shoulder all those years ago. Izzie could barely even see through the tears that poured out of her eyes.

"H-how... The wand...? And what am I feeling...?"

He smiled his classic Syrel smile that never failed to melt her inside. "I've been working on it for a while. You know I love tinkering. You deserve nothing but the best. I found a fragment of it after... well, you know. It still holds much of your power, and I think something about the ritual imbued it with something ancient. I also enchanted it with a couple spells of my own. I think it will enhance your already great power... quite a bit."

"Wait—enchantments? It's not going to talk, is it? One sentient inanimate object is plenty for me."

Syrel burst out laughing, wiping tears from his own eyes. "Absolutely not," he chuckled. "I think our little family of three is plenty."

"Awww you really do love me, don't you?!" said Baggie Smalls, who'd apparently been listening and observing the whole time.

"You know what," answered Syrel, "you're a part of Izzie, and I love every part of her... so yes. I do love you."

"You do know that you're talking to a literal bag, ya weirdo?"

"Oh knock it off! We all love each other, and you know it."

"He's right—we do all love each other." Izzie heard a small voice say from behind her. She spun around to see Lago, beaming. Next to her was Donrel, grinning from ear to ear, holding his husband, who was now awake. The last surprise guest, Arkan, also smiled at the newly engaged couple.

"You... I thought you went back... and Werna," Izzie stuttered, barely holding it together. She whirled back around to Syrel, who stood up, put both of his hands on Izzie's cheeks, and pulled her face toward his. Her whole body felt hot at his touch. Here they were, in the worst possible place to get engaged, surrounded by their closest friends. His lips touched hers, gingerly at first, likely not wanting to give the onlookers too much of a show. She didn't care. Izzie was overwhelmed with passion and love for Syrel. She couldn't contain it. She wrapped her arms around his back and pulled him deeper into the kiss, her tongue finding his. She ignored the hooting and hollering from the crowd behind her, losing herself in the wizard with whom she'd spend the rest of her life.

Izzie finally pulled back, worried that if they got too hot and heavy she wouldn't be able to reign herself in. They were, unfortunately, technically at work. She examined the beautiful handcrafted ring again. She could still feel the power of her former wand coursing through her body. The stone at the top, though simple, felt deeply powerful. It looked vaguely familiar. A portion of what looked like an ancient rune glowed a faint scarlet at the top.

"Syrel, this stone. Is it..."

"Yep. I chipped a small piece of rock off one from the ritual circle. Those stones were surprisingly sturdy, but this is directly from the wizard's stone."

She tried to read the rune on the top, but it wasn't complete. "What's it mean?"

He winked at her. "It's a secret."

"Okay, first, you know I hate it when you wink. Second, I thought we agreed—no more secrets!"

"Fine, fine." He winked again, this time just to irritate her. "It's a rune specifically about blood magic. I think it will make your Affinity even more powerful."

Their friends, unable to contain themselves any longer, surrounded the couple with hugs and handshakes all around. Donrel carried Werna, both smiling through the pain. Arkan produced a flask of liquor from her robe, and Izzie pulled out a few tankards from her bag. Anybody observing the scene must have thought they were insane. Two wizards, an elven general with his bodyguard husband, an orc, a talking bag, and a dwarf, passing around mugs of liquor, surrounded by the ailing victims of a brutal war. The sound of swords hitting shields, the thundering stampedes of minotaurs, and the rumbling shouts of giants provided the background noise. They didn't care, ignoring the horrors for just a moment. It reminded Izzie of a time in the Jerdalin Forest, so many years ago. When Syrel was telling his story and Arkan thought Pyke tossing him into the Wasteland was the funniest thing she'd ever heard.

Somehow, gentle flute music came from her bag, drowning out the sounds of war. Izzie grabbed Syrel's hand, and they danced like the world wasn't falling apart. Everybody laughed. Everybody cried. Blood sprites buzzed around them, attending to the wounded in their absence. Syrel sat on the ground and talked softly to Werna while she danced with Donrel. Arkan continued to fill their glasses with liquor and the motley crew grew drunker and happier.

Donrel rested his head on Izzie's shoulder and finally let out the tears he'd been holding back. She held him as he cried, grieving with him. Lago reminisced on times with her twin brother, who she couldn't believe was now the leader of the dwarf army. Arkan spoke of how much she loved being a mother. Every few minutes, even as they talked to their friends, Izzie would make eye contact with Syrel and her heart would explode all over again. She was going to *marry* the love of her life. At long last.

Eventually, they all collapsed to the ground. The booze was really starting to hit them, and night had fallen in the background like a flake of snow gently falling in the Frost Mountains. Her wizard's constitution made her particularly tolerant of copious amounts of alcohol, but Arkan was a heavy pourer. They all lay on the ground, staring up at the stars. Izzie drunkenly wondered what was out there. Before she could get too lost in her thoughts, Syrel pulled her to her feet. He softly kissed her hair, which was plastered to her head with sweat. He didn't need to say anything as he led her by the hand back to their shared tent. She smiled to herself as she thought about how he was about to be the luckiest wizard in Cosconia.

* * *

Day 101 of the Twelve Race War
Somewhere in the Northwest Wasteland

One hundred days. Dalfa had been without magic for one hundred days. Brutal days of fever, chills, nausea, vomiting, shortness of breath, and chest pain. She'd had no idea the consequences of burnout could be so severe. As she did every morning, she'd tested out a minor Affinity spell to see if her magic was back, and it had finally returned the day before. She still felt mildly ill, but she knew she was on her way to recovery. She confirmed she could still create as many copies of herself as before, which was a massive relief.

All she could think about was the letter from Izzie. For years, Dalfa had languished with severe anxiety and depression over the horrors she had witnessed. She was plagued with nightmares of freles dying, babies suffering. Many people, including some she deeply cared for, had perished during labor and delivery. She'd known pregnancy was dangerous in Cosconia prior to this... ritual, or whatever it was. But she had watched the situation grow worse and worse before her very eyes.

And it was all Izzie's fault. *She* was the reason Dalfa quit midwizardry, unable to handle the bleak outcomes. *She* was the reason freles were dying left and right in Cosconia. *She* was the reason Dalfa still couldn't sleep at night. She trudged through the Wasteland, making her way toward Gravipar. Toward Izzie.

When she really thought about it, *Izzie* had started this war. Not her. There would be no war in the first place without this damned failed ritual or whatever the hells really happened there. How could she have ever been friends with such a monster? Somebody willing to sacrifice the health of hundreds of thousands of Cosconia's most fragile and helpless individuals, just so she could get pregnant? It was sick. Twisted.

A fire loomed in the distance, and the scent was the unmistakable odor of burning flesh and hair. Every step brought Dalfa closer to her end goal. To confront Izzie and tell her what a monster she really was. Tell everybody how the land they were fighting over, the reason they even needed to fight in the first place, was all her fault. And for that, she would pay the ultimate price.

CHAPTER THIRTY-TWO

She's Gonna Be All Right

A hospital alone shows what war is.

—Erich Remarque

Day 153 of the Twelve Race War
The Eastern Wasteland

Pyke knelt down to examine a halfling with a deep gouge in his shoulder, likely from a human sword. She tried as best as she could to turn off her emotions and examine the "patient," as Izzie called them. It helped maintain detachment to think of them as "patients" instead of living beings; it was already too heartbreaking watching so many lives being snuffed out. Blood poured from his wound, and he was barely hanging on to consciousness. Before Pyke could determine if he'd make it to the midwizard's hospital, she watched the small creature take his last breath. She gently closed his eyes, giving him one final shred of dignity. She tried to reassure herself this likely wasn't his last life, that, unlike her, he'd reincarnate into another race as Sparilism taught. It was hard to believe in any god, much less twelve, when examining the scene around her.

She continued to wander the battlefield, numb to the horrors. She and her people were choosing to stay above the fray and not actively participate in the war, transporting the wounded and the dying. They were practically the janitors of the war by this point, moving the wounded to the hospital and carting the bodies off. The fighting would often cease at night, none of the armies wanting to risk harming their own soldiers in the dark confusion, which was when Pyke and thousands of other changelings would descend on the bloodied land and listen for the cries of the wounded. They knew more would take their place the next day.

The changelings had learned to perform a quick triage assessment to determine if the fallen could make the trip back to Gravipar, or if they would have to pray their god would take them before the fighting resumed the next day. Some of her comrades, when faced with the mortally wounded or somebody in excruciating pain, would hasten the job. It was a mercy, but it still weighed heavy on the conscience of the one performing the act. The changelings had something Baggie Smalls called "ambulances" to carry the wounded, which were really just repurposed cargo carts, previously used to transport weapons, food, water, and supplies to their camp.

She continued to push her cart, which already had several wounded creatures inside, over discarded shields, severed limbs, and corpses. *So many corpses.* Once it was full, she would return her ambulance to Gravipar and hope the blood sprites and Izzie's team could heal them. Judging by the number of dead bodies the changelings hauled off the island every day, Pyke knew many of the injured warriors she carted in would never again see the light of day. The dead bodies were brought to the former changeling encampment, which now held a funeral pyre that grew larger every day. The acrid scent of burning flesh permeated the days, and the macabre glowing light of the fire illuminated the nights.

The Apex Changeling reflected on the battleground around her. Nearly all races were now represented here, with Izzie being the only wizard choosing to join the war, and this battle was exponentially larger than any that had taken place previously. The camps of each army were less than a half-mile apart. It was quiet right now in the dead of night, a nearly full moon casting the war-torn land in an eerie haze, though some nights the fighting raged deep into the darkness. Eventually, each army would make a tactical retreat until everybody was back at their own encampment, licking their wounds. *Why can't it just be like this all the time?* Pyke wondered. *Everybody is here, in their own camps, coexisting.*

It was still deep in the night when the ground started to rumble softly. Pyke looked around but couldn't see anything yet. She morphed into an elf, which would heighten her senses. She directed her pointed ear toward the ground. *Minotaur stampede,* she realized. It wasn't a true stampede, since the minotaurs typically walked on two humanoid legs, but their powerful muscles granted them the ability to run far and fast. A classic minotaur army technique was to charge at an opposing army, baring their horns and ripping right through anybody in their path. Many would fall, but the devastation a minotaur stampede could cause was legendary. She had to get out of here. Plenty of changelings would take the risk of sticking around during the fighting to evacuate the injured, their altruism outweighing their sense of self-preservation, but Pyke had to prioritize her own life so she could continue to lead. Especially now that she'd finally won the loyalty of her people. She would never force anybody to be here, but she was moved by how many chose to do so of their own volition.

410

Pyke spun her cart around and made a beeline toward Gravipar. The sound of the stampede was getting closer, meaning they were headed in her direction. She morphed into her orc form so that her brute strength could assist her in pushing the cart along as quickly as possible.

"Help... me..." a weak voice called out as Pyke rolled past an unmoving pile of bodies. She stopped to examine the gruesome scene. A mangled mass of orcish, human, and elven corpses was stacked higher than she was tall. There were no signs of life in the huge pile, nearly all the bodies sporting evidence of water injuries—water cannon blasts, water spear punctures, and even a few who looked like they had drowned.

"Is somebody alive in there?" The rumble behind her grew louder by the second. "Speak now or forever hold your peace!"

"Yes, I'm here," a frele voice answered, the sound muffled by layers of bodies. "I can't move. Please help me."

Pyke glanced over her shoulder to see the dust rising above the stampeding minotaurs. She still had to pass the dwarf encampment to get to Gravipar, so that must be where the herd was headed. She reckoned she had about a minute until they arrived at this spot. She briefly considered morphing into a giant, but she was worried it would put a target on her back. Pyke began hefting corpses over her head, attempting to unbury the creature who had called for help. After tossing aside at least a dozen bodies, she uncovered a water fae who looked barely conscious. She started to pick the frele up, but she screamed out in pain, causing Pyke to hesitate and look closer. There was a sword driven through the frele's left bicep and straight into the ground. She was pinned. Pyke, still in orc form, wrapped her rough, blue hands around the hilt and attempted to pull, but the sword barely budged. The fae screamed at even the slightest movement.

Shit shit shit, Pyke cursed to herself. The stampede was drawing closer, maybe thirty seconds behind her. She made a judgment call.

"I'm sorry," she said, abandoning the fae to pull the rest of the wounded to safety. "There's no time."

"Please," the frele pleaded. "I'm pregnant. Please. I've been trying for years and it finally happened. I just felt the baby move for the first time today. *Please.*"

Pyke hesitated for a moment but quickly changed her mind. As a mother herself, especially one who so desperately missed her son, she couldn't abandon this pregnant frele to die on the battlefield.

"What's your name, sweetheart?"

"Ruta. Thank you for coming back," she whimpered.

Pyke yanked a leather belt off a nearby elf and cinched it around the fae's shoulder as tightly as she could. Instantly the fae's ebony skin started to turn pale as the blood supply was cut off.

"Ruta, I don't think you're going to like what I'm about to do. But it's the only way to save you." Pyke picked up a bloodied axe that lay on the ground.

"Wait wait what are you—"

She didn't give the injured fae time to finish her sentence. The sound of the axe falling through the air seemed to momentarily drown out the approaching stampede. The cold steel sliced cleanly through flesh and bone, just below the shoulder, liberating the fae from her arm. She let out a blood-curdling scream, and Pyke tossed her into the cart with the rest of the wounded. She quickly morphed into a minotaur and grabbed the handles of her cart so she could escape with her own life intact. The charging horde was less than a hundred yards behind her, their momentum spurring them forward. Pyke took off toward

Gravipar with the fae still shrieking and staring at the space her arm used to occupy. The fastest way to Gravipar was directly northeast through the dwarf camp, so that was the direction she headed. The border of the camp quickly approached, with hundreds of dwarves lined up at the ready, axes poised to defend themselves against the stampeding minotaurs.

"I'm a changeling medic!" she called, hoping the dwarves wouldn't kill her on sight. "Please, let me through! I have an injured dwarf in my cart!" That was a lie, but she was hoping that with a herd of angry minotaurs hot on her heels, they wouldn't take the time to verify her claim. Her cart jumped as a minotaur at the head of the pack rammed it with their horns. She kicked her own speed up a notch, the dwarves parting their battle formation just in front of her so she could ride through. The line closed behind her as she heard the sound of horn puncturing shield and axe slamming into flesh. She didn't turn around until she'd made it all the way to the other side of the dwarf camp.

She dropped to her knees when she saw the gruesome scene. Minotaur heads flew into the air as the dwarves' heavy battle axes cleaved through their necks. But just as many dwarves ended up on the business end of a pair of sharpened horns or under the charging herd. As if it couldn't get any worse, a massive deluge of water dropped on the clashing creatures, drowning several right on the spot. Pyke looked to the north, where a fae battalion was marching toward the already bloody battle, hundreds of fae with their hands in the air casting a group water spell. She quickly morphed back to her natural changeling form so nobody would confuse her for an enemy combatant. When she took the time to further examine her surroundings, she saw dozens of changelings in a similar position to her— headed toward Gravipar with looks of horror on their faces and carts full of fallen soldiers.

Pyke turned away from the bleak scene, which would only get worse as another army joined the fray. She had picked up the long, wooden handles of her cart and started toward the nearest bridge when she saw a water fae break away from his army just as it descended upon the dwarves and minotaurs. *I just can't catch a break here, can I?*

"I'm a medic!" she yelled at the mele who was now running full speed toward her. She morphed into her water fae form, ready to fight fire with fire... or, more accurately, water with water. *This war would be another beast entirely if there were fire fae in Cosconia.* She drew from the water in the air to form a water spear, but let it splash to the ground when the fae finally came into focus.

"*Doren*? Is that you?"

The fae didn't even acknowledge her. "Ruta? Oh gods Ruta, what happened?" he screamed, shaking the now unconscious one-armed water fae. "Ruta! Please, babe, wake up!"

"Doren!" Pyke shouted, attempting in vain to get the fae's attention. "Doren! You have to let me take her to the island."

"... Pyke? Is that you? What are you doing here? How did you find Ruta?"

"I've been bringing the wounded to Gravipar. She was pinned to the ground and I freed her, but I have to get her to Izzie."

"Is she alive?"

"Yes, and I intend for her to stay that way."

"Pyke, you have to save Ruta. I love her. I couldn't find her after a clash yesterday. I thought for sure she was dead. But..." He glanced at the hospital across the channel. "Will they really help her?"

Pyke nodded her head vigorously. "I promise you they will. But you have to let me take her. Now." He still hadn't seemed to process that his partner was down an arm, but the tourniquet wasn't able to hold back all the blood from the open wound.

Doren looked to his army, now deeply mired in the battle. In the distance, a group of giants could be seen making their way toward the ongoing engagement. The fae formed a water bubble with his hands, whispered into it, and pushed it toward his army.

"I'm coming with you. I just handed off control to my second-in-command. I can't send Ruta to be around *him* alone."

Pyke wasn't thrilled about bringing Doren to the island for a possible confrontation with his father's murderer, but she didn't think she had a choice. She had to get the wounded as far away from this battle as she could.

"Fine, but you have to promise to *not engage*. Gravipar is a place of *healing*, not fighting."

* * *

Day 153 of the Twelve Race War
Water Fae Encampment

Queen Luxor seethed. She sat alone in her tent, which had become her prison. She knew she was a liability, as mind control spells were unpredictable and poorly understood. As far as she could tell, her actions hadn't been controlled since the peace summit. There was no way to know if the spell was broken, however, and most experts postulated it couldn't be fully broken until the caster was dead. And even then, the long term effects were unknown. The fae had no idea where the mind mage was, in spite of their best efforts to find her.

She could hear the low hum of battle drift over the flat terrain. Doren had led their troops to the clash east of Gravipar several weeks before, and she hadn't heard any reports since then. The sound of fighting rarely died down, and she wondered how long this war could possibly go on.

Instead of being the hero who brought peace to Cosconia, she was the villain. The slaughterer. The monster. She'd been forced to cede control of her people to her own son, which hurt regardless of how competent a leader he was. While everybody else put life and limb on the line, she was stuck here under constant guard. She'd lost her alliances with the mermaids *and* the dwarves. She hadn't seen Pyke since she'd sent her to kill Syrel, which had also been a bust.

Queen Luxor felt like she didn't even know herself anymore. She used to be known for her kindness. Everybody she met would comment on her gentle and bubbly nature. But the day of the coronation had ruined everything. Her life had been nothing but a series of unfortunate events, each worse than the last, since that day. Nothing was going her way. And it all went back to one person: Syrel. If it weren't for him, she would be peacefully ruling her kingdom, far away from here.

"Guards!" she called to the water fae who were always stationed outside her tent, but there was no response. "Guards? Hello?" Still nothing.

"Help! The mind mage is back!" she shouted to no response.

She was alone. For the first time in months, she was alone. She formed a sharp blade of water and started to cut through her bonds. It would take days, but if left unattended, she could break free.

Everybody already thought she was a murderer, so she would prove them all right and kill Syrel if it was the last thing she did.

CHAPTER THIRTY-THREE

Reconciliation

---

*We need never be hopeless, because we can
never be irreparably broken.*

—*John Green*

Day 153 of the Twelve Race War
Unity Hospital

"Izzie! Izzie, come quick!" Syrel awoke to the sound of his fiancée's name being called with increasing volume and urgency. He rolled over to find she was already gone, even though it was still the middle of the night. For the past few weeks, she had been constantly performing ultrasounds on changelings who were showing up to Gravipar pregnant or in labor. He chuckled to himself thinking of the situation. Soldiers couldn't seem to help themselves from fornicating between battles, which was causing a baby boom in Gravipar. While Izzie focused on being the midwizard she was trained to be, her already potent blood magic still growing more powerful every day, he was doing his best to use his much weaker blood magic to stabilize and treat as many wounded as he could.

Gravipar was practically bursting at the seams with pregnant and postpartum freles, newborns, the sick, the injured, and the freshly dead. There had to be over ten thousand individuals on the small island at this point. With the war at its zenith and battles leaving hundreds more wounded every day, the hospital would soon have to start turning away the wounded. Izzie was constantly trying to figure out solutions to the overcrowding, but she hadn't come up with anything yet. She couldn't very well kick a bunch of pregnant freles and babies off the island into an active war zone, so they were in a bit of a pickle.

He climbed out of the tent he shared with Izzie to find the source of the voice yelling her name.

"Isadore! We need you! Help!" Syrel jogged toward the voice, only to find the two Cosconians who would most like to see him dead. His former changeling partner and the son of the fae he'd murdered in cold blood, standing at the edge of their crowded island. He felt sick seeing the fatherless child—who wasn't much of a child anymore—and leader of the fae army. But he was working on taking responsibility for his actions, accepting the past, and focusing on the future, so he would tackle this head on.

"Pyke, I—"

"Save it, Nesbitch. Where's Izzie?"

"I don't know. She left in the middle of the night. The hospital is at max capacity right now and she hasn't stopped delivering babies and taking care of pregnant freles."

"We have to find her right now. She has to help save this girl."

Syrel quickly assessed the water fae, who was bleeding briskly from her severed arm, in spite of the tourniquet in place. Her battle armor was soaked in bright blue blood, and her dark skin was pale and blotchy.

"She doesn't have time, Pyke. She's lost too much blood. You have to let me help."

418

"Absolutely not," Doren interjected, stepping between Syrel and the frele. His voice was fiery. "He'll kill her like he killed my father!"

Syrel couldn't blame him for feeling that way. He took a deep breath as he thought about what to do next. He had so much he wanted to say to both of these individuals, but it wasn't the time. There were no blood sprites nearby, Izzie was occupied, and the fae frele needed help *this instant*.

"Please, Doren, you have to trust me. I have to make the bleeding stop *this minute* or she's going to die."

Doren looked at Pyke, who hesitated a moment before nodding her head slightly.

"You have to trust him. We both do. He's changed. I think." Syrel looked at Pyke with genuine surprise before she turned back to Doren. "There's no other option."

The fire in his voice was extinguished by Pyke's words. He sounded defeated. "Please," he begged. "Please save her."

Syrel lifted his wand and cast the blood magic spell he used at least a hundred times a day. "*Dejasangra*." He and Izzie had practiced this one at length before the war, knowing that getting bleeding to stop would be the most important piece of magic they could have. He'd grown his Skill quite a bit by now, and instantly the bleeding slowed. It was too heavy for him to fully stop, even with his Intent at an all time high in an effort to make up for past sins.

"Okay, Pyke, go find Izzie. She's probably in the nursery, the structure around the Mother Tree." Without another word, the changeling morphed into an elf and ran off.

Though the bleeding had stopped, it was clear to Syrel the fae had lost too much blood. She wasn't going to make it long enough for Izzie to work her magic. He had to take a gamble here.

"Doren, are you willing to do anything to save her?"

"Anything," the despondent fae croaked. "I'll do anything."

"You're going to have to trust me. I need you to cut your arm open."

"What! Are you trying to kill us both? Finish the job you started by killing my father?"

Syrel took a deep breath. *I deserved that.* "She's lost too much blood. She needs some of it replaced. We've had good success transfusing blood from one individual to another. I would do it, but it's more likely to work if it comes from somebody of the same race." He pointed toward a jagged cut down his own forearm and explained how he'd had to do the same thing to save the frele he loved. "There is a risk her body doesn't accept it, but this is our only choice."

Doren eyed him suspiciously as he took out his dagger.

"I love you, Ruta. This is for you." The fae mele dragged the dagger from the crook of his elbow to the bend of his wrist. Blood immediately began to pour from the wound.

"*Sangrimovi,*" Syrel muttered, pointing his wand toward Doren's arm. The fae flinched as his mortal nemesis pointed a wand at him, but to his credit, he stayed stone still. Syrel slowly moved his wand from the mele to the frele, bringing the now floating blood toward her arm. The only other time he'd done this was when Izzie had been hurt. His Skill with the spell was low, so it took every ounce of Intent and focus he had within him to perform the transfusion. He wished Izzie was here. Her control over blood was unparalleled.

"*Regrasangra,*" he continued, forcing the blood into Ruta's bloodstream. He couldn't sense the circulatory system like his fiancée could, so he said a small prayer that the fae's body would accept it. If her body rejected the blood, Doren would blame him and probably try to kill him.

Syrel breathed a sigh of relief when some color started returning to the frele's lovely dark skin. She stirred slightly, the first outward sign of life she had displayed. He finished transferring the blood from Doren to Ruta, then tightened the tourniquet around her upper arm to prevent any further bleeding. He used *dejasangra* and then *pelocer* to stop the bleeding from Doren's self-inflicted wound, and then collapsed to the ground, spent from using the spell with minimal Skill and no Affinity. *I have to be careful or I'm going to burn myself out*, he thought, then wondered if that was even possible.

Doren didn't attempt to help him up, choosing instead to hang on tightly to Ruta. After several minutes of silence, her eyes cracked open.

"Wh... what happened? Where am I?"

"Shhh, shhh." Doren comforted her. "You're okay. You're safe. Remember Pyke? She found you and brought you to the island."

Syrel watched as a look of horror dawned on her face. "With the psychopath who killed your dad? Your mom will kill me if she finds out I came! You have to get me out of here before he finds you!" She must not have recognized him, and Doren didn't say anything.

"You're not going anywhere, sweetheart. You just rest and focus on feeling better."

"Who healed me? Was it Isadore? The midwizard you were named after?"

"Actually... it was the psychopath who murdered my father," he responded, gesturing toward, Syrel, who was still on the ground. The frele sat bolt upright, but then groaned and laid right back down.

Doren moved her head to his lap and stroked her hair. "He saved your life."

"He saved both of our lives, babe."

Doren covered the freshly closed laceration on his arm with his other hand. "Oh, this? It was nothing, just a flesh wound."

"Not you, silly," she said weakly, her voice fading. The fae put her remaining hand on her belly. "I'm pregnant, Doren." With those words, she drifted back to sleep.

Doren's mouth fell open with those words. "P-p-pregnant?" he stuttered. "But that can't be; I thought you couldn't get pregnant..." He trailed off, realizing the future mother of his child was asleep.

Syrel chuckled lightly. "This land really is special. Congrats, Daddio," Syrel said, but immediately regretted his choice of words. It seemed like poor form to even use the word "dad" to the man whose father he'd killed. They both lapsed into silence.

"Why did you do it?" the fae asked suddenly. "You could have easily killed us both, like you did to my father and grandmother. How come you didn't just finish the job?"

"Doren, I... I never meant to hurt anybody. What I did to your father... It haunts me. I think about him all the time. If I could sacrifice myself to bring him back, I would do it in a heartbeat. There are no words I can say to make it better, but I am so, *so* sorry for what I did to you and your family. I wish I could make it right," Syrel sobbed. "I'm so sorry."

"You're... sorry? I don't understand... My mom said..."

"Whatever your mother said about me, I'm sure I deserved that and more. But Doren, I promise you, killing your father is the worst thing I've ever done. From what I've heard from Izzie, he was a great and powerful warrior. I wish I'd had the chance to meet him. I know you won't believe me, but somebody told me Izzie was in danger. That the fae were going to kill her on the coronation day if I didn't get there first. I was blinded by my own desire to protect her."

The two enemies were silent for a long time. Syrel could see the fae's mind was running at a thousand miles an hour.

"I forgive you."

Syrel cocked his head, sure he'd misheard. "You... what?"

"I forgive you, Syrel."

Syrel was dumbstruck. Before he could respond, he spotted Izzie out of the corner of his eye.

"You're... Isadore, right? The midwizard?" Doren asked. She nodded in affirmation. "Can you make sure my girlfriend is okay? Her name is Ruta, and she just told me she's pregnant."

Syrel looked on as Izzie cast *vitalagra* and examined Ruta's circulatory system.

"She lost a lot of blood, but I can tell she's a fighter. I think she's gonna make it."

"What about the baby? Is the baby okay?"

Izzie pulled out her wand and the *majalir*. Syrel had watched her use the device practically nonstop now that the changelings were showing up daily with new pregnancies, but she barely needed it—she had yet to diagnose a single fetal anomaly, proving yet again the wonders of Gravipar. The device still occasionally showed flashes of what they assumed to be the future, but nothing as significant as the visions of war Izzie had seen before. The war that raged on at this very moment.

Izzie circulated a little bit of extra blood to Ruta's head, the same trick she'd used with Werna, to wake her up for the ultrasound. It was clear, even to Syrel's untrained eye, that she was pregnant. A tiny fetus bounced around inside her uterus, bringing smiles to the faces of everybody present. It was a moment of joy in the midst of relentless sorrow. Ruta looked up at Doren, who kissed her on the lips.

"If it's a boy, we should name him after your father." With those words, she closed her eyes again.

The image of the fetus inside the *majalir* disappeared when Izzie removed her wand, but it was immediately replaced with a new set of images. A solitary figure, headed toward the Mother Tree. Then a face—Queen Luxor's. And blood. So much blood.

Izzie threw the device into her bag, which spoke softly. "I don't like the looks of what I just saw. Especially with how accurate this accursed thing has been about this war so far..."

"Who do you think that was? Headed toward the Mother Tree?" Doren asked nobody in particular.

"I think I know," Izzie said after a long pause.

Syrel, Pyke, and Doren all looked at her. Syrel was nervous to say anything at all after seeing Doren's mother in the *majalir*.

"Who?" Pyke finally asked, fearing the answer.

"An old friend."

* * *

Day 153 of the Twelve Race War
Eastern Battleground

Abrido. Dalfa strolled through the battle, unseen and unheard. Over the course of the long journey from Wastetown, she had pushed her mental magic to the limit and confirmed she was back at full strength. Currently, she was using the effects of the *desparaco* spell, which harnessed mental magic to fool all those around her into looking right through her. It made her effectively invisible.

Abrido. She winced as she observed the wreckage. Corpses of every race lay strewn across the ground, which had slowly turned from cracked and barren to green and lush over the past few months, though now it was stained with the various colored bloods of thousands of Cosconians. Such a grotesque sight, all tracing back to Izzie's ritual. She'd watched from afar as the minotaur stampede took out a large portion of the remaining dwarves, only for the water fae to come in and rout the injured minotaurs. The giants had come next, using their massive size to shrug off the water attacks of the fae. The orcish army, which even *she* didn't know would be coming from the southeastern marshes, had done their best to avenge their clanmates who had been previously massacred by the giants.

Abrido. She had heard through the grapevine that her old friend Kurai had died in the battle, which was a shame. Though he'd grown from an ambitious soldier into a warmongering general over the years, she still had a soft spot for the only orc who had ever given her the time of day. Kurai was proof war was unavoidable—he was not the type who would have ever sat on his hands while Gravipar was settled peacefully. Dalfa looked on with surprise as changelings carted off the injured.

Abrido. Dalfa had plenty of time to think about her next steps, and she knew exactly what she needed to do. She needed to publicly expose Izzie and Syrel so everybody would know they were the instigators of this war, and then dispose of them. Then she would use her mind magic to broker a final peace agreement.

Abrido. It hurt her to think of killing her best friend, but it was the only just punishment for causing the deaths of tens of thousands of innocent freles and babies. She was worried about taking out the two wizards. Though they had committed themselves to healing for the past few months, she knew what they were capable of. She was planning to take advantage of her friendship with Izzie to get close enough to use her mind magic. She had practiced her non-Affinity combat Skill over the years, but she would much rather rely on her powerful Affinity.

Abrido. The carnage around her was staggering. Dwarves so full of holes they looked like cheese. Minotaurs drowned with their own saliva. Water fae crushed into pancakes. Giants with every single stony limb hacked off. Orcs who looked like they'd wandered into the middle of archery target practice. Elves spitted through with swords like rotisserie pigs. She told herself again this war was unavoidable, but she could never have predicted the death toll.

Abrido. The fighting had died down somewhat, mostly because there was barely anybody left *to* fight. From her time spent wandering around the battlefields unseen over the past few days, she guessed each army was down to only a few thousand soldiers, if that. Thankfully, there was still plenty of each race left at home in their own territories who could help repopulate Cosconia once the war was over.

Abrido. Dalfa continued to use the spell over and over, which would open the minds of those around her to the power of her suggestions. Unlike the *mentopo* spell, *abrido* couldn't force anybody to do anything, especially something they didn't want to. It did, however, make them susceptible to being spurred into action toward something they already wanted to do. In this case, everybody wanted the war to end. Dalfa couldn't imagine there was a single individual on this battlefield who wanted the horrific war to continue, so she would activate the spell exactly when she needed it.

Abr—the sight of a battle hardened orc cutting through everybody in his path with a gleaming gold axe distracted her from her spellcasting. *Maybe I was wrong about* everybody *wanting the war to end.* She continued walking, figuring the orc didn't need any mind magic to push toward a final confrontation, but she stopped after a moment. *Wait a second...*

She recognized that orc. Though his teeth were broken and his entire body was crisscrossed with old and new scars, she was certain this was Kurai. *He's not dead?* Dalfa released the effects of the *desparaco* and appeared in front of him.

"Oi!" He jumped as she appeared, and he lifted his axe to chop right through her.

"*Sivromo!*" she yelled, temporarily freezing the orc in place by severing the connection between his mind and body. The axe hovered just a few feet above her.

"It's me! Kurai, it's me—Dalfa!"

She watched as recognition crossed over his face, and she cut off the spell holding him in place. Kurai tossed his axe aside and wrapped her in an embrace.

"Yer alive! I thought ye'd died years ago!"

She returned his embrace, happy to be accepted by at least one person in Cosconia. "I thought *you* were dead!"

"Ay, they tried, they did. Little punt from a giant, nothin' yer old pal can't handle." He grinned.

Dalfa gestured at the surrounding carnage. "This is... This is..."

"Beautiful? Lovely?" he finished for her.

She gave him a withering stare. "I was going to say 'atrocious.'"

"Didn't ye once tell me without war, there can be no peace?"

Dalfa couldn't deny it. "I just... I didn't know it would be this bad."

Kurai shrugged, as if the deaths of thousands of Cosconians meant nothing to him. "Coulda been even more dead if it wasn't for that damned midwizard." He looked toward Gravipar. "*Other* midwizard," he corrected, seeming to remember Dalfa's former profession.

"I'm not a midwizard anymore. Are you talking about Izzie? You remember her from the stories I told you?" She was impressed by how well he had listened to her.

"'Member? I'd never forget the lunatic who tried to freeze me heart." He continued staring toward the Mother Tree. From there, he told her a tale she had never expected to hear. How he had met Izzie, long before she had, in an alley in Wastetown. How he'd simply said hello, and she'd frozen his heart and tried to kill him. He explained that when Dalfa had talked about her midwizard friend and her use of the *frijangre* spell, he had known it had to be her. Dalfa's frown grew deeper and deeper as he told her about sending Syrel to the coronation and his eventual imprisonment of Izzie and some dwarf. He recounted their escape and eventual reunion on the battlefield, where he'd almost lost his life.

"You... you imprisoned her? For years?" Dalfa's feelings were at war with each other. On one side, she was appalled at the orc for imprisoning and torturing her once best friend. On the other, she felt like Izzie deserved torture, imprisonment, and more for causing the deaths of so many mothers and children. It still felt wrong, in spite of Dalfa being on her way to finish Izzie off once and for all.

"Nobody messes with Kurai and gets away with it," he said. "And I ain't done with her yet."

She had to bury her feelings. Whether or not she approved of Kurai's methods, the war probably would have never happened without him, and she still believed in her heart it was necessary for the future of Cosconia. Right now, they had the same goal.

"It's time to put an end to this war once and for all," she told him. It would be bloody, but it would work. *What are a few more deaths on my guilty conscience anyway?*

Kurai answered with a wicked grin.

CHAPTER THIRTY-FOUR

The Mind Mage

---

*Enemies are often former or potential friends
who have been denied—or think that they have
been denied—something.*

—Idries Shah

Day 154 of the Twelve Race War
Unity Hospital

Izzie sat with a small group at the base of the Mother Tree. She could practically feel the Maternal Magic emanating from it. They were inside the cobbled together nursery, which was packed with halfling, dwarf, and changeling mothers and babies. Syrel had erected a small "conference room" inside the nursery for the gathered individuals to talk without worrying about prying ears. They had watched the battle in the distance fizzle out, but changelings were reporting tens of thousands dead or dying on the battlefield. Izzie had made the painful decision to ask Pyke and her crew to stop transporting the wounded onto the island, as they didn't have any more capacity, physically or mentally. The blood sprites were working nonstop alongside

Izzie, Syrel, Arkan, and Lago, who were all packed into the small room. Joining them were Donrel, Pyke, Doren, and Werna, who still hadn't regained any feeling in his legs. Without realizing it, they'd formed a multiracial council to discuss the end of the war.

"This war can't continue much longer. Every army has been decimated by now," Doren said during their discussion.

Pyke shook her head. "I think most of these armies will fight to the very last soldier."

"We're running out of resources on this island anyway," Lago said. "The original stores ran out, and we're subsisting off what the changelings have been able to steal from other camps. But running this hospital is unsustainable."

Izzie listened to the back-and-forth, not contributing much to the conversation. She didn't have any ideas. Thousands lay sick and dying under her jurisdiction, and there was simply nothing she could do about it. They were turning away wounded who attempted to stagger onto the island because there was no room.

Suddenly, the one-armed Ruta burst into the makeshift room. All eyes turned to face her.

"Doren. It's your mother. She's here."

"How did she escape...?" Doren started, trailing off as realization dawned on him. "I ordered every available soldier to the battlefield. Her guard must have left her." He paused. "We have to stop her," he finished reluctantly.

Pyke nodded in agreement. "I'm sorry, Doren. We don't know what she's capable of."

"I know," he said solemnly. "I think she's under the control of a mind mage."

Izzie's heart dropped into her feet. "What did you just say?"

"A wizard came to her before the peace summit. Ruta and I believe she put my mom under some sort of spell and forced her to order the massacre of the dwarves. I can't prove it, but I know my mother. She would never have done something like that."

Horror dawned on Izzie as she put the pieces together. She thought out loud. "Dalfa. It's the only explanation." She turned to Doren. "It never made sense for your mom to do what she did. I know your father's death changed her, but at heart she is a good frele. I know she is."

"Who is Dalfa?" Ruta asked.

"The one we saw in the *majalir*. The mind mage. She used to be a midwizard, but she got too jaded by the failing Maternal Magic. She quit the field, but when she found out about Gravipar, she insisted war was the only way Cosconians could one day coexist harmoniously here."

Ruta, who Doren had informed her was a scholar before she was a warrior, finished her thought. "And she needed a catalyst to kick off the war, so she took control of Doren's mom and ordered the flooding of the tunnel."

"We have to stop her," Doren added. "But please—don't kill her. She doesn't deserve that. We just have to figure out a way to break Dalfa's spell."

"We can do it," Lago added hopefully. Yet again, Izzie was impressed with the dwarf's optimism and fortitude during these trying times. With that, all those who had gathered around the Mother Tree trudged out of the conference room, through the nursery and out into the open, where blood sprites buzzed around injured members of every race. Donrel continued to carry his husband, not willing to let him miss a second of the action.

Queen Luxor was blitzing across the island like a halfling headed for second breakfast. She ignored the wounded and the dead, her eyes only focused on Syrel.

"Mom, please wait!" Doren called out as she approached, trying to make peace. "You're under the wizard's control again. Fight it mom, fight it! I know you can snap out of it."

She didn't even look at her son as he pleaded with her, but her words were chilling. "Nobody is in control of my mind except me." Far behind the furious water fae, the water of the channel started to coalesce into a mist surrounding the island. Izzie couldn't believe her eyes, as she was shocked Queen Luxor would have that kind of power. The mist had to contain thousands of liters of water, and typically fae could only control a small volume of water. The mist drifted from the moat toward the center of the island, threatening to wipe out surrounding visibility.

Pyke tried to reason with the enraged queen, even though she knew deep down it would be futile. "Lulu, please. There's so much you don't know. Can't we just talk this out?"

The fae raised her hands, drawing water from her surroundings, and blasted Pyke with one of the most powerful water cannons Izzie had ever seen. The changeling went flying, caught off guard by the brutal attack. *How could she possibly be controlling the mist* and *be blasting off water cannons? Nobody is that powerful...* Something was off here, and Izzie had an awful feeling in the pit of her stomach.

Izzie and Syrel were ready to prepare their own attack. She would stick with her vow to not kill anybody, but that didn't mean she was useless in a fight. Since blood was mostly water, her blood magic Affinity did give her some small level of control over water, and she was always working on her water spell Skills. Izzie raised her wand and shouted "*Glaciartus!*" to freeze one of Queen Luxor's water spears and prevent it from hitting Syrel. At the same time, he cast *cudrado*, a basic defense spell. The frozen water careened away from him and hit Arkan square in the chest, knocking her out instantly. Izzie took her focus away from the battle to quickly glance at the orc, who was thankfully still breathing. She returned her attention to Queen Luxor, who was now frozen in place.

From the mist emerged a face she hadn't seen in years. The face she used to see for breakfast every morning before class. The face she pictured as she wrote letters while traveling around Cosconia. The face she blamed for starting this entire war.

"Dalfa."

"Izzie. It's been a while."

"Why are you here? Come to finish what you started? Maybe wipe out a few thousand more dwarves?"

Dalfa grimaced. "So you figured out I was behind that. It was a necessary evil."

"It was certainly evil, I'll give you that much."

"That's rich!" Dalfa laughed harshly. "You're going to talk to me about evil? We wouldn't even be standing here if it weren't for you and your psychotic boyfriend. None of this would have happened without your *ritual*." She spat the last word. Dalfa seemed to notice the looks of confusion on the faces of Izzie's allies.

Dalfa laughed again. "You haven't told them, have you?"

Izzie clenched her jaw so tightly it hurt. "That's not relevant right now, Dalfa. This is between me and you."

"Between me and you? This is between all of us! All of Cosconia!" She turned to address Izzie's gathered companions. "Your beloved midwizard *created* Gravipar by sucking the Maternal Magic out of the rest of Cosconia. *She* is the one responsible for this war, not me."

"Izzie has been saving lives every single day for decades!" Lago said from beside her. "I don't care what you think she's done; you're a monster who tried to wipe out my entire race!"

433

Izzie was proud of the dwarf for speaking up, but she worried for her safety. She had promised to get Lago home safely so she could continue to raise her adopted child.

"And they say *I'm* the one who brainwashes people. You've convinced everybody here you're the hero, when really, you're the most wicked villain of them all."

"I know I've made my fair share of mistakes, Dalfa, but I'm doing my best to atone for them. I started this hospital. I kept on delivering babies, whereas you quit when the going got tough." Izzie instantly regretted her words, but the battle lines were already drawn.

The mist now almost completely surrounded them. Queen Luxor still remained frozen, leading Izzie to believe she was back under Dalfa's control.

Dalfa shook her head. "You're deluded if you think you're anything but a monster. No matter; it's time to put this war to an end once and for all." She magically amplified her voice. "Anybody who wants to live has ten minutes to evacuate the island." She looked directly at Syrel and then Izzie. "Unfortunately, the offer doesn't extend to you two."

Gravipar instantly devolved into bedlam. Anybody who could move, did. Izzie looked on as bloodied orcs and weakened minotaurs stumbled through the mist toward the bridges off the island. There were actually touching displays of camaraderie all around the island. She saw water fae put their arms around the shoulders of humans with missing legs and lead them toward the exit. A giant carried two halflings. Changeling and dwarf freles, babes in arms, streamed out of the nursery and dashed madly to the nearest bridge. The blood sprites emerged from hiding to fly away. A few elves, though they were injured themselves, assisted a group of pregnant halflings who could barely run with their giant bellies holding them back. Izzie hoped they could stumble through the haze and make it off the island.

"Pstttt!" came a whisper from her back. Baggie Smalls. "Is this a bad time?"

"It's certainly not a great time," she whispered under her breath. "Do you have any tricks up your sleeves?"

"Maybe if I had sleeves..."

"Do you have something useful to say?"

"Well not if you're gonna sass me!"

"Can we not do this right now?"

"Fine. I've been around you and Syrel for long enough that I've developed sort of an... eighteenth sense for the presence of magic."

What the hells? "Eighteenth?! You have seventeen senses? You're a glorified purse for cryin' out loud!"

"I'm going to choose to ignore that because I like you. I think you're going to want to hear what I have to say!"

"Yes yes, spit it out!"

"Why is nobody getting wet?"

"Excuse me?"

"The mist is completely surrounding us, but nobody is wet."

Izzie looked at her hands, which were bone dry in spite of the heavy mist in the air. *It must be some kind of illusion...* Mind magic, she realized.

"STOP! Everybody stop! It's a trap! Don't cross—" Izzie's voice caught in her throat. She tried to finish her warning, but the words wouldn't come. She tried to reach for her wand, but her arms wouldn't work. She couldn't move her body. She couldn't speak. With great effort, she was able to slightly swivel her head to see Syrel and Doren experiencing the same problem. Pyke and Ruta had disappeared into the fog to help the evacuation effort. Dalfa had her wand in her hand. She must have cast some kind of spell to freeze them.

She saw Dalfa grin before she spoke. "You're experiencing a little spell I developed myself. *Sivromo.* Mind magic that temporarily severs the connection between your brain and your muscles. Makes it awfully tough to move, as you're probably feeling right now." Izzie was horrified, but also slightly impressed by the way she was able to use her mental Affinity. "I guess I can let the illusion drop now."

In an instant, the air around the channel, which a moment prior had been completely obscured with mist, cleared to reveal soldiers of every race poised and ready to fight. Thousands of them. The chaos devolved into a slaughter. The giant who had been carrying two halflings was cut down by a water fae, who subsequently kicked the halflings off the bridge and into the water. Much to Izzie's surprise, mermaids started popping up in the channel. A trident skewered the murderous fae. Lursa surfaced and liberated the mermaid's arm from her body. Izzie tried to mentally communicate that, at least according to Pyke, the mermaids were on their side now, but it didn't seem to work.

A disfigured orc swung a heavy axe and murdered two pregnant dwarves. That face... *Kurai.* Izzie had thought for sure her one-time captor had died at the hands of the giants, but he must have survived. It looked like he had landed on his face when the giant had launched him across the battlefield, as his teeth were jagged and broken. His nose was almost completely gone, and scars covered his pale blue face. He walked with a slight limp. It didn't stop him from smiling in her direction as soon as he spotted her.

The remaining troops from every army started pouring onto the island. Skygyr leading battle-hardened giants. Eko at the forefront of armor-clad humans. Drago, Lago's brother, commanding a small battalion of axe-wielding dwarves. The elves were conspicuously absent, perhaps not wanting to join the fray with their fearless leader, who had remained on the island, wracked with grief. He still had yet to return to his army since Werna's injury. There were plenty of water fae, so clearly somebody had taken over command in Doren's absence.

This was it. The final confrontation of the war. Whichever army still stood at the end of this would control the fertile land, granting them the ability to regrow their population quickly and safely. Though Izzie hated to admit it, their motivations made sense. As things stood in Cosconia, going into battle was no more dangerous than getting pregnant. So many of these soldiers had likely watched their mothers and sisters die from pregnancy complications and hoped for a better future in spite of the cost. This was the final push for these armies, in an attempt to secure a future where starting a family didn't feel like losing a battle.

Everybody was fighting with reckless abandon. A general could throw as many soldiers into harm's way as necessary to come out on top, since the winning army would be able to take advantage of Gravipar's improved pregnancy outcomes, while the rest of the armies would take generations to recoup their losses. It was a gamble, but a worthwhile one for the winner.

The island turned into a close-quarters battlefield. Injured soldiers were trampled underfoot as minotaurs charged at giants. Human swords clanged against dwarven shields. Halflings scurried around unnoticed, using their daggers to stab unsuspecting fae. Orcs indiscriminately swung their maces and axes, occasionally even beheading their own comrades. The hastily-erected walls of the nursery fell, and Izzie could see terrified freles huddled in the corner, trying to protect their newborn infants. She was completely powerless to prevent the horror as she saw soldiers casually end lives that had just begun.

Izzie fought as hard as she could against the spell preventing her from acting, but she couldn't do it. It was obvious to her what was happening here—Dalfa had somehow used her mind magic to convince the remaining armies to make a last stand here and now. Out of the corner of her eye, she saw Werna pull himself across the ground by his upper arms. He was just below Dalfa's sight line, and he slowly snuck up on her. When he was close enough to reach her, he swung his arm up and batted her wand out of her hand, causing her to drop the spell she was holding Izzie under.

"Oh fuck," she heard the former midwizard say.

CHAPTER THIRTY-FIVE

All Wars End

The universal slogan of war, she'd learned, was simple: If it had been you, you'd have done no different

—Omar El Akkad

Last Day of the Twelve Race War
Gravipar Hospital

When Werna forced Dalfa to drop the *sivromo* spell, Izzie immediately went on the offensive. She wouldn't break her vows, but she could still use her magical abilities to render the attackers powerless. It was extremely difficult to kill a wizard anyway, so she would aim to disable her.

Izzie realized Queen Luxor was on the move again, Dalfa's spell on her broken as well, charging toward Syrel. Her hands were raised, gathering the water in the air into a sharp spear that would easily impale her fiancé. She knew he wouldn't fight back, since a part of him still felt like he deserved to die by Queen Luxor's hand. Thankfully, the queen's son intervened. He erected a barrier of impenetrable water between the fae and the wizard, stopping her in her tracks. Izzie couldn't believe her eyes. Thelonius's son was defending his father's murderer.

"Mom! Please! You're focusing on the wrong enemy!"

"*Dolara!*" Dalfa shouted, attempting to cast a spell on Izzie that would cause excruciating pain. She narrowly dodged the spell.

"*Pesangra!*" Izzie cast back, attempting to use the same spell to slow the wizard down that she'd used on Lursa. Dalfa blocked it with a flick of her wand.

Izzie had a moment to glance at her surroundings, and she saw Doren occupied with holding his mother back from Syrel, while Pyke, Donrel, and Syrel attempted to fend off the horde of warriors closing in on their position. Ruta positioned her body between Werna and Dalfa, fearing for the elf's safety after his direct attack on the mind mage. Izzie knew it was up to her to stop Dalfa.

In an effort to create some distance between herself and her attacker, she spun around and cast *cudrado* behind her back, deflecting a spell Dalfa hurled at her. Before Izzie could completely turn around, she ran face first into a massive orc. She didn't even have time to register what was happening before he grabbed her arms and twisted them behind her back. She felt something in her right shoulder pop and screamed out in pain.

"'Ello poppet," a familiar voice hissed into her ear. A lyonium dagger pressed into her throat, causing a trickle of blood to roll down her neck like a bead of sweat. "Say a word and this here knife goes right through yer gullet."

"The plan is still on, right, old friend?" Dalfa asked Kurai as he held Izzie in a vice grip. "We kill the wizards and then put an end to the fighting?"

"Ay, a deal's a deal," he responded, raspy voice hot in her ear.

"And you said you wouldn't kill any of the freles or babies," Dalfa said in a pained voice.

Kurai barked a harsh laugh. "All's fair in love and war, darlin'"

"You've truly sunk this low, Dalfa?" Izzie asked, each word causing the knife to dig further into her throat. "You're going to let this monster kill me?"

"It's high time you paid the price for all the lives you've taken."

"And what about you? When are you going to pay the price?"

"We all get what's coming to us eventually, but somebody has to usher Cosconia into this fertile and prosperous new era."

"Please, Dalfa," Izzie begged. "It's me. Can't we talk about this?"

Dalfa shook her head sadly. "Finish her off."

This was it. Izzie was trapped between a vicious orcish warlord who seemed like he couldn't die, and a powerful mind wizard who could probably kill her with a word. Her arms were at an awkward angle behind her back, and her wand was in the pocket of her robe. It didn't matter, since she couldn't use her magic with the lyonium dagger at her throat and in contact with her bloodstream.

"I've got other plans for the lovely wizard," Kurai responded. "She'll be coming with me."

"No," Dalfa answered coldly. "She won't. Either you'll kill her right here, or I will."

Is this really what my life has become? Two monsters arguing over whether to kill or kidnap me? She couldn't move her head for fear of the dagger digging further into her throat, but she cast her eyes wildly about her. There was no sign of Syrel or Pyke, who she knew were both wrapped up in their own battles. Ruta and Werna had disappeared. Doren continued to hold his own mother back from doing anything she'd regret. The intense fighting continued to rage around her, but the common soldiers seemed to be keeping their distance from the standoff. Izzie could still hear the wailing of the freles and babies in the nursery who were rapidly being displaced by the armies that had stormed onto the island.

This ending was fitting for her. Here she stood, in the very land created by her own magical ritual gone horribly wrong. When she had started hearing rumors of the war, in the back of her mind, she had always suspected this would be her fate. As the orc and the wizard argued about what to do with her, the cut on her neck growing wider every time Kurai moved, some of the major events of her life passed before her eyes, almost like they were appearing inside the *majalir*.

Coming to this very spot to perform a ritual that would leave her broken and barren and separated from her one true love for far too long.

Falling into a disgraceful epoch of binge drinking and terrible decisions.

Enrolling in midwizardry school.

Delivering her first baby.

Saving her first mom.

Meeting Pyke and Lulu.

Finally seeing Syrel again.

Reigniting their relationship.

Helping Lago become a badass nurse.

Syrel proposing.

She thought of the ring on her finger. It still seemed as if it pulsed with power, but she wasn't sure how she could harness it. Izzie was devastated she would die without getting to marry Syrel. She was even more devastated she would die without ever getting pregnant. Her whole life, having a child was what she had wanted more than anything. Being a midwizard was the most rewarding thing she'd ever done, and she would choose it again in a heartbeat, but it was absolutely brutal watching so many others live her dream. When she had decided to set up the hospital on Gravipar, it wasn't for entirely selfless reasons—she was hoping the more time she spent on the island and near the Mother Tree, the more likely it would be that she would get pregnant. Even spending the past few months in the shadow of the Mother Tree in the most fertile land in Cosconia couldn't give her a baby.

Izzie tuned back in when she heard Dalfa say, "She's too powerful to let her go." She lifted her wand and pointed it at Izzie. Izzie accepted her fate.

Then everything changed in an instant.

She felt Kurai's grip go slack, the dagger in his hand clattering to the ground. As Izzie started to turn around to assess what happened, the orc fell forward on top of her. At the base of the back of his skull was a knife, stuck in all the way to the hilt. Standing behind the dead orc chieftain, who had toppled over on top of Izzie, was Lago. She had a look of pride on her face.

"Lago? You... you saved me."

The dwarf beamed, standing over the body of her dead captor, finally getting revenge for the years of suffering at his hands. "I did it just like you taught me! Right through the brainstem so they don't have any chance of survival."

"How dare you?" Dalfa spat at Lago. "How dare you come here and kill my friend and ruin my plans?"

"Suck my—"

"*Mortala*," the wizard said simply, almost casually, her wand aimed at the dwarf.

Izzie watched as her confidante, nurse, and most importantly, her dearest friend, dropped to the ground. Dead, like the orc Lago had just slain.

Dalfa shot into the air, flying high above Izzie, clearly not wanting to continue their duel now that she was no longer restrained.

Izzie gazed at the dead dwarf. She felt completely numb. She'd promised to bring her home, safe and sound. But she failed. Another mother Izzie couldn't save. Death and pain had been lurking mere steps behind her for decades. She'd watched as those she cared about, like Sydyr and Thelonius, perished. She'd also seen untold hundreds of pregnant freles, babies, and new mothers pass. Since the start of the war, thousands more had met their fates before her eyes. Izzie felt like she was a harbinger of death and destruction. This war wouldn't have even started without her influence, no matter how many times Syrel told her to forgive herself.

For too long, she had kept the promise she'd made to herself in the dwarven halls many years before. The promise to preserve life. To do no harm. Izzie had firmly adhered to her commitment, focusing on healing and bringing life into the world. For decades, she had used her blood magic only for good. As her power had grown steadily over the years, she had continued to use it to heal more and more creatures. Bring more life into the world. Even when the war started and her power continued to increase by the day, still she'd used her abilities to keep her promise.

High above her, Dalfa floated ominously above the island. The battle around Izzie had simmered as everybody gazed up to the sky. At the edge of her vision, Doren held a sobbing Queen Luxor. Syrel, holding a still unconscious Arkan, and Pyke, bleeding profusely from a gash on her cheek, jogged up to Izzie. Donrel and Werna were nowhere to be seen. Syrel started to speak, but immediately sealed his lips when he saw the figure of the dead dwarf on the ground at Izzie's feet.

They heard a chant drifting toward them on the wind. At first Izzie couldn't make it out, but once she started seeing the effects, the words became hauntingly clear.

"*Do... la... ra!*"

"*Do... la... ra!*"

"*Do... la... ra!*"

All around her, creatures of every race began dropping to the ground, clutching their heads. The *dolara* spell, a mental Affinity spell cast by Dalfa with the utmost Intent, was incapacitating all those remaining on the battlefield with incessant pain. One by one, hardened soldiers who had survived the gory affair thus far fell to the dirt. She'd known Dalfa was powerful, but the mind mage had clearly been busy honing her Skills.

Izzie looked on in horror as pain racked all those around her. She started feeling a tingling in her head she knew would give way to exquisite pain in just a moment. She looked deep into Syrel's eyes. He was wincing from the pain, and after another second, he dropped to his knees. She looked at Pyke, drenched in a mix of her own blood and that of her enemies. She examined Lago, who appeared much more peaceful than those on the receiving end of the *dolara* curse. Only her constitution as a wizard was keeping her standing a moment longer than everybody else.

"*Fortangra*," Izzie said out loud, casting a blood spell on herself that would temporarily protect her from the effects of the curse.

Finally, something inside her snapped. All the evil she had seen welled up inside her, igniting a flame that would not be put out. *Could not* be put out. The tangible pain around her fueled the fire, Intent building within her. She was the one to start this war. Now it was time she ended it.

Fuck my promise, she thought to herself.

"*Altasangra*," she whispered. Instantly, she began to float directly upward. A satisfied grin crossed her face as the spell, which made her blood lighter than air, went into effect. She swam through the air until she reached the altitude of the flying wizard.

Suddenly, there were five Dalfas. Izzie knew it was an illusion, but there was no way to tell which was the real one. They continued the chant and split in every direction. The mind wizard had never been particularly Skilled in combat, but she could leverage her mind magic illusions to make it significantly more difficult for Izzie to find and stop her.

One of the Dalfas broke off the chant and pointed her wand at Izzie, but she didn't even give her a chance to cast a spell. She knew once she stopped the real Dalfa, the copies would disappear.

"*Sulfangra*," Izzie screamed, emotion overwhelming her. Her Intent had never been higher. She could almost *feel* her Affinity, like a tangible object. The curse turned blood to acid, and the copy fell from the sky as her own blood dissolved her from the inside out. It was unnecessarily gruesome, but Izzie didn't care. She had to make a statement. She was going to put an end to this godsforsaken war once and for all, no matter what it took. No more of her friends were going to get hurt. Not if she could help it.

"*Pesangra*," she yelled, putting her mind, body, and soul into the next curse. A second copy, her blood now significantly heavier, plummeted to the earth. After so much time spent only using her power for healing, it felt liberating to finally use it to mete out justice. She could mourn the breaking of her promise later—for now, she would make sure it was worth it.

Three Dalfas remained, meaning she still hadn't taken out the original. Two of them bolted one way and the third the opposite direction, and Izzie hoped one of the two was the real Dalfa. Izzie pointed her wand at one of the quickly escaping wizards. "*Sangracala!*"

The spell had its intended effect as the wizard's blood boiled and she exploded in midair. Izzie knew she was acting like a monster, but she didn't regret it. *It was always going to take a monster to end a war this monstrous.* Two Dalfas remained.

The other escaping copy, now a hundred yards in the distance, sped away with alarming speed. "*Regrasangra.*" Izzie cast a spell on the distant wizard. Usually, the spell was used to return blood to a wound. However, Izzie changed the Intent behind the word to force dozens of streams of blood to fly up from the ground, which was soaked in the colorful blood of the thousands who lay dead. The rivers of blood flowed in a swirling, grotesque rainbow toward the fleeing wizard, until they finally reached her. Izzie pulled the spectacles out of her bag to ensure the distant copy had been taken care of.

"Wow, you are going full murder hobo," Baggie Smalls said as she put the spectacles on her face. She watched as the wizard tumbled to the ground, drowning in a floating blob of filthy blood. She removed the farseeing device, not wanting to watch any longer.

"You don't approve?" she asked.

"Quite the opposite, my dear Isadore. It's about *damn* time!"

It was just the encouragement Izzie needed to finish the job. She slowly reversed the effects of the *altasangra* spell and drifted back to the ground where the final Dalfa, the real one, stood. Every inhabitant of the island, friend and foe, good and evil, mother and baby, lay unconscious on the ground after the wizard's mental attack.

She faced off with the former midwizard.

"You truly are a monster, Izzie. When will you accept you're the bad frele?"

A throaty laugh burst forth from Izzie. "Me? *I'm* the monster? You've been stoking the flames of this war from the background for decades, and you have the nerve to call *me* a monster?" Izzie stepped closer to Dalfa as she spoke. She gestured at the hundreds of dead and incapacitated around them. "This entire war is *your fault.*"

"*My* fault? That's pretty rich coming from the one who created this place."

The words stung because Izzie knew they were true. She really was just as much of a monster as Dalfa. Thankfully nobody else was awake to hear it. She ignored the jab anyway. "You're right," she admitted. "It wasn't my intention, but I did create this place. My actions *did* lead to this war. But now I'm stepping up to end it. *You*, on the other hand, ended thousands of innocent lives to control this land!"

"I don't want to control it. I'm going to get as far away from here as possible when I've finished you off. Then, *finally*, Cosconia can know peace."

"Do you even hear yourself? Do you *actually* believe you're doing this for the greater good?"

"I might be the only one who cares about Cosconia's greater good. Nobody else is thinking long term like I am."

"You really believe that, don't you? But taking lives to save lives is *never* acceptable. You preyed on people's hope for a better future and twisted their minds to convince them war was inevitable. You never truly tried to achieve peace." Izzie inched closer, ready to attack. "Dalfa, you are pure evil. But thankfully, evil never prevails in the end. It might prevail for a month, or a year. It might even prevail for a generation, or an era. But there's one *fundamental* problem with evil: It can't support itself. Evil is too selfish, too unconcerned with others to triumph indefinitely. Eventually, evil will self-destruct. But goodness? Kindness? Those will never fail. You can't keep good people down forever."

"And what? *You're* good? How can you even say that?" She gestured at the land around her. "You're more evil than any of us," she spat.

Izzie nodded slowly. "That may be true. I've done a lot of bad things in my life. But each day, I try to be better." Without warning, she shot off a spell at the evil wizard. *Frijangre*. Dalfa blocked it easily. She backed up, trying to get out of the line of fire.

"Today wasn't my best day." *Sangrimovi*, she shot off, but the wizard used the *cudrado* spell to ward it off. "Maybe tomorrow won't be either." Dalfa tried to cast a series of spells on Izzie, but she easily shrugged them off. "But I'm going to keep trying every day to do more good than I did the day before."

The repartee went back and forth between the two wizards, each trying to land the fatal blow. But Izzie was far too powerful. For years, she had practiced her blood magic. Day in and day out, she'd experimented with her power. Grew with it. Molded it. Shaped it. And now, she could control blood more naturally than she could control her own emotions. Her Skill was unparalleled, and Intent practically exploded from her veins.

"But before I can do that"—Izzie deflected another of Dalfa's spells—"the war has to end."

With that, Izzie cast a spell she'd never used before. One she'd only read about in the *Sangrila*, never believing she would have the strength to perform it. If she failed, it would likely burn her out. It may even kill her. She rubbed the wooden ring around her finger, made from her old wand. She could feel its power coursing through her now that her Intent was maxed out, which she would need to eliminate such a powerful wizard.

"*SANGRESORBA*!" the midwizard shouted, and a dense beam of crimson light shot forward from her wand and hit Dalfa square in the chest. The wizard sank to her knees. Blood seeped from every orifice on her body. Dark red blood poured from her nose and mouth. Her eyes and ears dripped. Her skin began to turn pale and wrinkled, like the very life was being sucked out of her.

Which was exactly what was happening. The blood that fell from her body flowed through the beam of light and into Izzie's wand. She was absorbing the wizard's life force, growing her own power in the process. Not only that, but according to the *Sangrila*, she would gain the wizard's mind magic Affinity in the process. Dalfa's crumpled body slumped over, an empty husk lying where one of Cosconia's most powerful wizards had been mere moments before. Izzie dropped her wand as the light faded away. She could feel Dalfa's power coursing through her.

Izzie tucked her wand back into her bag, who couldn't resist making a comment.

"That was totally WICKED!"

Izzie hadn't experienced absolute silence in months. Dalfa was dead. Her attack had left all the remaining combatants unconscious. She looked around and realized there were only a few thousand soldiers still alive. Donrel's logistics captain, Smise, had estimated there were a total of over one hundred thousand soldiers when the war started. Thankfully, the blood sprites had protected the nursery with their blood magic, so it seemed many of the pregnant freles, mothers, and newborns remained alive. A small bright spot on the darkest of days.

Izzie silently walked over to Lago's body and knelt down next to the fallen nurse. She gently closed the dwarf's eyes as tears dripped from Izzie's own eyes and splashed onto Lago's dirty forehead. She couldn't believe how much it hurt. Lago's death made her heart feel like it was being ripped from her body.

She wanted nothing so desperately as she wanted to lie down and sleep. Night had fallen during the final battle. No moon lit the sky, so only the starlight and a few torches lit the island. Izzie wished it could all be over, but there were still enemy soldiers scattered throughout the island, and she was afraid that when they woke up, the fighting would just resume. Which meant she had to keep going, even though she wanted to sit down next to Lago's tiny corpse and give up.

Dalfa's power still coursed through her body. She didn't know any of the spells, but she could somehow *feel* the mental Affinity she'd just gained. The ramifications of this... a blood wizard who could control minds? Izzie could be unstoppable if she so chose. She walked over to Dalfa's shriveled corpse. Her wand lay shattered on the ground, but Izzie noticed a bulge from her robe pocket. She investigated, pulling out a book. The faded cover contained one word in the ancient wizard language: *Mentala*. She knew exactly what it was. The equivalent of her *Sangrila*, except for mind magic. She'd had no idea other Affinities had guidebooks like this. *This will be extremely helpful if I decide to make use of my new Affinity.* She slid the tome into her robes.

Doren and his mother, along with Ruta, lay unconscious at the edge of the channel; both Doren and Ruta still tightly gripped Queen Luxor's arms. Pyke had converted back to her natural changeling form, jagged scars still fresh across her scalp, and blood trickled from her face. Syrel's body covered Arkan's, noble even in the face of danger. She spotted Donrel, who had positioned himself between a piece of debris and his husband. A role reversal, with Donrel acting as the bodyguard. *It's ironic,* Izzie thought as she examined the battlefield. *This is the most integrated Cosconia has ever been*. All the warriors who had fallen mid-battle were mixed and mingled. Minotaurs lay prone next to giants; orcs and elves had collapsed side by side; halflings and fae lay with limbs intertwined. *This is how it should always be...*

Izzie had an idea. An idea about how to put an end to this war once and for all. It would be awful, but it would work.

"*ULTRASONORIUM ENFOCARTE!*" the midwizard yelled at the top of her lungs. Sound waves so powerful Izzie could actually see the ripples extend from her body unfurled in every direction. Usually the focused ultrasonic attack drained her, but she barely registered the energy drain. *I guess the spell must be in line with my new mind Affinity*, she realized. She used the *altasangra* spell to float a few feet above the ground. The focused ultrasound attack jarred the inhabitants of the island from their unconsciousness. She saw Syrel and Pyke look up at her, confusion on their faces. Members of every race began to climb to their feet.

"Fellow Cosconians! The war is over. Look around you—is this what you want? Endless suffering? A never ending war? We are *all* Cosconians. We must live together in harmony. Instead of twelve territories, why can't we all live in peace in this wonderful, fertile land?" She watched as hundreds of soldiers glanced around themselves, taking in their gruesome surroundings. Most seemed nauseated.

"You're all here because you have hope for the future. Hope for a better world for all. A world where pregnancy is an exciting time rather than a dangerous one. Do you really want to keep fighting? Haven't enough of your friends, your family members, paid with their lives?"

Though many creatures seemed to take her words to heart, not everybody was convinced. A group of orcs charged toward her position, leading with their pikes and maces.

"*Paracorzra*," Izzie said simply, and fifteen orcs dropped dead, their hearts stopped. Simultaneously, about forty minotaurs charged toward her position, putting her friends right in the line of danger.

"*Sangracala*." Just as the orcs had, the group of minotaurs died immediately, exploding into a bloody, furry mess. Izzie winced at the destruction, but she had to make clear further fighting would not be tolerated. Nobody had ever seen blood magic so powerful. This quelled any further resistance. *Thank goodness. I don't know if I had another spell like that in me.*

"All hail Isadore, Queen of Cosconia!" a voice called out. *No no no*, Izzie thought. *This is not what I had in mind.* Several more called out the same words. Before she could respond, an ear piercing shriek silenced those calling out her name.

"Queen?! *QUEEN*?! *I* am the queen! Gravipar would be nothing without me!" Queen Luxor shouted, her voice frantic and pressured. Izzie was pretty sure the compulsion would be broken now that Dalfa was dead, but that didn't mean Queen Luxor had forgiven the mele who killed her husband. The fae queen charged toward Syrel. Izzie felt for her. The poor frele was just a grieving widow, driven mad by her own sorrow. Yes, Izzie sympathized with her, but she also couldn't let her ruin the bid for peace. Luckily, Syrel and Doren—the most unlikely conspirators—had come up with a contingency plan for this. Izzie triggered her mental connection with Lursa, who she knew was patrolling the waters frantically, doing whatever she could to help.

Yes, my friend, a voice spoke into her head. Izzie realized with a jolt that the new mental Affinity must give her the ability to communicate telepathically with her bonded companion.

"I'm sorry, Mom," Doren said softly. "This is for your own good." The young fae drew an enormous spout of water from the nearby channel and shaped it into a smooth ball about a foot in diameter. He slammed it against his mother's chest, and she flew backward, directly into the water. The sea monster rose from beneath the surface and grabbed the flailing fae frele in her mouth. Izzie knew she wouldn't kill Queen Luxor. The fallen queen would be taken, with an escort of mermaid warriors, to a prison in Lork. There she would await a fair trial.

Izzie remained floating in the air. "Are there any others who would stand and oppose the end of this war?" The crowd beneath her remained deathly silent. She saw a few giants shake their heads slowly. Donrel and Werna smiled at her from their spot amidst the rubble. Pyke wiped a bloody tear from her eye. Arkan glanced around, not seeming to believe peace was imminent.

"Wise choice," Izzie continued. Before the shouts for her to become queen could rise again, she proposed her solution. She'd gotten the idea from Baggie Smalls. "Cosconia shall henceforth be a republic, in which each race shall live in harmony under the guidance of chosen representatives. Each race will have an equal say, and Gravipar will become the capital and seat of power of the newly united Cosconia. Lay down your swords. Lay down your bows. Lay down your axes. We will usher in a new era of peace and prosperity. Together."

The sound of hundreds of weapons clattering to the ground was deafening. These soldiers were ready for peace. Cheers rose from every corner of the island. Izzie laughed as a giant lifted a halfling in the air in celebration. Humans and orcs hugged each other. Dwarves cried with elves, mourning their lost brothers and sisters. Peace had arrived in Cosconia at last.

"Return to your camps. Celebrate. Mourn. Laugh. Cry. Sleep. Choose your representative, and we will meet at midday here, around the Mother Tree, in two months' time to discuss rebuilding Gravipar and bringing Cosconia into a time of peace."

CHAPTER THIRTY-SIX

Era of Peace

---

*It takes a special kind of courage to hold power
and know when not to use it.*

—*Hafsah Faizal*

Day 60 of the Era of Peace
Unity Hospital

Izzie surveyed the familiar faces around her. She had the
privilege of recognizing many of the elected representatives,
though there were a few surprises. She called the meeting to
order as twelve individuals, including herself, sat at the base of
the Mother Tree. The sound of crying babies was constant, as the
area still acted as a nursery until a better solution could be
found.

"I call to order the first official meeting of the Twelve Lord
Council," Izzie intoned, her voice firm and confident. They had
decided each one of the twelve representatives would be known
as the lord of their citizens, and they would come together to
form the Twelve Lord Council, or the TLC. Many informal

meetings had taken place prior to this one, with the leaders and influencers from each race figuring out who belonged where.

"We will lead our people with humility and benevolence. We will serve as we wish to be served. We will let our words settle differences, not our swords. We will repopulate Cosconia and treat every race with dignity and respect." Izzie laid out the plan for the expansion of Gravipar, though she had taken no part in creating it—she didn't know the first thing about building a city from the ground up.

Currently, the channel created by the dwarves surrounded the island with the Mother Tree, which was where the Maternal Magic was the strongest. They would turn their field hospital into a permanent structure, using it to deliver the many babies that were expected to come into this world following the war. A massive baby boom was expected. The other side of the channel was the vast Wasteland that was currently home to army encampments, discarded weapons, empty tents, and tens of thousands of corpses. Each race would have a project that would turn Gravipar into the prospering capital of a newly unified Cosconia. She gave every leader the opportunity to speak their mind and let the group know how they would contribute to the rebuilding effort.

"The dwarves are choosing to trust again, though we still mourn the loss of so many of our kind from the fae betrayal," Drago began, "including my sister, Lago the Orcslayer Nurse." Izzie was happy Drago had been chosen as the representative, since they could share in their grief over Lago together. The rest of the TLC nodded along, everybody having lost somebody near and dear to them. They all knew his pain.

"We will dig another channel to complete the expansion of the city." Several dwarven experts had drawn up a plan for the city. It would consist of two concentric rings of water so all had access to fresh water. The inner island, Inner Gravipar, surrounded by the existing channel, would contain the hospital and the seat of government. The outer circle, Outer Gravipar, would be much larger and surrounded by the outer ring of water. It would be divided into twelve zones. One for each race, save the mermaids, who could now freely roam the Cosc River without the threat of Lursa or rogue fae. They had hesitated to divide the land by race, but it was purely a logistical choice. It didn't make sense to have housing and infrastructure for giants and halflings in the same place, so dividing Outer Gravipar into zones made the most sense. Plus, some degree of separation was likely for the best. Instead of a Mermaid Zone, there would be a zone for business, religion, education, gathering, and entertainment, open to members of all races—the Meeting Grounds. Eventually, Izzie planned to start her own midwizardry school in that zone. Each district would have a bridge to Inner Gravipar, and there would be no physical borders between them. Ever.

The giant delegate was next. Izzie wasn't at all surprised by the choice.

"We will build a permanent hospital on this island," the one-eyed giantess said. The midwizard had been forced to remove her injured eye after the war when Skygyr caught the rot. Izzie could never have known fifty years before that this giant baby she'd delivered—in still one of the most harrowing deliveries she'd done to date—would stand by her side to rebuild Cosconia. Skygyr really did fulfill the giant prophecy. There were thousands upon thousands of swords, shields, axes, and pieces of armor left over from the war. The giantess leader had an ambitious plan to use the steel from the discarded tools to build a multistory hospital. A structure that large had never been built out of metal before, but Izzie knew it would work. Who better to build a forty-foot tall structure than a forty-foot tall giant? After the war had ended, she'd realized this was exactly the building she'd seen in the *majalir* so many times. She trusted Skygyr—and hoped the hospital would turn out the way she envisioned.

Izzie's bag whispered from her side. "I can't tell if she's blinking or winking with the whole one-eye thing..."

She put her hand up to her mouth and stifled a laugh.

"Can I call her Cyclops?"

"What the hells is a Cyclops?" Izzie asked under her breath as the giantess spelled out her plan for building the hospital and the capitol building.

"It's a one-eyed giant, duh."

She supposed if that were true, it was a very apt nickname, but she still harbored a healthy fear of the giantess. "Go ahead; I'm sure after she rips you thread from thread, my next bag will be nicer."

"Sure, but probably without all the pop culture references and fourth wall breaking!"

"I don't know what either of those things are, so I'm not sure I would miss them. Now let me listen to this damn meeting!"

After their last-minute bid for power, Izzie still didn't trust the orcs. For that reason, she had strongly *suggested* they elect the leader *she* had chosen for them. They had, surprisingly, taken to her very quickly. Apparently Kurai wasn't too popular among their kind, so a frele who had escaped him and raised his baby without his knowledge instantly became a celebrity. In orc culture, a large frele was a sign of health and prosperity, so Arkan was practically revered by her kin.

"The orcs will lead the cleanup effort. There are innumerable corpses scattered throughout Gravipar and the surrounding area, and they will quickly lead to disease and rot. Our job will be to bring them far away and dispose of them," Arkan said. "My people already know that defection will be punished swiftly and severely, and the orcish culture of constant fighting has to end. They also know I have a powerful friend in my corner." She winked at Izzie. She was so proud of the orc. She'd truly transformed from the damsel-in-distress to a badass boss bitch. Having the orc lord also be a close friend and ally would be instrumental in keeping the TLC united.

Next was somebody who Izzie was shocked had survived the war: Smise, Donrel's great uncle and the logistics genius. She had hoped Donrel would step up and join the TLC, but he had announced his retirement the day after the war ended. He told Izzie he had already spent too much of his life fighting, and he wanted to live out the rest of his days with the love of his life after nearly losing him. In a poetic twist of events, Donrel would now be taking care of Werna, who had spent so many years protecting him.

The ancient elf would be in charge of logistics for the entire recovery effort. He would make sure citizens had enough food and water, materials would be shipped in and out appropriately, and the entire effort to build a city from the ground up would be a successful one. It was a monumental task, but if anybody could do it, it was Smise.

She smiled as the changeling lord announced her task. "The changelings are committed to the security of Gravipar. We expect many citizens from the rest of Cosconia to move here once the hospital and the rest of the city are built. I'm putting together an elite task force of secret agents to ensure peace is kept throughout the land. We bowed out of the war so we could assist in bringing injured members of all races to Izzie's hospital, so you can trust us to continue to put the needs of others above our own." The rest of the TLC was nodding along, and Izzie was surprised they seemed to trust the changeling. It was truly a testament to how much each lord wanted to avoid any further bloodshed. She knew as soon as this meeting ended, Pyke was going to return to Jubox to fetch her son. Izzie was excited to finally meet Capino.

"So if you marry Syrel," her bag whispered, "does that make Pyke's kid your son?"

Izzie had thought extensively about how to handle *that* whole situation, but she still hadn't come up with a solution that would work for everybody. "Technically my stepson."

"Well, I'm sure you four will figure out how to be one big happy family some day." Izzie smiled at the thought, however unlikely, of living in peaceful coexistence with Syrel, Pyke, and her son.

Flor, the blood sprite, was up next. They were one of the few sprites who could speak Fingol, the common tongue, so it was a natural choice.

"Flor heal. Sprite heal. We use blood magic for good, like in war. We stay here and work in hospital." The blood sprite didn't need to say any more. Their race had already proven themselves invaluable during the war, and Izzie was grateful they were going to continue their healing efforts. She didn't think the hospital could run without them. In the weeks since the war had officially ended, they had continued to work tirelessly at healing the wounded.

Labrite, the minotaur herd leader, had perished during the war, but his second-in-command, Vito, had survived. One of his horns was cracked in half, and there were missing patches of fur all over his body. He was a creature of very few words. He had pulled Izzie aside before the TLC meeting had started to let her know he was committed to peace, even if he had trouble expressing his thoughts. It was a very sweet gesture.

"The minotaurs... will provide food... for Gravipar." He stumbled through his statement. The minotaur herds were known for their agricultural acumen, and this contribution to the well-being of the city and its inhabitants was crucial.

Of the two brothers who had initially come to Queen Luxor's peace summit, Hortho had survived, but his brother Portho had not. The halfling was broken by the losses he had experienced. Izzie had found him sitting on the floor of the nursery after the battle, his brother's broken body in his arms. She'd found out later he was attempting to find his wife, who had delivered a set of triplets a few weeks prior. Of the family of five, only Hortho and his new son had survived. The rest had been murdered in the final onslaught.

He currently held the tiny baby in his arms, tears dropping onto his tiny, bald head. "Like me," he finally said, pulling himself together, "there are many Cosconians who have lost somebody. I lost my brother, my wife, and two of my children. Yet still, others have lost more. Everywhere you look, you will find widows and orphans. Wounded veterans and the unhoused. Single parents. Older siblings, forced to take care of little ones after the loss of their parents. The halflings are committed to taking care of those who need a helping hand. We will run Gravipar's nurseries and orphanages, its shelters and safehouses. We will be a light in the darkness. The giants will fix our homes, the minotaurs our fields, the sprites our wounded, but we will mend Cosconia's broken spirit."

"Wow, a government taking care of its veterans?" Baggie mumbled. "That's a first." Izzie was confused by the comment, as she couldn't imagine *any* government not taking care of the wounded heroes who were the only reason there was peace in the first place.

Eko, the human general, was the elected representative of the humans. Izzie had heard his wife, Jilette, had survived the war, but she was so traumatized she had entered a nearly catatonic state. She couldn't imagine what he was going through—Syrel was her rock during this tumultuous time.

"The humans have committed to running the finances and business of our shared new city." Izzie could see several other members of the council about to protest, but Eko continued. "In order to ensure fairness and equity, I will gather a subcommittee similar to this one, with one chosen member of each race, to preside over financial matters." This immediately placated all the other lords as they pondered who to choose as their delegates.

Floating in a bubble of water next to Eko was Baztia, the mermaid warrior. Prior to the war, she had been simply a border guard. During the war, however, she had distinguished herself not only through acts of valor but also by making the wise decision to lead the retreat to Lork when Lursa turned. This decision alone had likely saved the lives of hundreds of merfolk, earning her the vote of her kin as their representative. Syrel, Pyke, and Doren had all put their heads together to develop a system to transport the mermaid outside the water for brief periods of time, and with the support of several water fae creating a bubble using their water magic, she could now attend their council meetings.

"The merfolk are committed to protecting all of greater Cosconia from outside threats. We fear that travelers from other lands may hear of the wonders of Gravipar and attempt to invade. With the help of Lursa, we will guard our shores from evil." This was actually Syrel's idea. From his studies, he knew more of the land outside Cosconia than anybody else. Though there was essentially no information about life outside of this landmass, the citizens of Cosconia had to have come from somewhere originally, and he worried that an unknown threat may still be out there.

It came time for the final member of the TLC to offer his contribution. The fae, who had perhaps faced greater losses during the war than anybody else after Queen Luxor's traitorous act at the peace summit made them popular targets on the battlefield, had chosen Doren as their leader after he had banished his own mother. The respect for the royal blood ran deep in fae culture, so it was an easy choice, even though Doren adamantly insisted he didn't want the role. The eleven other members of the council stared at the silent fae.

"I... I don't know what to say. Besides I'm sorry. I don't know how we can help." The downtrodden fae hung his head in shame. Izzie couldn't blame him—he'd been present for every step of his mother's tumultuous reign, including the initial slaughter of the dwarves.

Izzie pondered the role the fae could take in the construction of Gravipar. She felt like all of the important jobs were already accounted for, but it would further isolate the fae from the rest of the races to leave them without a duty. It was somewhat unfair to pin hatred on the fae alone since all sides had committed atrocities during the war, but sometimes folks just needed a villain. The fae were an easy choice.

"Doren, I spent enough time in Pwise and..." She paused, not wanting to spill any secrets about the water fae Palace. "And other fae areas. If there is one thing you all are good at, it's beautification. Why don't the water fae take on the responsibility of turning the new city into a comfortable place to live? I'm thinking water features, koi ponds, fountains, sculptures... really anything your heart can dream of. This city could really use a little spirit! You can breathe life into this city as we welcome new life every day." She glanced around the circle to see a few of the other lords reluctantly nodding their heads.

Doren seemed reluctantly interested in the idea. "Yes... yes. I think that's a great idea. We can use our water magic for the good of Gravipar."

She clapped her hands together. "Welp... that's about it! What do you all say we wrap up for today so everybody can get started on their projects?"

As the crowd started to disperse, a small voice spoke up. "Uhm... excuse me, Izzie?"

Izzie looked at Hortho. He still appeared dejected, and she was surprised he was even speaking up any more than he had to. "Yes?"

"Pardon my ignorance... but I just want to ensure everybody is contributing equally... What are you going to do?"

Izzie smiled when she answered. "Make sure all you motherfuckers stay out of trouble... or else." She didn't mention she was also funding the entire operation, as the considerable sums of gold given to her by the dwarves—against her will—was going to be funneled right into the city so many had paid for with their lives.

"That could have gone worse!" Baggie Smalls said cheerfully from her side. They were leaving Inner Gravipar to head to the area that would be the Wizard Zone. Since the rest of the wizards had chosen to stay out of the war and Dalfa was dead, Izzie and Syrel were the only two wizards left in the Wasteland. That would change soon, since the moment the war ended, word had been sent to all of Cosconia that the fighting was over and some members of each race could come to enjoy the fertile land of Gravipar. Eventually, they would have to put population limits or length-of-stay restrictions on the area to prevent overpopulation, but it would be a while before that would be necessary. The goal wasn't to eliminate the need for any population centers in the rest of Cosconia, but rather to provide a place where the races could live together in harmony and trained professionals were available to aid with labor and delivery. Even with the significantly improved outcomes in the land practically bursting with Maternal Magic, Izzie knew there would still be plenty of need for assistance, so she wouldn't be out of work any time soon.

"You can say that again…"

"That could have gone worse!"

Izzie rolled her eyes. *After all this time, how do I not see those coming?* "Helpful. But seriously—I was shocked how docile and compliant everybody was."

"I gotta be real with you here, Iz… I think they're all terrified of you."

"Aw come on! I bet you every single one of those lords killed more individuals on the battlefield than I did."

"Yeahhhh… it was less the *amount* you killed, and more the way you kinda like… drained the life from a powerful mind wizard and blew a bunch of people up?"

Izzie grunted in acknowledgment. She still hadn't processed the fateful last day of the war, and she wasn't ready to yet. Even though it was what needed to be done, guilt wracked her days and nightmares plagued her nights. She had made a commitment to herself, and she had broken it. If she couldn't even keep a promise to herself, how could she make any oaths to anybody else?

"I'm not ready to talk about it."

"Don't take my comments for judgment. I thought it was extremely badass. And even if it wasn't, it had to be done. Izzie, you *ended* a war between twelve different races in one day… so don't be too hard on yourself?"

It was shockingly good insight, and she was grateful for it. "Y'know what, Baggie? Thank you. For everything."

"Go on," it interrupted.

She laughed at the comment. "Usually people say something to the effect of 'Oh, stop' or 'It was nothing' in these situations."

"Well, I don't think you've thanked me enough. It's about time, and it better be good!"

Izzie kept laughing as she responded. "Fair enough! In all seriousness, I wouldn't be here today without you. Not only did you save my life in Lork, but you did it again when I was trapped in Kurai's prison. You provide much-needed comic relief during dark times, and your weird references keep me calm when I'm starting to panic. Thank you for always giving me what I need, if not with a little pushback from time to time. I have no idea how you ended up the way you are, but I wouldn't have it any other way."

"Alright, that was an acceptable expression of gratitude; I'll take it."

"Aren't you going to say anything back?"

"Is the sidekick supposed to thank the hero?"

"Hmmm… fair point! Now are you ever going to tell me where you come up with your strange jokes and allusions? It almost seems like they're from some other realm."

"You're closer than you think… but nope! You're not getting it out of me that easily."

CHAPTER THIRTY-SEVEN

A Day in the Life

In the aftermath of war, the wounds may heal,
but the scars remain forever.

—Jennifer Robson

Day 234 of the Era of Peace
Unity Hospital

"Okay I need a nurse to go check in on the breastfeeding minotaur in room 4, somebody to grab food and bring it to 18 because if that halfling doesn't get a bite to eat after the labor she had I'm pretty sure we're going to have another war on our hands, and for the last time Jayd, how many times do I have to tell you to bring your enchanted forceps to work?!"

The group of medical providers in front of her grumbled but started their assigned tasks. Izzie sighed. While it was certainly easier than traveling around all of Cosconia, trying to run this hospital was brutal. From the moment she walked in the door before the sun rose until she left long after it set, somebody always needed something from her. *This is good*, she reminded herself. After the time of grueling warfare, the land was finally at peace. *We started this hospital so that every mom-to-be in Cosconia, no matter her race, would be able to deliver safely and with top-of-the-line medical care.*

Izzie was headed to see a patient she'd been eager to check in on since she'd left the day before, so she left her office after the rest of the team had dispersed and entered the massive courtyard. The hospital, which had been constructed using material from the massive piles of discarded weapons left behind after the war, was a square building with a large courtyard in Inner Gravipar. Hundreds of thousands of weapons had been melted down and reshaped into massive supporting beams that could be used to make houses, shops, and, of course, Gravipar's first official building—a hospital.

The hospital was by far the biggest structure in Gravipar, which wasn't saying much for the new city. That probably wouldn't be the case for long, however, since technology had been advancing at a rapid pace since the war. The colossal structure took up most of the island, with a little room left over for the TLC headquarters. Though much of it sat empty so far, the doors having just barely opened, Izzie noticed new rooms being utilized for the first time every day. Gravipar was growing rapidly.

She walked out of the edifice and into the courtyard, which was surrounded by the hospital on three sides, the south facing side of the U-shaped building being completely open. The grassy courtyard, which was still strange for Izzie to see in the formerly barren land, was dominated by the enormous tree in the middle. It towered over the four-story building, and it still seemed to be growing taller every day. Surrounding the tree were dozens of picnic tables, which were full of new mothers and their babies. Izzie smiled as she saw unadulterated joy on tired faces. Such a stark contrast from the pain and suffering she had seen here just a few months prior. The courtyard also included a deep, clear pool, which was connected to the channel surrounding the island on which the hospital was situated.

"*Burbujum*," she muttered, and a bubble appeared over her head as she jumped into the refreshingly cool water. Though there were no "rooms" in the underwater wing of the hospital, each "delivery bay" was marked on the surface with a number, so Izzie knew where she needed to descend. The part of the basin where most of the deliveries took place was only about fifteen feet deep. Izzie cast *pesangra* to make her blood heavier and sink herself to the bottom. By some trick of magic and engineering developed by a team of wizards and mermaids to clean the water passing through Mermaid Bay, the water was crystal clear.

When her feet hit the silty bottom of the water, she was immediately assaulted by three tiny creatures. Izzie's face lit up at the sight.

"You did it!" she shouted, though she knew it would be muffled by her breathing bubble. Three merbabies, no larger than her hand, swum in circles around her, occasionally bumping into her. Though she knew they would grow into beautiful merpeople like the one in front of her, they were born looking entirely like fish.

"It was all thanks to you, Izzie. I couldn't have done it without all the support you gave me yesterday. I was ready to call it quits, but your words of kindness and encouragement carried me through."

Tears welled in Izzie's eyes as she saw the unbridled joy written all over the merman's face. *That's the reminder I needed today. That's why I do this.*

Once she'd said hello to the merman, she ascended and jogged over to give a scheduled tour to the TLC. All of the members except Baz and Doren were present.

"This is our halfling floor—our first unit to reach twenty-five percent capacity! The halflings have been reproducing at an unprecedented rate, so I suspect in a few years we'll be at full capacity." Izzie paused, as she could see there was a question. "Sir?"

"How many mothers have you lost?" Hortho, the halfling lord, asked, apprehension evident in his voice.

Izzie smiled. "Great question. Last month we did fifty halfling deliveries, and we've only lost one mom."

The Council gathered around her immediately began turning to one another with smiles and surprised muttering.

"You're at a maternal mortality rate of two percent? Izzie, that's remarkable," Arkan said. The orc knew firsthand from her own personal experience how dangerous pregnancy could be.

Izzie nodded her head. "It's a small sample size, but it's extremely reassuring. While it's devastating any time we lose a patient, the halfling maternal mortality prior to the war was thirty percent. The outlook for the babies was even worse." She shuddered, remembering how awful it had been.

"Do I even want to know?"

"No," Izzie answered quickly. "That's in the past, and I hope we never return there. As you all know, halflings never deliver just one baby—usually it's twins or triplets, but occasionally they'll have up to six or eight. Previously, the frele's system couldn't handle it and the babies and mothers would often pass if there were more than two. But now, we're delivering quadruplets and even quintuplets with barely any problems!"

This drew more shocked looks between the members of the TLC. The halfling lord, unsurprisingly, looked to be the happiest of the group in front of her.

"Excellent work, Izzie. Absolutely excellent work!" he squeaked.

"You shouldn't thank me—there are hundreds of nurses, assistants, technologists, and even a few midwizards-in-training who keep this place running. We've been training new workers nonstop. I barely do anything these days."

With all the reconstruction projects underway, the TLC was starting to venture out into the community to assess the status of the rebuilding effort. They'd asked Izzie to give a tour of the hospital, which she was more than happy to do. The improvements in maternal, fetal, and neonatal mortality were staggering when compared to the numbers before the war, so Izzie was always thrilled to share with anybody who would listen.

"Well this has been quite informative and eye-opening, Izzie." The elf lord, Smise, spoke up for the first time, very obviously trying to wrap up the tour. "Is there anything the TLC can do for you?"

"Honestly? We just need bodies. It takes an insane amount of work to keep this place up and running. We need folks to help clean, deliver supplies, move patients, make food, provide security... The list goes on. And nurses. I've discovered nurses literally run this entire place. Anything you could do to..."

Eko, the human lord, who was in charge of finances in the new city, cut her off. Izzie wondered how his wife was faring since she'd enter a catatonic state after the war.

"Name your price. We'll give you whatever you need."

"Thank you, sir. You have no idea how much the support of the Council means to maintain this place. I'll have my assistant deliver the numbers to your team tomorrow."

As the TLC dispersed, a nurse came running in, out of breath.

"Izzie! We need you *now*. Come quickly!" She'd met the dwarven nurse once or twice, and while she was a dedicated worker, she had nothing on Lago. Not a day went by that she didn't think about that beautiful dwarf. Izzie followed the nurse to a room one floor down, where a one-armed water fae was lying on a delivery bed. The frele was covered in sweat, which was unusual—most fae had such fine magical control over water they didn't let themselves sweat. It was considered gauche in fae culture. The baby's head was practically halfway out, but she wasn't pushing. Izzie also noticed the hopeful mom-to-be looked extremely pale.

"What's going on, Ruta?" Izzie asked hurriedly. *That makes sense of why Doren was missing from the tour.* "Somebody give me an update."

"She has been pushing for a few hours. Everything was going fine until..." The dwarf gestured toward the fae's left shoulder. Izzie was so tired from running around the hospital, she hadn't noticed when she walked in that the stump of the frele's missing arm was soaked in blood. *She must have pushed so hard to get the baby out she popped a blood vessel in her stump. No wonder she looks so pale.* The expectant father looked like he wanted to say something, but he remained quiet. There was so much that Izzie wanted to say to Doren, but it just wasn't the right time. She swore she could hear his thoughts, which had been happening more and more lately. They hadn't spoken outside of TLC meetings in months.

Even though everybody in the delivery room seemed panicked, Izzie wasn't worried. This was a problem she could fix in her sleep. She wished she *could* fix it in her sleep. She put a hand on the fae's arm. *Burning up*, Izzie realized.

In quick succession, she cast two spells. *Glaciartus* to freeze the sweat on the fae's body and cool her down, and *dejasangra* to stop the bleeding from what was left of her arm. Instantly, the atmosphere in the room changed from one of trepidation to relief.

"Alright my friend, just one more big push and we're gonna have a birthday party!"

"I can't do it," Ruta said, her voice weak. "I don't have the energy..."

"Yes you do. I know you do. You've been through so much, and I've seen you survive worse." Izzie grabbed and squeezed her hand. "You've got this."

Resolve painted her face. At that moment, Izzie knew she was going to do it. The water fae took a deep breath in and snapped her mouth closed, focusing all of her effort on pushing.

"That's it!" Izzie shouted. "You're so close; keep it up!" Izzie got her hands into position as the baby's head started to deliver.

"Okay take one more deep breath for me, and do the exact same thing again," Izzie continued.

With one more powerful push, the fae baby made her appearance. She immediately started crying, and Izzie handed the baby, still attached to the umbilical cord, to her mother. Both mom and dad wept with joy, snuggling their new baby between them. Izzie watched as the new father seamlessly assisted his partner, who struggled to keep hold of the baby in her one arm. Even though she'd delivered thousands of babies, these moments still brought her an immense amount of joy. They also brought her an immense amount of sadness, knowing she would never experience it herself. *It's also a shame Lulu can't be here to see the birth of her first grandchild.* Doren had pleaded with the TLC to allow his mother temporary freedom from her imprisonment to witness the delivery, but they had rejected the proposal. It was part of the reason she and Doren were at odds.

She wiped a tear away with her enchanted midwizard robe, now standard garb at the hospital, and asked, "What are you going to name her?"

The couple both looked at her and smiled. "We're naming her after her grandfather. Izzie, meet Thela."

"I hope today is better than the day Thela's father was born," Baggie said, quietly enough that the new parents couldn't hear. Izzie congratulated the couple and looked at the setting sun, realizing it was time to head home.

Syrel had built a very small hut on the outer edge of the Moat of Peace, the inner channel having been renamed by the TLC after the war, which acted as their temporary home during the rebuilding efforts. She spent most of her days (and many of her nights) at the hospital, which was also currently serving as the TLC headquarters, so she didn't need anything extravagant. Syrel was committed to the rebuilding effort and was helping with city planning. She had no idea where he had learned to do that, but he was a mele of many skills, so she didn't question it. The moment she walked in the door, the overwhelming scent of fresh bread assaulted her.

She breathed in deeply, leaving the troubles of the day at the door. She and Syrel had agreed that for the time being, they were going to leave the past in the past. Some day, probably soon, they would have to process everything that had happened, including the definitive finale of the war, but neither of them were ready. They had already spent the past years of their lives either preparing for, fighting in, or rebuilding after the massive war, and they didn't feel like reliving it in their limited time at home together.

"Welcome home, sweetheart," Syrel said, floating over from the hearth to kiss her on the forehead. "How was your day?"

"A real Dalfa. Yours?" The couple had taken to using the term "Dalfa" as code for all the bad things they didn't want to talk about. Izzie knew it was inappropriate, but sometimes a sense of gallows humor was all that could keep them going.

"Same. You wanna talk about it?"

"Nope. You?"

"Definitely not."

"Glad we got that settled! Now what are you making?"

"You'll never guess!"

"Hmmm... Is it bread and veggie soup?"

"You nailed it," he chuckled. While Smise was working overtime to get as much food into Gravipar as possible, the rations were still slim. Vegetables, water, and flour were the only ingredients available. They had eaten it for dinner every night for weeks, and she looked forward to a time when they could indulge themselves again. Though she wouldn't eat unicorn steak anymore—in fact, she hadn't eaten one since their first meeting—she could go for a nice piece of chicken or a pork chop.

The couple sat down on the floor to eat their meager dinner. Syrel was the chef in the family, and he had a way of turning basic bread and soup into a halfway decent meal. She leaned over to kiss him after she took her first bite of the warm bread.

"This is delicious, darling. Thank you for always cooking for me."

He kissed her back. "Isadore, I missed too many days of doing life with you. I'll spend the rest of my life cooking"—he kissed her forehead—"cleaning"—then her cheek—"and whatever else you want." This time, he kissed her lips deeply. He pulled back briefly to emphasize his last statement. "*Whatever* you want." He winked and went back in to continue their kiss, but she playfully pushed him back.

"Too far! Can't I enjoy the soup while it's hot?"

"Ugh, fine," he pouted. "I just love you so, so much Izzie."

"And I love you, weirdo."

The engaged couple finished their meal in silence. Not the kind of awkward silence when you had nothing to say. The kind of silence that said everything. The kind that said you were so comfortable you could never say another word again and it wouldn't matter. The kind that made you feel known on every level. The kind that made it seem like even if everything else was wrong, this was right.

In Izzie's world, basically everything else *was* wrong, or at least had been for a long time. She had already spent too much of her life in mourning. Over not being able to get pregnant. Over losing Syrel. Watching patients die. Being imprisoned. Losing Lago. *That one hurt the most.* She could fill a book with the reasons she had to be sad... but she wasn't. She couldn't be. She was so happy she had found the person her heart desired, and she didn't need anything else.

While they cleaned up from dinner, they chatted idly. Mostly about nothing, which was okay with her. Since it was already late, they laid down in what passed for a bed in the small hut— really, it was just a straw mat that extended across the seven-foot width of the dwelling. The tall couple barely fit.

"Hey babe?" her future husband said out of the blue before she was about to drift off to sleep. Normally, she would be mad at somebody for waking her up, but he sounded serious.

"What is it?"

"We never decided where we're going for our honeymoon!"

Izzie considered and realized he was right. They had barely had time to start planning a wedding, much less a honeymoon. "Where were you thinking of going?"

"Well I've never been to Lork..."

Izzie elbowed him under the blanket. "You really want to go where they are holding the prisoner who tried to kill you? For our honeymoon?"

"Hmmm, that's a fair point. Where would you want to go?"

"Disneyworld?" Baggie Smalls suggested.

"How about you go wherever that is and we'll go somewhere else?" Syrel shot back.

"Unicorn Island?" Izzie asked.

Syrel groaned. "C'mon, that's so overdone! What if we just hopped on a boat and started sailing?"

"To where?" Izzie asked, bewildered. "We don't know what's beyond the sea."

He shrugged. "Maybe we could discover what's out there?"

"I'm not quite ready to leave behind Gravipar. I'm the wizard lord, remember?"

"You remind me every day you're my superior; how could I forget?"

Izzie chuckled evilly. "You better not forget, subordinate!" He was, after all, one of the only wizards living in her jurisdiction.

"What if we went to the marshes?"

"I—" Izzie was about to protest, but then she realized something. The marshes *weren't* dangerous anymore. The orcs had been cleared out, and the blood sprites weren't the murderous lunatics everybody thought. They were actually pacifist healers, and there would be thousands more corpses strewn around the Wasteland if it weren't for them.

"That's... actually a phenomenal idea! It's one of the few places neither of us has ever been."

"Then it's settled; honeymoon to the marshes! And then to the beach." He leaned over, cupped his hand around her cheek, and kissed her nose. She blushed. Somehow he still made her weak in the knees.

"Goodnight, my love. Dream of me!"

With that, he rolled over and was snoring within a minute. *Bastard*, Izzie thought to herself. She wished she had the ability to fall asleep the moment she decided to. Usually, she would be up late tossing and turning, envisioning the horrible scenes she had seen in the war or replaying the events that had led to her murdering dozens. But not that night.

That night, her head was full of dreams for the future. A romantic getaway to southeastern Cosconia where they could see the marshes, learn about the history of the blood sprites, and visit the fabled beautiful beaches that lay beyond Blood Sprite Territory. She dreamed of her life with Syrel—it wasn't how she had imagined it, with a house full of kids running around—but she still looked forward to it. Their relationship had grown stronger than the Mother Tree towering over Gravipar. Sure, there were still occasional fights and bickering, but they knew their love could overcome anything. It had already overcome so much. Izzie smiled as she thought about the plans they had together. Building and running the hospital. Designing their own home in the Wizard Zone. Spending time with Donrel and Werna, who had decided they would adopt the elven baby Lago had been raising. Visiting Pyke and Capino, Arkan and Sintu. For the first time in a long time, the future was bright.

Izzie drifted off to sleep with a smile on her face. Just before she faded into a dreamless sleep, she felt a strange sensation, deep inside her belly. A kick.

Epilogue

Day 234 of the Era of Peace
Wizard Zone, Gravipar

Syrel slid out of bed, not wanting to disturb his beautiful sleeping fiancée. It was before dawn, but his anxiety had awoken him. Typically, he could sleep for hours without stirring, yet he had been extremely disturbed for the past week. He slid on his clothes and tiptoed to the door, turning back to ensure Izzie hadn't woken up.

He gazed lovingly at his future bride. It almost hurt how much he loved her. That's what made lying to her so hard, but he still hadn't figured out the right way to tell her. He knew he would have to eventually. Before the wedding. But he felt like he had to get to the bottom of this mystery first.

He slipped out the door and slunk away from the small hut. After crossing the bridge to Inner Gravipar, he wound his way past the hospital. Several blood sprites waved at him as he walked past, most recognizing him from the time he had spent doing healing magic there during the war. He made his way across the artificial island to the Fae Bridge. One of the first projects after the war had ended had been to increase access to Inner Gravipar by building twelve different bridges connecting the island with the surrounding land, one for each zone. After crossing into the Water Fae Zone, Syrel walked several hundred more feet. There were a few hastily constructed buildings in the distance, but most of the early rebuilding efforts had gone toward Inner Gravipar.

Looking around to make sure nobody was watching, Syrel morphed into his water fae form. Though he'd spent many years as a wizard, it was still as natural as breathing to morph into whichever form he chose. Like Pyke, he would be considered an Apex Changeling by Cosconian standards, though he had been around far, far longer than the young changeling, and he certainly wasn't limited to the twelve races found in Cosconia like she was. He couldn't believe Izzie hadn't put it together by now, and he was ashamed at how many lies he'd had to spin to cover it up. He'd thought for sure she'd catch him when she started to question why the blood sprites didn't recognize him, or how he showed up on the island during the peace summit. He would have had no idea how to tell her that he was never even kidnapped.

One day, he'd have to tell her the ritual had never been intended to find his Affinity, since he could never have one as a changeling. One day, he'd have to tell her what the ritual had really been for. One day, he'd reveal his true origin from far beyond Cosconia. But today was not that day.

There were only a few hundred occupants of the Water Fae Zone after the devastating losses they'd faced during the war. Unfortunately, it didn't seem the losses were over for the fae. He walked into a small building at the outskirts of the budding city, where an older fae sat near a pale, young frele. The frele, who couldn't have been more than eighteen or nineteen by the looks of it, was ghostly white. Her shirt was rolled halfway up her abdomen, which revealed a deep wound. Her breathing was shallow, and her skin was clammy.

"Another one?"

The only reason he was in the fae camp that night was to look into what had happened the night before. A fae had been found dead in their camp with a deep wound across her abdomen, just like the frele here.

The elderly fae nodded his head slowly. "Just found her a few minutes ago."

"Don't you think you should bring her to the hospital?"

"Blood magic wouldn't do any good. She doesn't have any more blood."

Syrel's stomach dropped at his words. That was exactly what had happened to the other fae. He watched her take her last breath. Something wicked was happening here, and he was determined to find out what it was.

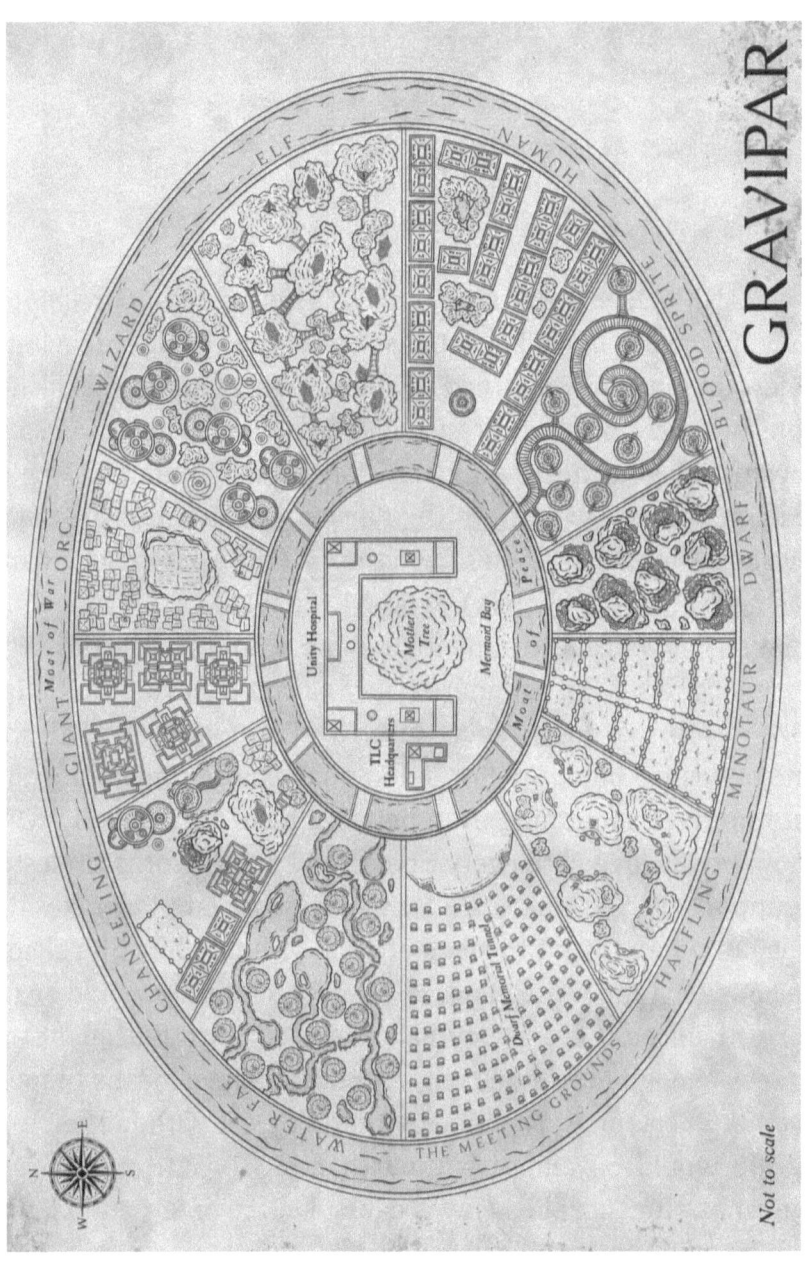

GRAVIPAR

Not to scale

Acknowledgements

THANK YOU for checking out *The Midwizard of Cosconia*! If you enjoyed the book, I humbly ask that you consider leaving a review on Amazon, Goodreads, Fable, or wherever you so desire. Indie authors like myself survive on your reviews! Already jonesing for your next fix of Izzie, Baggie, and Maternal Magic? Head on over to www.themidwizard.com and subscribe to my newsletter for short stories from the Call the Midwiz series and read a first draft of Book 2, Chapter 1 today!

My friend once asked me if I had more hours in the day than everybody else—he wondered how I could have a full time OB/GYN job, two dogs, a social life, travel the world, and still find time to write a book. Spoiler! I don't have more time in the day. But I do have something even better: I have a Rachel. My wife, whom I truly love with every fiber of my being, works tirelessly to support me. She makes dinner when I work late. She takes the dogs out when I want to sleep after a 24-hour shift. She cleans the house so I can write in peace. I think our society would be far more advanced if everybody had their very own Rachel. I can't express enough how much her support and love means to me. I owe her everything. This book wouldn't exist without her, and my life would be empty without her big, beautiful eyes and constant optimism. She is my greatest source of joy, and I know I can do anything with her by my side.

The second most important person in the writing process isn't a person at all—it's my sweet, sweet snoot. Penny, if you're reading this: first off, way to go! Our reading lessons paid off. Everybody told me I was crazy, but I knew I could teach you how to read. Second, thank you for being the softest part of my writing process. Most of this book was written with you curled up at my feet (but not touching me because we both hate physical touch, a doggie after my own heart.) Because every Penny needs a Desmond, at the time of this writing, we welcomed a new puppy into our home. But since I barely know the guy, and he's still a bit of a maniac, there isn't much I can say about him in the acknowledgements section. He's reallll freakin' cute though.

Thank you to my beta readers: Colin Johnson, Jordan Hauck, Ray Stapleton, Allison DeLuca, Jordan Schoppen, Kelsey Schoppen, Matthew Schoppen, and Tracy Schoppen. Your feedback was invaluable, and I appreciate you dropping everything to read my book and help take this book to the next level. Colin, thank you for starting the Fantasy WhatsApp, which was a great place to bounce ideas and learn more about fantasy. To all the members of the chat, even those who don't participate (we know you're watching), thank you for being part of my circle.

My family has been nothing but supportive in this entire process. I know you thought once I was done with residency my life would get less busy and you could see me more, but here we are. Brittany and Eric, thank you for letting me take a break from board games to do a little writing, and for always asking for a progress report and taking a vested interest. Jordan and Kelsey, not only did you manage to beta read while also raising a whole human (s/o Ro Ro), you've been nothing but supportive the entire process. Matt and Hannah, I vividly remember how excited you were when I talked to you about the book that day in our condo, and you jumped on board to help without hesitation.

Finally, my mother, who deserves her own paragraph. Things have not been easy for my mom, especially since my dad passed away from pancreatic cancer several years back. Yet she has never once wavered in her undying support for her children, friends, and family. You have been my biggest cheerleader, number one advocate, best friend, and confidante for so many years. I have never once questioned your love and support for me. Going through Hooked on Phonics with me nearly three decades ago, buying me encyclopedias to read as a child (I wish that was a joke), and encouraging my passion for reading got me where I am today.

Dad, I so wish you were here to read this book. The crazy part is—you would probably hate it since you didn't even like reading, but I know you would have read every word and been so proud of me. You shaped me into the man I am today with your kindness, generosity, humility, humor, and commitment to your family. I love you so much, and if *The Midwizard of Cosconia* ever makes into heaven's library, check it out for me.

Emily Dahl of Dahlhouse Editing turned my story into a book. Her developmental edit vastly improved my character development and pacing, and you really helped turn Dalfa into a great villain. To Zoe Cochlin, my line editor, thank you so much for letting me focus on the writing without worrying about the grammar and punctuation, since I knew you would get this book into tip top shape. Thank you to Katherine Nesler who helped design the OG cover, and Saqib at Book Cover Hub for bringing it to life.

I've saved the best for last: my readers. Thank you to every ARC reader who went out on a limb to read a book with a crazy concept by a brand-new author, and taking the time to write detailed and positive reviews. Your kind DMs and emails, social media posts, GR reviews, and everything did not go unnoticed— I am appreciative to each and every one of you. My street team (Jordan, Malvika, Alyssa, Teena, Loriana, Leighton, Sarah, and MaElrin), thank you so much for hyping up the book and starting a real movement. And to every other reader, thank you for picking up what I hope is the first in a long line of #MedicalFantasy. Head over to my website to check out a first draft of Book 2, Chapter 1!

Have you ever seen a pregnant elf? Halfling quintuplets? A tiny bearded dwarf baby or a six foot tall GIANT baby?

In a land where Maternal Magic once protected every mother and child, birth has become deadly. Fresh out of midwizardry school, Izzie is determined to use her blood magic to save the lives of every mom and baby she can.

Maternal Magic is waning each year. She's lost friends and patients. And no one knows why. Haunted by an ancient ritual that went tragically wrong, Izzie has sworn to do no more harm. But when Cosconia's twelve races vie for the formerly uninhabitable Wasteland, war threatens to consume the continent—and somehow Izzie ends up in the middle of the conflict.

What's a wartime midwizard to do? Izzie must face the trauma of her past—which might have more to do with their current predicament than she realizes—and possibly make peace with a very attractive, very annoying wizard.

Could the truth heal her dying land—or break it (and her) beyond repair?

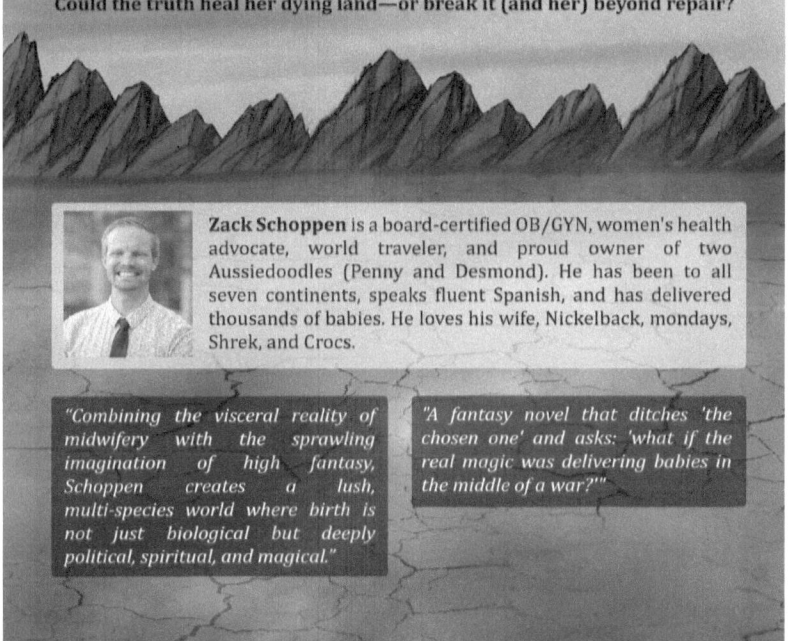

Zack Schoppen is a board-certified OB/GYN, women's health advocate, world traveler, and proud owner of two Aussiedoodles (Penny and Desmond). He has been to all seven continents, speaks fluent Spanish, and has delivered thousands of babies. He loves his wife, Nickelback, mondays, Shrek, and Crocs.

"Combining the visceral reality of midwifery with the sprawling imagination of high fantasy, Schoppen creates a lush, multi-species world where birth is not just biological but deeply political, spiritual, and magical."

"A fantasy novel that ditches 'the chosen one' and asks: 'what if the real magic was delivering babies in the middle of a war?'"

489

www.ingramcontent.com/pod-product-compliance
Lightning Source LLC
Chambersburg PA
CBHW032013110726
47901CB00004B/1066